Ripples

Ripples

Richard C Pizey

Book Guild Publishing
Sussex, England

First published in Great Britain in 2008 by
The Book Guild Ltd
Pavilion View
19 New Road
Brighton, BN1 1UF

Typesetting in Garamond by
Keyboard Services, Luton, Bedfordshire

Printed in Great Britain by
CPI Antony Rowe

A catalogue record for this book is available from
The British Library

ISBN 978 1 84624 250 2

For
Debby

Contents

Part One

In and Out and All About

1

Jessica and Alex had been co-habiting for two and a half years.

They'd met in the mid 80s, on an island in the middle of a river in Munich. Not so much an island, more a museum – the Deutches Museum, full of everything from aircraft to submarines, and crowded with all types of people; from gawping oiking-pogs, schoolchildren, students, tourists and lovers, to bemused, bearded, bespectacled professors.

It was in the coal mine; not a real one obviously, but a look-alike, work-alike, feel-alike and even smell-alike replica of a coal mine. There he was, Alex, groping about in the dark, when all of a sudden the Stygian air transformed itself into the soft, yielding form of a female.

'Bloody hell. Er, I mean, *Entschuldigung,*' he said, automatically. Quickly, he removed his offending hand from the woman's left breast. Given time he supposed that he could have come up with something slightly more original, but his mind had been on other things.

'Pervert!' was the immediate response.

Never at a loss for words, Jessica always managed to come up with a word or a phrase to suit every possible situation. Her answer threw Alex, or rather his mind, completely off balance and all he could muster in return was a feeble, 'Pardon?'

'Get your hands off me,' she continued. 'You can't just lurk in dark coal mines in the middle of Munich, waiting for unsuspecting females to fall into your clutches. Who do you think you are?'

This string of words ushered them into a corridor boasting slightly better lighting. Lighting that glistened on the most beautiful head of hair that Alex had ever seen, especially in a pit! It was still a little too dark for him to be able to make out the colour of her eyes but immediately he formed the opinion, as one does, that they must have been blue, to match the long blonde hair that had temporarily rendered him speechless.

Unable to remember exactly how they got there, Alex found himself a few minutes later sitting at a table in the cafeteria. He was stirring a cup of coffee with a bendy plastic stick, trying to apologize for his earlier behaviour, whilst endeavouring to discover more about the blonde goddess who'd just happened to visit a coal mine at, for Alex, the most propitious time possible.

It's not every day, he thought to himself, that one finds oneself down a mine, totally in the dark, only to fall against an angel sent from heaven.

'. . . and then Mum and Dad said they were off for the afternoon to do some shopping, so ... here I am.'

'Yes,' he said vaguely. 'I see.'

He didn't though. He didn't understand any of it. He was still in a daze.

'But how? I mean, how come you happen to be here? I mean, here in this museum?'

Maybe he'd missed something, he thought, realizing that he didn't even know for how long she'd been speaking. He didn't even know her name – he'd almost forgotten his own.

'Oh, easy,' said Jessica. 'In the hotel. In the lobby there's a vast mahogany table covered with little bundles of leaflets all extolling the virtues of countless interesting places to visit. It's

4

raining,' she shrugged, as though the wet weather was her reason for choosing the museum, 'and this place happens to be just round the corner.'

Well-educated, Alex surmised. Elegantly eloquent; not everyone extols virtues.

'Another cup of coffee?' he ventured, glancing at his watch. Quarter to four. Christ! He was supposed to meet his friend Nick at four in some Bierkeller near Isartorplatz, before they were both due to meet others at the Hoffbrauhaus for some Wildschweinbraten mit Steinpilzen, no doubt to be washed down with more beer.

Well, bollocks to that, Alex decided. Nick would have to amuse himself for a while, and hopefully they'd meet up sooner or later at Munich's famous watering hole.

Too late! Jessica had seen his watch.

'Quarter to four already?' She turned her head to peer through the window and, in the movement, Alex noticed a subtle hint of red underlying the luminosity of her hair as it trawled across her shoulders. 'Look, it's stopped raining,' she observed. 'I'll be able to walk back to Rumfordstrasse without getting soaked. I'm supposed to be meeting the folks at four, I think we're off to a concert this evening. Anyway, I'd better go.'

'Um, listen,' said Alex. 'You obviously enjoy visiting museums otherwise you wouldn't be here.' Fatuous remark, he told himself, mentally bashing his head against the table top. Oh well, in for a penny... 'There's one place in this town that you really shouldn't miss,' he told her, 'the Glyptothek. Have you been there?'

She looked doubtful, and again Alex realized that he still didn't know her name.

'Alex,' he said, standing up. 'Alexander Prentiss.' He helped her on with her coat. 'I really am very sorry about the coal-mine incident but it's been great talking with you, and, well ... tomorrow I'm going to be at the Glyptothek anyway. Perhaps we could meet and wander around together. I think it's so much more interesting to have someone to discuss the exhibits with, and...'

'Yes, okay. Why not? My name is Jessica. Not Jess, not Jessie. Jessica. I know where the Glyptothek is, I read about it in one of those leaflets and ... well, I've been meaning to visit. How about two o'clock?'

'Fine!'

Alex was shattered. Jessica had arranged something that he'd been summoning up the courage to arrange, and indeed might have got around to accomplishing by the time they'd stepped outside the museum, but she had done it all, in detail, before they'd left the table.

'Fine!' Now he was starting to repeat himself. 'Oh, and I hope you enjoy the concert.'

Jessica turned towards him, smiled. 'Bye. See you tomorrow.'

A hint of perfume, a swish of coat, and that was it. Jessica moved away into the distance.

Alex floundered.

2

PRIVATE AND CONFIDENTIAL.

What a giveaway.

These are the letters that head straight for the bin, before any of the others. Even before the final reminders printed in large, red, easily decipherable letters which herald to all and sundry that you haven't paid the gas bill, the electricity bill, or the poll tax.

PRIVATE AND CONFIDENTIAL.

Three words that send a cold chill spiralling down one's spine.

The overdraft has overflowed and the bank is getting edgy.

The credit-card company hasn't been paid for several months and wants to know why.

The bailiff is on his way round to collect some of your treasured possessions.

PRIVATE AND CONFIDENTIAL.

Envelopes that are propped up in front of you as you chomp away at the breakfast cereal, and then, thrust deep into some inner recess of your jacket, insidiously make known their presence during the remainder of the day.

'Should I open it?' Alex asked himself, maybe for the hundredth time.

No. Definitely not. Tear it in half, he thought. Then tear it into quarters, eighths and sixteenths and shove the pieces into a bin at the earliest opportunity.

Too late.

The envelope was already open, and it hadn't been Alex who'd done the opening. Despite those enormous black letters which shriek out 'danger lies within', *she'd* opened it. The envelope, which must always be destroyed before its contents can manifest themselves upon the unwary, had been opened at some stage during its voyage from the hall carpet to the dining table.

Jessica was like that. She had that type of nose. The sort that had always to weasel itself into anything that looked remotely interesting, mysterious or secret.

Useful at times, Alex found himself admitting, but at other times, he decided, there should be a mutual agreement of 'snouts out'.

'Would you like something to drink, sir?'

One of the nicest ways to be woken up. Pretty stupid question though, Alex thought. Of course he'd like something to drink, especially when that something to drink is free. Doubly so when, jolted out of a three-hour cat nap, one finds oneself in a metal tube, suspended thirty-nine thousand feet above the sea. Air hostesses are renowned for their efficiency, on the better airlines at least. Still, it nevertheless amazed him to see a gin and tonic materialize in a matter of seconds onto the little swing-down plastic shelf fixed to the back of the seat in front of him. He gazed at the lines of bubbles swimming to the surface as they struggled past the wedge of lemon and the three ice-cubes, seemingly all jostling for the best position. It looked so refreshing, so cool, sophisticated, and necessary.

Alex slowly began to move his limbs and suddenly realized what it must be like to exist as a paper bag that's been well and truly crumpled. Creased, wrinkled, deflated were adjectives that sprang readily into his mind.

'Ugh,' he said to himself.

Slightly louder than the noise of the rising bubbles and audible above the background murmur of the aircraft's air-conditioning, Alex had been vaguely aware of some sort of scraping hissing sound coming from his left. Twisting his head in that direction he spotted the source of irritation. It was a vicar. Well, not exactly the vicar himself, it was those little pads that were clinging to the vicar's ears. Quite trendy for a vicar, Alex thought, David Bowie sounding all thin and squeaky. He started to wonder what trendy vicars might preach about but supposed that the sermons couldn't be too way-out, otherwise they'd lose their congregations, but then maybe if the sermon was too dull...

He needed to pee.

Being nestled next to a window, Alex had to extricate himself without becoming entangled in the vicar's speaker wires, then he had to be careful not to knock over the baby bottle of claret on one knee, and the half-full glass on the other knee of the pin-stripe-suited man occupying the seat between the vicar and the freedom of the aisle. The man had taken the precaution of holding each object firmly in each of his hands and was sitting bolt upright staring straight ahead, at, but not seeing, the screen in front of him. Alex noticed the whiteness of the knuckles as he lifted his feet over the man's legs. Either he's in some kind of trance or he's scared shitless, Alex thought, making a mental note to be careful not to disturb the fellow too much when returning to his seat.

9

Having relieved himself, he closed the lid and flushed the loo, and grinned at the thought of his personal rain cloud being unleashed from the underbelly of the aircraft. Or was it siphoned away into a giant tank to form a holding-pattern, only to end up in a sludge-gulper when the plane was parked safely on the tarmac? This train of thought caused another grin as Alex pictured passengers emanating from one door, baggage from another, and his contribution to the world's precipitation being sucked from yet another of the aircraft's orifices.

He had an inquisitive mind and filed away the problem of inflight waste disposal, resolving to ask a mate who, when not too drunk to locate his aircraft in the parking lot, flew for one of the longhaul airlines.

It seemed a lifetime ago that Jessica had driven him to the airport, one hand on the steering wheel, the other on his leg – when she wasn't changing gear, something one doesn't have to do too often on the M4 at three in the morning when the motorway is as deserted as Chernobyl. After a hurried coffee and a piece of toast with butter and marmalade, they'd left the house in High Barnet at two-thirty, allowing plenty of time for the trip to Heathrow, Alex's flight being scheduled to depart at six.

Despite the early hour, and despite the fact that he should have been making last minute checks on the contents of his suitcase, Alex had re-read the confidential letter, leaving Jessica to check the case, the passport, the envelope containing dollars, and the time.

Private and Confidential

Dear Mr Prentiss

We are writing to you in the hope that you might be able to assist us with a problem which has come to our attention.

Enclosed you will find photocopies of documents which were unearthed during the upheaval caused by our firm's recent relocation. The original documents had been concealed beneath a desk-drawer in the office of one of our Partners, and came to light when the removal men started packing everything in preparation for transference to our new premises.

You will notice that a name appearing on one of the documents is the same as your own, and whilst we acknowledge it's highly unlikely that you are in any way connected, or indeed related to the person in question, we feel it to be our duty to contact you with regard to this information.

We are certain that should you have any interest whatsoever in this matter, you will also be aware of the importance of our discovery.

Likewise, in the event that you decide you are unable to give us any assistance or contribute further to our findings, we hope sincerely that you will not have been inconvenienced by this letter.

Yours

George Michelstraub
Meyer, Michelstraub, Meyer (Attorneys)
1473 Maple Avenue, Binghamton, New York, USA

The photocopies had given a rough outline of a shipment of goods belonging to one Arthur Prentiss. There was mention of a crate, a list of shipping in and out of Marseilles, and a sheet of paper detailing some kind of transit insurance. The print quality

11

of the photocopies was not good, and Alex surmised that the original documentation had suffered through continued exposure to sunlight. Perhaps it was just the age of the papers that made them almost illegible, but Alex persevered, and close scrutiny of the photocopies under a strong lamp had revealed a month, September, and a year, 1944. Also, towards the foot of another sheet of paper, Alex had been able to make out a figure which, although very faint, had enough zeros attached to place it in the realm of tens of thousands, maybe millions. But of what? Articles in the crate? Money?

Enough was enough.

Although Alex's natural curiosity had been roused, he'd remained a little dubious, and the story may well have ended here had it not been for the return ticket to New York, which had lain half-hidden amongst all the photocopies.

Doubt disappeared, intrigue blossomed.

'Definitely the right thing to do,' Alex had said for the umpteenth time, as Jessica had started showing signs of impatience. 'A free trip to the Big Apple. And it'll be good to get a handle on what this is all about,' he'd added, waving papers and ticket in the air.

Jessica had pointed at the clock and they'd exited the house, their passage to the front door causing the air to form swirling vortexes, heavily laden with the aroma of burnt toast.

Alex had never been to New York.

He'd never been to America.

Heathrow had been bad enough, but, JFK? Well, Dante probably would have felt quite at home. The noise enveloping Alex as he walked across the concourse in search of baggage-collect was horrendous.

For some unknown reason the place was full of schoolchildren. Maybe someone had informed them that Alex was coming, perhaps they'd followed him all the way across the pond. Magically, they would seem always to appear out of thin air, like flies round a bride. They seemed also always to be the noisiest children in the world, channelling decibels of unwanted child-speak and child-screams directly towards him.

Just like the neighbours, Alex reminisced.

'Brookside' was how he and Jessica referred to them-next-door. 'Brat-Pack' was another tag they'd bestowed upon their neighbours' kids. The parents yelled at the kids, the kids hollered back, each trying to out-yell the other. And now it seemed they were all here, with all their noisy peers running in circles around Alex and getting under his feet.

Then there was the carousel, which had a particularly nasty squeak and seemed incapable of holding onto the cases. They were falling onto the floor in their hundreds, all except Alex's of course. His was the last to totter down the chute, balance precariously on the edge of the rotating turntable and immediately become jammed, only to be verbally abused by one of the largest people Alex had ever seen. He was huge. His task, it seemed, consisted of little more than yelling at recalcitrant pieces of luggage, and his one great advantage was that the subjects of his relentless verbosity were incapable of any backchat.

Alex had learned that a pleasant smile usually does the trick and, sure enough, yet again it worked its charm.

He grabbed his case, circumnavigated the hulk and, having followed all the exit signs, wedged himself and his case into the relative safety of a cab.

Congratulating himself on his safe arrival, he settled back into the leather upholstery. A moment later he noticed that he was

13

being watched via the rear-view mirror and found himself staring into the eyes of the cabbie.

'Top o' the mornin' to ya. And where exactly would you be needin' to go?'

'Binghamton,' Alex told the driver, and went on to give him the name of the hotel, then, knackered, he dozed off. He was surrounded by large soft woolly clouds which tasted like candy floss and rained lemon sherbet onto the roofs of terraced houses, row upon row, stretching away into infinity.

Binghamton is the archetypal American town, the outskirts featuring neat houses, neat fences and neat letter-boxes neatly fixed to the neat fences. Neat kids with their neat pets loitering on neat lawns. Neatness rules, okay?

The hotel that Alex had checked in to slotted into the same category.

The receptionist, like the taxi-driver, turned out also to be Irish but then, Alex found himself thinking, over here wasn't everybody? Red hair, green eyes, and efficiency was her middle name. By the time he'd signed the register, his case had disappeared, he'd been offered a drink, a meal, a hire car at a very special weekend rate, and the soft 'ding' was the lift welcoming him into its inner sanctum.

The room was comfortable; a sort of olde-worldly charm, well-appointed and well-decorated, a haven of peace for weary travellers. The bathroom contained everything a bathroom should contain so Alex tested the lavatory, plunged into the shower and then, toothbrush clamped firmly between his teeth, he returned into the bedroom to switch on the television.

Revived and refreshed, he was ready for that drink and perhaps

14

also ready for something to eat, but, first things first. He picked up the phone and dialled London.

Jessica was jumping up and down.

At least that's the impression that Alex formed as he listened to her voice over the phone.

How was the flight? Was he suffering from jet lag? Were the natives friendly? Had he had anything to eat?

Fine. Not yet. Yes, and about to. Naturally he went into a little more detail. With Jessica, one always went into detail; it was filed away in her brain and made available for instant retrieval at a moment's notice. No need for a filofax, no need for a computer – the inanimate objects and modern technology would be out of their league, unable to keep pace or be as reliable, and they'd be nowhere near as attractive.

3

Thursday.

Ever since school days Alex had had a strange affinity with Thursdays. He remembered them as being biased towards English and geography in the mornings, French and sport in the afternoons. The main attraction perhaps used to be the proximity to Friday and the weekend. Yes, Alex decided, Thursdays were okay. Normally.

The rain bouncing off the pavement only intensified the autumnal atmosphere; sombre trees, dark and dull although crowned with magnificent glory. The American fall is something one always hears about, sees in the movies and in glossy magazines, but nothing can recapture the reality. Multicoloured leaves glistening in the rain, adorning every tree; beacons bright enough to dispel the gloom of even the darkest of days. Every shade from deepest red through the palest yellow, each leaf accumulating individual photons and generating within itself a living fire, a dazzling jewel.

As Alex rounded the corner he came face to face with a brass plaque conveying its message through baleful morning light: Meyer, Michelstraub & Meyer (Attorneys). He was about to ring the bell when the door opened to allow the passage of a pair of high heels, a cape and a Russian rabbit hat. He caught a brief glimpse of grey-green eyes as the figure swept past him and disappeared, floating down the street. A faint aroma of Chanel No. 5 invaded his senses as he collected himself together before effecting his entrance into the lobby of Messrs. Meyer, Michelstraub & Meyer.

The typewriter stopped clacking, just long enough to allow the secretary time to point Alex towards the waiting-area that, for some unknown reason, was in urgent need of attention from a decorator. Alex figured that these attorneys either were not doing too well and could not afford a few dollars on make-up or, they were doing extremely well and were therefore far too busy to clutter their premises with workmen. Then, noticing a pile of *National Geographics* stacked in a heap on the floor, he remembered that the firm had just moved office. He picked up one of the glossy magazines and had just started perusing an article on Vermont from a 1974 issue, when he was startled by the opening of a door.

Well, thought Alex, it had to be a Meyer or a Michelstraub. He chose Meyer – there were more of them.

'Nope. Michelstraub.' They shook hands.

'Ah. Well I've come from England in response to your letter.'

'England? In that case you must be...'

'Prentiss. Alexander Prentiss.'

'Exactly.' Michelstraub ushered Alex into his office.

Redolent of well-worn leather, the room exuded an air of Dickensian quality; book-lined walls, heavy oak desk and two deep armchairs, the whole shrouded in subdued lighting giving the impression of scholastic tranquillity.

'Sit down, sit down,' said Michelstraub affably, closing the door behind him.

Alex sat. Rather, he sank into one of the armchairs and had to haul himself back into an upright position. Michelstraub had seated himself in the other armchair and was peering at Alex, the way solicitors do.

'You're the first.'

'I am?'

Alex was rattled. He began to wonder if the differences between the English and American languages had drifted so far apart that they'd said their goodbyes, gone to their respective homes and altogether given up the pretence of similarity.

'Oh yes. Definitely the first. And all the way from England!'

Michelstraub was not making himself any clearer.

'I'm afraid I don't understand,' said Alex. Ignorance, he guessed, probably would be his best ploy in this situation. He was certain that Michelstraub would be the sort of person who'd delight in detail, telling him precisely what the whole matter was about. Alex began rummaging through his pockets trying to find the letter that had started him off on this caper.

'We certainly haven't heard from anybody else,' said Michelstraub.

This was getting silly. Michelstraub was proving to be an expert at proving a point but Alex was unable to fathom out just what the point was.

'You see, we wrote to all the Prentisses we could find, and believe me we found quite a few. It's strange that we haven't heard, as yet, from anyone in the States, but then...'

Alex let him ramble on. He had no choice really, his mind had gone into overdrive. Here he was in some American town, confronted by some American lawyer who obviously had no idea which particular Prentiss was going to be able to help him out of his dilemma.

Then there was the money.

My God, thought Alex, Jessica would be hopping mad. Her work, indeed her passion as a psychologist, gave her undeniable insight into the workings of the intellect. She'd guessed, correctly, how the meeting would transpire and had told him to raise the question of finance as soon as he entered the offices of Meyer,

Michelstraub and Meyer. Okay, he told himself, the airfare had been provided and, as he'd found out from the receptionist, the hotel room also, but no one had taken his time into consideration. It must have been the thought of Jessica's ire that launched him onto his next tack.

'What about expenses?'

Straight to the point, thought Alex. No messing about. Anyway, he mused, this is America and they're supposed to respect people being up-front.

'I mean, here I am at your beckoning, so to speak, and you don't appear to know if I'm the correct Prentiss! In a couple of minutes I could be walking out of this office, back to the airport and back to the UK with not so much as a "thank-you".' Alex was warming to his task. Once embarked on a collision course he was as unremitting as a tank.

'Mmm,' said Michelstraub. 'I'm under the impression that you don't want to be heading home until you've heard more about this scenario.'

'But...'

'You see,' Michelstraub continued, 'your curiosity has brought you this far. I guess ... no, I'm *certain* you'll be itching to know more.'

'Maybe, but...'

'And so far as expenses are concerned,' Michelstraub went on, 'there's no problem. We have a covenant, a deed. Found it with all the other documents. It'll cover all our expenses. Yours as well. Lunch?'

Each course was accompanied by idle chatter. The weather, the Boston Red Sox, or maybe it was the Chicago Bears, a recent

19

holiday in Florida; anything but the subject uppermost on Alex's mind. Michelstraub evidently was in no hurry to elucidate. He was engrossed in what must have been his second favourite occupation – the first making itself blatantly obvious, right in front of Alex's eyes: eating. Michelstraub presented himself as a perfect example of 'The Gourmet'.

During the course of the meal, every nuance, every movement, every gesture imparted a vision of his being at one with his environment. A pause, a sigh, a wine glass hovering in mid-air as the bouquet was savoured. A stare into space as the subtle flavour of a juniper sauce brought forgotten memories sweeping back into Michelstraub's ample head.

Ample, in fact, would be an excellent word with which to describe the build of the American lawyer, an outline that was expanding even as Alex watched. Michelstraub had just finished siphoning cherry pie and ice cream from his dessert bowl and was in the act of demolishing a stack of biscuits, each generously covered with layers of butter and thick wedges of cheese deftly selected from an impressive array.

It was late afternoon by the time they returned to the office.

Michelstraub ensconced himself in his armchair which seemed to embrace him as some long-lost friend, while Alex perched on the edge of the other armchair and waited for the oracle to orate.

'Mrs Carmichael lives in New York, Manhattan. She's eighty-seven years old with a mind as sharp as a slice of lemon.'

Who the fuck is Mrs Carmichael? Alex asked himself, beginning to wonder if the whole episode was some sort of fairy tale.

'The Carmichael family are legend in New York,' Michelstraub continued, answering Alex's unvoiced question. 'Their house is like a museum.'

Alex shook his head and sighed, frustrated but also amused. It was worth the frustration just to see Michelstraub's eyes twinkling and his jowls trembling as he picked his way carefully along each sentence, the words chosen and uttered with complete satisfaction as the story was coaxed from its hiding place deep within his large astute cranium.

'Wall-to-wall ectopia. Artifacts bound one to another by glutinous spiders' webs, surfaces awash with the detritus of time itself, a black hole. There must be one of everything in the Carmichael domicile, gathered and garnered from every corner of the world – known and unknown. Most of it useless debris.'

The oracle was in full spate while shadows shifted and blended, the light from the standard lamp gradually overpowering the waning daylight as evening approached. Michelstraub and the armchair morphed and became one.

'Ellie – that's Mrs Carmichael – couldn't have been more helpful. Directly we told her what we were looking for, she took us straight to it. Saved us days. To have gone through all those rooms, all those boxes, crates... Well, anyway, there they were...'

'What were?' Alex asked.

'The pictures.'

'What pictures?'

Alex was beginning to feel a little twinge nagging away somewhere in the space between his ears, and he believed it had absolutely nothing to do with the wine and the brandy he'd had with his lunch. It was just ... maybe a sixth sense, a sliver of light trying to penetrate the shadows hovering in the corners of his mind.

'Ah, yes.' Michelstraub's left arm broke free from the confines of the armchair, and he picked up a medium-sized folder from a table conveniently located just under the lamp. He thumbed through three or four sheets of paper, coming at last to the page he required. 'Item thirty-seven,' he read. 'Eight pictures, framed, each bearing the signature "A. Prentiss".' He glared over the top of his glasses, another trait practised by solicitors worldwide. 'Am I making sense?'

'No,' Alex answered. At that moment nothing made sense to Alex, except perhaps that the world was filled with too many Prentisses.

Michelstraub handed him the sheet of paper. Emblazoned and embossed at the top were the words 'The Repository', its Manhattan address and telephone number centred underneath. Typed down the page was a long list of articles, including item thirty-seven.

'I take it that this repository is now the home of your Mrs Carmichael?' asked Alex.

'Always was,' Michelstraub replied. 'Her husband was an art collector of some repute, as was his father, and his father's father.'

'That'll be his grandfather,' said Alex, always anxious to be of help.

'What? Oh, yes.' Michelstraub barely hesitated. 'Not just art. They collected virtually everything from paintings to porcelain, shark's teeth to seashells. Like I said, a veritable Aladdin's Cave. Anyway, after her husband passed away, Mrs Carmichael retained the place, keeping it just as he'd left it. A museum, but ... but not a museum, if you see what I mean. A shrine if you like. And over the years it became well known, a haunt for researchers from every walk of life. And Mrs Carmichael? Well, she became known as the "Custodian", a living directory of the Repository's contents.'

Alex passed back the sheet of paper and Michelstraub returned it to the folder which he replaced on the table, before once again fusing with the armchair.

'It transpires that Prentiss was quite well known in early-nineteenth-century Europe,' Michelstraub continued, 'although these particular pictures seem to be shrouded in mystery. The only documentation appears to be that which we discovered during the move. But – and here's the thing – two of the pictures are missing.'

'Down to six,' ventured Alex.

'Yes,' said Michelstraub. 'Down to six, as you put it.'

'So?' asked Alex.

'So,' replied Michelstraub, 'this maybe is where you come in.'

Or maybe not, thought Alex.

It had been quite an exposition, the most extensive outpouring Michelstraub had thus far managed. And, as if to substantiate Alex's observation, Michelstraub left the sanctuary of his chair and, from a drawer in the outsize desk, produced a bottle of port and a couple of glasses. A quick shuffle brought him back to base, whereupon he proceeded to fill the glasses with the thick rubescent liquid.

'Are you related?' Michelstraub asked.

'To my mother and father,' Alex answered.

'No no...'

'To an aunt and an uncle,' Alex continued. 'Then there's a handful of cousins and cousins removed, and first and second cousins...'

'To Prentiss the artist?' Michelstraub cut in.

'Shouldn't think so,' Alex replied. 'Circles and straight lines are my limit when it comes to drawing, and that's only with a compass and a ruler.'

'Pity.' Michelstraub rubbed his jowls between thumb and forefinger.

Things seemed to be getting a little less hazy, but Alex still had one question that needed an answer.

'The air ticket – surely you can't have sent one to all the Prentisses on your list?'

'No. No. It was a hunch. Based to a certain extent on intelligent supposition. The pictures ... the paintings, began life in Europe, so I thought it a safe bet that the missing pair would still be there. I narrowed the Prentiss search, for a start, to Britain – no language problems, and the London Directory gave me your address. Easy.'

'The London Directory would have given you a glut of Prentisses.'

'It did,' Michelstraub agreed.

'Then why me?'

'Superstition. As with our artist, your Christian name also begins with the letter "A".'

It was looking as though it was going to be a long evening, and as he had nothing else to do, Alex decided he might as well stretch out his legs, relax into the depths of the armchair, and slowly imbibe the proffered port whilst his host waxed lyrical.

The heavy lunch, the alcohol, the sonorous tone of Michelstraub's voice, not to mention the jet lag, were all catching up on him. It was as much as he could do to keep his eyes open, and a couple of hours later he made his excuses and left the offices of Meyer, Michelstraub and Meyer.

Although the damp evening air did its best to revive him as he wandered back to the hotel, Alex decided that the day had been more than long enough. On reaching his room, he lay on top of the large double bed, his hands tucked behind his head, powerless to stop the automatic reaction of his eyelids as they dragged themselves heavily across the aching surface of his over-tired eyes.

On waking the following morning, he had no recollection of climbing out of his clothes and crawling between the sheets but, as he tried to open his sleepy eyes, vague impressions of a dream, filled with dim, book-lined rooms, packing cases full of stuffed animals, and someone who wouldn't or couldn't stop talking, passed through his emerging conciousness.

Dreams are weird and wonderful things, Alex thought to himself as he stood under the stinging jets of the power-shower, and later, as he towelled himself dry, he found himself smiling at the idea that last night's dream somehow had provided him with a clue as to his plan of action.

4

Breakfast was coffee and orange juice.

Black coffee, freshly squeezed orange juice. Gallons of both. The full breakfast was just what the menu said it would be, but after yesterday's session of over-indulgence, Alex's stomach wasn't up to it.

Whilst the other residents sat behind their papers, Alex glared at the table cloth, downed the orange juice, sipped the coffee, and elevated his mind into higher gear.

Packing his case didn't take long, phoning Jessica did; more information to feed into her reservoir of knowledge.

Alex had given her the facts: documents, pictures, missing pictures, repositories – everything, and Jessica had assimilated, calculated, eliminated and regurgitated the correct response by the time he'd finished speaking.

'So, it's back to New York?' she'd said. Input and output.

To Alex, it seemed impossible that Michelstraub hadn't thought of it, but then it's often the simplest ideas that are overlooked.

The journey from Binghamton back to New York gave him the chance to ponder the pros and cons. Perhaps Mrs Carmichael had inadvertently placed the missing pictures in one of the other rooms. Perhaps she hadn't done anything inadvertently, had simply kept them for herself.

Although Michelstraub believed the missing pictures were still in Europe, Alex reckoned they were probably somewhere right under his nose, Michelstraub's nose. It may have been just an excuse for him to visit Mrs Carmichael's treasure-trove but, Michelstraub's description had fascinated him and, as a journalist, he thought there was a strong possibility that he'd be able to sniff out a good story, maybe earn a few pennies. Curiosity had got the better of him and, as he journeyed back to New York, Alex couldn't help thinking there was something strange about the facts that had been presented to him. He began to wonder at Michelstraub's interest in the recovery of the two paintings. And, having ruled himself out of the equation, certain there was no 'lost' artist lurking on a branch of his family tree, he asked himself, to whom did the paintings belong? Yes, fair enough, they'd been housed at the 'Repository' but ... why? Did they belong to Mrs Carmichael? Or maybe they'd been part of the collection put together by her husband? Alex resolved to stay on the case, to ferret about and ask some questions. After all, the paintings had been in Michelstraub's care for at least a month, yet no one had thought of returning to the Carmichael residence in order to search for the missing pair.

Except Alex.

And Jessica.

And, as it turned out, Mandie...

Michelstraub, however, had been entirely correct about one thing: the Carmichael intellect certainly was razor sharp.

Mrs Carmichael led Alex through a spacious hall, then through room after room until they arrived at a library, of sorts. There were more books here than one would find in an average municipal library. Shelves stretched right around the room from ceiling to floor with books overflowing everywhere, carpeting anything and everything that offered a flat surface. Alex looked around in amazement as he followed Mrs Carmichael on an erratic course between the mountains of books. Thin books, thick books, leather-bound tomes, paperbacks, whole sets of encyclopaedias stacked vertically, forming columns and corridors. They stepped into a clearing and stopped, suddenly, Alex almost colliding into his guide. He pinched his nostrils together to prevent himself sneezing as the dust of antiquity infiltrated his lungs. And there, interlaced with the heavy tang of leather, something else drifted through the atmosphere, inspiring Alex's senses to communicate with his brain. He left them on automatic, left them crunching numbers, hoping they'd discover the link.

They sat.

Mrs Carmichael, with her back to a window, took the only chair. Alex made do with an upturned crate. A couple of minutes later a maid brought a tray bearing a pot of tea, cups, saucers, and a plate of biscuits. She placed the tray onto a small circular table and withdrew, disappearing into the sea of literature.

'I do like my afternoon tea,' said Mrs Carmichael, pouring for both of them. 'Afternoon tea and biscuits,' she continued. 'It lends majesty to the afternoon and settles one into a state of readiness for the evening. Don't you think?'

'Quite so,' replied Alex, deciding it would be futile to argue with such profound Englishness, indeed, with such profound logic. He took a sip from the bone-china teacup. Earl Grey. He lowered the cup onto its saucer and balanced them on his left knee.

'Mrs Carmichael,' he began.

Not a bad beginning, he thought to himself. Not bad at all.

'Mrs Carmichael. You may recall that a few weeks ago, some paintings were collected from your house by a...'

'Ah, and what interesting paintings. All by the same man. What was his name now? Let me think. Ah, yes, Prentiss. Prentiss something, or something Prentiss.'

'Arthur,' Alex offered.

'Excuse me?'

'Arthur. Arthur Prentiss. That's the artist's name.'

'Arthur Prentiss,' Mrs Carmichael repeated slowly. 'Of course. And then there's that nice Mr Michelstraub, from out of town. Such a polite man. He really was quite excited you know, Mr Michelstraub, when I showed him the pictures. It's all a mystery to me. I mean, they must have been lying around in the games room for years and suddenly... Oh dear, you must excuse me rambling on, it's just that I don't have that many visitors these days, and ... dear me, I've quite forgotten what it was you were asking.'

'Well, I was hoping that you might allow me to rummage about in the room where the pictures were stored, because ... well, you see, there should be two more.'

'Two more paintings?'

'Yes, yes. Two more to complete the set of eight. You see, they're missing and I thought they might have been...'

'You've just missed her!' Mrs Carmichael responded enigmatically.

'I have?' Alex asked, feeling a little like the Mad Hatter.

'Yes.'

'Who?'

'Sweet girl. Such eyes. Blue. No, green. Mandie. Said she worked for Mr Michelstraub and could she... Well – she asked precisely the same as you. All to do with...'

All of a sudden the atmosphere coalesced and the connecting thread that had been hovering in space revealed itself.

Chanel No. 5. Rabbit hat. Binghamton.

Synapses snapped and the link was complete. Alex had to know more and Mrs Carmichael was telling him everything he wanted to hear, at least, she was trying to tell him. She'd stopped in mid-flow and was looking at him with suspicion.

'Are you quite all right?' she asked.

'Yes,' he replied absently, thinking that he must have looked pretty stupid while his brain had been attempting to catch up with itself. 'Yes, I'm fine.'

'Well, you looked a bit startled there for a minute.'

Alex smiled, took a gulp of tea and composed himself.

'Now. Where was I?' Mrs Carmichael collected her thoughts, then continued. 'Ah, yes, Mandie. Well, I showed her to the games room and she peered here and she peered there, and after several minutes she produced from behind a packing case a tightly wrapped bundle of papers. She brushed away the dust and we saw the name "Prentiss" handwritten on the edge of the roll. Her face really lit up and she said it was exactly what she'd been hoping to find.'

That was it. That was just too much. Another bundle of papers. Michelstraub was playing games with him and he wasn't happy about it, not happy at all. Alex imagined the man sitting at his desk, eyes twinkling in delight, as Michelstraub in turn was probably imagining Alex running around in circles.

'Could I use your phone?' he asked.

'Dear boy,' Michelstraub purred from the safe, familiar confines of his office. 'How are you getting on?'

'Listen,' thundered Alex. 'I'm here in Manhattan at the Carmichael place. Only there's someone else been here already. Someone you know.'

'Mandie.'

'Yes,' Alex agreed. 'Mandie. Who the hell is Mandie and why am I duplicating her moves? You didn't tell me there was anyone else mixed up with this business. Oh no, I had to go and find out for myself.'

'Ah. Well, it's a little involved. But really it's nothing for you to worry about.'

'Let me be the judge of that,' stormed Alex. 'This whole thing's involved. It's all ... topsy-turvy, and if you've any other little surprises stashed up your sleeves, maybe now would be a good time to tell me.'

This wasn't Alex, placid, calm, tranquil Alex. This was somebody else. But perhaps the wadge of notes Michelstraub had handed him in the office the day before had made him a lot more assertive. Also, he decided, it might just possibly have something to do with the fact that he wanted to meet this Mandie. She seemed always to be one step ahead of him and he wanted to know why.

'Yes. Well. Mandie. She's the daughter of one of my partners.'

'So she's a Meyer?' Alex's powers of observation were improving in leaps and bounds. Jessica would have been proud.

'No. She's a Baxter. She's married.'

'Ah.' Alex reckoned it had been a good try, so he tried again. 'So how come you failed to tell me about her before sending me out on this goose chase?'

'I suppose I thought it unlikely that you'd go bumping into each other,' Michelstraub explained. 'At least, not at such an early stage. You know, I thought if I had two people working on the problem we might cut to the chase sooner rather than later. So, now you know everything you may as well work together. I'll give you her number and tell her to expect your call.'

Alex recalled the brief glimpse in Binghamton and thought

that Mandie might well be the sort of woman with whom he wouldn't mind working. He also knew that Jessica would not necessarily be of the same opinion.

He replaced the phone on its cradle and turned to find Mrs Carmichael looking at him. 'Mrs Carmichael?' he asked. 'The paintings? To whom do they belong? Are they yours?' He paused. 'Or maybe they belonged to your husband?'

'Goodness, no,' she smiled, eyes sparkling. 'They were not to his taste, not at all.'

'Then they belong to Mr Michelstraub?' Alex pursued.

Mrs Carmichael swept a hand across the material of her dress, brushing at some imagined flecks of dust, as though erasing some irksome memory. 'No,' she replied quietly, 'they don't.'

'So why all the interest?' Alex asked.

'I suppose he's just trying to tie up the loose ends, you know?'

'You mean after the partner's death?'

'Yes,' Mrs Carmichael answered. 'After Charley's death.'

'Charley?' Alex queried.

'Meyer, Charley Meyer.'

It turned out that the Baxters lived in an apartment not a million miles from Mrs Carmichael's rambling jumble of rooms. A short ride in a cab brought Alex to his destination and, standing on the stoop with suitcase in one hand, briefcase in the other, he came face to face with a tough-looking New York City cop.

'Hey, you must be Prentiss, the English guy. Come in, have a beer. Howd'ya find New York?'

Alex was tired. Instead of making some smart remark such as 'I let the pilot find it for me', he dropped his cases onto the floor, slumped onto a sofa and gratefully accepted the offer of a beer. The New York City cop mumbled something about 'fixing a bite' and disappeared into what Alex presumed would be the kitchen.

His head revolved around three-hundred-and-sixty degrees taking in the surroundings, while his brain tried to work out why there was this policeman offering him a beer as though he owned the place. Then it dawned on him. Maybe the policeman *did* own the place, in conjunction with Mandie. After all, he thought, it sort of makes sense that a solicitor's daughter might chance to get entangled with a cop. Keep it in the family, so to speak.

Oh well, better keep on the right side of these people, he told himself.

The chilled beer had just begun to reach his nether regions when the New York City cop and Mandie entered the living room from different directions, only the cop no longer had the appearance of a cop. The distinctive blue uniform had been replaced with jeans, white shirt open at the neck, and a dark-tan leather jacket. He was carrying a dish piled high with tortilla chips. Mandie had a glass of beer. Had it not been for the faint aroma of Chanel No.5, Alex might not instantly have recognized her. Gone were the smart clothes she'd been wearing upstate. Instead, she sported a pair of tight, ass-hugging blue jeans and a primrose-yellow shirt, knotted at the front; evidentally a woman who'd look good in anything. Alex beamed, ready and willing to act out Michelstraub's charade.

'The man from England,' said Mandie, shaking his hand as Alex struggled to leave the sofa. 'No no, don't get up. Relax.'

She waved him back into the seat as she turned towards her partner. 'Dan, Alex. Alex, Dan.' Brief but efficient. The minimum of words and everyone knew everyone.

Mandie and Dan sat across the table from Alex on another of the deeply luxurious three-seater sofas.

'Well well,' Mandie said, smiling at Alex. 'You seem to be Michelstraub's blue-eyed boy.'

'How so?' Alex asked.

'He's just been on the phone. Seems pretty impressed with the way you responded to his letter.'

'It wasn't too difficult,' Alex explained. 'I just got on the plane.'

'Well, maybe it's your accent then. It's kinda cute.'

'That's not difficult either,' Alex smiled. 'It's natural, comes with my pedigree.'

'Anyway,' Mandie said, 'he seems to think that with the two of us chasing these pictures we'll come up with the goodies without too much delay, and he told me that you should be given all the help you need.'

'Michelstraub takes too much for granted,' Alex complained. 'How does he know what I'm going to do?'

'You took his money,' Mandie reminded him. 'You flew across the Atlantic. You're here.'

'True,' said Alex. 'Very true. But there are several details he's omitted to divulge. He didn't even tell me that you were involved in this caper.' He grinned. 'Mrs Carmichael gave that away.'

Mandie's return smile was disarming.

'I know,' she replied. 'Old George does enjoy his fun and games. He loves to keep hordes of people running round him, all working on the same problem, each totally unaware of the other. Sometimes it stays that way. Sometimes it happens that people bump into one another and questions are asked. But ... he is generous. I get two percent of the expected value of these paintings – if we find them. What's your deal?'

Deal? he thought to himself. Huh!

'I don't have a deal,' he said. 'Michelstraub gave me a few hundred dollars to keep me happy, but . . . shares, that's something else.'

Alex looked down at his shoes.

Mandie left her place on the sofa, crossed the room and shrugged her body into a full-length black coat. She moved back towards Alex and leaned across him to collect a long blue scarf which had been draped over the back of the sofa. She wound it around her long elegant neck and said, 'Let's eat.'

Americans seem to spend a large part of their lives eating. They're very good at it. They're also pretty good at providing a vast range of places in which to perform this particularly popular pastime.

New York features very few streets that do not boast at least one eating-house, more usually several strung together in a row. Mandie and Dan were fortunate in that their neighbourhood incorporated a wide variety; cheap, expensive, and everything in between. As they wandered along the pavements they encountered a multitude of fragrances; aromas from the Far East, the Middle East, Mexico and . . . the odour of hot fat and fried onions from the burger and hot dog stands.

Mandie and Dan escorted Alex round a corner into a small alley, dark and dingy. A pair of carriage lamps hung on the wall, emanating a dull yellow light, guardians to an immense wooden door inlaid with black metal studs.

Could be interesting, Alex grinned to himself, thinking of dungeons and things medieval; fair maidens, wenches with full heaving breasts clutching jugs overflowing with frothy mead, sawdust on the uneven stone floor, and bawdy laughter.

Dan opened the door to reveal the interior, a small, up-market Italian restaurant. The floor was tiled, black and white, chequered like a chess board. The table cloths were crisp white, the flowers fresh, and the music Italian, Vivaldi's 'La Stravaganza'. Within minutes, calamari, salade niçoise, garlic bread, a bottle of house red and a bottle of still water appeared on the table, along with four bottles of Peroni Nastro Azzurro to accompany the antipasto. The order was placed, the beer poured, and Mandie began in earnest to lift the lid on Michelstraub, the paintings, and life in general.

To be fair, it seemed to have started just as Michelstraub had stated in his letter, with the bundle of papers being unearthed when the firm had re-located to Binghamton. No one knew how long the papers had been lurking under the desk drawer; indeed, no one knew how they'd got there in the first place.

It was possible that old Charley Meyer might have known something about the documents' early history but if he had, he'd taken the knowledge with him to his grave, three or four months before their discovery. In fact, it had been his death that had prompted the move out of the city.

'Wait a minute,' Alex broke in. 'Didn't anyone think of asking Meyer's wife if she knew anything about the papers?' He thought it logical that she would have been privy to her husband's secrets.

'Yes, we did,' answered Mandie, 'but she's an elderly lady, not quite as with-it as our friend Mrs Carmichael. She knew nothing about the papers – didn't even know they existed. But, in the course of conversation, she did mention Charley's granddaughter. Seems that she, the granddaughter, was very close to Charley, always playing games together, that sort of thing. So we decided to go speak to her. Eve. She's around my age and we immediately struck up a friendship.'

'And?' Alex was hooked. He found that listening to Mandie

was far more entertaining than listening to Michelstraub. Her voice was captivating, an accent from the mid-South, not harsh, but soft and beguiling. She also had a fantastic smile that started at the corners of her mouth and slowly worked its way up her face to linger around those grey-green eyes. Radiant!

Dan seemed to be more than content to let his wife do all the talking, although it soon transpired that he also had been roped in to join the quest. Alex supposed that this would be pretty useful; Dan's uniform would open doors that might otherwise remain closed. Mandie was speaking.

'Well, it was actually Eve who'd suggested to her grandfather that he should hide the papers where he did. She recalled that he'd been in a great state of excitement about the documents, but admitted that after they'd been secreted away she'd completely forgotten about them. It was only my questioning that brought the whole episode flooding back. She reckoned they must have been slotted away in their secret location for at least fifteen years. Unfortunately, she had no idea as to their origin.'

Alex lifted his glass to his lips, took a deep draught of the chilled golden liquid and rolled it around his mouth, savouring the subtle flavours of the Italian beer. He'd been surprised to see the waiter pouring the beer into wine glasses, but after sampling the slightly effervescent beverage, he decided maybe it was a good idea and resolved henceforth always to drink bottled beer in this manner. He set the wine glass back onto the table.

'Tell me,' he said to Mandie. 'The other documents. What were they all about?'

'What other documents?' she asked.

'The ones you discovered at Mrs Carmichael's.'

Mandie looked at Dan, picked up her fork and lightly tapped the handle against the table top.

'Did you mention this to Michelstraub?'

'The other documents?' Alex shrugged. 'No, I'd forgotten all about them until now.'

'He doesn't know,' Mandie said. 'Thinks I came away empty handed.'

'Secrets?' Alex asked.

'Haven't decided yet,' Mandie replied. 'I'll let you see the papers when we get back to the apartment.'

'Yes, okay, but I don't understand why you haven't shared this information with Michelstraub.'

'Information is power, Alex. Remember that, and remember always to keep something up your sleeve.'

'Right,' Alex said, looking at Dan, who'd raised an eyebrow to regard Alex's response to Mandie's short lecture.

Mandie started pouring wine into their glasses and as she replaced the bottle in the centre of the table, she looked up at Alex with a little mischievous smile and said, 'We have learned something that you'll find intriguing.'

'Can't wait,' said Alex.

'The paintings,' Mandie said. 'They're a little delicate.'

'Delicate?' Alex repeated.

'Their subject matter,' Mandie explained. 'They portray human forms, male and female, in various stages of dishabille, striking poses of an erotic nature.'

'Dishabille?' Alex asked, perplexed. 'Dishabille?'

'Naked,' Dan translated. 'She's trying to tell you that the paintings are pornographic,' he continued, his face full of spaghetti, his eyes full of interest, 'only she's going all round the houses to get there.'

'Not by today's standards,' Mandie retorted. 'Just a little risqué. "Titillating" was the word George used to describe them.'

'George?' Alex asked. 'Who's George?'

'Michelstraub,' Mandie replied. 'George Michesltraub.'

'Oh yes.' He'd forgotten that Michelstraub was called George. Alex was agog.

Sitting in an Italian restaurant in New York, he found it quite amusing to learn that he was about to embark on a search for a couple of dirty paintings.

'These eight pictures. Do they form a set or are they just individual pictures?'

'We believe it's a complete set,' Mandie replied. 'At least, it would be. That's why George is so eager to locate the missing pictures. He thinks they were being brought together for some sort of exhibition and if he can find them they'll dramatically increase the value of the collection.' She paused. 'By the way, did he tell you that the original owner of these two pictures lived in London?'

'No,' said Alex, looking slightly confused. 'It seems he told me mighty little. But he did say that he thought the missing pictures would still be in Europe.'

'Good old George,' said Mandie. 'It's all there, in the documents he found under the desk drawer, and is really the reason why he was so interested in trying to contact someone from the UK. Someone with the name Prentiss.'

The missing link was no longer missing; it was disguised as Alex.

Michelstraub seemed meticulously to have thought of everything. The puppet-master had built the stage, set the scene, and was now manipulating his motley crew. Once again Alex pictured Michelstraub sitting in his armchair, rubbing his stubby little hands together in anticipation of the rewards that his puppets were helping to accumulate.

'Where are you staying, bud?' asked Dan, another forkful of pasta sliding down his throat.

Alex was brought out of his reverie. 'Um, actually I'm er, I'm not booked in anywhere. I went straight to Mrs Carmichael's when I got in from Binghamton, then came directly to your place, but...'

'Hell, Mandie, the guy can stay with us can't he? If he wants that is. It'll be much easier for both of you than if he goes to some hotel.'

Smart thinker, this man Dan, thought Alex. Of course he'd like to stay. Mandie might be married to the cop but she still had that amazing smile, and there was still a lot of planning to be planned.

The apartment was more of a house, or at least, an extremely large flat. Consisting of two levels, it was the last word in luxury. The living room Alex had seen already but had been too tired really to appreciate. It was almost the size of a warehouse, large and lofty, incorporating a dining area and a lounging area complete with a giant television screen and an enormous hi-fi set-up. There was also a cosy 'chat' area for people who might not want to watch television or listen to music, a sort of after-dinner sanctuary, Alex supposed. Off the dining area was a fairly large kitchen with plenty of work surfaces, storage cupboards, a breakfast bar and stools, and the largest spice rack he'd ever seen, outside Sainsbury's. He began to wonder who the cook might be, Mandie or Dan, then wondered if he'd get to sample any of the cooking. There was also a small loo, and a study-cum-library-cum-den. The upper level boasted three bedrooms, two bathrooms and another small sitting area.

American cops either were paid a lot of money to patrol the highways and byways, Alex thought to himself, or Mandie earned a lot as... He suddenly realized that he had no idea what she did for a living, so when everyone settled down again, he asked.

'Photography,' she said over her shoulder as she filled three large glasses with wine.

'Damn good one too,' added Dan who was slouched into an armchair, his legs dangling over the arm. 'Paid for all of this,' he said, indicating with a wave of his arm the expanse of the apartment and presumably everything in it.

'On average I have three exhibitions a year. My agent charges exorbitant prices and takes generous helpings, but I still manage a tidy return.' Mandie placed the glasses of wine on the long low wooden table in the centre of the seating arrangement. 'I enjoy my work,' she continued. 'Well, I suppose it's a hobby really. At least, it was until I realized I could make good money from it. Doug, my agent, is great. He does all the setting-up of exhibitions, deals with the finances, makes appointments and handles the arrangements for special commissions. All I have to do is point the camera in the right direction and trip the shutter.'

'Hey hon,' said Dan, placing an arm around her waist, 'tell the man like it really is. Tell him about the hassles with the models, the make-up, the clients who don't know what they want 'til they see the finished work. Tell him about the early-morning shots, you know, the ones that have to be photographed when the light is just so. Listen Alex, you wouldn't believe the half of it. I used to think that my job was pretty tough but Mandie's? Nah, wouldn't touch it.'

Mandie laughed. Everyone laughed. Everyone drank. Everyone went to bed.

Alex barely had time to appreciate the comfort of his room. It was all he could do to push a toothbrush round his mouth before collapsing into bed. He'd been in America for two days. It seemed like a month.

He slept.

*   *   *

Dan woke Alex at ten the following morning. It was his day off and he'd fixed some breakfast. Mandie had left at six-thirty to photograph some people on their way to work.

Strange things people want photos of. Still, if it paid as well as it obviously did, Alex thought, maybe he should go to night school and learn the trade for himself.

Dan's breakfast was vast. So was Alex's.

'So. Tell me about England,' said Dan. Over the meal Alex rambled on about pollution, traffic jams, recessions and the cost of living. They agreed that life was probably much the same on both sides of the ocean, except, thought Alex, over in England there was a bit of heritage, a bit of culture, and a large bit of his life called Jessica.

Making use of Dan and Mandie's phone he reported back to base, bringing Jessica up to date on the latest developments. She asked him to tell her all about Mandie, so he told her a lot about Dan – it was easier and didn't involve too much cross-questioning. She asked him if he'd heard about the hurricane which had just swept across the south of the country, and when he asked 'which country?', she called him stupid and informed him that a few tiles had been blown off the roof, that she'd lost three pairs of knickers from the washing line, and that every tree and gatepost along the street was cosily wrapped in black bin-liners, the original contents having been strewn hither and thither.

'Apart from that,' she concluded, 'everything on the home front is fine.'

Before hanging up, Alex informed her that he'd probably be home in a couple of days and that the missing pictures were in England. Possibly. On the other hand, they might not be. But he didn't say that. He kept that bit of information to himself.

* * *

When Dan discovered that Alex never before had been in New York, he offered to spend some time showing him the sights. It seemed like a good idea to Alex and although he'd heard that some of the city's districts were supposedly no-go areas, he thought that a tour with a policeman as his guide should be okay, even if Dan had left his uniform at home.

In the space of six hours Alex reckoned they must have seen all that there was to be seen. They'd visited the high spots, the low spots, and most of the in-between spots as well.

Greenwich, Fifth Avenue and the Empire State, down Forty-Second Street, through Times Square, up Eighth Avenue and onto Broadway. In and out of Harlem and back down Roosevelt Drive, through little Italy and into Soho.

Yellow cabs and subways. Manhattan! Manhattan! Manhattan!

Alex decided that he must have seen more during the course of the afternoon, than the average tourist sees in a week. Dan appeared to enjoy showing him around, saying that a quick spin through districts other than his own was good for maintaining his levels of awareness, not that Alex could see too much wrong with Dan's awareness as it was. Dan must have prevented Alex from being mugged or run over a dozen times – he was still finding it hard trying to get used to cars coming at him from the wrong direction.

At some stage they grabbed a couple of hot dogs to keep their inner reserves going and went through the lengthy routine of 'easy on the mustard, easy on the onions, easy on the ketchup, but gimme plenty of fries'.

'How's it goin', Detective?' asked the hot dog man, ladling quantities of fries into an inverted cone.

'Detective?' queried Alex, looking at the fast-food vendor.

'Yeah, Detective,' the hot dog man confirmed.

'Detective?' Alex repeated, looking at Dan.

'Yeah, huh?' said Dan. They collected their order from the stall and walked along the pavement, each immersed in their own thoughts, each concentrating on keeping the mustard and ketchup from dripping onto their clothes.

'I thought you were a cop?'

'Use't'be, 'til they decided to give me my badge,' Dan said.

'But the uniform?' Alex asked. 'That was a cop's uniform, right?'

'Yeah,' Dan answered. 'We put on all the glitz and glitter for special occasions, events and the like.'

'Uh huh,' Alex said.

'Yeah. Get inspected before we're allowed out. The sergeant has a thing about shiny buttons.'

'Shiny buttons,' Alex repeated.

'Shiny brass buttons,' Dan informed him

'Detective?' Alex said again.

'So now you know,' Dan told him, grinning at Alex and cuffing him across the shoulders. 'Now you know.'

It was about six o'clock by the time they finally made it back to the apartment and, upon entering, were greeted with wonderful culinary aromas. Alex smiled to himself, remembering that not so long ago he'd been wondering about who did the cooking. Now he knew – both of them. Dan's breakfast had been great and Mandie's dinner turned out to be superb; some sort of chicken casserole with chunks of lemon and lime, and cream swirled through before it was served up.

At the end of the meal the chairs were moved back and Dan, Mandie and Alex retired to the comfort of the sofas. Dan put some music on and, with Tamla Motown providing a relaxing background, they set about a second bottle of excellent claret and devised their plan of action for the retrieval of the missing paintings.

Mandie had gathered together the remaining papers she'd discovered at Mrs Carmichael's.

'Ah, these are what I was asking you about last night,' said Alex.

'Yeah, I know,' Mandie said. 'It went clean out of my head.'

'Mmm, mine too,' Alex agreed. 'Good food, good wine, good conversation, and the revelation about the pornographic paintings. There was no room for anything else.'

'Anyway,' Mandie said, spreading the documents across the coffee table, 'here we are. Look. Here's a list of all eight paintings, detailing titles and dimensions of each. And here, a list of all the original owners.'

'You mentioned something about an exhibition,' Alex said, idly perusing the list of owners.

'I did?' Mandie asked abstractedly, sifting through the remaining documents, mainly bills from various shipping agencies.

'Yes. Last night over dinner,' Alex reminded her, looking up from the list.

Mandie drummed her fingernails lightly against the sheets of paper.

'Reading between the lines,' she answered, 'it looks as though the paintings were being brought to the States for a private showing, you know, connoisseurs of pornographic art.'

'Titillating,' Alex corrected.

'Yes,' Mandie agreed.

'Back in nineteen forty-four?'

'Back in nineteen forty-four,' Mandie said, repeating Alex word for word. 'Pornography isn't something associated only with the eighties,' she smiled, 'it goes back to the dawn of time.'

'Back to Adam and Eve,' Dan suggested. 'You know, when we discovered we were different, man and woman, and...'

'Exactly,' Mandie said. 'Couldn't have put it better myself.'

Alex realized he still had his index finger pointing at the list of names. He looked down, scrolling towards the foot of the page.

'Goodness!' he exclaimed, stabbing the page with his digit. 'Michelstraub was right. Look, here's someone from London. Reginald Stanforth.'

'Excellent,' said Mandie. 'That'll be your starting point.'

'How do you mean?' Alex asked.

'Find out what the deal was.'

'Jesus, Mandie, the list is forty years old. There's no way this Stanforth will still be there.'

'You don't know that, Alex,' Mandie riposted. 'Anything is possible. Try to find some documentation. Proof of this exhibition would be a great help.'

'And here it is,' said Dan, grinning and holding aloft a sheet of paper. 'It's a letter from a Mr Glibstein of Boston. Reckons to have a hall which'd be just perfect for a select display of paintings.'

'Well, that's something we can check on,' said Mandie. 'I'll find the time to get out to Boston over the next couple of weeks.'

There was a little problem which had been floating about in the back of Alex's mind and he thought that now was probably a good time to mention it, to see if Mandie or Dan could shed any light on it.

'I've been trying to figure out why the two bundles of papers weren't kept together. I mean, it seems strange that Meyer didn't also possess this collection of papers,' he said, pointing at the documents spread out in front of him.

'Well, maybe he did,' said Dan. 'Who knows? Also, why did the paintings end up in the Carmichael house and, Alex, to use your logic, how come Meyer's documents weren't found together with the paintings? You know, tied up in the bundle that Mandie found.'

'There are too many loose ends,' Mandie agreed, 'but at least we've got a couple of possible trails.'

The three of them stared silently at the papers spread about on the table as though willing them to come to life and explain what happened all those years ago.

Mandie broke the spell.

'Well, it seems that if I can find out whether or not the paintings were put on view, it'll solve a large part of the mystery. Meanwhile, Alex, you return to London and try tracing those missing pictures. Tomorrow we'll get photocopies of all these papers so that you can take a set with you.'

'Why wait?' Dan said, gathering the documents together, adding that he knew of a little corner store where they had a copier, not too far from the Italian restaurant.

At last it seemed they were heading in the right direction so, when Dan returned clutching copious amounts of paper, they put their glasses together and toasted the project.

Jessica was standing with her back to the Avis counter. She looked gorgeous. With her fawn trench coat and blonde hair, she evoked memories of some secret agent from one of the Bond movies or maybe from an earlier time, when everybody crept about in the black-and-white world of *Casablanca*. She had an umbrella upon which she was leaning; it was raining cats and dogs.

'Has been all day,' she said, greeting Alex with a kiss, reviving his spirits which had been severely jolted by a none-too-gentle landing. Then there had been 'hunt-the-case', a game which had kept Alex waiting at the carousel for fifty minutes. Eventually, triumphant and with case in hand, he became stuck behind a family clustered around a trolley stacked with so much luggage, he thought it surprising that a tractor hadn't been hired to drag it around the concourse.

Alex felt good to be back on terra firma.

Jessica tucked her arm under his and hauled him off to find the car. On the homeward journey she asked him more questions about his new-found friends and he told her all about Mandie and Dan as if he'd known them for years. Jessica stole a glance at Alex when he mentioned Mandie's tight jeans. She watched his face, especially his eyes, as he smiled at the memory.

Provided they had the figure, girls in tight jeans were definitely 'in', as far as Alex was concerned. It wasn't a secret. Jessica knew it and she knew what kept him happy. She had a collection of jeans which moulded her perfect buns like paint on a statue.

Jessica offered to help Alex in his search for the missing pictures, but first, she told him, there were some more important things to attend to. Arriving back at their abode, as Alex put his case and briefcase on the floor, Jessica wriggled out of her raincoat, revealing underneath that she'd been wearing only a bra and panties. Black ones. Just the sight of Jessica's body had always been enough to cause Alex's prick to make demands on the elasticity of his briefs, and this time certainly proved no exception.

They didn't bother climbing the stairs to the bedroom, they just fell into the sitting room and made total use of the sofa.

They didn't even bother to draw the curtains, and in the light of the street lamp illuminating the scene from across the road, they made love, long and slow.

Jessica removed her underwear and positioned herself on the front edge of the sofa. She leaned back and placed her arms along the top of the sofa, presenting her perfect body for Alex's inspection as he knelt on the floor in front of her, a supplicant obeisant to the high priestess of desire.

His eyes focused on Jessica's breasts, which were not large, but neither were they too small; they were soft yet firm and jutted out, the nipples pert proud and erect, dusky brown, a sexy contrast to the light pigmentation of her areolae. Jessica watched his eyes as they tracked downwards across her rib-cage, downwards across her flat stomach, downwards past her heart-shaped bush until at long last, his gaze lingering upon her open sex, she felt her body melting, turning itself inside out. She sensed the tightness in her nipples and experienced the warm tingling deep within her soul, as though the insides of her belly were being stroked by an artist's brush, each stroke very light and very slow. Alex leaned forward and Jessica smiled. She eased her legs further apart and gave in to the abandonment of sheer pleasure as Alex's face pressed itself into the humidity between her splayed thighs.

Tasting Jessica's heat, Alex rasped his tongue against her hardened button of flesh. She moaned and thrust her groin hard against his mouth, her satisfaction complete. Finding himself unable to wait any longer, he moved his body forward and pressed his shaft into Jessica's warm, wet, yielding body. They watched as his stamen brushed aside the glistening petals and slid into the eager softness of her secret depths. She pressed her shoulders hard against the sofa, forcing her body down and forwards so as to impale herself further.

Then, pushing Alex away from her, she levered herself up and around to end up kneeling on the seat with her back towards him. Alex ran his hands lightly over her buttocks and hips, tracing the outline of her hip bones as his fingers reached down across her belly. Bending her body away from him she leaned forward, pressing her forehead against the back of the sofa. She forced her stomach downwards and, arched to breaking point, pushed herself backwards as Alex penetrated fully her pulsating openness.

It didn't last long. It couldn't. The arousal, the fierce sexual heat, the sensations, the tension and the desire coalesced and welled up to explode out of Alex's body and slam deep into the centre of Jessica's being. Alex slumped forward, allowing his body to nestle into the curve of her back.

'Jesus, Alex,' Jessica grunted. 'I'll have to send you away again if this is what you come back with.'

He spluttered a snigger into the back of her neck, turned his head to one side and said, 'Roger that, Houston.'

Jessica laughed, her convulsions causing Alex to bounce about on her back. 'The rogering's okay,' she said. 'Let's leave out the Houston.'

Later, much later, they shared a bath and lay back in the hot soapy water, lazily exchanging snippets of conversation and occasionally sipping at a drink, a gin and tonic for Alex, a Chardonnay for Jessica.

Eventually, their glasses empty, they decided to step out of the bathtub and used big white fluffy towels to dry one another before padding out of the bathroom and into the bedroom. They peeled back the duvet and with Jessica straddled across Alex's body, again, they made love. Afterwards, cradled in one another's arms, satisfied and satiated, they drifted into deep sleep.

50

5

The address of the house in Peckham as detailed in Prentiss's list, was that of the original owner of one of the pictures. It had not been hard to find but, as predicted, held no clues to help further their research.

The present occupants couldn't have been less interested.

'We ain't got no paintin's 'ere mate, 'cept them what the kids've sprayed all over the place.'

'Oh,' said Jessica, quite unperturbed. 'Well maybe you have some knowledge of a previous owner, someone by the name of Stanforth?'

The man on the doorstep turned round and yelled down the dank corridor stretching out behind him.

'Oi, Effel. You 'eard of some Stanforf geyser?'

He stood there scratching his behind and picking his nose, watching the slow progress of Ethel as she shuffled along the corridor to find out what all the commotion was about.

'Eh? Whadya say?'

'These people wanna know 'bout some bloke called ... wha's 'is name? ... Stan, Stan ... Stan somefin'.'

'Stanforth,' Jessica reminded him. 'Reginald Stanforth.'

'Yeah, Stanforf. That's it. Ain't 'eard nuffin' 'bout 'im 'ave yer?'

'No I ain't. Not 'eard nuffin' 'bout no one an' if I did I wouldn't say nuffin' 'cos it never does no good. Wha's 'e done anyway?'

'Never mind,' said Alex, seeing that they were getting nowhere. 'Thanks in any case.' Jessica and Alex turned on their heels, walking off down the street as the door slammed behind them.

They found a pub, the Three Bells, and marched in looking for a bite to eat while they mulled over their next move.

'Perhaps we're barking up the wrong tree,' Jessica said. 'This list of addresses is almost fifty years old, there's no way these houses'll be occupied by the same families.'

'Not unless we're very lucky,' said Alex.

'Fat chance,' Jessica responded. She pushed her empty plate to one side and wiped her lips on the bright scarlet serviette which had been brought to the table earlier as a tight roll containing a knife and a fork.

'I've been thinking,' she said.

'Always dangerous,' Alex grinned at her.

'If this Prentiss was all he's cracked up to be, there may be some mention of his works at one of the galleries. I mean, they must have records on just about every artist that ever was. Maybe we'd have more joy exploring that avenue.'

Sheer genius, thought Alex. Jessica had just earned her apple and blackberry pie, with cream.

On the bus heading towards the West End, Jessica asked questions. She wanted to know what other information Alex had about Prentiss. What type of artist was he? What was the subject of his paintings?

When Alex explained that the collection portrayed naughty nudes, Jessica giggled, a big smile working its way over her face as she suggested that this little adventure might prove to be more entertaining than she had at first imagined.

It took about forty-five minutes for the bus to reach Trafalgar Square. Forty-five minutes during which people got on the bus and people got off the bus. It's in the nature of things as is the fact that people are of immense interest, in their own way, especially to a person such as Alex. Looks, clothes, mannerisms, speech; all provide him with endless fascination, and today he was by no means disappointed.

They were sitting towards the rear of the bus on the lower deck, where they found themselves face to face with a couple who'd joined the cavalcade at Camberwell Green. In their thirties, she was slim, petite, dyed-blonde, and withdrawn; he wasn't. He was just the opposite; chubby, balding, boorish and loud, giving anyone and everyone within earshot free access to his views on everything; from the way he believed the government should tax the populace fairly, to the deep-hidden propaganda (his words) behind the television soap *Dallas*. No one was listening. Some were reading papers, others books, and a young man sporting a yellow-green-Mohican-pointy-thing on his head had the endemic baby loudspeakers attached to his ears. The rest were all looking out of the windows as the world passed them by.

Having grappled Alex with his eyes, the man wouldn't let go, and so Alex and Jessica learned that the only way to tax people was to return to the old rates system, which would be perfect because then he, Misstra Know-it-all, wouldn't have to pay any tax at all. He also informed them that JR was a revolutionary of Arabic descent, secretly trying to undermine the American oil industry, thereby granting a monopoly to the Middle East.

Jessica smiled sweetly, so did Alex, so did their talkative friend's wife; she'd heard it all before. Characters such as this are very good reasons why so many writers, artistes, directors, producers et al. often tend to travel by public transport. It produces a wealth of material for their books, plays, films and television programmes, and it helps to pass the time. The bus finally reached its destination.

* * *

Trafalgar Square.

An overcast day in late September. Ambient colour: grey.

The magnificent stone buildings merged with the leaden skies, creating a heaviness, solid and timeless. It wasn't raining but everything was damp, the streets and pavements coated with just enough moisture to reflect the sequential traffic lights and the mournful headlamps of cars, taxis and buses, following each other in some sort of ritualistic procession. The National Gallery stands large and formidable on the northern edge of the square, its imposing façade gazing imperiously across the endless streams of traffic at the nation's hero, standing frozen in time on top of his column.

Swiftly and succinctly, Alex and Jessica outlined their problem to the girl at the information desk. The girl summoned a security guard and told him to escort them to 'old Mr Symond's office'. They followed in the guard's footsteps as he led them ever deeper into the interior of the vast building until, well and truly disorientated, they were delivered into the calm oasis of Symond's domain.

'Old' Mr Symond was exactly the sort of person they required. His appearance suggested that he might even be able to recall the setting-in-place of the National Gallery's foundation stone, personally. The top of his desk was almost bare, supporting only a telephone, a pen, a well-sharpened pencil, and a shorthand notebook folded open to reveal a fresh sheet of lined white paper.

'Yes? And exactly how may I help you?' The smile was genuine, the eyes conveying academic interest and an eagerness to assist, and the formation of the question, exquisite. Here was a man whose love of art clearly encompassed everybody else's lack of knowledge and the desire to introduce them to his world, which so obviously rotated within the confines of this small office.

'Well...' Alex began.

'We're trying to find out all we can about a certain Arthur

Prentiss,' Jessica continued. 'We'd be very grateful if you could shed some light on...'

'Or have a record of his work,' Alex concluded. Together, the super-sleuths were dynamite.

'Which one?' asked Symond.

'Which one?' Jessica and Alex repeated in tandem. Alex looked at Jessica. Jessica looked at Alex. They both stared at Symond.

'Yes, which one?' Symond asked again.

Again, Alex looked at Jessica. Again, she looked at Alex. Again, they both stared at Symond.

'You see, there were two,' he elaborated, sailing above their obvious confusion. 'Arthur Prentiss, who died in eighteen twenty-three, and Arthur Prentiss the Younger, whose dates unfortunately are not known.' Symond beamed. Lofty intelligence shone from all quarters.

'Um ... well ... amongst the works of the Prentiss we're interested in, there appear to have been some er ... slightly risqué pic...'

'The Nymph Collection,' said Symond. 'Actually Prentiss's, the Younger Prentiss's claim to fame. They were all lost at sea, ooh, about forty years ago, although there is a belief that one or two may have missed the boat...'

'Really?' said Alex, quickly recovering from his embarrassment.

'Yes.' Symond steepled his hands and lowered his chin onto the tips of his fingers. 'And ... therefore there may be one or two still in existence.'

'There...' Alex began.

'There *may* be?' Jessica intervened rapidly, before Alex could finish. Indeed, almost before he started.

'Yes,' Symond reiterated. 'It's possible. Of course there's been no official word about this for years, it's only hearsay.'

Once again Jessica and Alex exchanged glances.

Symond picked up his pen, twirling it between thumb and forefinger.

A random beam of light reflected from the gold pen-top and crossed through space, a small yellow circle tracking hypnotically across Symond's forehead.

Alex found it mesmerizing. Almost.

Over the years he'd learned that when a person seated behind a desk picks up a pen, one is in imminent danger from a long serious discussion; the first, undoubtedly, having been delivered many years previously by his headmaster. It seems that the holder of the pen, by concentrating on the article revolving between his fingers, is able to focus his thoughts, marshalling them into the correct order of play, and thus speak at length on the chosen subject without let up.

Resigned to the fact, Alex winked at Jessica and leaned back into his chair, ready for the tale to unwind.

'Strangely,' Symond informed his audience of two, 'we don't have too much information on Arthur Prentiss. It is however almost certain that there is no connection between the two. Prentiss number one had no sons, nor did he have any brothers, or sisters for that matter. Just him. Prentiss number two, the Younger Prentiss, creator of our "Nymphs", seems to have been quite a shy, should we say reserved character. As I said, very little is known about him. Indeed, it wasn't until the fifties that anyone knew of his existence. Some photographs of the paintings,' Symond nodded, 'yes, the "Nymph" paintings, were discovered in Marseilles by a *Times* reporter who accidentally stumbled on them while researching another story. Well, to cut a long story short, the photos were sent here and close inspection revealed the name Prentiss. Thinking that the pictures were some unknown works by Prentiss number one, the Gallery sent a man to the South of France to dig around and see what he could find. A couple of weeks passed with no result, but our man was diligent and, having checked all the local newspapers, libraries and galleries on offer in Marseilles, a chance idle conversation with the custodian of one of the town's smaller museums gave him the idea of checking with some of the shipping agencies. And, bingo!'

Symond set his pen back onto the desk, picked up the phone and tapped out a number.

'Ah, Conrad. We need the file on Prentiss. That's the Younger Prentiss ... Under 'P' ... Yes ... Yes, in my office. Thanks.'

He replaced the phone on its cradle, picked up his pen and, resting his elbows on the desk, gazed at a point midway between Jessica and Alex. A couple of minutes passed, during which Alex and Jessica craned their necks trying to see what it was that Symond was staring at. Then, a knock on the door heralded the arrival of Conrad and the file.

'Thank you,' said Symond. Conrad was dismissed, the file was placed on the table, and opened. 'You will understand that I wasn't here all those years ago,' Symond said, smiling.

'Yes. Yes, of course,' Jessica agreed.

'But I do remember reading a report on Prentiss. Goodness, it must've been ten or fifteen years ago in the seventies.' He looked up from the opened file, his mind arrowing through the years. 'You know, these documents laid bare the massive extent of looting carried out by the Nazis, especially as the war dragged to a close. The cloven hoof of the Third Reich had been stomping all over Europe, garnering priceless works of art with which they became reluctant to part. It's amazing when you consider the logistics. These treasures had been taken from private collections and renowned galleries and were transported the length and breadth of the continent, passing to and fro right under the noses of the Russians, the British and the Americans.' Symond returned his attention to the notes in front of him. 'Yes, here we are,' he purred. 'Just as I recall. Not much in the way of information but, let's have a look anyway.'

He removed a few sheets of paper, carefully positioning them on his desk, face down in the order in which he took them from the file. Then he extracted an envelope from which, in turn, he took some photographs.

'Aha,' he enthused. 'Yes. Here we have it.' He shuffled the photos to and fro, backwards and forwards. 'Yes, yes. Now I remember. Nineteen forty-four. December. The paintings had arrived in Marseilles on a train from an unspecified starting point. Eight of them.'

Symond continued to expound, referring now and then to the papers laid out in front of him.

'They were loaded onto a freighter bound for Argentina but, and this is where the trail grinds to a halt, the ship was torpedoed and sunk by a British submarine just after clearing the Straits of Gibraltar.'

'What?' Jessica stood up and then immediately sat down again. Alex did nothing. He was rooted to his chair. 'Well, yes, that would bring the story to an end,' she said, throwing a glare at Alex. 'This information makes our project just about impossible … although, you did mention that some of the paintings may not have been included in the shipment.'

'Yes,' said Symond. 'So I did.' He picked up the pile of papers, turned them over and went through them page by page, until he selected a sheet boasting an impressive crest embossed at its head. 'A certain General von Oberstürm wrote to the shipping agency confirming the shipment order, adding that two of the paintings would be delayed as they were on loan to one of his colleagues.' Symond turned the page and clipped to the reverse was a handwritten note. 'Mmm. Our man in Marseilles wrote here that he visited the general's address, but to no avail. The house was in a place called Bad Wiessee, near Munich, and had been converted into a kindergarten. Of the general, there was nothing, no information whatsoever. Once again, the story came to an abrupt halt.' Symond lowered the paper, removed his glasses and smiled benevolently.

'And that,' said Alex, 'seems to be that.'

The smile changed and became inscrutably Chinese. 'Such is the world of art,' said Symond, enigmatically.

'Could I trouble you for a copy of the general's letter?' Jessica asked him.

'I don't see why not,' he said. 'It can do no harm, this being a closed case.'

Conrad was summoned. Conrad was dispatched. He returned in the space of three minutes and Jessica had her photocopy of von Oberstürm's letter.

'Thank you,' she said. 'Thank you for your time. You've been most helpful.' Once outside the office she turned to Alex. 'I rather fancy a little trip to Germany.' Her eyes sparkled.

The streets and pavements had turned to liquid gold, their rain-washed surfaces reflecting light from the late afternoon sun which had just emerged from behind a bank of densely dark clouds.

Alex grabbed Jessica's hand and dragged her though the traffic, through groups of tourists and flocks of pigeons, all of them looking miserable, going about their business in the rain. They passed down Northumberland Avenue and on to the Embankment. Alex's mind was in a spin, Jessica's as well.

'Listen,' she said. 'It's amazing. We know more than they do, the National Gallery! How many people other than us, Mandie, Dan and Michelstraub, know about the existence of any of these pictures?'

'Well, I suppose Michelstraub's secretary knows. Then there's Mrs Carmichael, and...'

'Okay, okay,' Jessica interrupted. 'But the point is that no one in the art world knows. So far as they're concerned, all the pictures, with the possible exception of two, went to the bottom of the sea, and there they remain. Finito. Thank God we left Symond before he started asking awkward questions.'

They were nearing Cleopatra's Needle and Alex slid his arm around Jessica's waist, drew her close and planted a kiss on her soft, receptive lips, a tactile tactic to which she was well accustomed. She kissed him back, a brief, tender caress. A kiss from Jessica was similar to having a butterfly land on one's heart; a hint, a mere suggestion of latent power within, enough, Alex knew, to make his stomach turn somersaults. It happened every time.

Smiling, Jessica said, 'Come on, time for a drink.'

Before leaving the riverside, Alex fished in his pockets for some change. His hand came out clutching a pound coin which he tossed into the air. They watched the spinning disc as it hovered for a split second, light reflecting from its faces, before it fell into the restless waters urgently lapping at the stonework several feet below the balustrade. It was a romantic token of love, a gesture designed to steer their project to a successful conclusion.

It was early evening, so the pub, situated between the Strand and Covent Garden, was packed with people who'd just left work. Also in evidence was a sprinkling of thespians partaking of a little Dutch courage to help propel themselves across the boards. The background music was soft and distant, the electronic machinery, pac-man and a couple of one-armed bandits, was loud, and the level of chatter was staggering. Alex ordered a couple of pints and returned through the multitudes to the vacant spot Jessica had found near the door.

'Right. Germany. When?' Jessica asked, straight to the point as usual. No messing about.

Alex lowered his glass, watched Jessica do the same with hers, and said, 'What makes you so sure we'll find anything in ... where was it?'

'Bad Wiessee,' she replied.

'Mmm, Bad Wiessee.' Alex paused, thinking. 'But Symond's man, he's already checked the place over.'

'I know,' Jessica agreed. 'I know. But maybe he was careless? Maybe he was getting pissed off? Who knows? I just think there may be something ... anything, just a hint. That's all we need. Besides,' she added, 'you've had a good snoop around Mrs Carmichael's house, I think I'd like to sniff around von Oberstruction's place.'

'Oberstürm,' Alex corrected.

'Über alles,' Jessica retorted.

Word association. It was one of their best-loved games although probably it annoyed quite a few of their friends. But what the hell, thought Alex, it's good for the brain, keeps the mind alert, and can be played anytime, anywhere.

A couple of people came and stood in close vicinity, effectively stopping the topic of conversation.

'Let's go and see what's happening over on the South Bank,' Jessica suggested.

They were in luck. An orchestra was playing Mozart, a piano concerto and a divertimento. After their encounter in Munich, it hadn't taken long before they discovered a shared love for several art forms, and of them, music was perhaps the strongest. Mozart being a favourite, they sat in utter contentment, letting the music transport them far away, far from the troublesome paintings. Light and shade, power and tenderness, just like Jessica's kisses.

Alex glanced at her from the corners of his eyes. She caught the movement, smiled, and lightly touched his arm.

Magic, thought Alex, sheer magic. The music was casting its spell; relaxing, soothing – and then, all too soon, it was over.

They plodded back over Hungerford Bridge, past the lonely sax player serenading the night, the river, and anyone who walked by. They headed on past cardboard city, and into the tube at Charing Cross.

It was a good twenty minutes to Barnet. Jessica snuggled up against Alex and went to sleep, whilst he remained awake, watching the passengers come and go as the train stopped at its various ports of call. Leicester Square and Tottenham Court Road saw a lot of people joining the train, Euston and Camden saw a lot get off.

And so it went, until, by the time the train had pulled into High Barnet, stopped and farted, there were only a few weary travellers left on board. Alex woke Jessica, and they joined the dozen or so other people as they shuffled along the platform, tripped up the stairs, and left the station. The night was cold but at least it had stopped raining. A few cars hissed along the wet streets pulling themselves along the beams generated by their headlamps. A short walk brought them to their home and as Jessica closed the front door, Alex opened the drinks cupboard. He was pouring a cognac for Jessica and a port for himself, when the phone rang.

'I'll get it,' Jessica called.

He took her drink over to her. She'd dragged the phone to

the sofa and was sitting curled up at one end of it, the lead trailing over the carpet. Alex sat himself at the other end of the sofa and watched her mouth 'MANDIE'.

Fifteen minutes later he went to pour another measure. Jessica held up her empty glass, so he replenished hers as well.

Obviously, she and Mandie had found much to discuss. Pretty good really, he decided, considering they'd never met.

Another fifteen minutes went by before she put down the phone.

'She doesn't want to talk with me then?'

'Not really. Said to give you her love but thought that we, she and I, had just about covered everything.'

'And more! At least it wasn't our call. Anyway, how is Mandie? How's Dan, how's America?'

'Mandie's fine, Dan too. America? Don't know. But Mandie's had no joy in finding out about the exhibition. Every avenue turned into a dead end. Nobody knows anything, and she found no more documentation.'

'Always had my doubts about that exhibition,' said Alex, 'or rather the lack of it. But why, why? I mean, someone goes to all that trouble, gathering the pictures together, shipping them to South America, and then the whole consignment gets lost, drowned at sea, it's...' He stopped, suddenly, took a large gulp of port.

'Yes?' Jessica was watching him closely, a look of amusement on her face.

'It's almost unbelievable ... but ... but somehow the pieces are beginning to fit.'

'Yes?' she repeated.

'Nineteen forty-four. The end of the war. Germany. Works of art. It couldn't...?'

'It could.'

'It couldn't. Well, could it?'

'Let's sleep on it,' Jessica suggested.

'Sleep on it? I can't go to sleep now...'

'Good,' she said. 'That's what I like to hear.'

She led Alex up to the bedroom, undressed him and told him to lie on the bed. He needed little encouragement. Jessica removed all her clothes apart from her knickers and proceeded to give him a full body massage, expertly, from top to toe, back and front. No inch was left unexplored and Alex began to feel good. He began to feel very good. He began to feel...

'Okay. My turn.' Jessica lay face down on the bed, arms and legs stretched to their full extent. Alex hooked his fingers into her panties and, easing them down over her buttocks, watched closely as the thin material separated itself from the confines of her sex. Then, perching himself lightly on her legs just below her marvellous ass, he let his dick, which was beginning to show an interest in life, rest in the crease. With one hand on either side he eased her cheeks apart and his member, obeying gravity, nestled down and became cloistered. Having parked his extension, his fingers set to work kneading the muscles at the nape of her neck, her shoulders and her shoulder blades. His thumbs applied firm yet gentle circular movements either side of her spine all the way down to her coccyx and, for the return journey to her shoulders, he raked his fingernails up along the sides of her body. Down, then up. Down, then up.

Alex swivelled his body through one-hundred-and-eighty degrees, sat on the small of her back and proceeded to administer the same treatment to her legs, his thumbs pressing into them as his hands travelled down towards her feet. He allowed his fingernails to scrape gently along the outside of her legs as he worked his way back up to her hips and over her ass. Under these manipulations Jessica's body began to move. She arched her behind upwards and

64

parted her legs, giving Alex full access to all her secret places. He changed the pattern and for the upward journey drew his fingernails along the inside of her legs, paying close attention to her sex, now moist with expectation. Reaching to the bedside table, he picked up a small bottle of oil, then moved himself a little further backwards, towards Jessica's shoulders. He poured a few drops of the fragrant unguent onto the small of her back at the point where it raised to meet the curve of her buttocks, allowing a few drops to disappear into her crevice. Using the tips of three fingers, Alex rubbed gently up and down her lower spine, his digits moving easily, sliding slowly back and forth through the oil. Jessica began to push against him, positioning herself, so that his hands found themselves caressing the skin stretched across the tightness of her behind. She felt the oil spreading towards her crease, the warm liquid oozing through the deep dark valley, felt it creeping relentlessly onwards and downwards to drip sensuously into her eager openness. Moments later, Alex lifted himself from her body, his manhood standing proud.

'Turn over,' he said.

'Apple?' Jessica asked.

'Crumble.' Alex rejoined, continuing the game.

'Wrong. You got it wrong,' Jessica mumbled from the depths of the pillows, her body quivering with laughter.

'Shut up and enjoy,' Alex told her. There was a time and a place for everything. Right now was the time for sex, word association could wait. Alex was rampant.

Giggling, Jessica turned over. She parted her unbelievably long legs and, joining them together behind him, used her feet on his ass to push him slowly into her.

6

It's just as well, Alex informed himself, that the Germans speak such good English. They'd spent most of the flight from London swapping the few German phrases they'd latched onto during their previous visit to Munich, and had decided that 'Ich will heute abend nicht arbeiten, weil ich sehr besoffen bin' probably would not be of much use. But then again, one never knew.

They strode purposefully across the airport's foyer in the direction of the hire-car kiosks.

'Guten Morgen. How may I help you?' Miss Avis herself, smiling from ear to ear. In fact it was just possible that the smile went all around her head; the Germans have ways.

Having been informed exactly how she could help, Miss Avis told them the price, picked them off the floor, and led them out to a car of German extraction: Vorsprung Durch Technik.

Happily, the airport was situated on the correct side of the city, making it unnecessary for Jessica and Alex to traverse through the centre, a task that would have proved quite exciting what with the untried, untested experience of dodging trams. Instead, they headed east to the outer ring road, followed it clockwise, then joined the E11 southbound to Holzkirchen, where they left the autobahn and drove along the German equivalent to an 'A' road, following it to Gmund and Bad Wiessee.

* * *

Huddled at the foot of the Alps, Bad Wiessee sprawls along the shores of picturesque Lake Tegernsee. The main street is lined with Swiss-type chalets, each bristling with window-boxes sprouting flowers and foliage left, right and centre.

The Bavarian way of life is far more relaxed and more easy-going than that of the northern domains. One can sit and imbibe steins of beer and chew on giant pretzels at almost any time of day or night.

Alex and Jessica came across a restaurant that overlooked the tranquil lake and, having parked the car, they walked to a group of picnic tables bunched together on a strip of lawn that sloped down to the water's edge. They sat on one of the benches and gazed across the serene outlook. They watched the ducks cavorting in the shallows, close to the shore, and laughed as the birds tipped themselves upside down to investigate life beneath the surface. Alex told Jessica the story of an acquaintance from his earlier days in Munich who'd grown tired of the concrete jungle, and had been in the process of taking over a small inn somewhere in the vicinity of Bad Wiessee.

'Convenient,' said Jessica, 'how you remember these little details at the eleventh hour. All we need now is an address.'

'Shouldn't be too difficult,' said Alex, heading towards the restaurant. The door slammed behind him as he threaded his way past the heavy dark wooden tables and chairs. A waitress appeared from nowhere and moved into position behind the bar.

'Bitte?' she asked.

'Um...'

He raised his right hand to his ear, little finger and thumb extended as if holding a phone, then, with both hands on top of the counter, he pretended to be turning the pages of a book.

The waitress looked on, bemused at the antics of the strange Englishman. She looked up and their eyes met. Alex smiled and said, 'Name.'

'Renate,' the girl said.

'No,' said Alex, shaking his head. 'Telephone.'

The waitress picked up the receiver and held it towards him. Alex took hold of it and replaced it on the set.

'No,' he said, waving his arms. 'Book of names. Telephone.'

'Book of names?' the girl repeated slowly. Her accent was not at all bad, Alex thought, before realizing that the three words hardly constituted anything remotely approaching hazardous pronunciation. He nodded vigorously.

'Book ... ach so,' she smiled and pointed at a large volume in green covers, half-hidden beneath a stack of menus.

Alex unearthed it and, making the motion of a rugby pass towards the door, asked the girl if he could take the directory outside.

She stared at him blankly.

Alex pointed at his eyes, pointed at the book, pointed at the dim lights spaced around a wagon wheel suspended from the ceiling, pointed at the book and shook his head.

The waitress raised both hands, sighed, and disappeared through a small door cunningly concealed in the wall of wooden panelling behind the bar.

'What took you so long?' Jessica demanded as Alex returned to the outside world.

'Language,' he replied.

Before becoming too befuddled with the ale, they applied their eyes to the directory. Krabbe, Krebs, dozens of Krebs with one 'B', and then with two, Krohne – there were several of them as well. But there was only one Krohne-Stube.

'Typically Germanic, naming the place after himself,' Alex informed Jessica. 'Good old Wolfgang.'

Then, changing his mind, 'No, Voolfy. That's what everyone calls him.'

'Voolfy?' Jessica mimicked. Then she repeated the name, 'Voolfy.'

'Yeah,' said Alex. 'They have problems with their "W"s. You should hear them say werewolf!'

Jessica laughed. 'I suppose wigwam would be quite difficult?' she asked and, after a short pause she added, 'Then there's always Edward Woodward.'

Alex shook his head and waved his arm at the waitress who'd come outside to observe the couple sitting at the picnic table. She glided across the grass and came to a halt at the end of the table.

'Bitte?'

'Die Rechnung, bitte,' Jessica said.

The waitress smiled sweetly and informed them that the bill was eighteen marks. Alex put twenty marks on the table and pointed at the directory, still open at the relevant page. He ran his index finger down the lists of names and brought it to a halt at the entry for Krohne-Stube.

'Where?' he asked.

The waitress looked at him.

'Wo?' Jessica asked, correctly turning the W into a V.

Fortunately the girl knew the area and gave them directions. Alex looked to and fro between the two women as, with much gesticulation and not many words, the information was passed from one to the other. Finally, Jessica nodded.

'Vielen Danke,' she said, this time turning the V into an F. The waitress grinned at her. Alex also grinned at Jessica, visibly impressed at her mastery of the German language.

'Yes,' she told him as they ambled back to the car, 'I'm a genius.'

They backtracked out of the village and after a couple of kilometres turned left, away from the lake, and drove along a narrow road that snaked up into the hills.

Krohne-Stube.

It was like something out of an Andersen fairy tale; a chalet with a steep-sloping roof, an inverted 'V' reaching down on either side almost to the ground. Window-boxes perched on every windowsill and flower baskets hung from the eaves. The small garden encircling the house was bordered on every side by a dark mysterious pine forest. The trees on the hillside above seemed almost oppressive, forming a heavy mantle rising to ever greater heights. Beneath the house, the trees, although of the same variety, seemed less domineering, less malevolent as they fell away in a graceful sweep towards the distant lake.

Wolfgang was coming to meet them, his footsteps crunching across the gravel.

'Alex! Guten Tag! How are you? Good?' Another who spoke almost perfect English – albeit with a heavy Bavarian accent. It was better at least than the faltering German practised by Alex and Jessica.

'Yes,' Alex replied. 'I am good.'

After the introductions, Wolfgang invited them to follow him. 'Come, come,' he said, leading them towards a huge, studded wooden door.

As effusive as ever, Alex observed.

Gesturing Germanically with his arms, Wolfgang ushered them into his home. The hall was spacious and lofty and featured a fireplace large enough to walk into. On the right-hand side a wide staircase led towards the first floor, unknown gentlemen staring gloomily out of heavily framed paintings hanging evenly spaced and parallel to the well-polished banisters. A door to the left opened onto a long room containing a massive dining table surrounded by fourteen upholstered chairs, six to a side, and two carvers, one at each end. Jessica and Alex were led through this room and out through French windows onto an east-facing timbered balcony. The view was fantastic: a panorama over the trees to the lake spread out far below, a giant puddle with toy-like boats plying their way, criss-crossing the placid water to leave vivid scratches in their wake.

The visitors were invited to sit down and were quickly presented with small stubby bottles of Paulaner and heavy, pebbled glasses from which to sip the Bavarian brew.

Uttering the words 'Ach, but you must be hungry, yes?' Wolfgang vanished, only to reappear a few moments later carrying plates laden with cheese, cold meats, bread, and a large bowl of salad.

It was true; they were hungry. They hadn't eaten since the in-flight meal, and had only nibbled at the giant pretzels when they'd stopped in the village by the lake. Moreover, something of substance was needed with which to soak up the beer.

'Voolfy,' Alex began. 'This,' and he waved his arms to indicate the whole caboodle, 'this place is wonderful.'

'Oh yes,' Wolfgang beamed, re-adjusting his large glasses so they sat more comfortably on his nose. 'Yes, it is wunderbar. But business is not. The summer visitors are gone and the winter ski-people are not arriving until Christmas or maybe after. But ... is okay,' he chuckled. 'At least I am having plenty of room for you, yes?' Again, he beamed. Opening more bottles of beer, he asked, 'Now, why are you here in Bavaria? Is it your holiday? But why did you not inform me?'

'No no. Ah, well, sort of.'

Alex received an intense stare from Jessica, a look which had 'CAREFUL' stamped all over it.

'Um, yes, it is a holiday, but we're also doing a spot of investigation.'

'Wie?'

'Investigation. We're looking for something,' Alex explained.

'Here? In Wiessee?' Wolfgang asked.

'Um. Well yes. I think so. Aren't we?'

This was aimed at Jessica, who by now was sitting bolt upright, watching and waiting to see how Alex would manage to extricate himself from the pit into which he'd dug himself. Alex also was wondering if he'd gone too far, and how he might call a halt to the interrogation.

'But what ... what is this thing for vhich you are looking?' Wolfgang asked, re-positioning his spectacles, displaying a soupçon of agitation.

Gazing out over the lake beneath their vantage point, Alex began thinking how typically Germanic was the construction of Wolfgang's last sentence. But then again it was also perfect English. Better, he thought in his humble estimation, than to leave the preposition at the end of the sentence. Although ... it wasn't just a sentence, it was also a question. Oh well, he decided, never mind all that, back to the here and now and life's little necessities.

'Well Voolfy, actually it's a house. Long ago it used to belong to some general but apparently it's become a kindergarten and, for the rest of the story you'd better ask Jessica, I need the loo.'

'Was?'

'Die Toilette, und schnell!' Pretty good, thought Alex, although he realized he was near the limit of his knowledge of the German language. Anyway, there was no time to ponder the intricacies of the subject, his bladder wasn't going to wait.

Wolfgang pointed towards a door leading from the dining room and, being careful not to bounce too much, Alex disappeared.

Returning to the balcony, Alex found Jessica and Wolfgang engaged in earnest conversation. Jessica had brought her chair closer to the large round table which bore the remains of their alfresco meal. Her elbows were planted on the edge of the table and her chin was resting in the cup formed by the palms of her hands, fingertips nestling under her earlobes. She'd pushed her sunglasses up onto the top of her head and was staring at Wolfgang whose large frame posed a totally different attitude. He'd pushed back his chair, letting it come to rest against one of the neighbouring tables, and had shuffled his body downwards until it became recumbent, his legs stretched out straight in front of him. From top to toe he resembled a frankfurter at rest although, with his hands clasped over his rather large belly, the frankfurter took on the appearance of being in the latter stages of pregnancy.

'It's there, or at least some of it's there,' Jessica told Alex, still with her eyes fixed on Wolfgang. 'It's in the process of being converted into something a little more modern. You know, larger rooms, bigger windows, better facilities for the children and the teachers. More money being taken from the tax-payer's pocket. Same sort of thing we do back home,' she smiled. 'Wolfgang says he'll take us there tomorrow morning, but he doesn't think we'll find much. He says the contractors've just about gutted the place although a few walls are still standing, along with one or two of the original rooms.'

Wolfgang nodded his head in agreement, enthusiastically.

Alex began to nod his own head; rather, it nodded itself. He was beginning to feel not a little weary. It had been a long day and the intake of beer wasn't helping his thinking process.

'Ja. Is good. Tomorrow we go hunting but now I am showing you a room and you must relax. Ach, you are travelling all day and ... what is it you are saying in England? Oh ja, now you are putting up your feet.'

Who am I to correct him? Alex thought to himself, deciding in any case that it sounded better the way that Wolfgang had said it.

Chortling to himself, the benign Bavarian led the way back into the house, through the dining room, through the hall and up the flight of stairs, at the top of which a corridor ran the full length of the house with doors leading off on either side.

'You shall have the best room in the house,' said Wolfgang, magnanimously throwing open a door on the right of the corridor. 'See. Everything is here. Television, radio, coffee, and ... through here, your own private bathroom.' Shoving his glasses, yet again, further up his nose, he said, 'Sometimes it is good that the place is empty, so now I can look properly after my friends.'

Looking slightly awkward, Wolfgang stood uncertainly in the centre of the room. His appearance became even more awkward-looking when Jessica went up to him and planted a great big kiss on the side of his face. She grabbed both his hands, looked him straight in the eyes and said, 'Voolfy, you are a brick.'

Wolfgang shot a glance at Alex who shot a glance at Jessica. All three burst out laughing.

'Ja, brick. Voolfy is a brick,' Wolfgang agreed, none the wiser. Now I go to prepare a meal. I have no cook when the season is over.' He grinned, backed out of the door and closed it gently behind him.

Jessica went to the window, threw it open and breathed deeply. 'Oh Alex,' she said, 'this is wonderful.'

'Ja. Zis is vunderbar,' Alex agreed.

'Just breathe in that air,' Jessica directed, filling her lungs with the pungent scent. 'The essence is so heavy, you can almost taste the resin.'

Alex moved a few paces to join Jessica at the window and together they looked out over the canopy of trees towards the lake, half of which was lying in deep shadow cast by the hills ranged behind the two watchers. On the far shore, still bathed in bright sunlight, the dolls' houses perched on the lower slopes of the mountainside captured the rays of the sinking sun on their window panes, turning them into sparkling jewels suspended against the verdant backdrop. The old magic was working and they turned to face each other.

Alex placed his arms around Jessica's waist and pulled her close. She reached up to put her arms around the back of his neck and their lips met in a long breathless kiss. Jessica pressed herself against him. Their bodies were created the one for the other, moulding together like the interlocking pieces of some sensual, sinuous jigsaw puzzle.

After many moments of monumental magic they unlocked their embrace, Jessica saying that she was going to wallow in a deep, hot bath. Alex removed his shoes and lay on the king-size bed, setting the radio alarm to ring after two and a half hours. Everything was beginning to take its toll; the journey, the beer, the heady scent of pine forests...

It was seven-thirty in the evening when the alarm bell rang, waking Alex from his slumbers.

Jessica was sitting at the Tyrolean dressing table, applying a touch of make-up. She looked immaculate. She was wearing her long grey jersey-dress in which she always looked stunning. A pearl necklace was strung around her neck and her long blonde hair, which she'd obviously just hot-brushed into large open curls, hung down over her shoulders, set off to perfection by the contrasting colour of her dress. Poetry in motion. An old cliché, Alex thought, but nonetheless, a good one.

There was something moving somewhere and he swivelled his eyes around, attracted by the flickering television screen in a corner of the room. With the sound turned off, it was trying to convey its message by making the pictures leap around the screen; quite hypnotic really and, as if under its spell, his eyelids started to droop.

Unknown to Alex, Jessica had been observing his every movement reflected in the mirror, and as his eyes began to close, she said, 'Oi. You've been sleeping for more than two hours. Come on, wakey-wakey. We've a dinner to attend.'

Alex dragged himself off the bed and fell into the bathroom.

A shave and a shower later and he was feeling more human, more in control. To complement Jessica's outfit he'd donned an Italian designed dark suit, white shirt, and a bright tie with colourful squiggly things printed all over it.

'You'll do,' said Jessica, patting his behind as they sallied forth to see what delicacies Wolfgang had been preparing.

They'd wondered if they would be eating at the vast dining-table, and had sniggered as they'd thought of the three of them sitting miles apart, having to slide plates, condiments and other paraphernalia up and down the length of the table. However, as they reached the foot of the stairs, Wolfgang came flying round the corner and led them in another direction, away from the

76

dining room. At the end of the house they came to a room with windows on three sides. Two of the windows had heavy drapes drawn across them but the third, uncovered, enabled the occupants to peer through the autumn evening at the twinkling lights of Bad Wiessee, the navigation lights of the boats on the lake, and the moon as it emerged from behind the mountains to take its place in the dark velvet of the Alpine night. In the room, the only source of illumination came from two tall candlesticks placed side by side at the centre of the table. Similar to the tables on the balcony, this one also was circular, but its melamine surface had been covered by a crisp white table cloth.

Wolfgang certainly knew his onions. He'd thrown them into the soup, along with chunks of French bread which were groaning under the weight of layers of cheese, and struggling to remain afloat in the piping hot, rich brown broth.

Alex picked up a goblet of the deep red burgundy that Wolfgang had poured, lifted it towards his host and said, 'Toast!'

Jessica and Wolfgang raised their glasses and looked at Alex, expectantly.

'Um, to Voolfy, a close friend, and to ... to the winter season. May your inn be filled with happiness and ... guests.'

Jessica and Wolfgang moved their glasses towards their lips.

'And...'

'Oh get on with it,' said Jessica. 'The soup's getting cold.'

'Ja, und I am needing a drink,' said Wolfgang.

'And ... to Bavaria and its magic,' Alex finished.

'Bavaria, and its magic,' Jessica and Wolfgang intoned.

They smacked their goblets together, chanted 'Prost', and gulped down a couple of mouthfuls of the heady wine.

After the soup came Schweinshaxe mit Kartoffeln und gemischter Salat. At least that's how Wolfgang described it. Whatever it was, it was delicious, cooked to perfection by Herr Host who, during the course of the evening, regaled his visitors with tales of his life as an inn-keeper.

Time passed and the conversation, punctuated here and there by the noise of a knife on a plate or the chink of glass as Wolfgang poured out more wine, ebbed freely to and fro between the three friends.

'That was delicious,' Jessica thanked Wolfgang. 'Simply wonderful.'

'Yup, Voolfy,' Alex echoed. 'Wunderschön.'

Having scraped their plates clean, they helped him clear the table, then waited in the kitchen while Wolfgang prepared coffee. A few minutes later all three trooped into the lounge, Wolfgang carrying a large pot of coffee, Alex a tray bearing cups and saucers, glasses, plates and forks, and Jessica bringing up the rear, holding another tray upon which there reposed a large Schwarzwälder Kirschtorte and a bottle of Asbach. Jessica and Alex both claimed that they'd eaten far too much already, but the cake looked so fresh, so yummy, so enticing, so … they had some, a great dollop each. Wolfgang poured three generous measures of brandy, raised his glass and said, 'To my very good friends. I am hoping you will be enjoying your stay, and will be coming soon again to visit.'

They raised their glasses, clinked them together, and quaffed the golden nectar. The gâteau was light, fluffy, not at all stodgy, and contained enough liquor to make the brandy almost superfluous. The chocolate and the cream melted on their tongues, the sweet gooeyness contrasting sharply with the hot bitter coffee, combining effortlessly with the smooth round sensation provided by the Asbach Uralt.

Jessica and Alex quickly ran out of superlatives, but it didn't really matter. Wolfgang just nodded knowingly, a beatific smile creasing his face.

As the evening wore on, the food, the wine, and the brandy began to take effect, and it wasn't long before yawns were being stifled behind hands. Jessica was first to give up the unequal struggle.

'Come on my love,' she said. 'If we don't go now I'll never make it up the stairs, and I'm sure Voolfy is just as tired as we.'

They both embraced their German friend, praising his cooking and saying how much they'd enjoyed the evening.

'Okay okay,' Wolfgang acknowledged. 'Now we haff things to do.'

Stumbling up the staircase, Alex found himself thinking that the alcohol must have infiltrated Wolfgang's logic control and, as he followed Jessica along the corridor towards their room, he smiled to himself, realizing that the alcohol certainly had affected his own.

7

Alex's nostrils twitched rabbit-fashion and one eye opened. He drew the duvet round his neck and backed up closer against Jessica's sleeping warmth. As consciousness slowly reclaimed his body he noticed a chill air pervading the room. The window was wide open and he recalled the previous evening when Jessica had opened it before tumbling into bed.

'Bugger,' he said, extending his right arm from under the cover and groping blindly around the carpet until his fingers came into contact with the towel which he'd flung down only a few hours earlier. He slid his frame out of the bed, wrapped the towel around himself and padded over to the window.

The scene before him was pure fantasy. The sun had just cleared the mountaintops and was painting the valley with brushstrokes of rich autumnal light. The lake was invisible, cloaked beneath a layer of mist which extended over the town, blanketing houses and connecting the sides of the valley with an unbroken skein of fleecy opalescence.

Alex reached out and pulled shut the window, then, to disperse the chill from his limbs, he went into the bathroom, turned on the shower and stood under the stream of piping hot water. Afterwards, while shaving, it was necessary intermittently to wipe at the mirror which persisted in misting over, due to the sauna-like atmosphere caused by the steam from his shower.

Fully awake he returned to the bedroom to find Jessica sitting up in bed, a tray across her legs. Breakfast; croissants, butter, black cherry jam and a large pot of coffee. The smile on Jessica's face said it all. There is something deeply darkly satisfying about croissants and black cherry jam.

Finally, breakfasted and dressed, at nine-fifteen they trotted downstairs to discover Wolfgang in the process of putting together a picnic.

'Lunch,' said Wolfgang. 'I thought we could go into the mountains. It will be warm when the mist is going.'

'Yes,' said Jessica, always ready for a picnic; wherever, whenever. 'Good idea,' she continued, 'then tonight we will take you out for a meal. There must be some little restaurant that you'd recommend? Other than your own.'

Wolfgang hesitated, but not for long. When Jessica made a decision it wasn't a good idea to hesitate – it annoyed her. It was something that Alex had discovered fairly early in their relationship, so he seconded her suggestion and that was that. Wolfgang stood not a chance.

The hamper and a couple of rugs were loaded into the hire car and they set off for the kindergarten. With Wolfgang directing, it took only ten minutes for them to reach the location.

The place was deserted. Suddenly, it occurred to them that it was Saturday.

Good, thought Alex. It'd be easier for them to probe the ruins without teams of workmen impeding their progress and questioning their every move.

A crescent-shaped drive led up to and past the front of the derelict building, and they left the car half-way around, outside what once would have been the entrance.

A faint sensation of spookiness emanated from the site, a sensation augmented by thin wreathes of wood smoke drifting out of the trees, gathering ethereally around the piles of shattered bricks. Maybe it was the lack of any noise and the fact that the place was no more than a hollow shell, that gave the impression of something slightly sinister.

However, though only glimpsed fitfully through the smokey haze, the sun was shining and the chill of the early morning had disappeared; there was no reason for them to dawdle on the periphery. So, Alex leading, they advanced through a hole in a wall and entered the remains of what used to be General von Oberstürm's residence. In its heyday it obviously had been a mansion of some standing.

Sunlight slanted over the jagged tops of gaping walls, golden beams penetrating the mist to focus on a scene of total destruction. Here and there the original floorboards were still in evidence, although the majority of the surface was littered with debris resulting from the renovation – broken bricks, shards of glass, weird sculptures of twisted metal, pieces of timber, and over everything, a thick carpet of dust.

The three of them stood in awe, probably all thinking the same thought: what a waste of time, they'd never find anything in this scene of annihilation. Alex picked up a metal pole that lay half-concealed beneath a heap of bricks, and started poking disconsolately at the desolation surrounding him in every direction. Wolfgang clambered across the stacks of rubbish and began his own personal investigation of an enormous fireplace, blackened by years, perhaps even centuries of use. Alex caught himself smiling at Wolfgang's spirit of adventure, his desire to assist in the search despite having no idea of what it was he was looking for.

Then he stopped smiling, suddenly realizing that none of them knew exactly what they were looking for. It had been just a feeling, a gut reaction, to come here to this little German town nestling at the foot of the Alps with its fairy-tale chalets, its window-boxes, its placid lake and its kindergarten. A hunch that had expanded into reality when Jessica had suggested this trip, an expensive trip, only to find a pile of rubble at the end of it.

He turned round to see what she was doing and noticed that she'd disappeared. He glanced over at Wolfgang, who was still prodding away at the fireplace. As he watched, Wolfgang straightened up from his exertions and, with the stick he was using as a prodder, pointed towards the ruined entrance. Alex looked in the direction being indicated, and saw Jessica skipping over the littered floor as though she were a mountain goat bounding across some boulder-strewn precipice. She moved straight through the centre of the decimated entrance hall and on through a heavy wooden door, set in what seemed to be the building's one remaining wall.

'I've found the cellars.'

The sentence echoed back and bounced from brick to brick, before finally coming to rest at a point equidistant between Alex's ears. He and Wolfgang picked their way over the lumpy floor in the direction of Jessica's voice and, once through the door, followed her trail through the dust to the top of a flight of stone steps, which led in a spiral towards the basement. Jessica had paused on the fifth step to switch on the torch she'd collected from the car, giving Alex and Wolfgang ample time to catch up with her. She set off again, her feet following the small pool of light as it wound down and around the staircase. Alex experienced a feeling of déjà vu. As the darkness closed in around him, his mind was transported back to the Deutches Museum. Two and a half years later, and they were still groping around in murky spaces.

Movement was easier in the cellars; the reconstruction, or rather demolition work, hadn't yet reached this section of the house, and the floor was therefore free from impediments. They trailed from vault to vault following Jessica and her little circle of light. It soon became evident that the cellars were quite extensive; they were also quite bare. Just as they were on the point of retracing their steps, the torch light caught the outline of a wine rack filling a wall from floor to ceiling. Jessica played the beam over the whole rack and they were disappointed to see that there were no bottles of wine, not one. A sturdy bench had been fixed securely to the wall just to the right of the wine rack and used, presumably, as a surface upon which to place the bottles selected for functions hosted by Herr General, in times gone by. Sweeping the light over and beyond the bench, they noticed a large crate half-hidden in the space underneath it.

'Okay. What have we here?' asked Wolfgang. The first words anyone had uttered since entering the subterranean world.

No one answered. The atmosphere, dark and foreboding, held on to its secrets.

Wolfgang bent forward and grabbed one end of the crate, Alex grabbed the other end and together they hauled it clear of the bench. Its lid was fastened by means of a clasp but had no padlock attached. Gingerly, they lifted the lid and peered inside.

Nothing. Nothing at all. More disappointment.

'Ach zo. This is too bad,' said Wolfgang.

Understatement humongous, Alex thought to himself, as they shoved the crate back into its niche under the bench.

'Never mind, Voolfy,' he began when, all of a sudden, Jessica dropped to her knees and began examining the floor, running her fingertips over the flagstones, tracing through the dust which formed a perfect skin, unbroken, except where it had been scuffed by their footsteps.

The edges of the flagstones formed a straight line, a groove, running towards the centre of the room. Following the line with her fingers, Jessica found another, joining at an angle of ninety degrees. Then, about three feet along the new line, there was another ninety-degree join, and another groove which ran back towards the wall behind the bench. After a little further exploration, Jessica located an iron ring set into the flagstone, close to the edge of the shorter groove in the centre of the room.

'Mein Gott!' said Wolfgang.

'Just like something out of the Famous Five adventures,' said Jessica, standing up to survey the scene, staring at the floor and the rectangular outline she'd traced through the dust.

They gazed at the little ring buried in the floor then, while Jessica held the torch, Wolfgang and Alex inserted the metal bar that Alex had been carrying, until an equal length protruded from each side of the ring. They took up positions on either side of the rectangle.

'Ein, zwei, drei, und...'

They strained, they heaved. The bar began to bend a little and then, whoosh, the whole section of floor flew upwards with such ease that they were knocked completely off balance. Quickly regaining their composure, they jumped to their feet, joined Jessica and peered into the bowels of the earth.

Six large stone steps led down into a small chamber about eight feet long, six feet wide and only about five feet in depth.

'Go on then,' said Jessica, ushering Alex towards the top of the steps, 'see what you can find.'

Descending one step at a time, Alex advanced towards the floor of the secret sepulchre whilst Jessica illuminated the scene from above, keeping the torch beam at a constant distance in front of his feet. Leaning against the back of the chamber were some shallow crates of varying dimensions.

It didn't require the services of a genius to imagine the contents of these boxes. A few minutes later, the crates, all five of them, had been removed from the chamber and were lying side by side, arranged in a semi-circle on the dusty cellar floor, the three speleologists standing at the centre.

Wolfgang produced a Swiss Army knife from one of his pockets, and set to work on the first of the crates. Alex took the torch from Jessica and kept the beam trained on the work area. As the blade slid under the lid they all held their collective breaths. The room resounded with high-pitched squeaks and creaks as the plywood cover was forced slowly over the heads of the retaining nails. The temperature in the cellars had been freezing when first they'd entered, but gradually became a little warmer due to the heat generated by their bodies. Beads of sweat, caught in the torchlight, glistened on Wolfgang's forehead as he worked his way round the edges of the wooden box.

Time appeared to stand still and the noise of splintering plywood grew in intensity, amplified by the echoing cellar walls.

At last Wolfgang placed the knife on the flagstones and, inserting his fingers into the gap, gently removed the lid.

'Bollocks.' It was Alex's turn to comment on the proceedings which, at this stage, were not going too well.

The crate was empty. A shell containing nothing but air. Thin air.

Passing the torch to Wolfgang, he knelt down, picked up the penknife and set to work on the next crate. Once again it seemed to take an eternity, but eventually the moment arrived when he managed to claw his fingers under the lid and hauled it away from the casing.

Again, a blank. Again, a box full of nothing.

Alex rose slowly to his feet and stood glaring at the open crate, his arms hanging loosely at his sides in a display of utter dejection.

Jessica, shaking her head from side to side, took the knife from Alex's hand and set to work on the third crate. It was a little like playing Russian Roulette, maybe not quite as dangerous, but just as unnerving.

Another aeon went by while Jessica worked her way methodically round the edges of the crate and then, fingers under the lid, she heaved upwards and ... eureka! The plywood lid came away in her hands to reveal a large rectangular shape, protectively wrapped in brown oiled paper.

The silence was profound, the atmosphere expectant. The passing flight of a neutrino would have appeared to make as much noise as the passage of a tube train, lumbering round the tight corners in the tunnels far beneath Bank and Liverpool Street Station.

'Is this a picture, or what?' Jessica asked no one in particular. The question hovered in the stillness.

'Let's lean the crate against the wall,' Alex suggested, 'and find out.'

By the light of the torch, Alex and Jessica each grabbed a corner of the precious cargo, carried it over to the wall and propped it up against the brickwork. Alex angled the crate slightly forwards so that the package slid gently out of its shell into Jessica's waiting hands. He moved the empty case to one side and helped Jessica lean the tightly-wrapped parcel against the wall.

'Wolfgang,' Jessica said, taking the torch from his hands, 'you've helped us get this far, why don't you remove the paper and see what we've got?'

She picked up the knife, handed it to Wolfgang and stepped back to give him room in which to work. At first a little hesitant, he set to work loosening the paper from the edges but, progressing from top to bottom, he soon became absorbed in his assigned task. With his culinary expertise it was entirely appropriate that it was he who was performing this operation, akin to peeling an onion. Layer after layer of heavy oil-impregnated paper soon littered the floor around the base of the object. Then, another eureka.

A bloody huge eureka.

A painting, nestling in a gilt frame, serenely surveyed the trio from across the cellar as they in turn stared back, transfixed.

'Ach zo. Very interesting,' observed Wolfgang.

Another colossal understatement from their Bavarian accomplice.

'Not only interesting, but also...'

'Puzzling?' Alex queried.

Jessica gave him a look. One of *those* looks. A 'Jessica' look that said everything. And more. Evidently she hadn't enlightened Wolfgang totally as to the information regarding their sojurn in Germany.

'Wait a moment,' he cried. 'This is a ... how you say? A picture of fame? I am seeing it in a book. I haff many books on paintings, on art. Oh ja, I have seen this. Yes. Is gut. Is gut.' He beamed at the painting, his face rapt in admiration. Whether the admiration was for the work of the artist or for the fact that he thought he recognized the picture, he wasn't saying, and Alex and Jessica weren't about to ask him. They had other matters on their minds.

'Um, Wolfgang, who is the artist?' asked Jessica. 'Can you tell us who painted this picture?'

She glanced at Alex and Alex glanced at the picture. He had no idea, didn't have a clue. No bells were ringing in any department of Alex's brain.

Wolfgang scratched the end of his nose and hitched his glasses up to the bridge, James Brown fashion. He was deep in thought.

'Ja. Nein. I am not sure.' He turned to face Jessica. 'You see, I like paintings but I don't know. I think I must look first at my books.'

'Have a guess,' Jessica suggested. 'A wild guess.'

'Well...' Wolfgang hesitated. 'I am thinking maybe Rembrandt, but it can't be. Not here in Bad Wiessee. It has to be a picture by someone else who is painting in the same way.'

'Rembrandt!' Jessica dropped the torch, caught it again and shone the beam full into Alex's face. 'Rembrandt. It can't be. Rembrandt?'

Shock, horror, total disbelief. At least that's what Jessica told him later. It was written all over Alex's face in large bold letters.

'Rembrandt.' This time it was Alex. This time it was just a whisper.

'No,' said Wolfgang. 'No way. I am making a big mistake, but I am checking when we get home.'

Jessica grinned, took the penknife from Wolfgang who seemed to have forgotten he was still holding it, and passed it to Alex.

'Might as well open the other two,' she told him, smiling. 'You never know, we might find something valuable.'

It was a strange grin.

8

The light was dazzling. The transformation from the dark dank depths of the metamorphic mansion to the scintillating sunshine of the outside world left them breathless.

Not quite understanding what they'd just discovered, the trio stood uncertainly in the bright light, squinting as they readjusted their vision. Wolfgang burst out laughing and pointed at their clothing. Looking down, they noticed great patches of dust clinging to various prominent places, and this resulted in a lot of leg and thigh slapping as they tried to dislodge as much of the grime as possible. If only they'd been wearing lederhosen they could have claimed to be practising a traditional Bavarian dance routine. As it was, it created a safety valve, mirth and merriment as they struggled to come to terms with their individual thoughts on the meaning of their find.

Of the remaining two crates, one had been empty, but the other contained another painting which caused them to forget, temporarily, all about the possibilities held by the discovery of the first painting. The new find turned out to be a naughty 'Prentiss Pose', one of the missing pair. Unframed, it had been attached to a thin sheet of hardboard and mummified in yards of oiled paper.

The empty cases had been returned to their secret hiding place and the segment of floor lowered back into its well-engineered recess. It was a bit like the sealing of Tutankhamun's tomb, in much the same way that the removal of the paintings was analogous to the robbery. The three friends were certain that the desecrated crates would remain undiscovered and undisturbed as they had for many years already.

Alex had carried the framed painting and Wolfgang the other while Jessica did her best to illuminate the floor under their feet. Up the stairs, over the builders' rubble, and out through the front of the house onto the drive and into the warm welcoming sunshine. Jessica had opened the boot and the paintings were placed in their new temporary home. She placed a few sheets of the oiled paper between and on top of the pictures, and threw a rug over the lot before hastily slamming shut the lid to hide the contents from prying eyes. Not that there were any, not hereabouts in any case.

'Okay Voolfy, picnic time,' said Alex, as they clambered into the car. 'Which way?'

The dust particles were still settling as they drove away under Wolfgang's directions, heading towards the mountains and a well-earned lunch.

Having been so engrossed in the almost clandestine peregrinations, they'd lost all track of time. Amazingly, they discovered that they'd been scratching away at the dust and unravelling bits of brown paper for a good couple of hours.

Twenty minutes after passing through the lop-sided wrought-iron gates at the entrance to the drive, they parked the car in a clearing half-way up the side of a mountain.

Shafts of golden sunlight filtered through the towering pine trees, weaving fairy-tale patterns on the lush grass carpeting the glade, Tolkienesque to say the least. At any moment a troupe of trolls or a handful of hobbits could well have emerged from the dense forest to march across the open space on some mysterious unknown mission. Alex reckoned that he, Jessica and Wolfgang would not have been in the least bit surprised.

Wolfgang and Jessica were unpacking the contents of the hamper onto a picnic table. Onion bread, cheese, cold meats and a salad, accompanied by a couple of bottles of Piesporter Michelsberg, which had spent the morning keeping cool in a freezer bag. Wolfgang was doing them proud; the perfect host.

Jessica collected her battered but beloved Zenit from the car and spent several moments balancing it on another of the picnic tables before setting the auto shutter-release and racing back to join Wolfgang and Alex in a toast to their endeavours.

Click.

Captured on film for posterity: the three heroes celebrating a productive morning's work.

A mouthful of bread and cheese washed down with the light refreshing wine was all that was needed to launch them into earnest conversation. Jessica started the ball rolling, her enigmatic smile returning to her face.

'Voolfy is right,' she announced, the smile becoming self-explanatory. 'I'm sure it *is* a Rembrandt.'

'Ja. The picture is Rembrandt,' Wolfgang agreed. 'I am all the time knowing this.'

'Thought so, Voolfy,' Jessica nodded. 'It's difficult to believe but I think it's genuine, not a replica,' she continued. 'Although I didn't think we'd actually find anything, I did have vague suspicions that we might unearth something ... I don't know, another document maybe? But this? Fuck me, this is absolutely brilliant.'

'But Rembrandt?' Alex interposed. 'I mean, that has to be worth something, right?'

'And this is where we have to be extremely careful,' said Jessica, giving Wolfgang and Alex one of her special 'Jessica' looks. 'Wolfgang has been dragged into this and now he's part of it. So, when we return to Krohne-Stube, he's going to have to find a suitably secure storage place for both pictures until we decide on our next move. And, for the time being, let's not say anything to our American friends. I need to think this one through.'

'No problem,' said Wolfgang, his voice betraying an underlying trace of nervousness, although it may well have been excitement. Very probably it was a mixture of both.

By the time they got back to Wolfgang's house it was nearly four o'clock. Jessica and Alex washed up the picnic things while Wolfgang prepared a giant pot of fresh coffee, which they took outside and placed on one of the tables on the verandah.

The paintings meanwhile had been spirited away by Wolfgang. 'Somewhere safe,' was all he'd say.

There was no reason to doubt him. In a place the size of Krohne-Stube there must have been at least a dozen hidey-holes, all of which would be almost as secure as the secret chamber beneath the ramshackle kindergarten.

Ever since the discovery Alex had found himself thinking back to a conversation that, not so long ago, had taken place in London.

The disappearance of works of art during the last few months of the Second World War. Valuable collections vanishing without trace, only to turn up years later, piece by piece, in various locations throughout the world and being sold for small fortunes. Sometimes not such small fortunes.

'Art fraud,' said Wolfgang, echoing Alex's thoughts. His merry eyes danced behind his glasses as he crunched on a Lebkuchen. 'Ja?'

'Ja. I mean yes, Wolfgang. It's an idea we toyed with before leaving London, but it was such an overwhelming thought, us being enmeshed in bogus works of art, I suppose we didn't really want to believe it. It's the sort of thing you see in films and, yes, historically it actually happened, but to step right into the middle of it is...'

'A step in the right direction,' Jessica finished for Alex. 'It's a chance in a million, and we have to consider very carefully how we're going to handle this situation.'

'What is enmeshed?' asked Wolfgang.

'Enmeshed,' said Alex. 'It means mixed up, connected to something. Like a fish trapped in a net.'

'Ach zo,' said Wolfgang. 'I understand. We are feeshes caught in a trap.'

'Mmm,' Alex agreed. 'Sort of.'

Just as it had done the day before, the setting sun started to bounce its rays off the windows of the houses dotted around the far side of the lake. Once again the pure magic of the Bavarian countryside unfolded in all its breathtaking glory.

Photography couldn't have done justice, even an artist would have had an almighty struggle, trying to capture the myriad shapes forever changing their hues, as the sun slowly relinquished its power to the gathering night.

Watching the line of shadow chase its way down the side of the hill upon which Krohne-Stube reposed, they leaned back into their chairs and drained their mugs of coffee. As the chill of the evening air became more tangible, Jessica pulled on a musk-pink sweater. Her head popped out of the neck and a rogue ray of sunlight glinted in her hair as it spilled down around her shoulders. The deep gold of the sun enhanced the underlying reddish tones and transformed her into a Titian goddess, straight out of a Raphaelite painting.

'And what would you be staring at?' she asked, a smile playing around her blue eyes.

'A Titian goddess,' Alex replied. 'A beautiful Titian goddess.'

Jessica looked embarrassed. Wolfgang looked embarrassed. Alex looked at his watch.

'Wolfgang. Can you rediscover that picture of the naughty nudes? I'd like to see if we can remove it from its board.'

He wasn't absolutely sure what good this would do, apart of course from making the picture easier to transport. In the back of his mind Alex was thinking that at some stage they'd have to take the painting to London and, more than likely, all the way over to the States.

They moved back into the house and while Wolfgang went to retrieve the painting, Jessica and Alex covered the large dining table with sheets of newspaper, protection for painting and table alike.

Face up, under a couple of bright lights, the provocative picture was given close inspection. Down in the cellar they'd given it only cursory observation, just enough to establish whether or not it was one of the missing paintings. Now, the picture flooded into reality, the detail swimming into clarity in front of their eyes.

'Titillating' was the description used by George Michelstraub. He hadn't been wrong. The centre of the picture depicted a man sitting on an armchair, his arms draped round the shoulders of two women who were straddling the arms of the chair, one on either side. The trio, completely naked and with their hands groping in certain obvious places, were facing out of the picture directly towards the viewer and, but for the judicious positioning of a few cushions, the painting certainly would have been deemed pornographic. As it was, it could have been said to exude a high degree of eroticism; what the eye doesn't see, the mind will conjure up. The work had been effected in soft pastel colours, feathery brushstrokes leaving much to the imagination, despite the lascivious expressions and suggestive poses portrayed by the subjects in the tableau.

Wolfgang's spectacles were slipping slowly down his nose as waves of concentration flitted across his forehead.

Jessica was closely examining one of the corners of the painting, gently touching the surface with the pads of her fingers.

'Look,' she said. 'It's slightly discoloured here, almost as if something brushed against the paint while it was drying.'

Wolfgang's eyes swivelled in their sockets, re-focusing on the area indicated. His glasses had come to rest at the tip of his nose and he fixed Jessica with a glare over the top of them.

'It is reminding me of a painting I saw in a gallery in München. Apparently, the canvas had been damaged by the rain, und the paint looked a leetle like this.' Squinting at the discoloured area of the picture, he began also to jab at the paint with one of his fingers.

'Oi you two, don't do that,' Alex reprimanded them. 'You'll end up putting a hole in it.' Before any further damage could be done, he sauntered off to the well-equipped kitchen in search of a palette knife with which to lift the canvas from its hardboard base. The job proved easier than he'd imagined. Over the years, the glue bonding the two surfaces together had lost its adhesive

96

quality, and the knife made short work of the few remaining globs which seemed to have the consistency of chewing gum.

Chewing gum!

Word and thought association caused Alex to start wondering about Mandie and Dan, and how best to impart the staggering news. He visualized Mandie's smile winding itself around her face when told of the probability that the missing pictures were no longer missing. Magic.

'Hello?' Jessica was calling from across the ocean. 'Which planet are you on?'

'Oh, sorry. I was just trying to figure out when we should tell Mandie and Dan.'

'He always goes funny when he thinks of Mandie,' Jessica explained to Wolfgang. 'It seems he's found my Yankee equivalent.'

'Nowhere near my love. Yes, she's attractive. Yes, she's intelligent. Yes, I think she's nice ... Oh hell Jessica, what are you driving at?'

'Just a joke.' She smiled and blew a kiss in his direction, across the top of the dishevelled canvas. Jessica and Alex had that kind of relationship, a special kind of relationship, or so they thought. They would inform one another that they found so and so interesting, or funny, or even attractive, but, at the same time, they knew there could never be another.

'Okay. It's five o'clock and tonight we're taking our mate Voolfy out for a meal.' Alex was adept at stating the obvious, the facts that everybody already knew. 'After today's expedition,' he continued, 'I for one would like to go and wash away the dirt and dust before changing into something more suitable.'

Wolfgang agreed. Jessica nodded assent. It was unanimous.

Brilliant, thought Alex. He had other things on his mind.

'You've got other things on your mind, haven't you?' Jessica whispered as they climbed the stairs. She grabbed one of his arms with both hands, adding, 'So do I.'

When it came to sex, Jessica and Alex both thought alike. Nothing had to be stated, it was just there, automatically, a genetic code, a magnetic force, a *raison d'être* so wonderful and so superbly full of magic.

Closing the door behind them, they threw off their clothes and flung their bodies onto the unmade bed. Placing his hands round each of her breasts, Alex squeezed, the firm pressure forcing them into tight, small cupolas, perfectly presenting her semi-erect nipples. He bent forward, lightly brushing each nipple with his lips, then with his tongue, and as each nipple responded and became rigid he took them between his teeth, gently pulling and teasing with light bites. He moved his right hand down over her stomach, over her pubic hair, and with his index finger began to massage the smooth sensitive area of her abdomen immediately above her sex. At first he used tiny circular movements but after a while his finger caressed her skin with a slow up and down motion. He brought his hand up to Jessica's mouth and inserted a finger to collect some moisture from her tongue, before returning to the slow digital manipulation, occasionally sliding his finger a little further to touch the protective sheath of her bony protuberance.

Jessica moaned and parted her super-slinky legs. Her body knew best, the invitation was there and Alex accepted. He began a long, slow, languorous movement, a concerto, composing a medley of the senses. Jessica pushed up to meet him and as his tongue located her miniature penis, she placed both hands behind his head and pulled his face deeper into her sex. She felt the hot tendrils of pleasure drawing rhapsodies throughout her stomach,

98

the waves building, building, building, pushing her euphoric body upwards towards the crest.

'Yes. There. Right there.'

Alex stopped, lifted his head.

'Alex!' She moved her fingers between her legs, discovered the moisture lubricating her delicate membranes. Alex took hold of both her hands and used her fingers to open her folds. For a few seconds he just looked at the roseate entrance then, very slowly, he introduced his swollen member into the liquid velvet glove.

'Fuck,' Jessica gasped. 'Jesus Fucking Christ.'

'C'mon, c'mon,' Alex implored, feeling his own peak rushing up to engulf him. He moved his hands onto her breasts, his fingers squeezing the sensitive, turgid nipples. His tongue found her mouth and forced it open, Jessica's teeth scraping against the eel-like invasive intruder. She moved her tongue to slide alongside his and tasted the sweet bitterness of her sex. She felt him deep inside her, felt her muscles contracting around his throbbing manhood. The waves mounted, one piling up on another, a crescendo licking her vitals from within, lifting her, lifting her up and over the summit.

'Yes. Alex, yes!' The detonation flooded throughout her being as she experienced the sudden engulfing heat as Alex's body shuddered to a climax. It was always fantastic, a perfect amalgamation of two souls becoming one. They lay in each other's arms for several minutes savouring the afterglow, sharing kisses and words of love.

It wasn't long before Jessica, eager for more, began applying mouth and tongue, composing new variations on an old theme. It worked. It worked every single time. She moved around, straddled Alex, and with her sex tightly gripping the culmination of her ministrations, she looked down at him, her eyes taking in every movement, every nuance of their lovemaking.

And so it goes.

The restaurant was run by a friend of Wolfgang's so everybody knew everybody; well, almost. Made to feel welcome, they were ushered to a corner table and presented with drinks on the house.

They'd taxied from Wolfgang's home. It was a policy of Alex and Jessica's never to drive when going out for a meal – there was no point, especially when living in a city. The act of eating is synonomous with the act of drinking, while the act of drinking is anything but synonomous with the act or even the art of driving. So, a taxi was a prerequisite.

Situated right on the water's edge, the restaurant was small, intimate and cosy. In an earlier life it had been a boathouse, a very elegant boathouse large enough to accommodate two sizeable yachts, black-and-white photos of which decorated the simple wooden walls. The table, positioned next to a window overlooking the lake, allowed for an awe-inspiring view.

Darkness was swiftly descending and the vast mass of water took on the aspect of a large slab of slate, punctuated here and there by the few boats still making their way back to the little harbours dotted around the lake's periphery.

The candles were lit and the menus were set in front of them, the evening had begun; a lot of wine, a substantial amount of food, and plenty of laughter were followed by further toasts to their successful outing, although not a word was spoken about the day's more sensitive activities. Walls have ears, so it was decided to retire to Krohne-Stube and the privacy of Wolfgang's sitting room for after-dinner coffee laced with a little brandy and further discussion.

100

'I've been thinking,' Wolfgang stated, his deep tones sliding through the relaxed atmosphere.

The room was lit dimly; four wall-lights with low-wattage bulbs gave illumination sufficient to add highlights to the deeply burnished wood of the leather-covered armchairs, yet impotent against the shadows that leeched from the four corners of Wolfgang's comfortable retreat.

'Thinking about our conversation,' he continued.

'Our conversation?' Jessica asked.

'Art fraud und the war. You see, there is something else, but ... well, maybe I should not be saying it.'

'But you will,' Alex prompted, his smile lost in the shadows.

'You know,' Wolfgang said, pulling himself into an upright position, suddenly serious. 'It's not just here that the treasures of Europe ended up. The Nazis took their ill-gotten loot with them, und when the Führer's armies stormed into Denmark, Poland, Austria, Bohemia und Moravia, the treasures ended up in the headquarters of the occupying generals. Copenhagen, Paris, Prague, Vienna, wherever there was a Nazi High Command, there would be also a display of plundered art.'

'Shit, I never realized,' Alex said.

'Zo,' Wolfgang replied. 'Not many people did. It vas like the Jews, not many people were knowing of their disappearance, these things were not made public knowledge. It was a secret shared by the Nazi elite, who liked to surround themselves with beautiful things, other people's beautiful things. I suppose it gave them an added sense of importance, a reminder of their achievements, the crushing power they wielded over so many countries.'

'Hmm, you sound just like an historian,' Jessica said, smiling, as she and Alex went on to quiz Wolfgang further about his knowledge of art.

It was almost two o'clock by the time Jessica and Alex climbed the stairs and fell into a deep, well-earned, alcohol-aided sleep.

Peas in a pod.

Dormice.

Something or someone was growling at Alex from behind a boulder. Peering around the giant rock he came face to face with a wide-mouthed troll. It leered at him in a manner common to trolls and bade him follow into a hole that had just materialized in the side of the boulder. Like an idiot, he followed. Just like that. The passage was totally devoid of light, so he reached out both arms to full extent on either side. Horrible squelchy things brushed under his fingertips, and he noticed that the corridor was becoming steadily narrower. And then, pop. He was catapulted through a clammy veil into a cavernous chamber dimly lit by incandescent spheres, seemingly suspended in thin air way up above his head.

Beneath the spherical lights the air was thick, heavily laden with incense and draped with strands of gossamer, floating freely throughout the grotto. The filaments, lit in pastel hues, shifted every so often to reveal scenes of utmost debauchery. A tendril of gossamer lightly caressed Alex's face, gradually insinuating itself into a well-known form that began to make quiet but insistent love with him.

Jessica. Alex woke up and immediately tried to go back to sleep, to return to that state of Nirvana. But it wasn't to be, Mr Sandman had run out of sand.

He sidled up against Jessica's back, gently kissed the nape of her neck, caressed her long golden tresses and lay there thinking about the meaning of life, and about the conclusions at which they'd arrived during the previous evening.

Wolfgang had consulted, checked and double-checked his art books, but had been unable to find an exact match for the unearthed painting. The style, however, was unmistakably that of Rembrandt. Having established the fact, they'd decided that the best plan was for the painting to remain in Krohne-Stube, at least for the time being. Wolfgang had salted it away in a safe place, in a cupboard behind a cupboard containing vacuum cleaners, brooms, mops and a whole plethora of cleaning paraphernalia.

The other painting, the Prentiss Pose as it had become affectionately labelled, was rolled up and packed into Jessica's suitcase. It was to accompany them back to London where its fate would be decided upon.

The following morning they took their leave of the Krohne-Stube and bade Wolfgang a fond farewell. Jessica hugged him, kissed him on both cheeks and smiled.

'We'll be in touch soon Voolfy. Very soon.'

Wolfgang and Alex clasped hands.

'Take care Voolfy, and thanks for everything.'

'Oh ja. Everyzing is good. Call me soon, yes? Tchüs.'

The morning mist was melting under the sun's onslaught, and as the car crunched down the gravel drive, they wound down the windows and waved to Wolfgang, who was standing on the doorstep.

'Nice guy,' said Jessica as she moved the gears into third. 'You have some good friends, und Ich liebe Dich.'

'Ich auch,' Alex replied.

The drive to Munich was uneventful apart from the fact that, as they motored along the autobahn, they decided to return to

England by rail rather than making a quick dash through the skies. Not only would it prolong the mini-holiday, it would also satisfy their penchant for train journeys, and Munich to the Hook is a worthy distance.

Having successfully negotiated the streets of Munich, dodging trams and pedestrians, and recognizing one or two street corners upon which they'd loitered, or around which they'd strolled during their last visit to the city, Vorsprung Durch Technik was checked into the Avis ranks outside the Hauptbahnhof.

Today, Munich was full of sunshine. A perfect autumn day with clear blue skies. But, despite the sun, there was a slight chill in the air; harbinger of winter and the sub-zero temperatures often experienced in this part of Germany.

The Hauptbahnhof was surprisingly deserted. Alex had always remembered it to be crowded with people, a seething mass of humanity. There were of course a few inveterate students with their obligatory backpacks, clutching European Rail Passes and vast well-thumbed tomes of incomprehensible timetables. A handful of bedraggled old men sat slouched over a couple of metal benches, taking swigs from beer and whisky bottles, the empty evidence overflowing from a nearby litter bin and steadily piling up around their feet. With bleary eyes the men stared morosely at a couple of extremely high-heeled, leather mini-skirted women, who patrolled ceaselessly backwards and forwards across the expanse of the concourse. Endemic to any large rail terminus, the down and outs, the ladies of the street and the itinerant students form a stable population, a population which becomes massively swollen twice a day. Rush hour. They rush in, they rush out. They rush here, they rush there. *They:* the workforce. In the mornings the suburban trains slide into the stations and disgorge their human cargo; in the evenings the trains return and the process is reversed.

104

Jessica and Alex's footsteps echoed their way to the booking-office where, with many repetitions of '*Nein*' and '*Ja*', they managed haltingly to purchase their tickets, little passports that would safely guide them along the gleaming parallel lines to Liverpool Street Station, via a four-hour sea-crossing between the two H's, the Hook and Harwich.

Having a few hours to kill before their train even entered the station, they stashed their luggage into a lock-up and made their way to Neuhauser Strasse, Munich's central pedestrianized shopping-street. Near to the Frauenkirche they found a café and ordered some soup, some pasta, and a couple of glasses of the local Löwenbrau. The arrival of the soup made them realize how hungry they were, and they found it hard to wait for it to cool a little before attacking it with gusto.

The café was effectively sheltered from the chill air, so they sat at an outside table and watched the inhabitants of the Bavarian capital as they criss-crossed to and fro, going about their business. It was all there; lederhosen, feathered hats, jeans, big brightly coloured chunky sweaters, business suits; high fashion, low fashion, and even one or two fur coats. On the corner opposite the café stood Hertie, one of the country's largest department stores, and Alex and Jessica found it fascinating to watch the comings and goings through the portals of the vast emporium. All shapes, all sizes; cosmopolitanism at its utmost.

Appetites satisfied, they sauntered further along the walking street to Marien-Platz and arrived to the sound of the glockenspiel chiming the hour, five o'clock. The famous clock, let into the façade above the entrance to the city hall, features figures from German mythology which shuffle round the clock twice every day, out one side and back in the other, a superior version of a giant cuckoo clock. It's a big tourist attraction, and today Jessica and Alex were tourists with time on their hands, and a big clock above their heads.

At a leisurely pace, they retraced their steps, stopping now and then to peer into shop windows. There was a motley collection from which to choose: fashion boutiques, confectioners displaying row upon row of mouth-watering chocolates, furniture stores, chinaware and glassware, racy lacy lingerie, and several kiosks selling newspapers, magazines, souvenirs and knick-knacks.

Back at the station, they collected their luggage, checked the indicator board for the correct platform, and found the train waiting for them. Their carriage was about half-way along the length of the train, conveniently close to the dining car. They prowled along the corridor and located their cabin, colliding with the attendant as he was backing out. He asked to see their tickets and, having ascertained that they were indeed the correct occupants, with a flourish of his hand he gestured for them to enter the cubicle. It was a six-berth cabin with the minimum of floor space, and they claimed the upper-bunks by throwing their baggage onto them. Alex found himself thinking that it sort of made up for all those towels on deck chairs. Pulling the window down they leaned on it and watched their fellow travellers meander about the platform.

Luggage trolleys were pushed up and down as the pushers searched for the correct carriages, and mobile hamburger-kiosks trundled around describing erratic circles, the vendors trying to entice the passengers to buy the succulent frankfurters on offer. Suddenly, the train was moving. No whistles, no announcement, just a hoot from the engine somewhere a long way up at the front as the train began to glide slowly out of München Hauptbahnhof.

For some unknown reason continental trains tend to make far

less noise than their British counterparts – a fact borne out as the train effortlessly and soundlessly slipped through the city suburbs and into the countryside, on the first leg to Augsburg. It was just after seven and the light was fading, but Jessica and Alex remained standing at the window, devouring the scenery flashing by ever faster as the train picked up speed. It was only a matter of minutes before they heard one of the sounds that Alex associated most with European rail travel; the clanging bells of a level crossing, the pitch changing with the Doppler effect as train, passengers, and Alex's ears thundered past. They saw the glare of headlights from a car waiting to cross the tracks, a memory of red warning lights flashing on the horizontal barrier, and then, the rapidly diminishing sound of the bells lost in the slipstream.

They closed the window and closed the compartment door, sealing themselves into their own little world, and it wasn't until they relaxed, sitting on one of the lower bunks, that they realized how tired they were. Looking back, it had been quite an active day. The drive from Bad Wiessee followed by the concentration required to thread their way through Munich, the wandering up and down Neuhauser Strasse, all adding to the exertions of the previous day. They drifted off, lulled to sleep by the hypnotic motion of the speeding train.

A knock at the door dragged them out of their catnap. It was the attendant with information that the dining car was open, and would they 'please to take their seats'. They stared at him through half-closed eyes, yawned, stretched, and wobbled to their feet. A couple of minutes later they placed their bums on chairs, one on either side of a table. It seemed as though the train was fairly empty – there were only a dozen or so people in the dining car.

They ordered glasses of wine and a bottle of mineral water,

and propped their heads on their hands while they studied the menu. After a couple of sips of wine they began to revive and rejoined the world at large. Alex ordered a pâté, Jessica had smoked fish, and that was it. The starters proved to be so generous that they skipped the main course and the dessert, and went straight for the coffee.

Looking out of the window, there wasn't much to be seen beyond their own reflections. The occasional light blinked into existence and then blinked out again, small outposts of humanity signalling their presence to anyone who happened to be passing by. From time to time the train sped over more level crossings, the ringing bells sending twinges of aural delight along Alex's spine, as though Jessica had drawn one of her fingernails lightly down the length of his back.

The sound of bells. The sound of a multitude of things.

Sound. The first of the senses. We use it even before we're born, Alex thought to himself. We use it whilst still swimming around in the amniotic sac, sure as eggs is eggs, swimming about just waiting for something to happen, preparing ourselves for action. And that's when our sense of hearing manifests itself, sounds of our progenitors yabbering away at each other, sounds of vacuum cleaners, dogs barking and, if you're lucky, the sound of music. No, he told himself, his private conversation becoming quite extended and involved, not the film score but something perhaps slightly more inspiring, such as a string section from a Haydn symphony. Possibly, he decided, quite possibly that's how some of us grow up with a love of music. Food for thought.

That was it. His personal soliloquy was ended.

As they lurched their way back to their cabin clutching the half-empty bottle of mineral water, they sensed that the train seemed to be slowing down. It was almost imperceptible, just a hint of a slackening of pace, probably another station they guessed.

They entered the compartment and before clambering into the upper bunks, they quickly threw a few clothes around, making it appear well-inhabited so as to deter any inquisitive passengers. A few doors slammed, a few guttural voices said 'Gute Nacht', and the train slithered out of the station. Squinting out of the window Alex watched the word STUTTGART move from right to left then, more rapidly, another STUTTGART moved from right to left. The next time the name went by it passed as a blur, and then Jessica monkeyed her way across the chasm separating the two top bunks and snuggled up against him. Stuttgart was instantly forgotten.

'We needn't have worried,' she said.

'What?'

'Well, it seems as though this train is virtually ours. There's hardly anyone on it.'

'Good,' said Alex.

'Good what?'

'Good night!'

Jessica groped. Jessica pinched. They giggled. They fell asleep.

9

The picture had sailed straight through customs, untouched, in Jessica's suitcase.

With Alex it had been a different story. The officious official must have had a foot fetish; he'd unrolled all Alex's socks, even the dirty ones which had been lurking in an inner pocket of his holdall.

'Perhaps if you told me what you're looking for?' Alex had ventured.

An icy stare. They're good at icy stares. There's probably an H.M. Customs College that teaches nothing but icy stares, although possibly it specializes also in unintelligible language, the primal grunt indispensable to the men in navy blue sweaters. They'd be press-ganged into attending evening classes in how to be totally devoid of humour and even the most basic of manners. They refused to re-pack Alex's socks and just left them lying about, discarded like autumn leaves, woolly ones.

'Under no obligation, sir.'

Venom. Pure unadulterated venom.

Alex had had to attend to his socks himself and was frowned upon for taking too much time.

After the hiccup at Parkeston Quay they'd caught the boat-train to Liverpool Street and then tubed to Barnet. The journey took forever. It's always the same; the closer to home one gets, the longer the last few miles seem to take. They unpacked, poured a couple of drinks, collapsed onto the sofa and fell into lengthy discussion.

In the evening they telephoned Mandie and Dan, telling them much of what they'd been up to. However, they didn't tell them everything, they didn't mention the Rembrandt, although they did divulge the finding of the Prentiss Pose.

Mandie was ecstatic. 'Bring it over, bring it over,' she ordered.

Jessica told her that they would indeed ferry the picture across the pond, but added that before travelling to the States she had a few loose ends that needed tying up.

Mandie was incensed. 'Hey, c'mon guys. What's there to sort out? Bring the picture over here. We can go see George, get the whole thing straightened out and claim our share of the booty.'

Jessica bypassed the barrage and calmly stated that they'd be over as soon as possible, then signed off. She was certain that the Prentiss Pose was a red herring, a painting holding a lot of secrets up its sleeves. So, over the weekend, she'd set up a meeting with Christine, one of her old school friends, who now worked at the Tate.

Alex and Jessica had taken the weekend to relax, to recover from their whirlwind trip to Germany and to marshall their thoughts with regard to the situation and their recent discoveries. Saturday and Sunday, two lazy days, forty-eight hours in which to do as little as possible. Except...

On Saturday afternoon Jessica suggested a visit to Waitrose in order to replenish the sad looking interior of the fridge.

'All we've got is yogurt, some frozen bread, some cans of beer, and a few limp sticks of celery,' she announced, closing the fridge door. Alex picked up the car keys and they motored the short distance to the High Street.

An hour and a half later they returned to the house, whereupon Jessica told Alex to go and have a bath while she prepared some spag-bol. 'And take a drink with you,' she yelled after him as he started up the stairs.

Alex came back into the kitchen and yanked a beer can out of the fridge. 'What's this then?' he asked, watching Jessica peeling an onion.

She looked up from her work. 'A beer can.'

'No, I mean, you know, you preparing dinner while I go and have a bath?'

'How do you mean?' Jessica looked at him.

'It's something I could get used to.' Alex smiled and put on a northern accent. 'It's like slippers and a G and T when hubby comes home from t'office.'

'Go on,' said Jessica, busily chopping, 'and take your time.'

Before starting up the stairs again, Alex sauntered into the living room and put some music on the hi-fi, Beethoven. He cranked up the volume so he'd be able to hear the music while he wallowed in the bath.

Thirty minutes later he dragged his prune-like body into an upright position and stepped out of the tepid water. He smiled as he towelled himself dry; the music was still playing and a mouth-watering scent of herbs and cooked meat wafted through the air. He pulled on a pair of jeans and a well-worn rugby shirt and, humming along to Beethoven, padded down the staircase and went into the kitchen.

'Jessica?' he called as he prodded the bubbling food with a wooden spoon that he noticed resting on the work surface. 'Jessica, what about the spaghetti?'

112

He lifted the spoon to his face and, using his teeth, carefully removed the few pieces of mince that sat in the shallow wooden depression. 'Mmm, tasty,' he muttered softly.

He fetched a saucepan and sloshed some water into it before setting it on the hob. He lit the gas and then went in search of Jessica. Thinking that maybe she'd gone to change the music, he walked to the living room. 'Jessica?' he called as he walked through the open doorway. The room was empty, although full of Beethoven. Alex moved across to the hi-fi and lowered the volume. Turning, he went back to the hall and called up the stairs. 'Jessica?'

No reply.

He climbed the stairs and peered into the bathroom. Empty. He looked briefly into the spare room, then hurried to their own room and clicked on the light. Again, empty. 'Now what?' he asked himself, staring at the bed.

He returned to the kitchen half-believing that Jessica may somehow have been there all the time. The mince simmered gently and the water for the spaghetti was beginning to boil.

'Shit,' Alex said, before adding, 'Jessica, this isn't funny!' He switched off the gas under both pans and tipped the meat into a dish which he covered and put in the oven. 'Bollocks,' he muttered under his breath. 'Where the fuck is she?'

Alex turned the oven to one hundred degrees and then walked to the front door. He went out, down the steps, through the wrought-iron gate and onto the pavement. Nothing. No movement anywhere. He squeezed between two parked cars and looked up and down the street.

'Jessica,' he called, then again, 'Jessica.' Across the road at number ten a dog started barking, a stupid toy dog with a high-pitched yappy squeak. 'Shut the fuck up,' Alex yelled at the diminutive pooch, thereby causing the wretched animal to wind itself into a small-dog frenzy.

Alex ran through the covered alley which divided the two houses, theirs and the neighbour's, the house filled with the noisy population from Bangladesh as opposed to that of the 'Brat-Pack'. He peered into the garden thinking that maybe Jessica had gone to pick some herbs. It was dark, the light from the street lamps didn't penetrate the area behind the houses, so Alex squashed his eyes tightly shut. He paused, then opened them again and still saw nothing. He walked round the perimeter of the pocket-handkerchief-sized lawn, brushed past the hypericum and startled the cat.

'Shit,' Alex hissed as the cat moved to a safer position, sat and gazed at him.

'Where is she?' he asked. The cat just stared.

Alex made his way back down the corridor, turned right, turned right again and retreated into the house, closing the door behind him. He returned to the kitchen to make sure Jessica hadn't materialized out of thin air. He was running out of ideas. He looked at his feet and realized that he'd been running around without any shoes. He raced upstairs, put on a pair of gym shoes, then came back down, two steps at a time. He picked his jacket off the hook on the back of the front door and, as he shrugged into it, he saw the blue-green light illuminating the controls of the hi-fi. Moving across the room to switch off the equipment, he noticed the telephone. Alex sat down on the sofa and glared at the phone, willing it to ring.

'Come on you stupid fucking piece of machinery, make a noise.'

He shook his head as he thought through his dilemma; go out and search the streets or stay at home and wait for the phone to

114

ring? Alex looked at his watch and realized he'd left it in the bathroom. He walked into the dining room and looked at the grandfather clock. Eight forty-five. He'd give it thirty minutes and if Jessica didn't come back or if the phone didn't ring, he'd go out and patrol the streets. He returned to the living room and sat bolt upright on the sofa; there was no way he could relax. His eyes, channelled as if by magnetism, kept returning to the phone, while his mind went into hyper-drive. He went over in minute detail everything he'd said, everything he'd done, and came up with nothing.

'But,' he told himself, 'something's caused this.'

So he went over everything again; the lazy morning, the pub lunch, the trip to the supermarket, the journey home. He racked his brain trying to remember all the conversations, the things he'd said, the things that Jessica had said.

Nothing.

Alex got up and went to look at the clock. Ten past nine. He left the house and turned right, heading down the street. A light drizzle had begun to fall giving everything a brilliant sheen, the tarmac had the appearance of a dark, deep, mysterious river. Again, there was no sign of any movement, no traffic, no figures loitering suspiciously in the shadows. Alex continued to the end of the street, made another right and started up the hill towards the High Street.

'What else?' he asked himself.

There was nothing else. Jessica had walked out leaving no clues, no hints as to where she might have gone.

She'd done it before, one night a few months ago, after an argument about how to cook a curry for some friends they'd invited to dinner. Alex had been in the kitchen happily throwing all the ingredients into a large pan, when Jessica had marched up behind him and told him he was doing it all wrong.

'Excellent,' Alex had said, 'you've come to give me a hand.'

'The fuck I have,' was Jessica's response. 'I'm just pointing out that what you're doing is wrong.'

Alex had continued gently frying the spices then, when he added the garlic and onions, Jessica told him it was too early to start adding the other ingredients.

'Fine,' Alex had said. 'If you want to take over, feel free to jump in at any moment. Show me how to prepare the perfect curry.'

That was all it had taken. Jessica had stormed out of the house and hadn't returned until just after midnight, meeting their dinner guests as they were saying their goodbyes on the doorstep.

'Good was it, the meal?' she'd asked as she'd flounced into the hallway. 'I bet it was. I bet it was superb, cooked to perfection by Superchef Alex.'

'Jessica... '

She hadn't waited to hear what the guests had to say; by the time the first word had been uttered, she'd reached the top of the staircase, entered the bedroom and slammed the door.

'This is crazy,' Alex told himself.

He'd reached the High Street and was passing the entrance to Waitrose. He peered through the plate-glass windows and saw the late-shift stacking the shelves, making everything neat and tidy for the following day when the life cycle of the supermarket would repeat itself. He crossed the street and started walking back in the other direction. It was pointless, there was nowhere to go, nothing he could do. As his feet took him automatically along the pavements he began again to think about the relationship, about the hopes and dreams they shared. He was just about to turn left for the final leg back to the house when he remembered that Jessica used to have a flat overlooking the station in New Barnet. He'd been there once and recalled it as being a bit of a dump. He'd told her so.

'Yes,' Jessica had replied, 'but it's perfect for the station, I can get up at the last possible moment...'

'And still miss the train,' Alex had finished for her.

'And still miss the train,' Jessica had agreed.

Alex smiled at the memory as he made his way along Warwick Road.

A taxi went past him, spraying him with water as it splashed through a puddle.

'Bollocks,' Alex said as he turned to watch the taxi. It stopped and started reversing.

'What the fuck are you doing here?' The question came through the open window in the rear door of the cab, followed by a head outlined with blonde hair flying wildly in the wind as the taxi came to a halt in line with Alex.

'Taking the dog for a walk.'

'Get in.'

Alex walked around the back of the taxi and got in on the other side.

'What are you waiting for?' Jessica shot at the cabbie.

In the whole history of taxi journeys it must have been the shortest; it was certainly the quietest. No one spoke, it seemed as though no one breathed.

Outside number seventeen Jessica darted out of the cab leaving Alex to pay. She didn't have a key for the front door so she stood in the drizzle, fuming with impatience.

'What now?' she demanded as Alex made his way towards her, the taxi remaining where it had stopped, chugging in the way that only London taxis do.

'Money,' Alex answered. 'I didn't know I'd be using a taxi.'

'Well, fucking hurry up.'

Alex unlocked the door and opened it and was swept aside as Jessica flowed into the house and made her way into the kitchen. He collected some money and returned to the waiting taxi. When he came back into the house he found Jessica seated at the table in the dining room, an open can of beer in her hand. Alex went into the kitchen, switched on the hob and rummaged around in the kitchen drawer for a bottle opener. He collected a wine glass and, returning into the dining room, found a bottle of red wine and sat down at the table on the side opposite to Jessica.

'Do you want to talk, would you like me to put on some music, or perhaps I should just go outside and shoot myself?'

'That's what I hate about you, you're so condescending.'

'Or maybe Jessica, maybe you'd prefer it if I knocked you about a little and asked you what the fuck you've been up to?'

'That's not your style.'

'Precisely.'

Jessica sipped from her beer can while Alex poured himself some wine.

'The choice is yours,' Alex said. 'We can forget all about it, pretend that it never happened, we can confront it head on and try to see where the problem is, or...'

'For fuck's sake Alex, stop being so ... methodical.'

'Practical, Jessica. The word you're groping for is practical.'

'Jesus, there you go again.'

'You're the one who walked out into the night while I was

soaking myself in the bath tub. No note to say where you'd gone, no phone call to say that you were okay.'

'Are you my boss, do you own me?'

'No Jessica, I'm not your boss and I don't own you.'

Jessica shook her head then stopped and looked at the beer can, she rotated it between her thumb and third finger, the soft scraping sound of tin against wood filled the room. Alex stood up and walked around the table to position himself behind her. He put his hands on her shoulders and massaged gently as he leaned forward to place a kiss on the crown of Jessica's head.

'I don't know,' he said. 'I just don't know.'

Jessica raised her head and turned it towards Alex. He kissed her softly, letting his lips brush teasingly against hers.

'Mmm,' Jessica breathed as her tongue probed into Alex's mouth. 'That's what I need, love and attention. How long until that meal's ready?'

London.

It's always there. Solid. Never changes. Not really.

The streets become more heavily littered, the people become meaner, the tourists more obnoxious. The old buildings grow more tatty, while new constructions obliterate the skyline with their hideousness. Apart from that, it never changes. Old Father Thames just keeps rolling along; if only the river could communicate.

They were next to the river, opposite the entrance to the Tate.

The rolled-up Prentiss Pose had been placed in a cardboard tube to protect it from the elements, and now it was protruding proudly from Jessica's shoulder bag, like a large salami sniffing the air, the London air. Different to the Bavarian air, it lacked sparkle, it lacked clarity. Instead, it was heavy, enervating, and from their vantage point close to the river, it was salty and damp.

They made their move into the gallery and collared the commissionaire, asking to see Christine.

'Eh?'

'Christine,' said Jessica. 'Christine McAuley. She's in administration.'

'A mini what?'

'Straight on,' answered Jessica, leading Alex across the entrance hall towards some vastly imposing doors.

'Oi, come back here. I haven't given you permission.'

Before managing to get half-way across the foyer they were met by a tall, auburn-haired woman in a black-and-white checked suit. Very debonair, very elegant, and very assertive. Grabbing them by their arms, she wheeled them round, past the astonished commissionaire and out onto Millbank. They were escorted through a succession of streets and soon were ensconced in a small coffee bar.

'Ever so pleased to meet you,' said Christine, shaking Alex's hand. Her eyes said the same. 'I've heard so much about you.' This with a glance at Jessica.

Alex also glanced at Jessica. He hadn't heard a thing about this Christine, she'd emerged from nowhere, straight into Jessica's plans in the space of a weekend.

'Strange,' Alex told himself, thinking that he'd met all of Jessica's friends.

'We go back simply ages,' said Christine, as though catching his train of thought. 'Don't we?'

'Yes, we do, but we don't see that much of one another. Mostly we just chat on the phone. In fact it's been four ... five years since last we met.'

120

'Really?' Christine asked, looking doubtful. 'Has it been that long?'

'Yes, the school reunion, remember? That's when you told me you were working at the gallery.'

Jessica's computer brain was marvellous, storing information and reproducing it at a moment's notice.

Christine's dark brown eyes were looking Alex up and down, appraising. He just stared back. He wasn't going to be intimidated, and made a mental note to speak to Jessica about this 'friend' of hers.

Christine, her hair cut in a bob, French style, higher at the back and sort of falling down and forwards towards her pointy chin, had the bearing of a polymath. During the ensuing conversation, and later when Jessica revealed a few more facts about her, this observation was proved to be correct. In fact this is why Jessica had made contact in the first place. 'If there's anyone who'll be able to help us, it's Christine,' she'd announced.

'I thought we were doing pretty well by ourselves,' Alex pointed out. 'Why do we need assistance from an outsider?'

'We're not experts,' Jessica had replied. 'We know next to nothing about the art world and if we're to find out more, my sweet love, we have to go to the mouth of the horse.'

Simple, Alex had thought. The perfect answer.

The conversation was under way and in full flow, and Alex surfaced into the direct line of fire.

'What picture?' Christine asked.

Jessica tapped the tube, the top just visible above the edge of the table.

'In there?' Christine was visibly stunned. 'I thought you said it was valuable?'

'It might be.' Equanimity. Jessica smiled back at Christine. 'It might well be.'

'Okay,' countered Christine. 'Who's the artist?'

The scales were level. It was a joy to behold the two women fencing with each other. Scholastic parrying, a game evidently having its origins back in their school days. 'Prentiss. Arthur Prentiss. To be exact, Arthur Prentiss the Younger.'

'Prentiss.' Chistine repeated the name, closing her eyes, suddenly opening them. 'Prentiss. Yes. We've had a memo about Prentiss. From the National. Apparently they're showing interest in this artist.'

'Curiouser and curiouser said Alice,' said Jessica.

'That's what I thought,' Christine agreed.

Three cups of cappuccino were plonked onto the table, most of the froth slopping over the rims. The waiter was sullen, unshaved, and sported a ring the size of a hula hoop in one of his ears.

'Sorry,' he mumbled, turning away to fetch the taramasalata, pitta bread and olives that they'd decided to have for lunch.

'Look,' said Christine. 'Obviously I can't take the picture into work with me.'

'Obviously,' Alex concurred, in a manner suggesting that he thought he was dealing with a customs officer.

Jessica's eyes smouldered. Christine's eyes were volcanoes. Pure magma.

'Well,' Alex acquiesced, 'it would be unwise.'

He fiddled with the table top then, plucking up courage, stabbed a piece of pitta into the mound of taramasalata. 'So what do you propose?' he asked.

'I propose you both go for a walk, maybe take in a movie, and meet me at six. Here.'

'And?' Jessica questioned.

'I'll have a surprise waiting for you.'

Two of a kind, thought Alex. Jessica and Christine. No, three of a kind, he corrected himself. Jessica, Christine and me. 'Fuck,' he said to himself. 'Who am I kidding?'

Christine left to return to work, leaving Jessica and Alex to mull over all that they'd learned, which wasn't much. She'd told them nothing. But then, to be fair, she hadn't seen the picture.

'Give the woman a chance,' Alex told himself, remembering her soft Scottish accent and deciding that it was actually quite attractive.

'Can we trust her?' he asked.

Immediate character assassination. He didn't mind admitting it. He was worried, to say the least. If this painting was as important as everyone was making out, he reasoned, then the fewer people who knew about it, the better. He wasn't too happy about Christine's revelation concerning the National Gallery's interest in the Prentiss works. Gordon Bennett, he thought.

'Yes,' Jessica had replied.

'Yes what?' He'd forgotten what it was that he'd asked.

'Yes, we can trust her. She's a bit weird, but she's honest.'

'But what about the National Gallery? She said they were asking questions.'

'I suppose that's 'cos we were asking questions.'

'Mmm, maybe. Even so, it's a bit coincidental,' Alex said, worried.

'Coincidental, that's all,' Jessica replied. 'Yes, they have records of the Prentiss Poses, but no proof of their existence, remember? Lost at sea, Davy Jones's locker.'

'And the two that missed the boat? Won't they start wondering about those?'

'They can wonder all they like,' Jessica smiled in answer. 'We've got them.'

'Yeah, well, I hope you're right.'

'Mmm,' said Jessica. 'So do I.'

Alex was startled. Here was his darling, his oracle, mentor and fount of all wisdom. Here she was and for once she seemed unsure. There had to be a reason. There was. Jessica finished her cappuccino and set the cup back onto its flooded saucer. She took a deep breath, looked him straight in the eyes and said, 'Here we go.'

Alex blinked. Twice. He stared back, waiting.

'The Prentiss Poses, I don't think they're genuine.'

Alex was all agog. He dragged his chin back off the table top and continued to gaze into those blue, blue eyes.

'I think it's a cover,' she continued. 'A camouflage to hide something else. Remember what we were talking about before we left for Germany? Nineteen forty-four? End of the war? Works of art?'

Jessica paused while the waiter threw the bill onto their table. It landed, one corner catching the pool of coffee in Christine's deserted saucer. Alex and Jessica watched the blotting-paper effect as the stain spread slowly across the check, stealing its way through the printed name of the coffee bar.

'I'm certain that the Rembrandt we discovered in Wiessee was destined to become a Prentiss Pose, only something occurred to prevent it happening.' Her eyes were bright. They had to be to keep pace with her brain.

'Funny,' said Alex. 'I was thinking along the same lines.'

'You weren't.'

'I was.'

It was one of the many things they had in common, minds that travelled along the same tracks. It'd been that way ever since the day they'd met. Once, it happened in the car. They'd been motoring along for several miles in complete silence when suddenly, and for no apparent reason, they'd both uttered the same phrase, simultaneously. Along with their many other similarities, it led them to believe that they'd been carved from the same block, albeit with a few years in between.

'Yes of course,' Jessica agreed archly. 'You would've been.'

Both of them had realized, or at the very least suspected, that all was not as it seemed when they'd found the paintings side by side in the long forgotten chamber in Bad Wiessee. Alex recalled Jessica's look, *that* look, when the Rembrandt had been unearthed. Yes, he decided, it had been at that precise moment when all the pieces of the jigsaw had started to fall into place.

Before it became totally coffee-logged, they rescued the bill from its landing place and carried it reverently over to the till. Le patron took the proffered piece of paper and after giving it a cursory look, told them that they owed him twenty-three pounds.

'Twenty-three pounds? For three cups of lukewarm cappuccino, most of which was in the saucers, a mound of turgid taramasalata and some leathery pitta? You must be joking?' Jessica went for the jugular.

The owner retrieved a half-smoked cigarette from behind the Gaggia and jammed it into a corner of his over-large mouth, an unmistakable act of concentration. 'Yeah. Cappuccino, three pound each; fish eggs and bread, fourteen pound. And that don't include no service.'

'Service?' Alex echoed. 'What service?'

The over-sized mouth manipulated the cigarette from one side to the other, an unmistakable act of aggression. Stone-age man with stone-age brain, Alex decided, taking an instant dislike to the swarthy character.

Not really having another option, because they had to return to the overpriced eatery to meet Christine, they paid the twenty-three pounds.

'I bet we paid for someone else's bottle of wine,' said Jessica. 'Bloody foreigners. The fuckers should go back to counting beads and rearing sand dunes.'

'Oh well, never mind,' Alex reasoned. 'That was paid for by good old George, part of the expense account.'

Jessica smiled, reached out and took hold of one of his hands. 'Let's go see some stuffed animals.'

'I *am* a stuffed animal,' Alex retorted. 'In more ways than one.'

They set off for Pimlico, and the tube.

N.H.M. Nasty Hairy Monsters. AKA the Natural History Museum.

Alex hadn't been there since being propelled around the lofty halls as a small child. 'Look Alexander, a mammoth. Look at those tusks!'

He recalled that in those days it had been almost obligatory for parents to march their toddlers around all the city's museums. Certainly, he mused, it was much more the done thing than nowadays. Today's children rebel against any suggestion of an educational outing, whilst today's parents are forbidden by law to contradict their offspring. What a dilemma; children running riot in every direction with adults powerless to do anything about it. A national epidemic; hordes of unruly, uneducated malcontents laying waste to anything and everything that gets in their way, 'fuck everything' being the common anthem.

126

Alex found the urge to summon up a selective massive natural disaster, something overwhelming. Something was needed to purge the cancer gnawing at society throughout the world.

A dinosaur's head seemed to nod in agreement.

'Well, my friend,' he said to the monster. 'Something certainly put an end to *your* cavortings.'

It grinned. At least, Alex liked to think it did.

Although on the surface they were just killing time until the rendezvous with Christine, Alex and Jessica always made sure they never killed time without in some way being constructive. They had an in-built ability to have an interest in everything; even the bendy coffee stirrers at the Deutches Museum had come under pretty close scrutiny, and that was on their first meeting! It's a sin to waste time, they'd agreed, life's too short.

They peered at this, prodded at that, gasped at the other and gawped at everything; pros on the museum circuit, every now and then pausing to comment upon some exhibit. It's the way they were, bouncing facts and information off one another, the best way to learn. They took time, whilst journeying between cases of this and cases of that, to discuss the Prentiss Pose still resident in Jessica's shoulder bag. They realized, however, there wasn't much point in making firm decisions until they'd discovered what the six o'clock surprise was going to be.

Four-thirty found them sitting in the cafeteria, pushing another plastic stick around a couple of cups of coffee. The restaurant was almost deserted; in fact, the museum as a whole was not well attended. There were, however, still one or two characters worthy of observation.

A couple of teenagers, one male, one female, sat in a corner.

They were sitting at opposite sides of a plastic-topped table, gazing intently into each other's faces. Young love and natural history, a good combination. Perhaps it was their first date, Alex found himself thinking; after all, his own first date with Jessica had taken place in a very similar environment.

Two tables separated the lovers from a woman of indeterminate age, sitting with a cup of tea in one hand while with the other, she occasionally turned the pages of a thick paperback which lay in front of her on the table.

Alex smiled. It was one of his favourite occupations whenever he found himself in such a place with time to spare, or even in John Lewis's on a Saturday afternoon. It's a simple pleasure; a crêpe laden with morello cherries, a coffee and a good book. From time to time one can steal surreptitious glances around the immediate vicinity to see what's going on, to take in one's surroundings. People-watching.

At five-fifteen they left the museum and headed back towards the meeting place to await Christine and her surprise.

The surprise took the form of what later transpired to be Christine's man, Terry, about five-foot ten, longish dark hair, slim and good-looking, according to Jessica's summation. He also exuded an air of erudition, but then he was with Christine, so maybe it was to be expected.

The introductions complete, Christine strode off leading them back towards Pimlico. It was as though they were going round in circles, having set out in exactly the same direction only a few short hours ago. However, Jessica and Alex were relieved that they hadn't had to re-enter the outlandishly expensive coffee bar.

Following Christine and Terry, they found themselves continuing beyond the station, turning right up Belgrave Road and heading into Warwick Square, where the couple lived. The flat was vast and reminded Alex of a certain apartment over in New York. Filing into the living room, they sat on sofas lined up facing each other across a low-slung coffee table, liberally littered with coffee-table-sized art books.

The room itself displayed evidence that its occupants were of a studious nature. A large desk at one end of the room was positioned in front of a French window overlooking the gardens in the centre of the square. The desktop was clear except for both volumes of the Shorter Oxford English Dictionary stacked to the left, a couple of sharpened pencils on the right, and a sheaf of blank white paper placed dead centre. Christine switched on a wrought-iron table lamp that cast a warm glow over the leather desktop. It also illuminated a couple of framed photos, one of Christine and one of Terry. Close, but not together, Alex noted.

The desk was probably a communal work place, in the same way that Jessica and Alex used their dining table when spending evenings writing together, the atmosphere conducive to creative thinking. Add some wine, some olives, some Mozart, and inspiration begins to flow.

'Okay. First things first,' Christine announced. 'Let's have a drink.'

'This,' Alex said to himself, 'sounds like an excellent idea.'

Christine handed a bottle of claret to Jessica, who extracted the cork like the professional she was. The bottle was passed around and they all poured for themselves.

'Cheers!'

Glasses were lifted and lips were smacked in appreciation of the Bordeaux which, although it had only just been opened, still managed to impart a full body, a woody nose, and a warm glow to the oesophagus.

Using her glass to point towards Terry, Christine started the ball rolling.

'Terry here is involved in the art world. His field, his speciality, is the restoration of paintings, so he should be able to shed some light on your little problem,' she said, turning to face Alex and Jessica.

'Just what we need,' said Jessica. And, as if on cue, she began to recite the story of their involvement with the Prentiss Pose. Without going into all the details, she gave a fairly full synopsis of the picture's history, along with her and Alex's suspicions.

'. . . obviously the fewer people who learn of this, the better,' she ended, gazing pointedly at Terry.

'Yes of course, I quite understand,' he said. He had a pleasant voice, well-spoken, giving the impression of having an abundance of authority on the subject in question. 'I also understand that you have the painting with you, rolled up in that tube?' he continued, guessing, a smile playing about his face. 'Mind if I see it?'

Jessica and Alex exchanged glances, but their hesitation was brief. 'No. No problem,' said Jessica as she took the tube from the floor and handed it to Terry.

The moment of truth was nigh. They held their breaths as he coaxed the canvas out of its temporary shelter, unrolled it and spread it out on the coffee table, shunting the piles of books in every direction.

Once again the erotic images lay stretched out in all their glory, open for inspection. The only sound to be heard came from the stubble on Terry's jowls. More exactly, it came from the motion of his hand as it passed to and fro across the day-old growth, while he gazed at the painting and pondered.

'Mmm.'

The collective breath was released. Terry had spoken. Admittedly he hadn't said much, but as far as his audience was concerned, he might as well have been Zarathustra.

'Mmm.'

There it was again. The definitive sound that summed up the mind of the picture restorer.

'Can you take that a stage further?' Alex enquired. 'Sort of "Mmm", what? Is it a good "Mmm", or is it a bad "Mmm"?'

Without taking his gaze from the picture, Terry asked Christine if she'd any nail polish remover and some cotton-wool balls. Without answering, she rose to her feet and padded off in search of the requested items.

'This *is* interesting,' said Terry.

'We think so,' said Jessica.

Terry pursed his lips and the magnetic lock between eyes and picture was sundered.

'Yes, very interesting,' he continued, fixing his eyes on Jessica. 'Tell me. This damage in the corner ... here,' he pointed. 'Was it there when you found the picture, or did it happen when you removed the canvas from its backing?'

'It was there already,' answered Jessica. 'Why, would it have made any difference?'

'No, not really. It's just something that aroused my curiosity.' Terry glanced at both of them. Not exactly sheepishness, but something akin was manifest in the look he bestowed upon them. 'Would you mind if I carried out a minor experiment on this painting? I won't damage it any further, but I'd just like to...'

He trailed into silence as Christine returned bearing a phial of varnish remover and a handful of cotton-wool balls.

Alex looked at Jessica. She shrugged her shoulders non-

131

committally, but her eyes said 'yes'. 'Well, we've nothing to lose, have we?' she said.

'Not really,' Terry assured her as he unscrewed the top of the phial. Inverting the bottle, he allowed a little of the contents to soak into some of the cotton wool. 'This stuff isn't really strong enough to do the job properly, but for the time being it'll have to do,' he explained.

Jessica and Alex leaned forward to observe the work being carried out on the picture.

It was inspiring, equivalent to a musician's fingers drawing sublime textured nuances from an instrument. It takes infinite patience, enduring practice, and consummate concentration to attain such heights of artistic perfection.

With the lightest of touches which, to Alex, was instantly reminiscent of one of Jessica's meandering massages, Terry teased at the edges of the damaged area. He moved the ball of cotton wool in gentle concentric circles and paused after each contact, in order to assess the progress of his work.

Ten minutes later and, although the others were unable to perceive a change, Terry grunted, apparently satisfied with the way things were going. He sat back in his chair. Alex and Jessica also sat back. They looked at Terry. Terry looked at them. Christine poured some more wine and then disappeared to find another bottle.

'It's a painting on a painting,' said Terry. 'Much as I'd expected.' He lifted his glass, took a mouthful of wine and savoured the moment.

'So. What happens now?' asked Jessica.

'It depends,' said Terry. 'Depends how much you need to know.'

'Everything.' In tandem and stereophonic. Jessica and Alex had hit the play button at the same instant.

132

'Okay.' Terry replaced his glass onto the table. 'That's going to take time.'

'How much time?' More dual discourse. The dynamic duo were on form.

Christine started to laugh. 'You two are amazing,' she chortled. Her giggles were infectious and they all started to laugh, the tension had been lifted.

Terry hurriedly rolled up the painting and returned it to its cardboard container. 'Just in case the wine is spilled,' he explained. 'Let's order a pizza,' he suggested, 'to soak up the rest of this bottle.'

Alex began to unwind, his initial uncertainty as to Jessica's trust in these people's discretion, melting away as mist under the warmth of the sun.

Within thirty minutes a giant four-seasons pizza had materialized, courtesy of a spaceman with a motor bike. A large bowl of green salad had also appeared, thrown together by Christine and Jessica.

Despite the size, it didn't take long to demolish the pizza. Terry brewed a pot of coffee and from somewhere a box of chocolate mints was produced. The scene was set, and once again the characters took their places around the coffee table.

'It's a long process,' said Terry. 'Painstaking, deliberate, methodical. Quite boring really. Well no, not boring.' Smiling, he corrected himself. 'Actually it's like placing a sheet of photographic paper into developer and watching the picture slowly being revealed – it's fascinating.' He paused to bite into a mint.

Alex took the opportunity to gulp a couple of mouthfuls of coffee. This was a brand new science that was being explained, new to Alex anyway, and his appetite for learning was voracious.

'As you saw earlier,' Terry continued, 'it takes a long time to work away at the layers of paint. The Prentiss was executed in a mastic-varnish to which various pigments were added as necessary. To remove this mixture will take several weeks of repetitive swabbing, with workshop solvents such as acetone or toluene.'

This was brilliant, Alex decided. Mysterious wonders were unfolding before his eyes. 'That's all very well,' he said. 'But how do you stop the process from damaging the original painting, when you eventually get down to the last layer?' Me and my inquisitive mind, Alex thought, as he threw an After-Eight into his mouth to aid his powers of concentration.

'The fact that the original painting is oil based gives it a certain amount of protection,' Terry answered. 'But in reality, the overriding factor is the deliberate slowness of the entire operation. As each successive layer is methodically removed, one can judge the precise moment when the varnish becomes oil, and that's the moment to stop. A little leaching can sometimes take place, but very rarely does this give rise to any major problems.' He paused and grinned. 'Of course, it helps if one's an expert.'

'Several weeks,' said Jessica. 'We're going to have to think up some subtle ways of keeping Mandie and Dan and dear old George at bay.'

'It should be quite easy,' said Alex. 'We'll just tell them the truth.'

'What? About everything?'

'Just enough to make sure they stay over on their side of the ocean. We'll tell them that the painting is being examined by an expert...'

'To verify that it is indeed a Prentiss,' Jessica cut in. 'Yes, that should do the trick. It might annoy them, but it'll certainly show them that we're taking the business seriously.'

'Here's to Prentiss,' said Christine, raising her glass.

'To Prentiss,' the others chorused.

10

It's guaranteed always to quicken the pulse, the haunting sound of a wailing siren. Especially in the middle of the night.

The rain which had been drumming against the windows for the past hour or so added a certain urgency to the alarm as the emergency vehicle hurried through the darkness on its secret mission.

Quarter past two and the phone rang.

Then it stopped.

Dragging himself drowsily across the bed, Alex reached out to cuddle Jessica, only she wasn't there. Drearily he dragged himself further across the bed until he fell off it and onto the floor without encountering Jessica's body on the way. Semi-alert, he found a dressing gown, shrugged into it, and shuffled off in search of Jessica and the other phone.

'What? Here in the UK?'

'Here in Barnet,' Jessica told him.

'Here in Barnet?'

'Here in Barnet. They're coming to stay with us for a couple of weeks.'

'They can't!' Alex said, panic in his voice.

'They can and they are, in...'

'When?' he asked.

'. . . a couple of days.'

'Oh bloody hell.'

'It's no good. I tried to put them off. Anyway, you're the one who's met them, you know how persuasive Mandie is.'

'Well, what are we going to do? I mean two weeks! Jesus!'

'Since you're fully awake, we're going back to bed.'

'Jessica!'

That was as much as Alex was allowed to utter before she applied her lips to his and, unfastening his robe, lightly drew her fingernails across his body, from his throat all the way down. Down over his chest, stomach, abdomen and. . .

'See?' said Jessica.

Alex didn't need to look, he could feel. It was always the same for both of them, immediate response.

Taking him in both hands, she looked him in the eyes.

'Okay, that's enough encouragement,' she announced, raising an eyebrow and smiling. 'You light the candles, I'll get the oil.'

The bedroom had been furnished and decorated by Jessica; plenty of soft furnishings, cushions and drapes in all directions. There were also shelves that stretched all the way round the room, full of books of every description; fairy tales to Hardy, Kafka and Koontz to encyclopaedias.

The candles stood in a couple of glass containers on Jessica's dressing table, and when lit they transformed the room into a mediaeval chamber, creating an atmosphere of warmth and passion.

Letting the gown fall to the floor, Alex climbed onto the bed and lay face down on the sheet awaiting Jessica's soft caresses.

He didn't have long to wait.

She bounced onto the bed and, kneeling first on one side, then on the other, and finally between his legs, she drew wave upon wave of pure pleasure throughout his entire being. The oil

136

was warm and aromatic, Jessica's hands were silky smooth and her fingers fondled fantastically, pressing, squeezing and pinching as they traced over every inch of his body.

Turning him over, she straddled him and slowly eased herself down onto his erection. For many moments they stayed motionless just gazing into each other's eyes, enjoying the closeness, luxuriating in the love and tenderness, the oneness of their relationship.

After a while Jessica began to move, lifting away from him until the swollen head of his member became visible in the folds of her sex, then she plunged back down to embrace his pubic hairs with her own. She leaned towards him and Alex raised his head to kiss her breasts and take her nipples into his mouth. Leaning further forwards Jessica crushed her breasts against Alex's chest and forced her body backwards, pressing the front of her sex against his member, feeling the pressure against her engorged nub. Alex ran his hands down her spine and massaged the small of her back, before allowing one finger to press gently into the crease of her backside as Jessica thrust her tongue deep into his mouth. She climaxed a split-second after him and, forcing her arms under his body, embraced him tightly, her face snuggled against his neck.

'You're fantastic,' he told her.

'You're fantastic,' she told him.

'We're fantastic,' they informed each other in unison as the candles flickered.

Sleep was just around the corner.

Zing.

The toaster popped up with two bits of toast, depositing a few crumbs onto the work surface.

'I've been thinking,' Jessica announced. This usually meant either that monumental troubles were about to take place, or that Jessica had managed to dissolve all the problems that might have been in the way, thus restoring peace, calm and tranquillity to the domestic domain.

'Scotland,' she said. A simple statement.

'Scotland,' Alex repeated as he methodically buttered a piece of toast. 'What about it?'

'We'll take them to Scotland,' Jessica explained.

The piece of toast fragmented in Alex's hand. 'But that's ours,' he protested.

'In a manner of speaking, yes,' Jessica agreed. 'I know it's our favourite place, our retreat from life's hurly-burly, but it might be fun to show them some of this island's more beautiful parts. And it'll keep their noses out of London.'

Zing.

The toaster offered up another couple of pieces of toast and scattered more crumbs over the work surface.

Breakfast was still the most important meal of the day, Alex thought to himself, especially when about to put out the welcome mat for their American buddies and embark on a trip to Scotland.

Several rounds of toast and a couple of coffee pots later found Jessica and Alex trundling into the living room, and from one of the book shelves they took down a well-thumbed guide to recommended hotels in Great Britain and Ireland. They'd stayed at a few of the listed establishments and all had been excellent, so the manual became known as 'The Book', its pages pored over whenever they travelled in the UK. Alex still had some of the money that Michelstraub had pressed into his hands when he'd left the office in Binghamton, and he saw the trip to Scotland as being a good way of using it.

The morning was spent on the telephone, booking hotels. The tour of the North was arranged with meticulous precision, ensuring that the hotels would never be more than three hundred miles distant; after all, a holiday should be just that, a holiday.

In the afternoon they rang Christine to find out if there was any news from Terry, and also to inform her that they'd be out of town for a couple of weeks. It had been a week since they'd left the painting in Terry's hands, a week during which they'd asked themselves again and again if they'd done the right thing giving him the picture in the first place. Eventually they'd decided they'd had no option, so there was no point in fretting. The painting had to be cleaned, and it had to be cleaned by an expert. Terry happened to be just such an expert, and at least Jessica had known Christine long enough to be sure that any of Christine's friends, albeit that this one was her partner, would be completely trustworthy.

She had little news, except that Terry was progressing, slowly but surely. 'This sort of thing takes time,' she reminded them. 'It can't be hurried, it's painstaking.'

'It's frustrating,' Alex complained to Jessica. 'How difficult can it be to sieve through a few layers of paint?'

'Infinite patience, consummate concentration. Remember?' Jessica said.

Alex packed a suit, a couple of shirts, jeans and a sweater. Jessica packed a dress, a pair of jeans and a sweater. Their walking boots were slung into the boot.

It was like old times. Memories revisited.

They drove to the airport via the M25 and the M4, just as they had when first they'd embarked upon this adventure, a mere three weeks ago. This time was different in that there were banks of fog drifting over the countryside.

They were late arriving at Heathrow, as was the flight. Nothing changes. Two cups of coffee and two Danish pastries and suddenly, there they were, as large as life, Mandie and Dan.

They looked in great shape. They sounded in great shape.

'Hi, buddy!' Dan pounded Alex's arm up and down as if it were an old village pump. 'And this'll be Jessica?' He kissed her on both cheeks as though he'd known her all his life.

Mandie kissed Alex on both cheeks. They were all friends at this gathering, from the word go.

Mandie and Dan were travelling light, one case between them. Into the boot it went and the foursome piled into the car. With Jessica at the wheel they set off for the first port of call.

'So where's this home of yours?' Dan asked.

Jessica moved her hand from the gearstick and placed it on Alex's knee. 'Barnet,' she answered.

'Barnet,' Dan repeated. 'Say, is that hereabouts or do we have a ways to go?'

'It's near here, but we have a ways to go, 'cos we're not going there,' Jessica replied obliquely, picking up on the phrase from the New World.

'If that sounds Irish, there's a good reason for it,' Alex endeavoured to explain, but seemed only to add to the confusion.

'Excuse me?' said Mandie. 'I think maybe I missed something?'

'Well, Jessica is half Irish and sometimes comes out with strange expressions.'

Alex smiled broadly at the dashboard, pleased at the way he'd managed to handle the situation.

140

'No, the bit before that,' Mandie countered. 'The bit about having a ways to go, about not going to your home.'

Rats! Alex turned in his seat and transferred his grin from the dashboard to Mandie and Dan. They grinned straight back.

'Welcome to England,' he said rather lamely and belatedly, as they joined the M25 swinging north towards South Mimms and the A1.

Before reaching their initial Cambridgeshire destination, they'd imparted the idea about the Scotish trip, reasoning that, as there was nothing more to be done about the Prentiss Pose, they might as well take time out to enjoy themselves.

'Scotland! That's part of England isn't it?' asked Dan.

'Almost,' Alex replied. 'Only don't ever let a Scot hear you say that.'

'But it is, isn't it?' Dan insisted.

'Well, it's part of the UK, the United Kingdom. It's like your United States except you've got, what, fifty-two of them, fifty-three? We've only got four: England, Scotland, Wales and Northern Ireland. We're all fiercely independent, to such an extent that the Irish are trying to throw us out and the Scots are pressing for self-government. It goes back a long way, to the Romans in fact, who built a wall from one side of the country to the other to keep the marauding Picts at bay.'

'You don't say?' said Dan.

'Again,' Alex went on unperturbed, 'I suppose it's a little similar to the situation that you've got. We hear that folk in New York look upon the folk in California as being not much more than pill-popping beach bums. Presumably the denizens on the West Coast see the citizens of New York as unhealthy office-bound pen-pushers?'

'Yep,' Dan agreed. 'That's about the size of it. Oh, and by the way, it's fifty.'

'What is?' Alex asked.

'States. We got fifty,' Dan informed him.

Over dinner, Alex and Jessica recounted the story of their trip to Germany. They spoke of their meeting with Wolfgang, of their attempts at the German language, and immersed themselves in descriptions relating to the beauty of the Bavarian countryside. They recounted the visit to the kindergarten and the discovery of the Prentiss Pose, but had decided not to spill the beans about the Rembrandt until later. Much to Alex's chagrin, Jessica was still a little wary of the Americans.

'So, just one picture?' Dan asked, dejection apparent on his face.

'The seventh Prentiss,' Jessica confirmed. 'One down, one to go.' Well, she thought, it's not exactly a lie.

Alex looked across at Jessica and shook his head, doubt furrowing his brow. He was at a loss. The exhumation of the paintings had been mind-blowing, especially the unearthing of the Rembrandt, and Jessica's resolution to keep the secret hidden from his friends was causing ripples of concern. Wavelets of uncertainty washed through Alex's conscience as he wondered at Jessica's powers of reasoning. The fact that she didn't trust Dan and Mandie must mean that she didn't trust him, that she thought him incapable of making a sound judgement in his choice of reliable persons. Bollocks, he thought, reliable persons? These were his friends, Dan the policeman and Mandie the photographer. How reliable does one need to be? Didn't she realize that, with open arms, they'd welcomed him into their apartment and into their lives, no questions asked?

Jessica met his gaze and looked at him, deeply, darkly, as if seeking inspiration.

'Alex and I have spent some time discussing the war and the involvement of the Nazis in the wholesale rape of Europe, the plundering of cities and the disappearance of countless valuable artefacts.'

'And you're thinking...' Dan started.

'We're thinking,' Alex jumped in, picking up the flow, 'that the Prentiss paintings may have constituted a tiny part of this enormous military acquisition, a few paintings spirited away by some high-ranking officer with a penchant for erotic studies.'

'Certainly a possibility,' Dan agreed.

'Hmm. But what if...?' Jessica began.

'It's more than a possibility,' Alex enthused, cutting into Jessica's question. 'It's a certainty.'

'But what if...?'

'How so?' Dan asked.

'We have the general's name,' Alex answered. 'One General von Oberstürm.'

'Jesus!' Dan exclaimed. 'Where did you rustle up a name like that?'

'But what if what, Jessica?' Alex asked, peevishly, realizing she still hadn't finished her question.

'Nothing,' she replied, looking slightly sheepish. Then, brightening a little, she answered Dan's question. 'It's information we got from the National Gallery.'

Three faces wore blank expressions.

'The information about the general,' Jessica explained. 'He must have been the central cog in these machinations, after all, we found the painting in his house. And, the fact that he was a general would have made it easy for him, no one would have dared to ask questions.'

Candlelight reflected from the wine glasses and suffused a warm glow over the table, as the dialogue flowed back and forth across the plates of food. Fortunately the restaurant was not busy, so there was no fear of the conversation being overheard by inquisitive ears.

'Shit,' said Mandie, grinning widely. 'You guys seem to have opened up an ants' nest. Imagine stumbling over that! Rake around in the dust for long enough and everything traces back to the Nazi war machinery. Shit.' She paused for a few seconds, then, 'Talking about dust,' she continued, 'reminds me of Mrs Carmichael's house and my discovery of those documents. I've thought long and hard about that lucky break and have come to the conclusion that it was just one of those things.'

'What things?' asked Jessica.

'One of those things that just … happens.'

'Care to elucidate?' Jessica invited.

'Well, the more I thought about it, the more certain I became that the papers must have been stored away along with the six paintings, you know? I mean, it stands to reason. But, when Michelstraub was ushered straight to them, and especially when the dust covers were thrown back, it's my guess that the bundle of papers became dislodged, fell to the floor, and rolled away out of sight. With all the excitement that would have been evident at such a moment, no one would have thought to go crawling about looking for documents.'

'Hmm,' Jessica muttered, 'psychologically sound, but still, it doesn't explain why the two sets of documents were in two different places.'

'Maybe there's a simple solution,' said Alex, 'like the idea that Mandie's just put forward.'

144

'Yes?' Jessica asked, pushing, probing.

'Maybe,' Alex continued, thoughtfully, 'maybe Charley didn't want to have sheaves of paper cluttering his secret hiding place in his desk, but at the same time thought it necessary to keep some form of reference close to hand.'

'Of course,' said Jessica. 'That'll be it. There were only ... what? Three or four sheets of paper concealed beneath the desk drawer? And, presumably, that would have been enough for Charley's peace of mind. He had the list in a secret yet accessible place, while the rest of the documents were stashed away with the paintings. Perfect.'

Later that evening, leaving Mandie and Dan at the bar, Alex and Jessica retired to the sanctity of their room, where Jessica ran a deep bath to which she added some bubbly stuff, courtesy of the hotel. Alex searched through the mini-bar and found some mini bottles of brandy, which he carried through to the bathroom and, joining Jessica, they sipped at the amber liquid as they lay immersed in bubbles.

'Listen baby,' said Jessica. 'We just can't afford to let this cat out of the bag.'

'Which particular cat would this be?' Alex asked.

'The Rembrandt,' Jessica replied.

'Why? They're our friends. They know about everything else.'

'The Rembrandt changes everything,' Jessica said, running a bar of soap along her left arm.

Alex waited. He said nothing. He watched the slow languorous movement as the soap travelled across Jessica's chest, and then, as she changed hands, he watched her move the bar along her right arm. She, in turn, was watching him, looking at his face,

145

trying to find some sort of reaction. There was none.

'Well?' Alex asked, shuffling further under the water until his chin became level with the layer of foam.

'It's my contention that the Rembrandt was due to become a Prentiss Pose,' Jessica stated.

'What?' Alex exclaimed, sitting upright, and in the process managing to slosh water over the edges of the bath.

'It's simple,' Jessica explained. 'The perfect foil. A few erotic paintings, possibly having some aesthetic value, would not have attracted as much attention as a grouping of pictures by the likes of Rembrandt. You know, in case somebody started to ask questions?'

'Incredible. And you think this was all engineered by von Oberstürm?' It was Jessica's turn to remain silent. She just gazed into Alex's eyes. 'But I still don't understand why you didn't tell Mandie and Dan about the Rembrandt,' he asked.

'Do we have to tell everybody everything?' Jessica responded.

Alex thought he noticed clouds forming in the pools of her eyes, big, ugly, dark black clouds.

'Okay,' he said. 'But what if...?'

'What if what?' Jessica replied, rinsing the soap from her body.

'I don't know,' Alex told her. 'That's why I'm asking.'

'What do you mean?'

'After dinner,' he explained. 'You came out with "but what if?", and I'm wondering where that was going?'

'Oh. Nowhere. It was going nowhere,' Jessica replied.

'Okay.'

'It was just that...'

'Yes?'

'No. It was nothing.'

Jessica climbed out of the bath, wrapped a towel around herself

146

and perched on the edge of the loo, cleaning her teeth. Alex stared fixedly at his toes, which were peeping at him from the other end of the bath.

'Women,' he told his little pink digits, 'are funny things.'

11

Candy was a hooker. A call-girl, a visiting masseuse, a lady of the night; too posh to be a street-walker. She was a member of the service industry; you pay your money and choose from the menu.

'The sessions are supposed to last thirty minutes according to my controller, but sometimes it's all over in five ... sometimes even less. It all depends.'

This was interesting stuff. It's amazing the amount of information that can be gleaned from idle conversation in a hotel lobby at three in the morning.

'You see, it may be that the guy...'

'Yes, yes, I think I get the drift,' Alex told her.

'But...'

'No. It's quite all right. The sordid details you can leave to my imagination. But tell me, how did you get into the business?'

'Needed the money.'

She glared at Alex and then her minder-cum-chauffeur sauntered in, nodded, and together they left, disappearing into the night, leaving Alex perched uncertainly on a stool.

Jessica poured some milk onto her branflakes.

'You're so strange,' she said. 'Wandering around hotel corridors and lobbies in the early hours, talking to complete strangers. Whatever next?'

148

'I might write a book about it,' Alex mused aloud. 'Mmm, *Strange Encounters...*'

'*Brief Encounters*,' chirped Mandie, 'judging by what you told us. Only five minutes!'

'Or less,' Jessica reminded them.

'*De-Briefed Encounters*, sounds more to the mark,' said Dan, not wishing to be left out of the verbal parrying.

'Anyway,' said Alex, looking towards Jessica. 'Not being able to sleep and not wanting to disturb you, I thought I'd see if room service was on the go...'

'At three in the morning?'

'Well...'

'It was obviously more than room service that was on the go,' said Dan, wearing a grin the size of the Grand Canyon.

'Thank you Dan,' said Mandie.

'Yes. Thank you Dan,' Jessica agreed, adding, 'So, what else did you discover during your nocturnal meanderings?'

'Is this the Spanish Inquisition or what? I only mentioned it because I thought you might find it interesting. You know, more information to store away in your treasure trove of trivia.'

'Yes my love. Yes, yes, yes. Tell me more.'

'Well,' said Mandie, showing moral support for Jessica. 'Chatting up strange ladies in the middle of the night, what do you expect? Total compliance, complete understanding, or just a gentle ribbing?'

Alex grunted and ferreted about in the Cornflakes box.

The A1 was deserted. Well, comparatively deserted.

There was the occasional pantechnicon, the occasional coach, and a sparse selection of cars. The day was bright, crisp and cold, ideal weather for driving. They didn't pause to wonder at the lack of traffic but just enjoyed the open road, as they headed north towards the border.

North Yorkshire, and Mandie and Dan were introduced to their first English pub. They'd left the main road in search of a watering-hole and had found one in a little village near Richmond.

Roast beef sandwiches were the order of the day and when they arrived, turned out to be the biggest sandwiches anyone had ever seen. Door-step sized chunks of bread cradling cold roast beef, the quality of which can only be found 'Oop Narth'.

'This is the life,' said Dan as he downed a pint of the local bitter. 'I think I can manage another sandwich, and another of these to go with it,' he said, pushing the beer mug across the table top.

Heads swivelled at the sound of the American burr, then swivelled back again, their owners having ascertained that all was well.

Three brimming pint glasses were soon on their way to the table, one for Jessica, one for Mandie, and one for Dan. Someone had to drive, and Alex reckoned that despite the absorbency of the sandwiches, one pint of beer would be more than adequate.

The landlord bore a striking resemblance to Eric Morecambe, even down to the twinkling eyes behind thick glasses.

'Ay. People come from far and wide to sample our roast beef, and our steaks ... they're on the menu this evening.'

Dan's tongue was hanging out but managed to find its way back into his mouth when Alex reminded him that by then, they'd be in Scotland.

'Perhaps on the way home,' Alex consoled him.

'Just look at that, hon,' Dan directed.

150

The view, admittedly, was fantastic. A sight that Alex and Jessica had already seen two or three times previously, but nonetheless it managed to take away their breath on this occasion also.

To their right the tubular colossus of the rail-bridge monopolized the panorama, its rusty-red outline stretched like a giant adjustable arm linking the banks of the Firth of Forth. To the left the setting sun turned the river into a golden highway, majestically drawing the eye toward the west.

'That's just incredible,' said Mandie, busily pointing her Pentax in every direction. 'A little like the Golden Gate, but that rail-bridge is something else.'

At that moment, as if by divine inspiration, a train rumbled onto the bridge, sunlight painting the carriage windows with burnished gold.

'Oh look, a little train!' said Mandie, clicking frantically.

Jessica delved into her mine of information and revealed that the up-keep of the bridge was a never-ending occupation. 'They paint it constantly,' she told them, 'one end to the other. When they finish they go back to the beginning and start all over again.'

'They don't?'

'They do.'

'Oh wow,' said Dan. 'A job for life.'

Discussion on the merits of this observation brought them to their next oasis, a hotel a few miles west of the M90. Standing in its own grounds, the building commanded excellent views over the low undulating terrain towards the Ochil Hills.

The foursome entered the hotel, walked through the lobby and rang the little silver bell which they found on the reception desk. No one came, so they wandered up and down deserted corridors, in and out of a deserted dining room, and eventually were drawn along another corridor towards the sound of voices. They came to a door with a plaque bearing the legend 'LOUNGE BAR'. Alex swung the door open and was immediately confronted with a sea of people, thirty or forty of them, all dressed up, all holding well-charged glasses and all in merry mood.

'Bloody hell,' said Alex, trying to steer a path towards the bar.

'It's a party!' exclaimed Dan.

'It's a convention!' exclaimed Jessica.

'It's a wedding reception,' said the man who'd just appeared at their side. 'Follow me.' He led them back through the door and along the corridor to the lobby. Stationing himself behind the reception desk he said, 'Aye, it's just as well you booked. For sure there'll be a few people the worse for wear tonight. The rooms could get scarce.' The Scottish accent was of the soft, lilting variety, reminding Alex a little of Christine. 'And will ye no be havin' a wee welcoming dram?'

Mandie and Dan were lost immediately, uncertainty scrawled across their faces. 'Uh, say what?'

'It's time for a drink. A proper drink. A malt,' Jessica explained.

The laird handed over a couple of giant old-fashioned keys attached to giant chunks of wood. 'Up the staircase, turn right, rooms sixteen and seventeen at the end of the corridor. When you're good and ready come back downstairs and I'll put four malts on that table over there in the bay window. Unless of course you'd prefer to join the party in the bar?'

'No no, the bay window's fine,' Jessica assured him.

'Dinner's at eight, and the dining room...'

'We know where that is,' said Alex, picking up his travel bag. 'Down that corridor over there.'

* * *

'I could get used to this,' said Dan, pushing his chair away from the table after a superb dinner, leaning back and clasping his hands behind his head. 'This is pretty damn fine.'

Everyone was sublimely content. Everyone was in need of rest and a good night's sleep. Everyone trooped upstairs to their rooms.

The room assigned to Jessica and Alex was above the entrance to the hotel, overlooking the tree-lined drive, and although they'd fallen asleep as soon as they'd crawled beneath the duvet, Alex was woken at two in the morning by the sound of an engine. Intrigued, he clambered out of bed and peered through the window to discover the source of the noise. It was an old bus, its motor chugging away discharging clouds of blue smoke into the frosty night air. Alex saw no sign of the driver, and supposed he'd entered the hotel to find the late-night revellers who'd still been in the bar when the foursome had finished dinner. It had seemed as though the wedding guests were set on celebrating throughout the night.

'Bollocks,' Alex said as he returned to the warmth of the duvet, pulling it up around his ears. It was no good. The thrum of the diesel pounded at the threshold of his subconscious, preventing a slow glide into oblivion.

Forty-five minutes later he was still awake and mightily pissed off. Then, bang. He heard the front door being opened and thrown wide to disgorge twenty or thirty drunken Scots.

The cacophony of 'Good nights' accompanied by hoots of laughter, the crunching of gravel and the grinding of gears was enough to ensure that Jessica also was aroused from her slumber. She crossed the room to join Alex, who'd returned to the window, and together they watched as the bus and its noisome cargo trundled away slowly down the drive. They heard the front door as it was slammed shut, the bolts rammed home. Tranquility returned and they became captivated by the sight of moonlight dancing across the frozen lawns, each blade of grass momentarily transformed into a brilliant sparkling diamond. Snuggling back under the quilt, they turned onto their sides and Alex stretched out, pressing himself against Jessica's back. He nuzzled the nape of her neck and gently nipped at her earlobes until, their bodies becoming still and inert, sleep overtook them.

What's this then?'

Dan captured the object in question on the prongs of his fork, raised it into the air and awarded it minute inspection.

'Black pudding,' Jessica informed him in a bored, disinterested voice.

'Black pudding?'

'Why must you repeat everything I say?' Jessica grumbled, staring steadfastly at her plate. 'Black pudding. It's a sausage.'

'It's like no sausage I've ever seen,' said Mandie, suspiciously eyeing the dark congealed mass vibrating at the end of Dan's fork.

'Pig's blood, crushed oats, fat...'

Dan hurriedly lowered his fork, depositing the black pudding at the edge of his plate.

'...oatmeal, salt, pepper. All good wholesome stuff,' Jessica concluded as she looked around the table, judging the effect the list of ingredients had had on the assembled multitude.

Alex looked embarrassed and opened his mouth as though to make some comment but, deciding not to break the uneasy silence, he hefted some fried egg and tomato onto a piece of fried bread and munched thoughtfully on the tasty combination.

'So. Where are we off to today?'

Dan. Good old Dan. Alex raised his eyes towards the ceiling, making silent communication with whatever force holds the universe together.

'Perth, Pitlochry and all points north until we reach Inverness,' Jessica announced, oblivious to the drama she'd unwittingly engineered.

Part Two

Centrifuge

1

The Highland Fling had come to a grinding halt in Inverness. The Scottish trip that had begun well enough had turned into an unmitigated disaster. Although at the outset it had been Jessica's idea, she'd begun to find fault with it and with just about everything else.

The hotel had been incredible, the best yet. For Jessica, however, it had amounted to nothing. The sumptuous meals, the fine wines, the splendour of the enormous bedroom with its equally enormous bathroom featuring a cast-iron bath and ancient plumbing, the swimming pool and sauna in a log cabin across the lawn; none of this had been enough to alleviate the depths of depression that had seemed to hover above Jessica's head. She'd been sulky, spending long periods alone in the room, and when finally she'd appear, she'd been withdrawn, staring quietly into space. When the others had tried to draw her into conversation she'd snapped at them, leaving them puzzled and not a little curious as to the cause of her sudden change in character.

On the penultimate day of the holiday, she'd appeared at breakfast and calmly stated that she'd had enough, laying the blame for her misery fairly and squarely in Alex's lap. She'd got up from the table, stalked out of the dining room and into reception where she'd ordered a cab to take her to the airport, and then had returned to her room to pack her bags.

Mandie had followed thinking that maybe woman to woman in the privacy of the bedroom would allow Jessica to unwind a little. But no, she'd found Jessica to be in complete control and, while she'd sat on the edge of the bed watching her pack her few clothes into her holdall, she'd listened wide-eyed as Jessica told her that she'd made up her mind; she wanted a new life, away from Alex, away from everything.

'But why?' Mandie had asked, shocked.

'No reason. Well, yes there is. It's me ... it's just me.'

And that was it. The taxi had come and taken her away.

Dan, Mandie and Alex had spent the rest of the day picking up the pieces and trying to decide on the best course of action.

On their last evening after Jessica's departure, they'd repaired to the log cabin and the heated swimming pool. Dan had thrown a handful of American coins into the deep end and they'd dived into the water to see who could gather the most coins during one visit to the bottom. Dan had been the first to surface, then Alex, and finally Mandie, who'd been laughing so much she'd started to choke and had had to be helped to the side of the pool.

'Yeah,' she exclaimed as she deposited a fistful of change onto the wet tiles. 'I'm a champion.'

'You're a seal,' Dan told her. 'Long, lithe and slippery. Go on, clap your hands and bark.'

They hauled themselves out of the pool and sat on the edge, their legs dangling in the water.

'I don't know...' Alex started.

'No,' Dan said. 'Don't go there.'

'No, no. I just want to say I'm sorry for the ... oh shit, for the stupidity of it all. I just don't understand. One moment everything's fine, next, it's all fucked up.'

They looked deep into the pool as though searching their inner souls for something to say, when Mandie leaned forward and slipped into the water. She swam a couple of lengths breaststroke; clean, neat, precise, hardly disturbing the water before coming to a halt in front of Alex and Dan, sitting at the end of the pool. She knelt down, her head going under, then, straightening her legs, stood with her belly button just clear of the surface. She looked up at the two men, water cascading down her body leaving her hair matted to the shape of her head.

'Get a grip Alex,' she said, straight to his face. 'It's a bum deal. Shit happens.'

'Jesus, Mandie,' Dan responded. 'Why don't you tell it like it is?'

'We're his friends, babe,' she replied, hauling herself out of the water and onto the edge between Alex and Dan. 'If we don't say it, no one else will.'

'Say what?' Alex asked, looking from one to the other.

'Alex. We didn't like her.'

'Fucking hell,' Alex said.

'Jesus, Mandie,' Dan repeated, seemingly stuck in a groove.

'There's something about her. I picked up on it at the airport.'

'But that was days ago. You'd only just met her,' Alex protested.

'Yep.'

'What?' Alex asked.

'Excuse me?'

'What something? What was it you picked up on?'

'Her eyes,' Mandie replied. 'They were cold. There was something she was saying ... something about the picture, but her eyes were saying something else.'

'What is this Mandie?' Alex stood up and wrapped a towel around himself. 'What are you saying?'

'I don't know. It's intuition. Woman's intuition.' She looked at Dan who was staring at the ripples he'd been causing by clenching and unclenching his toes just below the water line. 'Dan, Alex, believe me. It's the way people deport themselves when speaking. The eyes, the mouth, the set of the shoulders. Body language. And her body language was alien to her verbal language.'

'Jesus Fucking Christ,' Alex retorted, almost parroting Dan's earlier summation. He folded his arms, then unfolded them. 'Two years.'

'I know.'

'Two years Mandie, and nothing, no sign...'

'There probably was, but you couldn't...'

'Why didn't *I* see this body language?'

'You were too close,' Mandie continued. 'You were like a fly stuck to paper, cocooned, no room to manoeuvre.'

'I just don't understand. How...? Fuck.'

Alex removed the towel from his waist, advanced to the edge of the pool and launched himself into the water, splashing Dan and Mandie in the process. Although the pool measured only eight metres, two lengths proved to be enough for Alex, who speared through the water in a fast crawl, not once raising his head for air. He ended up back at the feet of his friends, gasping for breath.

'Better now?' Mandie asked.

'No. But thanks for asking.'

They dried off and wrapped themselves in thick robes in order to make the quick dash back to the hotel, a short distance across the frozen ground. Their breath formed white clouds which disappeared into the still night air, and glancing upwards, they noticed the stars burning bright in the winter firmament. They

162

burst into the hotel via the back door and found themselves in a corridor which connected the kitchens to the reception area. Tiptoeing through the hall and past the reception desk, they were just about to step onto the staircase when the manageress caught up with them.

'Och, you poor wee things. Just look at you. Go now and get yourselves changed and I'll bring you a wee dram.'

Thirty minutes later the three friends had reunited in the lounge, standing in front of the fireplace, each clutching a glass of malt and reading the menu propped up on the mantelpiece.

'This is the beauty of these small private hotels,' Alex said, relishing the heat from the logs burning in the massive grate. 'There's no way you'd get such personal attention in one of the big chains.'

Mandie and Dan readily agreed.

'You know,' Alex continued, looking into the hearth, 'there's something I've been meaning to tell you. It's something that I think is pretty important and it's been weighing on my mind. Heavily. It's to do with Jessica.' He shook his head. 'Christ, everything's to do with Jessica but ... but this is more, and now she's not here I feel, hmm ... you know what it's like when someone lets you down?'

'What's on your mind, Alex?' Dan asked, concern showing in his eyes.

'It's Jessica, it's Germany. It's a secret that we've kept from you.'

'A secret?' Mandie gasped.

'Yes. A secret, and I feel so bad ... so, I don't know ... I feel like I've betrayed your friendship, your trust, you know?'

'Jesus, Alex. Must be a big secret?'

'It is. It's to do with art fraud.' Alex sank into one of the large brown leather-covered armchairs that were arranged in a semi-circle facing the fire. He was exhausted. The burden of obeying Jessica and carrying, for days, the secret about the Rembrandt had been too much. He sipped his whisky and felt the tension ooze out of him, and at the same time experienced a sense of relief, happy that at last he could divulge to his friends the important information he'd been withholding for so long.

Mandie and Dan had followed his example and had settled into the other armchairs that completed the group. They had said nothing, and still they maintained their silence, showing respect for Alex and his decision to include them into his inner circle.

'We, Jessica, Wolfgang and myself, found another painting.'

'Another Prentiss?' Dan asked, guessing wildly. 'That'll be eight, that'll be the complete set, the whole caboodle.'

'Rembrandt, Dan. We discovered a Rembrandt.'

'Rembrandt?' Dan said, stunned. 'What about Prentiss? What happened to the other Prentiss?'

'It was destined to *become* the other Prentiss,' Alex informed his friends.

'Christ, Alex, stop drinking that fire water. You're talking in riddles.'

'Alex, start from the beginning,' Mandie suggested, 'I think we've got some catching up to do.'

'Yes,' Alex agreed, still staring at the flickering flames. 'You have.'

* * *

'I still don't understand why a work of art, such as the Rembrandt, should have been lying in a box next to one containing a painting by Prentiss?' Mandie asked, her confusion evident.

After dinner the three friends once again had repaired to the lounge. The meal had been sumptuous, and had had an intense yet comical edge attached to it. Mandie and Dan had been trying desperately to glean more information from Alex but, due to the proximity of other diners, Alex had been unable to assuage their appetite. He had found it amusing to watch the hunger on his friends' faces, as he'd dangled in front of them a few unconnected morsels relating to the discoveries in the wine cellar.

'This,' Alex said, 'is the pivotal point. And the only possible solution that we could come up with was, art fraud.'

'What exactly do you mean?' asked Mandie.

'Well, as I mentioned earlier, the Prentiss is in London, and is being inspected by a picture restorer, an expert who will tell us what, if anything, is buried beneath the artist's beguiling brush strokes. Destiny certainly was smiling on us when we noticed the damaged paintwork, a clue that led us, Jessica, to conjure up the idea of camouflage.'

'So, let me get this straight,' said Mandie. 'We've got six Prentiss Poses in New York, or Binghamton. We've got one Prentiss Pose in London, and we've got a "joker", the Rembrandt.'

'Yes.' Alex concurred. 'And it's the Rembrandt that was our Rosetta Stone, the link that paved the way to our belief that the Prentisses really were ... poses, fictitious – licentious paintings hastily executed to conceal real works of art, that the Nazis were smuggling out of Europe when they realized their position was untenable.'

'Hold on,' said Dan. 'This puts into doubt the whole question of Prentiss's authenticity. The name "Prentiss" might be a pseudonym dreamt up by whoever was responsible for camouflaging the original Masters.'

'No,' said Alex. 'No, that's not possible. You see, the National Gallery has documentation proving his existence and ... Christ!'

'Christ?' Dan echoed.

'I just remembered something that Symond said ... about Prentiss. Something about not learning of his existence until the nineteen-fifties.' Alex recalled the tiny reflected spot of light that had glistened on Symond's pate. 'He told us also that the paintings were Prentiss's claim to fame. Um, the "Nymph Collection", that's what he called them.'

'So what are you saying?' Dan asked.

'I don't know,' Alex answered. 'I'm not even sure what I'm thinking.'

'I do,' said Mandie, 'and Dan's right. The poses were applied as a cover up, and the name Prentiss was attached to them to maintain credence. Our mysterious artist could just as well have been called ... Reagan. Hmm ... maybe not. And...'

'But that,' Dan interjected, 'means that George has a collection of priceless paintings right under his nose...'

'While he's under the impression that he's the proud owner of a set of erotic studies by a minor artist,' Mandie concluded.

'And this,' Alex informed them, 'places us in a fine pickle. Loaded with this information, the three of us become responsible for the safety of eight works of art. Pieces which don't even exist, as far as the rest of the world is concerned.'

'Three of us?' asked Dan. 'What about Jessica? What about George?'

'Mmm,' Alex answered pensively and, after a short pause, continued, 'Jessica seems to have become a loose cannon and, as such, will require close monitoring, and George ... well, let's wait and see what mysteries lie hidden beneath the bogus painting.'

'And,' said Mandie, 'talking about Jessica and loose cannons...'

'Yes?' Alex asked.

'And talking about pivotal points...'

'Mmm, I know what you're going to say.'

'You're going to tell me that my intuition was right.'

'Yes, Mandie, your intuition was spot on.'

'See! We girls are pretty cool when it comes down to it,' Mandie said, laughing.

Alex woke up struggling.

Although he couldn't remember any detail, it had ben a strange, frightening dream. He sat up, banging his head against the upper berth and promptly lay down again. Detail! Momentarily, he'd been unable to remember where he was, and had wondered why his world was rocking from side to side.

Of course, he realized, thinking back to the previous morning, when they'd made the decision to put the car on the train and save themselves the long arduous drive back to London.

'Slowly does it,' he said to himself, gritting his teeth and swinging his legs over the edge of the bunk. 'Nice and easy, don't go banging your head again.' Feeling foolish, he poked his head up into the space between the upper bunks and took in the fact that both were empty. He looked at his watch. Half-past eight. Pulling on jeans, sweatshirt and jacket, he emerged from the cabin and set off along the corridor in search of Dan and Mandie.

He reckoned he'd walked the entire length of the train before he found the dining car but, on opening the connecting door, his senses were assailed with the aroma of coffee and bacon and, as if by magic, the fuzziness that had been loitering at the edge of his reasoning dissolved, leaving his mind bright and breezy, open to reception.

'Hey. Good morning sleepy head,' Mandie said with a sunshine smile.

'Hi.'

Alex sidled onto the seat next to Dan, his movement aided by the motion of the train as it lurched over a set of points.

'Thought we'd leave you sleeping,' Dan said.

'It was the snoring,' Mandie giggled. 'We just had to leave.'

'Sorry,' Alex said, remembering the previous evening, and the bottle of brandy that Dan had produced as the train slid out of Inverness at the start of its long southbound journey. It had been intense, the conversation swirling around the compartment in errant patterns, like a ball-bearing coursing around inside a pin-ball machine. But it had helped. By the time they'd fallen into booze-induced slumber, there was nowhere left for the dialogue to go. Alex had railed and ranted, proclaiming the depth of his love for Jessica and arguing his belief in her love for him, all the while holding onto the slender chance that her sudden character change had been nothing more than a crazy aberration.

Dan and Mandie had been patience itself. Calm, cool and collected, they'd listened, reasoned, reflected and dissected each avenue, each meandering branch of Alex's tortured soul.

The train jolted Alex out of his reverie as it traversed the network of junctions and crossings at the approach to Euston. The intercom crackled into life as the conductor intoned, 'Euston. London Euston. The train terminates here. Please remember to collect all your baggage and thank you for travelling with Network North East.'

Mandie winked at Alex. 'In your case, you should forget all your baggage, you're a free man.'

'Yes,' he agreed. 'I suppose I am. Bugger.'

Dan cuffed him on his back and sent him lurching down the corridor in the direction of the compartment.

Alex drove the car off the train and onto the streets of north London.

'So now we get to see where you live?' Dan asked as they passed Camden, heading for Hampstead and the Finchley Road.

'Guess so,' said Alex, concentrating on not being squeezed out of the race between two double-deckers. He put his foot down and charged ahead as the buses closed rank behind him.

'Close,' Dan observed. 'Just like home.'

''Cept we don't have these large red buses to contend with,' Mandie corrected.

They approached the Tally Ho Corner and Dan spotted a sign pointing to Friern Barnet. 'Must be close,' he said. 'Look, Barnet, to the right.'

'No no,' said Alex. 'That's Friern Barnet. We're going to High Barnet.'

'High Barnet?' Mandie exclaimed. 'How many Barnets are there?'

'Enough,' Alex replied, listing them. 'East Barnet, High Barnet, New Barnet, Barnet itself, Friern Barnet...'

'West Barnet?' Mandie suggested.

'Nope, but there's a Chipping Barnet,' Alex informed them. 'And a Barnet Vale.' He was about to expound further on the possibilities of a bridal veil, but realizing that his friends might not understand the connection, he lapsed into silence.

'And, here we are,' he said, easing the car into a tight space next to the kerb on a tree-lined road. 'Number seventeen.' He undid the deadlock and, inserting the yale key and twisting it to the left, swung open the dark blue front door. 'Welcome,' he said. 'Welcome to number seventeen.'

Mandie and Dan followed him inside and up the stairs to the spare room.

'This is you,' Alex told them, walking through the bedroom to make sure there were some clean towels in the en-suite. 'Make yourselves at home.'

He returned to the landing and went to the large double bedroom at the front of the house to deposit his bag. On opening the door he noticed the difference right away. The little wooden dressing table was devoid of all Jessica's stuff. Her make-up, hair spray, perfumes, even the two small photo frames were gone. Alex crossed the room, looked in the chest of drawers, pulling open each drawer before slamming them back again. Then he went to the wardrobe, pulled it open and stood there gazing at the empty hangers.

'Cunt,' he said. 'Cunt, cunt, cunt.' He turned round to see Mandie and Dan standing at the door. 'Bollocks,' he said, climbing down the scale of profanities. 'Bollocks, bollocks, bollocks.'

Mandie went to him and embraced him. 'I know,' she said and kissed him tenderly on the side of his face. 'I know.'

'C'mon,' said Alex disengaging himself. 'There's a pub round the corner. I need a pint and a breath of fresh air.'

The pub literally was just round the corner, and it was deserted.

'Three pints, Jack, and a bag of scratchings,' Alex said to the man behind the bar.

'You just missed your other half,' the landlord responded.

'*Ex*-other half,' Alex quipped.

170

'Oh. Oh! Well she said to give you this,' Jack said, proffering an envelope across the counter. 'Said you'd most likely be in here before too long.'

'Well, she wasn't wrong was she?' Alex replied. 'Thanks.'

He took the envelope and went across the room to join Dan and Mandie, who'd seated themselves at a small round table next to a glowing coal fire. 'Look,' he said, flapping the envelope to and fro under their noses. 'From Jessica.'

'Give it here,' said Mandie, reaching across the table as the landlord arrived with a tray bearing three pints and a packet of scratchings.

'Where've you been?' he asked. 'Haven't seen you for weeks.'

'Here and there,' said Alex. 'Round and about.'

'Anywhere in particular?' Jack persisted.

'No,' Alex answered.

'Oh. Well, anyway, these are on the house.'

'Thanks, Jack.'

The landlord opened his mouth then, changing his mind, closed it and drifted off back to his enclave behind the bar, where he busied himself filling little dishes with an assortment of peanuts, pretzels and crisps, and placing them along the counter.

'Nice,' said Dan, looking around him. 'Good place you've got here. You go away for a few weeks then when you come back they give you free beer.'

'Yeah, well, I'm a regular.'

'An irregular regular,' Mandie chimed in.

'Not really,' Alex replied. 'I've lived here for quite a few years and have always used this place as my office, coming here to write up my reports for the newspaper. It's so convenient, and Jack's a good lad. He's often pulled the curtains and let us stay well past closing time.'

171

'Aha. Jack the Lad!' said Dan.

'Yes,' Alex agreed. 'Hey, Jack. Have one on us,' he called across the room and, gesturing towards Mandie and Dan, added, 'These are my friends from the USA.'

'Right,' said Jack. 'Welcome to Barnet, UK.'

'Okay, okay,' said Alex.

'It's a great place,' said Dan. 'Especially when everyone gets free drinks.'

They all laughed.

'So, Alex?' Dan asked. 'How come you've got so much time on your hands? I thought reporters were run off their feet?'

'The newspaper folded,' Alex answered, smiling wryly at the metaphor. 'The *Totteridge Weekly* ran out of readership. No sales, no jobs.'

Mandie slid a finger under the flap and tore open the envelope. She removed a card and read, 'Sorry.'

'That's it?' asked Alex. 'Nothing else?'

Mandie turned the card over.

'No. It's just a post card. A reproduction of a Max Ernst painting it says here.' She screwed her face in disgust. 'Ugh. Heavy stuff. Deep green, bottle green. Don't like it.' She handed the card to Alex.

'Hmm, "Joie de Vivre",' he said, reading the legend. 'Basle, Galerie Beyeler.'

'That's where you met, isn't it?' asked Dan.

'That's *when* we met,' Alex corrected him. 'Nineteen eighty-four, in Munich.' He turned the card to read the message. 'Hmm,' he said. 'Short, sweet and to the point. Typical Jessica. Insert the blade and twist.'

'It's going to take time,' Mandie said, glancing at Dan. 'But I stand by what I said in Scotland.'

'What did you say in Scotland?' Alex asked.

'I didn't like her. She was using you.'

'Oh yes,' Alex nodded. 'Now I remember.'

'Alex. Come and visit. Whenever you like.'

'Thanks, Dan. I will,' Alex replied, looking down at his beer mug. 'I will.'

Heathrow seemed busier than usual with groups of people standing below the indicator boards, looking up trance-like, waiting for some deity to tell them which gate to flock to. Alex noticed that several flights had been delayed, including the American Airlines flight to New York.

'Don't wait around, bud,' Dan told him. 'We'll get our bag checked in, then go get something to eat.'

'I'll come with you,' said Alex as they joined the queue.

It took forever to reach the desk but eventually they were standing in front of the efficient, smartly dressed check-in woman. She smiled as she took the tickets and Dan and Mandie's passports. Dan placed their case on the conveyor belt and they watched while the woman peered at her computer screen. She handed the documents back to Dan and attached the official flight-tag onto the handle of the luggage, before sending it on its journey to the baggage handlers somewhere in the depths of the concrete jungle beneath the world's busiest airport.

Heading back through the crowds they crossed the concourse and found a self-service cafeteria. They ate baked potatoes and drank fresh orange juice, Mandie and Dan stating that they never consumed alcohol before a flight.

Alex grinned at them. 'Yeah,' he said, 'and I've got the M25 to deal with.'

After their meal, Alex went back to the counter and asked for three coffees. The assistant pointed to a dispenser and told him to help himself. Alex fed a pound coin into the slot, punched a button labelled coffee, and watched a jet of hot brown liquid squirt out of a nozzle and disappear into a grating. Just as the stream of coffee ceased to flow, a plastic cup was ejected into the space beneath the nozzle. Alex looked across at the assistant.

'Amazing,' he said to the man with the white cap on his head. 'Come and look at this.'

The assistant emerged from behind his counter, looked at the empty plastic cup and shook his head. 'Coffee's off,' he said, ambling back to safety behind the till from where he handed Alex a printed card, telling him to write to the address and claim his money back.

'Happens often then,' Alex asked, 'this sort of thing?'

'All the time,' the assistant informed him confidently.

'Right,' Alex said. He marched back to the table and shrugged. 'Seems we don't get coffee.'

'Never mind,' said Dan. 'We'd have been peeing all the way to America.'

Mandie and Dan stood up and the three traipsed back towards the departure area. Mandie embraced Alex and told him to look after himself. 'Remember,' she said, 'we're only a phone call away.'

Dan gave him a bear hug, said, 'Any time, old buddy, come on over.'

Alex waited, watching his friends clutching tickets and passports head toward the barrier, and as they turned before disappearing into the duty-free zone, he raised his hand and waved.

Dodging through the crowds on his way to the car park, Alex felt his eyes beginning to smart. He located the car and made a quick search of the interior to make sure that Dan and Mandie hadn't left anything behind. He opened the boot and felt around in the dimly lit enclosure. His hand encountered something at the back of the boot and he drew the object forward, out of the gloom and into the daylight. A boot. A walking boot. One of Jessica's. He recalled the moment only a few short days ago when he'd put their walking boots into the car, prior to their trip to Scotland. A few short days ago when life had been good, when he'd been happy and deeply, madly in love. A few short days ago when there had been a future. He slammed down the lid of the boot and got into the car. He gripped the steering wheel in both hands and tried unsuccessfully to fight back the tears.

Alex was alone.

2

Simultaneously, as the alarm clock began to announce dawn, Alex's hand found the cut-off button. An automatic reaction honed to perfection during twelve years or more of rising and shining at the same time each and every day.

One leg followed the other over the side of the bed and he shuffled his way to the bathroom where, propping himself up with one arm held straight out against the wall in front of him, he emptied his bladder. As his eyes slowly adjusted to the bright light of the bathroom, they focused on the jet of yellow liquid as it left his body.

Satisfied that he'd managed to pee into the bowl instead of over his feet, as had happened once or twice before when he'd come round after a heavy night of drinking, he shook himself dry. One or two globules of liquid detached themselves from the sharp end of his dick and he watched them fly through space, seemingly in slow motion, to land on his legs, just above his knees.

'Bugger,' he said. 'So near and yet so far.'

He stomped into the bath tub and turned on the shower. 'Shit!' he exclaimed. The water was freezing and he danced about from one foot to the other, waiting for the hot water to make its way along the ancient system of pipes, from the immersion tank in the spare bedroom cupboard to the bathroom. 'C'mon, c'mon, c'mon,' he invoked the showerhead. 'Hurry Up!'

As soon as the temperature was bearable he directed the flow onto his legs and rinsed off the offending liquid. He turned off the shower, stood in the bath drying himself and noticed that his mouth felt as though it had been stuffed full of cotton wool. He took a slug of mouthwash, sloshed it back and forth between his teeth and spat into the basin. Looking into the mirror mounted on the front of the medicine cabinet, he pulled at the skin below his eyes. He wasn't pleased at what he saw: red lines criss-crossing in every direction, and he was certain that the dark bags under each eye had grown substantially larger in the space of only a few hours. Switching off the bathroom light, he returned to the bedroom and collapsed in a heap on top of the rumpled duvet. That's when he noticed that the wind which had been howling around the windows all night, had intensified to become what sounded like a hurricane. He thought vaguely that he should go outside and do something, like check the tiles or take the laundry off the line, but he couldn't remember whether there were any clothes out there in any case. He rolled to one side and pulled the duvet over him, plumped the pillow under his head and thought no more.

Three hours later he opened his eyes and registered the fact that daylight was creeping round the edges of the curtains. Propping up his head against the sloping bed head, he practised a few callisthenics, opening his mouth as wide as it would go and shutting it again. He rolled his eyes around their sockets and twisted his head from side to side. 'Excellent,' he announced to himself. 'It all works. I'm alive.'

And that's when it dawned on him.

Christmas.

The immovable feast when everyone has to pretend to be

happy, pat small children on the head, over-indulge in just about everything, visit some freezing church to listen to carols, and sit in front of the television listening to the Queen.

Load of old bollocks, Alex thought as he sat on the bed staring out of the window. Rain, together with the wind, had removed the few remaining leaves from the trees lining the street. Lime trees which, uniquely, still retained their lower limbs. All the nearby streets also lucky enough to be adorned with these trees, had seen the council out in force, lopping off the extraneous branches.

Alex thought he felt sorry for the leaves; they'd been there all summer, brilliant green and shimmery whenever the sun had managed to appear and enhance their natural radiant luminescence. Now, several colour changes later, they'd all gone, despite having held on for so long with the tenacity of a kitten clinging to one's back, when it decides it can't, or won't, climb any further.

'Christmas, huh?' Alex said to himself as he pulled on his jeans and headed towards the kitchen. He half-filled the kettle and left it to boil while he returned upstairs to shave.

Seven weeks had passed, during which Alex had plumbed the depths and scaled the heights. Hades and Heaven. Funny how they both begin with 'H', he mused, scraping the shaving foam to and fro across his face, but then he paused, recalling Harwich and the Hook. He chided himself for thinking back to those days of Arcady, days when he'd imagined himself to be living life to the full with the woman of his dreams.

'She screwed me,' he said, pursuing his chain of thoughts. 'Royally, regally, mentally, physically. Totally fucking screwed me.' It had been a close shave, closer than the work of art he'd just completed with his Bic razor.

'But that's what friends are for in times of trouble, Mother

Mary said to me,' he sang to himself. Words of wisdom from another age. 'Bollocks.' Another word of wisdom and one of Alex's favourites, directed not so much at the nick just beginning to make its presence felt on the side of his neck, as at the complete and utter insanity of the Jessica débâcle. 'Stupid fucking cow.'

Back in the kitchen, Alex again switched on the kettle, and poured the re-boiled water over a heap of coffee granules which he'd shaken straight from the jar into the coffee cup. He reached into the cupboard over the fridge and selected the bright yellow Weetabix box. He put two of the chunky biscuits into a bowl and then added a third, placing it on its side, wedged upright between the others. Familiar with the way the tightly compressed flakes soak up liquid, he poured a generous amount of semi-skimmed milk into the bowl, enough to cover the horizontal cereal bars. He transported the bowl of cereal and the cup of coffee into the dining room and placed them on the table, then returned to the kitchen to collect a jar of molasses sugar. Clutching the jar in his left hand, Alex walked through the dining room into the hall, and picked up the newspaper from the carpet before retracing his steps to sit at the dining table. He opened the jar and used his dessert spoon to break up the dark brown sugar, some of which had stuck together in solid lumps. He sprinkled a spoonful of the unrefined sugar over the cereal, propped the newspaper against the jar, and began to ferry bite-sized chunks of Weetabix into his mouth.

'Much better than Christmas pudding,' Alex declared, his fingers tracing downwards across the smoothness of the girl's shaven abdomen. She laughed and he felt her body trembling. At least

179

she seems to be enjoying it, he thought to himself, before realizing that he'd paid her to enjoy it.

Mind you, he mused, moving the tip of his tongue to lap at the smooth miniature plateau situated just above the hood of the philosopher's altar, we pay for it all the time, one way or another.

Smiling at this latest revelation, he lowered his head and allowed his tongue to graze lightly along the crinkled edges of the cleft so starkly outlined against the hairless skin. The body, under his ministrations, stretched sensuously, the legs sliding a little further apart as though inviting closer attention. Alex looked up to see the girl peering down between her legs, eyes wide with amazement that a client should be ... should be so easy to deal with, he supposed to himself.

Fuck it, he thought, at least this was some form of exchanging Christmas presents.

He got up off the floor and stood, watching with mild amusement as the girl popped a condom into her mouth and proceeded, with oral dexterity, to unroll it down the length of his rampant dick. Kneeling on the edge of the bed she began to fellate him, occasionally glancing up to ascertain his readiness to come. Alex noticed that she had huge round eyes with dark brown pupils and was just about to start wondering where she came from when...

He clasped her head between his hands and forced her away from him. Quickly the girl rolled onto her back, took him in hand and guided his cock into her. He lay on top feeling her tiny breasts flatten under his chest as he thrust away. It was all over in a matter of seconds.

'Shit,' he said.

'Don't worry love,' the girl reassured him. 'Been long, has it?'

'Long enough,' Alex grunted in reply as the girl removed the package from his limp member and then handed him a couple of tissues. He looked around the room and noticed how large the bed was, or at least how large it seemed to be. There was hardly enough room to walk around it, so maybe it was the room that was quite small. Either way, there he was, clutching a couple of tissues round his prick while the girl was slipping back into her thong, jeans and T-shirt. She moved towards the door and opened what appeared to be a wardrobe but was in fact a closet with a bidet.

'There you are, love, you can wash yourself in there if you like.'

The smile was vacant, the eyes too. The warmth and the interest had gone, replaced by a professional detachment. 'Let yourself out when you're done.'

Alex approached the bidet and sprayed water at himself. Fuck, he thought, do I give her a tip or what?

It was all new. Never before had he found himself in this predicament and he wondered what the fuck he was doing. Was it Jessica's fault, he asked himself? Was it some sordid reaction to the vagaries of the failed relationship? Was it the manifestation of repressed, suppressed anger, some way to avenge the impenetrable depths of the female psyche, or maybe some complex method for berating oneself? Then again, he wondered, could it be just a simple matter of sexual frustration?

Alex looked down and saw himself sitting on the bidet, his bits dangling in the warm soapy water. Oh well, he thought, one of life's philosophies was that one should experience everything at least once. Good enough, he decided. He'd paid his money, the girl had been attractive, had had a stunning body and the sex, for him in any case, had been adequate and, a definite plus, there was no down side; no argumentation, no negativity. Still, Alex was a romantic and he'd rather be in love. But then again, as he told himself, 'If you can't be with the one you love, honey, love the one you're with.'

Strangely, despite a lurking suspicion that he'd crossed some sort of boundary and therefore transgressed some moral divide, Alex felt no guilt. He thought the whole experience had been akin to an experiment in social behaviour. 'The fuck it was,' he said to himself, threading his arms into his shirt sleeves.

He smiled ruefully as he descended the stairs, grinned shyly at the Madam as she handed him a business card, and exited into the bright winter sunshine. He turned up the collar round his neck and, walking furtively away down the street, he looked at the card still in his hand. He read the legend and had to laugh: 'Carpet Cleaning Service' and a telephone number, there was even a picture of an oriental rug. Well, he thought, that's one way of putting it. He slipped the card into his pocket and turned the corner.

And came face to face with Jessica.

He stopped in his tracks, raised his arms then let them fall to his side.

'Alex!' Jessica exclaimed.

He shoved his hands into his pockets, his right hand coming into contact with the business card. He shuffled it over and over in his palm, eventually sliding one edge under four fingernails.

'Hi,' he said. He looked at the pavement then looked up at the buildings, tall ones crowding the narrow street. He felt trapped. He *was* trapped.

Jessica was looking at him, her trench coat billowing in the chill winter breeze.

182

'Well?' he asked. He didn't know what to say. He was transfixed, speechless. He felt instant guilt as his mind flipped backwards, replaying the vista of the sordid overheated room and the angular spread-eagled limbs of the naked young prostitute. Then the guilt disappeared, to be replaced by anger. The fault was hers, Jessica's. She'd left him.

'What?' he changed the question.

'What do you mean, "What"?' she parried.

Alex took a deep breath, filling his lungs with freezing air, then slowly blowing it out between pursed lips. 'I don't know Jessica. I just don't know anymore ... 'bout anything.'

Their eyes locked and she imparted one of her looks, a look laced with hatred and contempt. Alex stared back and more images tumbled through his tortured mind. He saw himself in his car driving back from the airport after saying goodbye to Mandie and Dan. He felt the tears as they'd tracked down his face, he experienced the loneliness, the abandonment, the sheer uselessness. He remembered the pain, the incredulity, the embarrassment when Jessica quite literally had flown out of his life. He recalled also the moments of unparalleled happiness, moments of love, tenderness and togetherness. He saw the two of them standing at a window, gazing down over tall dark pine trees at the moonlit lake huddled deep in the Bavarian valley; he saw the sparkling diamonds hanging on frozen blades of grass in the tranquil setting of the Scottish lowlands.

And he understood nothing.

Then, for some reason unknown, he recalled the time he'd spoken to his toes, telling them that women were funny things. Just about sums it up, he thought to himself, shaking his head. The ultimate excuse. 'The ultimate fuck up,' he said softly.

'Alex, I ... I have to go. I have to see a friend. I have to visit someone. He's ill you see, this friend, and...'

'Jessica,' Alex stopped her. 'What the fuck are you talking about?' He looked her up and down, saw the fragile beauty, the fairy princess who had entered his world via a coal mine. He saw himself teetering on the edge of the chasm that had placed itself between them. The depths beckoned.

She looked wild, the wind had played havoc with her hair and her eyes began to flicker hurriedly from side to side, as though striving to find something upon which to focus, something that wouldn't, couldn't torment her anymore than whatever demon was preying on her soul at that instant.

'I'm sorry Alex. I can't, I just can't say. I ... I love you. I'll call.'

Alex took his hands out of his pockets, raised them towards her. 'Jessica,' he said. 'I don't understand. Any of it.'

Jessica thrust her hands deep into her coat pockets, a mirror image of Alex's former stance, and before his hands could reach her, she'd turned and walked away. He watched as she overtook an elderly couple and then he began to follow, but soon decided that it would only aggravate whatever it was that she'd found so aggravating. 'Let it rest,' he told himself. He shoved his hands back into his pockets and turned to make his way towards the tube. 'No, fuck it. I'm always letting it rest,' Alex said, coming to a sudden halt. He turned round and chased after Jessica's disappearing figure. He caught up with her, grabbed her arm and spun her around to face him.

'How long have we been together?'

'What?'

'How long have we been together?' he repeated, slower this time.

'Three years, give or take.'

'On average, good or bad?'

The pause was minimal. 'Good, I suppose.'

'You suppose?'

'Yeah. Okay, good.'

'So?'

'So?'

'So what's going on? I mean ... shit, Jessica, what the fuck's going on?'

'Nothing.'

'Nothing? Nothing's going on? I give up.'

'I put you on a pedestal...'

'What?' It was Alex's turn to be confused.

'... and didn't want you to fall off.'

'Jessica, in English.'

'I don't want you to fall off your pedestal. I don't want you to fall in love with anyone else.'

'But...'

'You know, I couldn't live with myself if you met someone else.'

'Bloody hell Jessica, where the hell am I going to find anyone like you? You know, if I was looking? Which I'm not.'

'They're everywhere.'

'Who?'

'Women.'

'Jesus, Jessica, I never noticed.'

'That's another thing.'

'What is?'

'You're so flippant, you never take anything seriously.'

'I take the important things seriously.'

'The important things?'

'Yes. You, me, paying the bills ... Scotland.'

'Scotland?'

'It's ours, remember?'

Jessica reached up and touched Alex's left cheek. 'I need some space, I need some time.'

'Have you become Stephen Hawking?'

'Be serious!'

'I'll be serious when you stop talking in riddles. I'll be serious when you tell me what it is you want, or what it is you think you want. What the hell's making you act like this?'

'Like what?'

'Like this, Jessica, like you are now. Christ, you always had both feet on the ground, you were assertive, you were Jessica, remember? Jessica, not Jess or Jessie. You were the woman who could deal with everything.'

Jessica looked past Alex, looked instead at the shop window behind him and saw her reflection staring back. 'I'm so ugly,' she said.

'Jessica, you're the most beautiful woman to walk the face of this planet.'

Jessica smiled. 'Yeah,' she said. 'I know.'

Alex put his arms around her and pulled her close. 'That's better,' he told her. 'A smile is all you need.'

'But what happens if I stop being perfect?'

'You mean like now?'

'I'm so mixed up, I just don't know which way to turn.'

Alex looked into her eyes, kissed her mouth.

'How long have you felt like this?' he asked.

'Have you turned into a psychologist?'

'Touché,' Alex grinned. 'But, one per household is ample sufficiency.' He began to feel a little happier with the situation, thinking that maybe his decision to confront instead of letting go had been the right one to make. 'So, do you want a coffee or something?'

186

'No. Alex, I have to go.'

'Yeah, I know, to see a friend.'

'Yes, well he's ill.'

'He?'

'Yes. No. Yes. It's not what you think, it's...'

'What *do* I think?'

Jessica became flustered, once more her eyes flickered from side to side.

'Come on, what do I think?'

'Alex, it's no good. I have to go. I don't know what you think, but whatever it is ... I love you.'

Alex let out his breath, slowly, one long exhalation. He felt his body slump as he realized he was back to square one, the exact same position he'd been in before he'd decided to catch up with Jessica and have it out with her. Snakes and ladders. The higher you climb, the further you fall.

He groped for Jessica's hands, found them and lifted them up to his mouth. He opened them and kissed each one, left and right, in the centre of the palm, then let them go and watched as they dropped to her side. Alex shook his head, turned and walked away. He didn't look back.

He rounded the corner into Neal Street and almost collided with a bunch of evil-looking bastards who seemed intent on mugging him. He wasn't in the mood to be mugged and let out a barrage of choice profanities. The volley of words turned the would-be attackers into a pack of bug-eyed puppets, seemingly totally overawed and completely perplexed at Alex's knowledge of 'street talk'. They looked at one another uncertainly and shuffled about in their enormous boots as they tried to come to terms with this bolt out of the blue. Then, with one accord, they about turned and slouched off in different directions, pretending that nothing had happened; no loss of face, the hardest form of degradation for a low-life to have to undergo.

The stairs at Covent Garden are endless, a descent into the bowels of the earth. Still, better cork-screwing down the countless steps than waiting for the lift, especially when in the sort of mood in which Alex found himself.

On reaching the platform he discovered a minstrel singing plaintively, 'Where do you go to my lovely?', not to anyone in particular, but to everyone in general, although the station was uncharacteristically deserted. The tiled walls made an excellent soundboard for the singer's voice, and the melody bounced off them before evaporating into the dark tunnels.

'Fucking marvellous,' Alex said, as he wondered why it was that the itinerant had elected to air that particular song. 'I suppose it's pretty easy for you, you know, three chords?' he asked the musician. 'Repeat, repeat, repeat. It's all repetition.'

'Seven actually,' the busker informed him. 'But you're right about the repetition.'

'Bollocks,' Alex said, as a train lumbered into the station drowning all chance of further conversation. He fumbled in his pockets and found a fifty-pence coin which he dragged out and dropped into the open guitar-case. Lugubriously he watched the coin spin on one of its edges, and before fate determined whether it was to be heads or tails, he fished out the calling card and flicked it through the air, sending it on its way spiralling into the gap between the carriages and the platform as the tube train shuddered to a halt.

3

The struggle had been titanic, Alex found himself thinking, as he humped the last of the cardboard boxes onto the top of the pile which already was teetering precariously. 'Cardboard boxes,' he muttered, leering at the floorboards. 'My life in cardboard boxes,' he declared to the woodlouse, which he'd noticed as it made an unhurried inspection of the secret world in the gap between the floorboards and the skirting board.

He walked into the bathroom, pulled a sheet of loo paper from the roll, back-tracked to the bedroom, picked up the beetle, transported it back to the bathroom and magnanimously flushed it, shrouded in tissue paper, down and around the U-bend. Having dispatched the errant creature on its underground journey to the sea, Alex returned to the bedroom and, with a bottle of beer in hand, sat on the floor and leant back against the towering cardboard boxes, as he took a breather to recover from the exertion of moving all the cartons up the stairs.

It was February, and the comings and goings had been prolific. Well, they'd come and they'd gone.

Jessica had moved out, immediately, on her sudden return from the Scottish holiday at the beginning of November. Shortly afterwards Mandie and Dan had returned to the States, and Alex had gone round in circles muttering 'bollocks' and 'cunt'. It hadn't helped. Not much had, not even his visit to the young lady in central London. And as for bumping into Jessica, well, that just about took the biscuit.

'It's doin' me 'ead in,' he would tell himself, frequently, although he wasn't too sure why he used a cockney accent. Maybe, he thought, it was the only accent to use when stating such an emotion. One out, two away, and a lunatic, he thought, grinning as he did so.

Game, set and match.

When Jessica moved out before Christmas, she left the house devoid of Jessica's belongings, not only her make-up and clothes, but everything; Jessica's books, Jessica's CDs, Jessica's sheets of music, pots and pans, ornaments, paintbrushes, the lot, all gone. After Dan and Mandie had returned to the States, Alex had wafted around the rooms looking for a trace, a suggestion, a mere hint of Jessica's presence. There was none to be found save a white cushion on the armchair and, hanging above the bed, the photograph he'd taken of her during a blissfully happy sunny Sunday at Belvoir Castle. That had been it. No warning, no discussion, just betrayal. The ensuing weeks had found Alex at the lowest ebb of his life.

The inner torment had led almost to total destruction. He'd given everything to Jessica. His love, his trust, his entire life had been devoted to her happiness. He'd been one hundred per cent in love with her and, so he'd believed, she with him. They'd even joked about it, 'one hundred and one per cent' Jessica had told him, on more than one occasion. Now it was all gone, Alex's dream shattered into a million tiny pieces. His friends had rallied round, had been magnificent, and somehow had managed to prevent his sliding down into that huge black bottomless pit.

Mandie and Dan had been pillars of strength, calling once a week from their Manhattan apartment, asking questions, laughing, joking, and gently cajoling him into some semblance of recovery.

He had been lucky also in another direction. Having decided to put the past behind him, to move and find a new life, he'd spoken with the landlord and had managed to get him to agree to terminate the rental at the end of January. Meanwhile he'd searched for another property, slightly smaller but still north of the river. Again, fortune had smiled upon him. He'd found a house in nearby Southgate and, on the first of February, he'd moved in.

Yes, the struggle certainly had been titanic but, unlike the stricken liner, Alex had managed to kick his way back to the uncertain surface.

He levered himself up and away from the boxes, went downstairs into the kitchen and made himself a coffee. Instant, black, no sugar. He hadn't unpacked the cafetière and had no idea where it was and, in any case, he was definitely out of 'proper' coffee. So, when in Rome...

He pulled the phone off its hook on the wall and dialled New York. Dan answered and yes, of course they'd like for him to visit... 'Yep, whenever.'

'But I'm thinking about this weekend?'

'Fine. Book the flight,' had been Dan's response.

So forthright. So friendly, warm-hearted and welcoming. So American. He could almost smell the home-baked cherry pie. Or was it apple?

*   *   *

Once again Alex found himself in a long metal tube, rumbling along the tarmac at breakneck speed. The wheels left the ground and the rumbling stopped only to be replaced half a minute later by a buzz, a whirr, and a clunk as the landing gear retracted and imbedded itself into the warm underbelly of the mother craft. As the jet lumbered upwards into the indigo sky, Alex peered through the perspex at the pinprick strings of light demarcating the streets of Greater London. He pressed his nose hard against the window and realised that somewhere down there, somewhere beneath the aircraft, his former life had foundered to an end. Time to move on, he told his blurred reflection.

The plane shuddered as it rode a patch of turbulence.

That's it, Alex realized. Turbulence. Pass through it and come out the other side. He smiled at the passing hostess and, ignoring Dan and Mandie's maxim about not consuming alcohol before or during a flight, he ordered a gin and tonic. 'Double, please.'

February 5th. Five months since his first visit and JFK hadn't changed. It was still bedlam. It reminded Alex of Liverpool Street Station at rush hour, streams of humanity flowing in ever-changing, never-ceasing motion. Microbes sloshing about on a specimen plate. However, there was a difference; most of *these* microbes were attached to trolleys piled high with baggage. Alex watched the dance, the circumnavigation as trolleys and humans performed their symbiotic ritual. Fuck me, he thought, someone should put this to music.

He collected his bag and, on heading away from the turntable, walked straight into the towering bulk of the attendant. Alex backed off, looked up to say sorry and felt a giant hand on the back of his neck.

'Alex!' Dan was all teeth, grinning from ear to ear. 'It's okay,' he said. 'Sol's used to it. He just has a problem getting out of the way in time.' This, with a smile in Sol's direction. 'Sol, meet my pal Alex.'

The giant looked down at Alex. 'Any friend of his is a friend of mine. Man, you British?'

'Yes.'

'Well, you couldn't be in better hands.'

'C'mon,' said Dan. 'Places to go.'

They took their leave of Sol and exited the concourse.

'Christ,' said Alex, adjusting his eyes. 'Snow!'

'What else?' asked Dan. 'It's winter. There's always snow.'

'But there's so much of it,' Alex continued, looking around in amazement.

'Not now there isn't. Should've been here last week, although maybe you shouldn't. The airport was closed, clogged right up and the city was at a standstill. Fun.'

Alex paused to take it all in. There were mounds of snow everywhere; on the sides of the pavements, on the sides of the roads, and all the cars had a deep layer of the soft white fluffy stuff on their roofs, bonnets and boots.

'It never gets this bad in London,' Alex informed Dan.

'No? Well, it does here. And worse.' Dan led the way past a couple of taxi ranks, stepped into the road and with thumb and first finger gave a loud whistle. A sleek police car drew up in front of them and Dan ushered Alex into the front seat, alongside the driver. Dan climbed in the back and grinned at the look on Alex's face. 'We have our perks,' he explained. 'Okay. Let's go.'

* * *

'How's your geography?' Dan asked.

'Geography?'

'Yep.'

'Well, I know that I've just flown across the Atlantic.'

'No, I don't mean general stuff, I mean, for instance, where are we now?'

'JFK.'

'Brilliant. Alex, you're definitely an "A" student.' Alex grinned stupidly and looked across at the driver, who was shaking his head in amusement.

'Yeah, JFK. We're on Long Island, about fifteen miles from Manhattan, suppose the same sort of distance that Heathrow is from central London. Anyway, we're off to Long Beach for something to eat, there's a neat little restaurant on a jetty where the crayfish are the best in the world.'

'He's right,' the driver nodded in agreement, 'best in the world.'

''Specially with a glass of Chardonnay,' Dan added.

Alex twisted his head back and forth as the two men continued to rave about the delicacies on offer.

'And Mandie?' he asked.

'There already,' said Dan. 'She's been doing an evening shoot on the coast. Can't understand it. Prannying about in thick snow and freezing weather. Not my idea of fun. Still, expect the money's good.'

'Christ, the models must be frozen solid,' Alex suggested.

Dan laughed. 'What models? She's out there shooting lumps of driftwood for some arty-farty advertising agency.'

'Christ.'

'You know, all that moody crap. A poncey piece of drift-wood propped up on the beach with a dramatic background.'

Alex looked out of the window and noticed that it had started

194

to snow; big white flakes briefly illuminated as they drifted past the street lamps, reappearing as they fell through the beams of the headlights.

Mandie was sitting at the bar waiting for them, a glass of white wine at her elbow which was resting elegantly on the bar top. Alex noticed that she was dressed for the occasion; fur lined boots, tight jeans, a thick charcoal-coloured sweater and a navy blue parka, unzipped and open. Gorgeous as ever.

'Alex!' She got off the stool, embraced him and kissed him full on the mouth.

'Great to see you,' Alex said, fumbling with his coat.

'Hi Bry,' Mandie called to the driver, as she put an arm round Dan's waist and led him towards a table next to a huge plate-glass window.

Alex put his hand against the glass and looked out at the winter night. The snow was falling faster, spinning through the pools of light cast by the large old-fashioned metal lamps that were spaced along the jetty. He could just make out the dark roiling water that shifted uneasily beneath the timber walkways, the restless oily surface reflecting some of the yellow light that managed to penetrate the gaps beneath the ancient boards. He shivered and focused his vision on the interior; wood. Wooden walls, wooden floors, and high wooden gables with wooden beams and rafters, wooden tables, wooden chairs, and wooden toothpicks. And, covering the floor, a light sprinkling of sawdust.

Mandie had thought to order the food and although, as yet, the crayfish had not made their appearance, the table was well stocked with two bowls of green salad, a basket of obliquely sliced French bread, and a bowl of steaming new potatoes glistening under a drizzle of melted butter, topped with finely chopped garlic and basil.

Dan took the bottle of wine from the ice bucket and poured generous measures. 'Alex,' he said. They all clinked their glasses together as the crayfish were brought to the table.

'Cheers,' said Alex, slightly abashed at the camaraderie. 'And, er, thanks for the welcome.'

'Jeez,' said Bry. 'That's got that over with. Let's get into it.'

They unfurled their napkins, loaded their plates with food, and for a couple of minutes silence reigned supreme.

'So you're a Brit? Dan's told me some stuff about you.'

'He has?'

'Yeah. Like you come from London.'

'Right.'

'That's it ... pretty much.' Bry seemed to have finished.

'Well,' said Alex, 'glad to...'

'So what brings you over here?' Bry asked, suddenly returning to his interrogation.

'We do,' answered Dan. 'We thought he needed a break. It's a stressful life you know, living in London. All that rain, all that low-lying cloud, not to mention the drizzle.'

'Yes,' Alex agreed. 'Not to mention the drizzle. And the high cost of petrol and the strikes, and litter all over the place.'

Mandie cracked open a crayfish claw. 'Actually, we're just returning the favour. We were looked after like royalty on our visit to the UK.' She raised her glass. 'Thanks, Alex.'

Alex looked back at Mandie, looked down at the glass in his hand, then raised it. 'Here's to good friends.'

The plates were cleared away along with the empty bowls, only to be replaced by dessert, with coffee and cheese bringing the meal to a close as Mandie, Dan, Alex and Bry enjoyed the easy company and shared stories and recollections.

On leaving the restaurant, Mandie steered Dan and Alex to

her car and they said their goodbyes to Bry, who went to his police car parked behind Mandie's four-by-four. They spent some time clearing the snow from the windscreen then, with Mandie at the wheel, slowly made their way to Manhattan. Alex went to sleep in the back and missed the journey through Queens, over the Brooklyn Bridge and down Pearl Street towards Dan and Mandie's home.

Alex pulled the cord and opened the blinds. Sunlight streamed through the spaces between the slats, sketching a zebra-crossing over the tousled bed. New York glistened. Nothing moved. The cars, which overnight had been parked along the street, had been transformed into dolmens; softly curved mounds exemplifying the power of the motor industry, petrified and silenced under a blanket of whiteness.

Alex found the cord that raised the blinds and brought them halfway up the window. He released the catch, opened the window and …. shut it. Immediately.

'Fuck. Fuck. Fuckity fuck,' he said, launching himself back onto the bed to disappear beneath the duvet. A couple of minutes later, he poked his head out from under and lay propped up on the pillow, blinking in the dazzling sunlight.

He'd forgotten that New York could be so cold but, as he thought about it, he remembered how every year he'd read in the papers about the 'big freeze', and recalled the grainy black-and-white press photos depicting scenes of winter chaos on the streets of New York and Washington. He seemed even to remember a picture of snowbound JFK, and was glad to be safe and snug and warm on the left-hand side of the Atlantic, rather than being pissed off, tired, dejected and stranded at Heathrow, watching harassed airline staff run round in circles trying to placate irate customers.

A knock on the door heralded the arrival of Mandie with a mug of coffee and a big bright breezy smile.

'We're off. Dan to the station house and me to the agency.'

'You're not going out there? You can't.' Alex pulled the duvet higher around his shoulders as though to emphasize the impossibility of venturing onto the frozen streets of Manhattan.

'Yeah, we're invincible.'

'Mmm, and a little crazy.'

'You get used to it. After a while.'

'S'pose so,' said Alex. 'In London we get used to rain.'

'Same deal,' Mandie agreed. 'So, anyway, take it easy. Get up when you want, raid the kitchen, and ... here's a key if you want out. But remember, it is cold.'

'You're not kidding. I opened the window and closed it again in the space of a...'

'Nanosecond?' Mandie suggested.

'Less.'

'Okay. We'll see you around one-thirty, two o'clock.' She kissed him on the lips, then was gone.

'Blimey,' Alex said to the empty room.

Mandie and Dan appeared at two-thirty and found Alex seated at the kitchen table, nursing a coffee and a slice of buttered toast.

'Hey, how ya doin'?'

'Good. I'm good thanks Dan. How's life on the streets?'

'Full of assholes, no change there.'

'Oh,' Alex responded, trying to picture an asshole on the street.

For a full minute all three looked at the table top, lost in their thoughts, until Mandie lifted the pot of coffee, collected a couple of mugs, and poured for Dan and herself.

'Refill?' She looked at Alex.

'Refill? Oh, yeah,' said Alex. 'Refill. Thanks.'

'Where were you?' asked Mandie.

'Where was I?'

'You were miles away. Different planet,' she told him.

Alex shook his head slowly from side to side. 'Yeah, that'll be about right.'

'Listen,' said Dan. 'There's not much point in going anywhere this afternoon, it's colder out there than a frog's hole, so let's settle down and catch up on how you're doing with the Prentiss stuff.'

Alex chuckled. 'The Prentiss project.'

'It's been what, three, four months since you discovered those pictures in Bavaria?'

Alex looked at Mandie, nodded. 'Yep, thereabouts.'

'And?' Mandie asked.

'Nothing.'

'Nothing?' Mandie exclaimed.

'Nothing, nix, zilch, nada,' Alex confirmed. 'And, to be honest, I've sort of lost interest, what with...'

'Lost interest?' Dan interjected. 'Lost interest? You can't.'

'I know I can't, but I have.'

'Alex. You can't,' Mandie said, agreeing with Dan. 'Just 'cos that stupid woman decided to fuck off?' Mandie was all heart.

'Yeah, and stop calling me a can't.'

'A can't?' Mandie gazed at Alex uncertainly, then shrieked as she realized what he was saying.

'So we still don't know what's under the other Prentiss Pose?'

Dan asked, sticking to the serious business upon which Alex seemed to have given up.

'No, Dan,' Alex answered. 'We don't.'

'Well, me and Mandie, we, uh, we...' Dan hesitated.

'Got an idea,' Mandie finished for him.

'Yeah. Works like this,' Dan continued. 'You should pay a visit to Binghamton, have a chat with the man. You know, see how the land lies.'

'And maybe ask for some more resources,' Alex suggested.

'Resources?' Mandie asked.

'Mighty mighty dollars to pay for the return trip to Germany I'm going to have to make.'

'When?' Mandie asked.

'Soon,' Alex replied.

'Excellent,' Dan observed, removing his coat and handing it to Mandie. 'Now we're getting someplace and it seems like Alex is back on the rails. I'll talk to the boss tomorrow, see if he can spare me a day next week. Shouldn't be a problem.'

'Sounds like you've got a good boss,' Alex said.

'We're gonna have a family day out?' Mandie asked.

'We're gonna have a family day out,' Dan confirmed.

'Sounds like we got ourselves a plan,' Alex stated.

Dan, whose thought processes normally resided two steps ahead of everyone else's, was mooting the idea of putting snow-chains on Mandie's car, even though it was a four-wheel drive.

'Good idea, honey,' she agreed, 'but they've been on for a few days already.'

'They have?' he asked, looking up from his plate of toasted bagels.

'They have,' Mandie confirmed. 'Thought you were a detective?'

'Yeah, huh?' Dan replied, grinning at Alex.

They drove north out of the city along the east side of the Hudson, crossed over Washington, and motored along the west side of the river before heading north-west towards the Catskill Mountains, the Susquehanna, and Binghamton.

The journey took just over two and a half hours, longer than usual as they'd encountered one or two fairly deep drifts.

'See, honey?' Mandie said, as they felt the heavy-duty chains bite into the compacted snow. 'It was a good idea.'

'Mmm,' Dan replied.

'Seems everybody's got snow-chains,' Alex observed, gazing through the windscreen.

'Yeah,' said Mandie. 'The world got wise.'

'You never know what to expect,' Dan added. 'It can be pretty gruesome upstate, what with strong winds and stuff. For that matter, it can be pretty gruesome in the city.'

'It looked pretty gruesome a couple of days ago when I looked out the bedroom window,' Alex informed them. 'Everything was white. Everything had disappeared.'

'Happens every year,' Dan said. 'You get used to it.'

'Yeah,' Alex agreed. 'That's what Mandie told me.'

'C'mon, coffee,' Dan announced as Mandie pulled up at a respectable looking coffee shop. 'They do the best blueberry muffins north of the Apple.'

'But what about lunch?' Alex asked.

'That's next,' Dan answered as he opened the car door and crunched across the snow.

Alex looked at Mandie who was wearing a large smile. 'He likes to enjoy himself when he's not being a detective,' she explained.

*   *   *

Michelstraub was as effusive as ever.

'Mandie. Alex. A pleasure. And this'll be...?'

'Dan,' Mandie told him.

'Ah yes, Dan,' Michelstraub echoed.

'Dan. My other half,' Mandie explained.

'Ah yes, Dan. Of course.' Michelstraub appeared a little flustered. 'I'm a little flustered, you'll have to excuse me,' he said as he ushered them into his office. 'Sit down, sit down,' he invited, gathering together sheaves of paper which lay strewn across his desk. 'Dear me, dear me. My secretary's been off for a few days with the flu, and, and ... where's Jessica?'

'Jessica's in England,' Alex informed him.

'What? Already?' Michelstraub looked shocked.

Alex, Dan and Mandie also looked shocked.

'What do you mean, "already"?' Mandie asked, the first to regain composure.

Michelstraub had collapsed into his chair, his head in his hands. 'I don't understand,' he said, mumbling into his palms.

'You don't understand?' Alex asked him. 'What you mean, you don't understand?'

'Well, she was ... she was here.'

'How? When?'

'This morning. Jessica was here, in this office.'

'But it's still this morning,' Alex informed Michelstraub. 'Well, just about.'

'Precisely.'

'Well, how do you mean she was here this morning?' Alex asked.

202

'She was here,' said Michelstraub. 'She was here.' He looked sort of hopeless, holding out his hands as though trying to indicate the exact location of Jessica's earlier whereabouts.

'Fuck!'

Everyone looked at Alex.

'Excuse me?' said Michelstraub.

'Are you sure?' asked Alex. 'Are you certain it was Jessica?'

'Does the Pope piss in the wild woods?' Michelstraub answered with a question.

'Yeah, something like that,' Alex grinned.

'She was here, sitting in that chair,' Michelstraub reiterated, pointing at Mandie. 'Large as life.'

Alex and Dan looked at Mandie, expecting to see her transform into Jessica.

'Said you'd asked her to come over,' Michelstraub continued, 'while you were away in Germany, seeing ... someone. Can't remember the name.'

'Wolfgang?' Alex suggested.

'Absolutely. Absolutely. Wolfgang.' Michelstraub sat back in his chair looking relieved, believing the interrogation to be over.

'Alex...' Mandie started.

'I know,' Alex replied.

'Alex, the painting. You've got to call Wolfgang.'

'I know.'

'What's happened?' Michelstraub asked. He sat upright again and looked at the three faces in front of him. 'What's the problem? What painting?'

'The problem is that Alex is no longer with Jessica,' Mandie informed him, ignoring his question about the painting.

'But...'

'Therefore...'

'Therefore,' Dan interrupted, 'we've got to get in touch with her and find out what she's up to.'

'But we don't know where she is,' Alex said. 'Only that she was here this morning. Jesus Christ, what a fuck-up.'

Michelstraub started to say something, then thought that perhaps he wouldn't.

'What, what?' Alex asked him. 'If you've got something to say, say it.'

'It's just that she, Jessica...'

'Yes, yes?' Alex insisted.

'She asked me if I could release some funds for her to travel to Germany,' Michelstraub answered. 'Something about needing to meet this...'

'Wolfgang?' Alex asked.

'Yes.'

'Bollocks she did,' Alex said.

'He's English,' Mandie explained to a startled Michelstraub. 'We'd say, "balls".'

'Can I use your phone?' Alex asked Michelstraub, grinning at Mandie. Michelstraub passed the old-fashioned bakelite phone across his desk.

'Thanks,' said Alex, taking the phone in one hand while the other fished in his wallet for a list of phone numbers. All eyes were on the instrument as Alex dialled the international code followed by a number that would connect the office in upstate New York to a small hotel on a hillside in faraway Bavaria.

'So wha'ddy say?' Dan asked, exasperation written across his face.

They were back in the car, headed south on route 81 through

204

Pennsylvania to Dunmore. After his conversation with Wolfgang, Alex had handed the receiver to Michelstraub, shaken him by the hand and said, 'We're outta here. Mandie, Dan, let's go.'

'So wha'ddy say?' Dan asked again. 'And how come we left George's office so goddamn quick?'

'Said he was expecting a visit from Jessica. On Friday,' Alex answered. He compressed his lips together, tighter than those of an obstinate clam.

'Friday!' Dan exclaimed.

'Yeah, Friday. Hey, Mandie, can we stop at the next service station? I need to make another call to Wolfgang.'

'But you've just spoken to him,' Mandie pointed out.

'Yeah,' Alex agreed. 'And now I need to talk to him again.'

'Why?' Mandie and Dan asked at the same time.

'There's more I need to say,' Alex replied, nonchalantly.

'But why didn't you talk this through at Michelstraub's?' Dan asked.

'Because right now I don't know who I can trust,' Alex explained.

'Alex...'

''Cept you two.'

'Gas station coming up,' said Mandie.

'Now maybe we'll get some lunch,' Dan said as Mandie swung the car into a slot in front of a diner.

'It was only an hour ago you demolished that muffin,' Alex reminded his friend.

'That was then, this is now,' Dan responded. He swung open the door and led the threesome into the restaurant. 'Make your phone call, then come join us at the table.'

By the time Alex returned and sat down with his friends, Dan had ordered three all-day breakfasts, with everything.

'So?' Dan enquired.

'How long have you known Michelstraub?' Alex asked Mandie. Direct. Eyeball to eyeball.

'Why?' Dan asked.

'How long?' Alex persisted.

'Maybe ten, eleven years,' Mandie answered.

'Do you trust him?'

'He's a lawyer,' Mandie replied. 'He's one of Dad's partners for God's sake.'

'Do you trust him?' Alex repeated.

'Trust George?' Mandie responded. 'Sure. He talks a lot...'

'Eats a lot,' Dan added.

'... and takes the long route to get to the point. But, yeah, I trust him,' Mandie finished.

'Yeah,' Alex said, twiddling the knife that had just been placed in front of him on the table. 'Yeah, okay.'

'Alex, what is it?' Mandie asked him.

He twiddled some more and succeeded in making the knife spin round, once, twice. It stopped, pointing at Mandie. Alex picked it up and tapped the blunt handle against the table top, emphasizing each word. 'I don't fucking know,' he said. 'You think you know someone. You think you know them inside fucking out, but still...'

'We get that all the time,' Dan interrupted. 'You get to the point...'

'Where you don't know where you stand,' Alex cut in, completing the sentence.

'Where you stand, where anybody stands,' Dan agreed. 'So?'

'So that's why I decided to wait until we'd left Binghamton,' Alex explained.

'Poor old George,' Mandie laughed. 'He's okay,' she assured him, her grey-green eyes steady and sincere. 'He's fine. He's harmless.'

206

Three giant oval plates arrived, piled high with eggs, bacon, tomatoes, sausage, grits and hash browns, and pancakes on the side. 'Eat,' said Dan, picking up his cutlery. 'Eat and enjoy.'

The adrenaline rush of the past few minutes had made Alex quite hungry and he launched into attack mode, managing almost to keep pace with Dan as they set about the mountains of food.

'I told him to tell her that I had the painting,' Alex stated, waving a pronged segment of sausage through the air. 'You know, the Rembrandt.'

'Jesus, Alex,' Dan said. 'Why?'

'Obviously that's what she's after,' Alex answered.

'Yes, but you haven't got it, have you?' Dan prompted.

'No, of course not, but I had to say something. I can't just let Wolfgang hand it over to her.'

'No,' Mandie agreed. 'And what about the other picture you found, the one that's still being cleaned?'

'Huh,' Alex chuckled. 'That'll be another problem.'

'How so?' Dan asked.

'I don't know where it is,' Alex replied.

'Yes you do,' Mandie told him. 'It's with that restorer person...'

'A friend of a friend of Jessica's,' Alex cut in. 'I know, I know.'

'And?'

'And I don't have the address.'

'But Alex, you've been there, haven't you?' Dan urged.

'Yes. Somewhere near Victoria.'

'Who's Victoria?' Mandie asked suspiciously.

'The station. Victoria Station,' Alex explained.

'You don't have the number?' Dan asked. 'Any number, street or phone?'

'No,' Alex replied. 'No number.'

As if on cue, they each picked up their cups and took gulps

of hot strong coffee. Alex sat back from the table, put his hands in his pockets and his fingers touched a piece of paper. 'Ah. Wait a minute!' he exclaimed. 'Wolfgang gave me this number. Said that Jessica told him to call if he had a problem prior to her visit.'

'So give her a call Alex,' Mandie suggested.

'No. No way,' Alex replied.

'Give me that paper,' Dan said. 'I'll call her.'

'What'll you say?' Alex asked, handing the piece of paper across the table.

'Dunno. I'll think on it.' Dan look into his empty mug. 'Now then. Refill anyone?'

'God it's cold,' Alex stated when they trooped back outside.

The sun was setting on the wintery scene and everything seemed brittle, the snow crackling underfoot as they headed towards the car. Alex rubbed his hands together and breathed into them while he waited for Mandie to get the doors unlocked. Dan grinned at him over the top of the car. 'Next time we'll give you some gloves.'

'Next time I'll come prepared,' Alex replied as they climbed into the car. 'Anyway, how come we're going back a different way?'

'We were going to take you to see Lake Wallenpaupack,' Dan told him.

'Lake Wallenpaupack!' Alex exclaimed. 'And I got into trouble with Barnet!'

'Only because there were so many of them,' Dan laughed. 'Barnet this, Barnet that...'

'Okay, okay, you've made the point,' Alex acquiesced. 'So what happens at Lake Wally ... can't even remember the name?'

'Wallenpaupack,' Dan reminded him. 'Nothing. Oh, a bunch of people like to fish, and it's a popular place for sailing, but the scenery is outstanding, and there's a restaurant...'

'Might've guessed,' said Alex.

'Yeah, well, we've had our lunch and it's getting dark...'

'And it's bollock cold,' Alex added.

'And it's bollock cold,' Dan agreed, mimicking Alex's British accent. 'So we'll leave it and head on home.'

Alex stuffed his hands into his coat pockets and shivered.

'Won't be long,' Mandie told him. 'This car warms up pretty quickly.'

'Last time I was this cold was in Munich,' Alex informed his friends. 'The hotel had one of those revolving doors, and when the segment I was in came into contact with the outside air, I just kept on going round and went back indoors. The people at reception told me it was minus twenty degrees.'

'It can drop to minus fifteen, twenty, here,' said Dan, 'and if there's a wind, we do what you do. We don't go out.'

'Only to visit Binghamton,' Alex observed.

They reached the exit for route 380, which would lead them south east towards New Jersey and back to New York.

'What about Germany?' Dan asked. 'When do you need to head over there?'

'Soon as possible,' Alex answered. 'But I'll let Jessica do her thing and maybe fly to Munich at the end of next week.'

'She's going to be mighty pissed off when Wolfgang tells her that you've got the painting,' Dan observed.

'Yes. She is,' Alex agreed. They both giggled helplessly while Mandie drove on into the gathering night.

* * *

'Where's Dan?'

'He's on the phone, Alex,' Mandie told him. 'He'll be through in a minute.'

She poured a glass of red wine and held it out to him. 'Here, get this down you. I'm making some soup. Thought it'd be nice and warming. Also we've got some bread and cheese. Sound all right?'

'Sounds bloody marvellous,' he told her. 'Thought I smelled something cooking.'

'Seems like Jessica's got a new man,' Dan announced.

'What?' Mandie and Alex shouted simultaneously.

'Seems like Jessica's got a new man,' Dan repeated. 'Just been talking to him. You know, on the phone.'

'Who?' Mandie asked.

Alex sat down at the table, clutching a handful of cutlery.

'Said his name was Terry,' Dan told them.

'Terry?' Alex asked. 'Terry?'

'Yeah,' said Dan. 'Terry. Know him?'

'Know him?' Alex replied. 'That bugger's the picture cleaner. What a cunt. Oh, sorry Mandie. How come you spoke to *him*?'

'He's the bugger who picked up the phone,' Dan replied, becoming adept at picking up on English idioms.

'But why ring him, Dan? Of all the people to choose, why...'

'I rang the number on that bit of paper. And ... bingo! Terry answers.'

'That means...' Alex paused.

'It means nothing,' Dan said. 'It's probably just like Wolfgang told you. You know, a contact number for when she's in Germany, so she can keep...'

'Fuck off. When she's in Germany she'll *be* with Wolfgang and he's the one she gave the number *to*, and ... and, when she's there he won't need it because, well, because she'll be there, and … shit, I'm all confused.'

'It's probably just a contact number,' Dan repeated, as he too sat at the table.

'I bet it isn't,' said Alex. 'I bet she's wheedled her nose in there.'

'Wheedled?' Dan queried.

'Or wheeled,' Alex said. 'With her nose it would not be impossible.'

'That's my man,' said Dan. 'Still retains his sense of humour, even in his darkest hour.'

'Yeah, well, it's necessary,' Alex told him.

'Sure is,' Dan agreed.

Alex was restless.

Whichever way he tried lying, he found it impossible to sleep. On his side, flat on his back, one pillow, both pillows – it was useless. His mind was incapable of relaxing. It was like a cauldron, a seething mass of turmoil; questions, ideas and possibilities rising to the surface of his conscience, one after the other.

What was Jessica up to? Why had she travelled all this way to meet with Michelstraub? Had she told him about the Rembrandt? About the Prentiss Pose? Of course she'd told him, Alex thought, she must have, otherwise he wouldn't have given her the money to fly to Germany. Shit, shit, shit. But then, he remembered, Michelstraub had said very little. There had been no mention of Rembrandt, no mention even of Prentiss. And, what about Terry? Had Jessica become a part of his life? And Christine?

Jesus, Escher's pictures had nothing on this, it was too involved, and the detail, as with the intricacies of Mr Escher's cunningly constructed diagrams, revolved haphazardly in a never-ending circle through the connective tissue in the centre of Alex's head.

Part Three

Jessica

1

Half-past seven and it was still sheeting down.

Finchley Road was deserted, the gutters full of swirling water as the drains struggled to cope with the torrential rain. Traffic lights drifted through their sequence, the display witnessed by a solitary pedestrian whose trench coat and broken heel lent a touch of pathos to the sodden winter's night.

The figure shuffled towards a bus shelter and slumped onto the wooden bench. She slid the strap of the leather travel bag from her left shoulder and placed the case beside her on the seat. Bending forward she removed the broken shoe, ripped off the offending heel and, after a moment's hesitation, repeated the process with the right shoe, flexing the heel back and forth until it snapped off. She looked around her, left and right, assessing the situation, then, one after the other, she hurled the useless heels across the water-logged street.

'Fucking hell,' she announced, staring at the drifting curtains of rain. 'Poxy, pissing English weather.'

The woman unzipped the pouch at one end of the travel bag and removed a pack of Marlborough and a bright purple plastic lighter. She flipped the lid and tapped the carton against the palm of her left hand, smiling briefly as a cigarette slid half its length out of the pack. She put the filter between her lips, lit the tip and inhaled deeply. She held her breath for seven, eight, nine seconds before releasing the smoke in a dirty-white cloud, blowing it through her lips which were slightly apart, forming a shape as though making a silent whistle. With thumb and middle finger she removed the cigarette and contemplated the glowing cusp, her mind imagining a fine film of tar coating the beautiful pink interior of her lungs.

'Urggh,' she uttered, flicking the cigarette into the raging water running level with the top of the kerbstones. She watched as it was swept along for a couple of yards then, entranced, she gazed as the little white stick performed a counter-clockwise dance, trapped in an eddy swirling around the top of a storm drain.

Jessica sighed, slid her left arm through the bag's shoulder strap and, flat-footed, slouched off in the direction of Eileen's two-up, two down.

She put the key in the Yale lock, twisted towards the jamb and shoved the door open.

'Jessica?'

'Nah. Father Fucking Christmas,' Jessica answered as she dripped onto the oatmeal-coloured carpet.

'Good timing, Santa,' Eileen called from the kitchen, 'albeit a couple of months late. Come on, you're in luck. Tomato soup with a drizzle of gin and a stale French twig, sliced and floating on top.'

'Bloody hell,' said Jessica. 'What are we celebrating?'

'Another rainy day in the Big Smoke,' Eileen replied. 'Here, I've just opened a bottle. Get yourself a glass and I'll pour you some of this Spanish stuff.'

A few minutes later she placed two bowls of steaming soup onto the small round wooden table wedged into a corner of the kitchen. 'Sit down, sup up,' she instructed her friend. Jessica, still encased in her trench coat, sat and supped as directed. 'Jesus, Jess, you look like shit,' Eileen observed.

'Thanks.'

'Well, you know,' Eileen floundered.

'Yeah, you're right,' Jessica admitted. 'Look like shit, feel like shit.'

'And?'

'And I need a long, hot...'

'Penis?' Eileen suggested.

'Bath,' Jessica answered.

Both giggled as they lifted spoonfuls of hot potage into their mouths.

Ninety minutes later Jessica wandered into the living room dressed in knickers, a floppy grey sweatshirt and a pair of thick hiking socks. Eileen had Weather Report on the hi-fi and had transported the bottle of red wine through from the kitchen. She was sitting on the large cream-coloured sofa, her legs tucked under her bum. 'Feeling better are we?' she asked.

'A whole new person,' Jessica answered, lowering herself to sit lotus-fashion on the carpet. She nodded towards the CD player. 'Good choice,' she said. 'A bit of sophistication.'

Since schooldays the two had been like-minded on music. On books, films ... and, until recently, men.

'Goes well with the wine,' Eileen said.

'Which is?' Jessica asked.

'I told you. It's Spanish, Navarra. Deep in tannins, hint of plums, aftertaste of liquorice and is excellent with chocolate,' Eileen pretended to read from the label as she handed Jessica a large slab of Cadbury's Fruit and Nut.

'Mmm, heaven,' Jessica said, relishing the taste of the thick, creamy chocolate. 'Pure, unadulterated heaven.'

'And? Tell me about Wolfgang. Did you, did he...'

'Nah. He's like you.'

'He is?' Eileen asked.

'Yes.'

'How so?'

'Walks down the other side of the street,' Jessica explained.

'You mean he's gay?'

'Mmm,' Jessica mused. 'Moroccans mainly. Young ones.'

'What? Boys?'

'Yup,' Jessica confirmed. 'Boys.'

'Can't be too many of them in the middle of nowhere?' Eileen pondered.

'He finds them in Munich,' Jessica told her friend. 'Reminds me of a story that Alex told me. Apparently...'

'Allegedly,' Eileen corrected.

'Apparently,' Jessica continued, 'several years ago, he and Wolfgang were downing a couple of beers in the Englischer Garten when Wolfgang had indicated a throng of people. "See him?" he'd asked Alex. "Zat fellow over zere?" Alex had looked round and noticed a group of young lads at a nearby table. "Ze one wiz ze little moustache," Wolfgang had pointed out.'

'Your accent ist zehr gut,' Eileen chuckled, holding two fingers horizontally against her upper lip, her right arm extended in front of her. 'You vill tell me more.'

'Well, apparently, Alex had burst out laughing. "He's too young, he's too small. He can't be more than five foot!" he'd told Wolfgang. "Ach so," Wolfgang had replied, grinning at Alex. "Zis is all true. Is vunderbar, no?"' Jessica started to smile as she continued with the story. 'Alex had put his head in his hands and said, "But Wolfgang, he is very short, how do you, you know, how...?"'

218

' "Makes the little fucker stand on a chair," a voice at Alex's side had said, as Wolfgang and the newcomer had burst out laughing.'

Eileen giggled and slid off the sofa to refill Jessica's glass. 'I can just picture it,' she said. 'Slappen ze tize und bumpsen mit der lederhosen.'

'Mmm,' Jessica agreed, pensively.

'And?' Eileen prompted, noticing the shadow of annoyance flicker across Jessica's face.

'And I think Alex should go fuck himself.'

'You don't beat around the bush, do you?'

'No,' Jessica answered. 'There's no point. If you're going to say something, say it, don't fuck about.'

'So, why should Alex go fuck himself, apart from being your ex?' Eileen asked.

'Because, because... because Wolfgang no longer has the painting.'

'What? But who has? Where is it?'

'I suppose it's here in London,' Jessica replied. 'Oh, I don't know. It could be anyfuckingwhere.'

'Well, if it's here, how'd it get here?' Eileen asked.

'Alex.'

'Crafty fucker,' Eileen observed.

'Mmm.'

'But then they're all crafty fuckers,' Eileen continued.

'All who?' Jessica asked.

'Men,' Eileen answered. 'All of 'em.'

'Yes Eileen,' Jessica concurred. 'Your viewpoint on the subject is well documented.'

Eileen raised a hand and drew the tips of her fingers lightly across Jessica's lips. 'Great isn't it?' she purred, 'my viewpoint?'

Jessica smiled and reached for her glass, inadvertently causing her arm to brush against Eileen's breasts. 'Oops, sorry,' she said, looking down at the carpet.

'It's okay,' Eileen smiled.

'What...?'

Eileen raised one of her arms, placing her hand on Jessica's left shoulder. The hand squeezed gently. 'It's really okay.'

Jessica raised her glass to her mouth and took a long sip. She forced the red wine back and forth, sluicing it between her teeth, her eyes fixed in a stare, seeing nothing. 'Anyway,' she said. 'I've got to think what to say to Michelstraub.'

'Don't say anything,' said Eileen. 'Not for a few days. He doesn't know you're back in the UK, does he?'

'No. You're right,' Jessica nodded in agreement.

'See?' said Eileen. 'It'll all work out. Meanwhile, pass me that chocolate and tell me about the trip. Everything.'

Jessica passed the chocolate.

An hour later Jessica uncrossed her legs, stood up, and almost fell over. All feeling had disappeared from her lower limbs. 'Huh. That lotus position is supposed to help one attain a sense of relaxation,' she grumbled.

'It does,' Eileen told her. 'You become so relaxed, your muscles go to sleep. Try bending your knees a few times.'

Jessica wobbled slightly as she flexed her legs.

'That's it,' Eileen encouraged. 'Bend. Straighten. Bend. Straighten.'

'Do I give you the impression of a dying swan then?' Jessica asked her friend.

'No, not really. You're not as graceful.'

'That's it. No more entertainment. I'm off.'

'G'night then Jess. I don't think I'll be far behind you.'

Jessica chewed her lip as she climbed the stairs. She never let anyone call her Jess. She hated the shortened form of her name. She hated the shortened form of any name, including that of her partner, ex-partner, but Alex had been adamant; he'd been Alex since the day of his christening, he'd told her, and the subject was not open to discussion. She let it be known that she thought it common, and on the odd occasion when she'd met individuals who'd actually been christened Tom, Sue, Doug or Ally, she'd informed them boldly that their parents should have known better. The ensuing arguments had been legendary, but Jessica had never backed down. 'Take it or leave it,' she used to say. Some did. Some didn't. But, amongst all her acquaintances, there was great respect for Jessica and her tenacity when it came to her beliefs.

She went into the bathroom, picked her toothbrush off the shelf above the basin, and squeezed a minute dollop of Euthymol onto the row of bristles. She clenched the head of the toothbrush between her teeth as she dragged her knickers to her knees and sat on the loo.

'Bugger,' she said as she began to pee. The slight discomfort that had been there when she'd had a pee at thirty-five thousand feet had been the warning sign she'd feared.

'Bugger,' she said again, realizing that the chocolate binge would not have helped the situation. Very gently she dabbed herself dry, dropped the tissue into the bowl and pressed the flush. Back at the basin, she used one hand to flip the toothbrush around her mouth while the other pulled and pushed at her face. Jessica peered into the mirror and scrutinized the skin as various parts of her face came into sharp relief. She never wore a lot of make-up and was always scrupulous about removing every last vestige at the end of the day. 'It'll do,' she said to the mirror. 'It'll have to, it's the only face I've got.' She stuck out her tongue at her reflection, pulled the light switch and drifted across the landing into her bedroom.

Jessica moved to the bedside cabinet and opened it to pull out a litre-and-a-half bottle of mineral water. It was full. She unscrewed the top and downed almost half the contents. 'That'll take care of it,' she told herself, referring to the cystitis. She lay back in the bed and turned off the light. It was never truly, totally, impenetrably dark in London, and as her eyes accustomed themselves she was able to make out vaguely the pieces of furniture dotted around her room. There in the corner next to the window stood a chest of drawers, old-fashioned and dark. Jessica thought it might have been made of mahogany but, not being an expert on all the different types of wood, she wasn't too sure. The dim light limning round the edges of the curtains reflected off two framed photos propped up on top of the chest. The pictures had stood on her dressing table when she'd lived with Alex and, as she lay wide awake in the single bed, Jessica couldn't help wondering why she kept them on display. Then she began to wonder what he might be up to.

What a mess, she thought to herself. What a total fucking mess.

She switched on the light and sat up, her back against the headboard, and took another couple of mouthfuls of water. She'd have to be careful for the next few days; no milk, no butter, no fruit juice, no chocolate, definitely no wine or alcohol, and no stress. She reckoned that the cystitis had been caused by all the travelling, first to the States and then to Germany. Anyway, if it wasn't the travelling, she told herself, it was certainly the stress factor she'd suffered when Wolfgang had come up empty-handed, even more so when he'd told her that Alex had the Rembrandt.

Loads of black coffee and loads of water; Jessica was quite an authority on cystitis, having suffered from the condition, on and off, for many years. She remembered that she'd undergone a bad attack after her flight from Scotland, but the old remedy had weaved its spell and purified her system.

Jessica switched off the bedside light, turned onto her side, pulled her legs up into the foetal position and nestled her head into the pillow. She wrapped her arms around her legs and pulled them tight against her chest, then let go and rolled onto her back. Sleep was a million miles away. Jessica was over-tired, her mind in perpetual motion. The day had been too long with too much visual stimulation. There had been the snowstorm, a blizzard that had swept in from the frozen Russian steppes causing a two-hour delay for her British Airways flight out of Munich. The Bavarians were extra cautious when it came to clearing runways, the disaster of 1958 still lurking in the minds of the authorities. Jessica recalled the tension pervading the atmosphere as the aircraft finally had sped along the runway, the almost audible sigh of relief when the passengers realized that the take-off had been successful, and the nervous self-congratulatory smiles as the wheels had thunked into their housings. Mercifully, Jessica had been travelling light and had everything packed into her small shoulder bag, so the baggage handlers' strike at Heathrow had not impeded her passage through the terminal. The go-slow on the underground, however, did. Along with hundreds of other co-travellers, Jessica, standing to attention like a vertical sardine on the edge of the tightly packed platform, had fumed at the injustice and inefficiency of the system. When eventually a train had whooshed into the station, she'd been swept into the carriage like a piece of flotsam balanced on the crest of the Severn Bore. As the tide of humanity flowed through the doors she'd flung out one of her arms and caught onto a stanchion, managing to swing herself round into the seat next to the glass divider. She'd pulled her shoulder-bag onto her lap and had watched as the sea of people shoved and jostled. From somewhere behind her, somewhere the other side of the window, a voice had called out telling everyone to 'Move along please. Move down inside. Make room'. Heads had turned this way and that, bodies pressed against other bodies, and a few more atoms of air had been squeezed out, expelled from the carriage. The doors slid shut and the train had pulled itself out of the station and into the tunnel. And then, it had stopped.

Jessica turned back onto her side in a vain attempt to shut everything out of her mind. It was useless. If it wasn't the memories of the journey that kept her awake, it was thoughts about Alex, about Wolfgang, about the pictures.

'Those fucking pictures,' she announced into the depths of her pillow. The more she thought about them, the stronger became her frustration and, as the Rembrandt loomed large in her mind, she wondered where it was, where its new hiding place would be. She wondered what Alex intended to do with it, what *could* he do with it? Her thoughts travelled back to the dusty cellars, to the moment when the work of art had been revealed. Shit, she'd been so happy. It had been like Christmas, the three of them scrabbling about in the torch light, merrily unwrapping the giant parcels, exposing the gems that had been sealed, preserved like mummies. And what about the Prentiss Pose, she wondered? What would that reveal?

'Tomorrow,' she whispered, half asleep. 'Tomorrow I'll find out.'

And then her mind started crawling around the edges of perception, through mists and imaginations to enter the shadowy area between dreams and reality. Jessica moved one of her hands and placed it between her legs, a haven of warmth, softness and comfort. She smiled to herself as she remembered the erotic permutations stretched across the canvas; it was as if they were coming to life.

Her fingers started to move.

2

The radio blared away, announcing the eight o'clock news across the small kitchen. Eileen was preparing a cafetière, and didn't see or hear Jessica as she pulled out a chair and sat at the table. Jessica opened a box of Cornflakes and removed the peg clamped onto the inner bag. The golden flakes cascaded into her bowl and she replaced the box, still open, on the table, noticing that Eileen yet had to help herself to the cereal. Eileen turned round, cafetière in hand.

'Morning sunshine,' she said, beaming at Jessica.

'Good morning,' Jessica smiled back. She reached for the milk carton, pressed back the cardboard wings and poured semi-skimmed milk onto the flakes.

'Sleep well?' Eileen asked.

'No. Terrible.' Jessica answered. 'Too many things on my mind.' She set the carton onto the table.

'Well, you can rest today, can't you?' Eileen asked as she poured coffee for both of them.

Reaching for her coffee, Jessica looked across the table at her friend and, instead of locating her cup, her hand knocked against the milk carton causing it to fall over.

'Shit!' Jessica exclaimed, watching the milk pool across the table towards Eileen.

'Never mind,' said Eileen, stemming the flow with a handful of kitchen paper. 'You're just getting clumsy in your old age.'

'Clumsy?'

'Yep. Last night it was my tits. Now it's the milk.'

Jessica blushed as she recalled the contact.

'Not to worry though,' Eileen continued. 'There's a connection somewhere.' She grinned.

Jessica raised a spoonful of cereal towards her face and smiled sweetly.

As they munched their way through breakfast, Jessica informed Eileen of her plan to visit Christine and Terry.

'Somewhere down near Pimlico, isn't it?' Eileen asked.

'Mmm,' Jessica concurred.

'Maybe we can meet up later on? Lunch or something?' Eileen suggested. 'I'm temping at the moment. A solicitor's office near Victoria. I'll be just round the corner.'

'Yeah, okay. Maybe later though? How about a drink this evening? I'll meet you when you finish with your solicitor.'

'Great. There's a bar in the station itself. Opposite platform five. Or maybe it's six. Anyway, six-thirty?'

'Six-thirty,' Jessica agreed.

Jessica stepped out wearing her pinstripe suit. Jessica meant business.

'Damn,' she said as she exited onto the doorstep. It was still raining. No longer the heavy tropical downpour of the night before, but something infinitely more annoying – a light misty type of drizzle that found its way everywhere. It floated up under her umbrella, coating her face with a fine sheen and making her hair go frizzy.

Jessica followed the curve in Lyndhurst Gardens, dog-legged into Nutley Terrace, continued past the school and found herself on the Finchley Road. She crossed over to the station, bought a return ticket to Victoria and descended into the bowels of the earth. It was a pity about the rain, she mused, otherwise she would have emerged at Green Park and then enjoyed the walk through the park, across the front of the Palace, down towards Victoria and along Belgrave Road, eventually turning right into Warwick Square. She looked up at the adverts above the windows on the opposite side of the carriage, then noticed the schematic for the Jubilee Line and saw that if she stayed on the train, she'd end up at Charing Cross. Not being averse to changing horses in the middle of the stream, she decided to delay her visit to Terry and Christine. She'd do that in the afternoon and then, afterwards, she'd be able to saunter along to Victoria to meet Eileen.

Leaving the train, she joined the queue of people waiting to get on the escalator, rode up to ground level and came out in the middle of Charing Cross Station. She crossed the Strand and made her way to the National Gallery, feeling proud of her navigational skills and her knowledge and familiarity with the map of London.

Jessica entered the gallery and picked up a printed guide.

'Rembrandt, Rembrandt,' she muttered to herself, her eyes scanning the document.

'Ah, here we are,' she said, her index finger tracing the route up a staircase and along several corridors to a chamber, in which there appeared to be a display of works by Rembrandt.

She wasn't impressed. She'd seen two of the paintings before and one of them, 'The Night Watch', on loan from the Rijksmuseum, she remembered as being pretty scary. Rembrandt's use of contrasting light and dark served only to dramatize the dismal scene, and made Jessica think of stuffed marionettes. She studied the painted faces, the ludicrous expressions, and wondered at the significance of the strange woman who seemed to have a dead chicken hanging from her shoulder.

Weird, she thought, and shivered involuntarily before moving to the next painting, a religious scene – the Nativity, 1646 style, with a benevolent Mary and Joseph being visited by an astonished group of locals, and a dog with red eyes. Probably considered by those 'in the know' to be a masterpiece, Jessica thought, as she stood in front of what she could only think of as a 'brown study'.

Jessica had never been one to appreciate the intense, oppressive paintings of the Dutch Masters, she found them deeply dark and depressing. And it wasn't just Rembrandt. Whenever she viewed the mounds of flesh stretching endlessly across the canvases of the Flemish Rubens, she felt overpowered and anxious, ready to find something lighter in expression, lighter in mood.

Jessica's idea of art moved more in the direction of surrealism; she loved the works of the German painter Max Ernst, and the Spaniard, Salvador Dali, both of the twentieth century, although in truth, Ernst began life nine years before the century did. She loved the fantasy, loved being made to see things differently, her fascination drawing her into the depths of the artist's mind. She was interested also in the technical, architectural drawings of Ruskin and, as a concession to earlier epochs, she was impressed by the sixteenth-century work of Holbein the Elder, and the nineteenth-century Gothic melancholy of Friedrich. If there was one connecting thread, Jessica supposed it would have to be the lavish attention to detail found in all her favourite paintings.

She moved to another picture, a portrait of Saskia, Rembrandt's first wife. It did nothing to change Jessica's mind about the heavy brooding atmosphere of the artist's work, so she turned on her heels and walked off in the direction of the bookshop, where she managed to locate a huge tome dedicated to the works of Rembrandt. On the shelf above, she noticed a slim paperback titled *Baroque – A Guide*. Jessica's education stretched far enough to enable her to know that Rembrandt came within the Baroque period, so instead of paying a mortgage for the coffee-table publication, she spent four pounds seventy-five on the lighter volume.

Once again, Jessica's in-built knowledge of London locations found her, a little later, heading north along St Martin's Lane. After a couple of minutes, she turned left into St Martin's Court and found the little Italian restaurant just as she remembered, tucked away behind a theatre. It was only twelve-thirty so the place was virtually empty, save for a couple of men sitting at the bar, drinking coffee. Jessica chose a table at the window and, gazing out, was able to see the stage door as it opened to emit a group of people. Stagehands or actors? she wondered idly, not recognizing anyone famous.

When a waiter appeared at her side, she ordered a glass of house red and asked to see the menu. Having no other customers to worry about, the waiter promptly returned and placed the glass of wine and the menu on the table. Jessica selected a starter of endives with Roquefort cheese and olives, and a main dish of pollo cacciatore.

Leaning forward, she loosened her coat, withdrew her arms from the sleeves and let it drape itself over the back of the chair, before reaching into her bag to find the paperback.

She flipped through the pages; Carracci, Caravaggio, Rubens, van Dyck, Bernini. Jessica narrowed her eyes as she moved into unexplored territory. She'd heard of van Dyck, and Rubens she'd always lumped together with Michelangelo; thick thighs and lumpy butts. She smiled inwardly, realizing that the world of art

230

cognoscenti would label her as a Philistine but, 'Hey,' she told herself, 'we're all entitled to our opinions.' She flicked some more. Boucher, Lorrain, Poussin, Rembrandt.

'Aha,' she said to herself. 'Here we are.'

The starter arrived before she managed to get stuck into the chapter on Rembrandt although, before closing the book, she happened to notice that his full name had been Rembrandt Van Ryn. This was something she hadn't known, and as she swept the cheese-covered endive leaves into her mouth, she worried about why Rembrandt was known as Rembrandt, and not as Van Ryn. After all, she went on to reason, no one refers to van Dyck as Anthony.

She finished her starter and while waiting for the chicken dish to arrive, Jessica once again dipped into the paperback, searching for more information about Rembrandt. She wanted to be *au fait* with the life of the master of Dutch portrait painting, wanted to be one step ahead of Terry, who undoubtedly would expound deeply his knowledge on the subject.

The waiter arrived to remove the empty plate and Jessica gave him her empty glass, asking for a refill.

She read about Rembrandt's early years, during which success gained him considerable wealth. However, he was to lose it all in later life when, in 1642, his rich young wife died, forcing him to sell the house and put their collection of paintings and furniture up for auction. He moved to the poorest area of Amsterdam and though beset by hardship, it was in this later period that he produced his most profound works. His vast output of portraiture included paintings of his son, Titus, and several of his lifelong friends and, Jessica read, he seemed to have spent much of his time painting portraits of himself.

The pollo cacciatore arrived and while Jessica enjoyed the

flavours of onion, peppers, garlic and basil, she reflected on the fact that it was so often the way that artists of all genres seemed to produce their best work when in a state of penury, Mozart being perhaps the most obvious example.

'Fascinating,' she told herself as, absorbed in the printed word, she continued to read and came to realize how little she knew about the world of painting.

Although she remembered the number, the house was easy to locate due to the vividly bright yellow door and the black wrought-iron railings. The portal stood out like a sore thumb, especially vibrant in the sombre, dismal, leaden-hued atmosphere. Jessica pressed the brass button next to the legend 'Hastings'.

'Hastings,' said a voice from the metal grille set into the wall next to the front door.

'Jessica,' said Jessica.

'Who?' the voice asked.

'Jessica,' she replied.

'Jessica?' the voice queried.

She waited and started counting, slowly.

'Jessica?' the voice repeated.

'Five, six, seven, eight, nine...'

'Oh. Jessica?'

'Is this going to take a while, or are you going to let me in?' she asked.

'Ah, yes. Hang on.'

Something buzzed angrily and Jessica pushed against the door. It opened, swinging inwards to reveal a very modern hallway.

'Are you there? Are you inside?' the metallic voice enquired.

'Both,' Jessica answered, unsure whether her reply would be

heard now that she'd entered the building. She climbed the stairs to the first floor and knocked on the door which opened almost as she touched it.

'Jessica,' Terry said, extending a hand towards her. She was slightly wary, remembering that Terry had an exceptionally strong handshake.

'Aaah,' she said, feeling her knuckles being compressed, one against another. 'Terry!'

'Goodness, Jessica,' Terry said. 'I'm terribly sorry.' He unclenched his hand and Jessica retrieved her squashed fingers. 'Christine is always reminding me to be careful. Says I don't know my own strength. Coffee?'

'Black. No sugar,' Jessica informed him.

'Go through into the living room. I'll be with you in a moment,' Terry announced. She watched him as he disappeared into the kitchen. Entering the living room as directed, she looked about her and noted that the desk in the window was draped in a large white sheet. She moved across the room and peered down at a picture resting on top of the sheet. It was beautiful. It was tiny. Jessica judged it to be no more than four inches by six, and that included the plain gilt frame.

'It's an icon,' said Terry as he returned to the living room. 'The face of Christ.'

Jessica looked up as Terry approached, then her gaze returned to the picture. 'Christ?'

'Yep,' Terry confirmed.

'But it looks like Michael Jackson. A beautiful Michael Jackson, before he had his face changed.'

'Yeah. A lot of people say that,' Terry chuckled.

'But it does. It looks just like him,' Jessica insisted.

'It's the black Christ. Comes from Russia.'

'Russia?' Jessica exclaimed.

'*Came* from Russia,' Terry corrected himself. 'It lives in Manhattan now. Private collection.'

'Jesus, it's beautiful,' Jessica enthused.

'And priceless,' Terry informed her. 'So, let's move over to the coffee table.'

Jessica sat down on one of the sofas as Terry went off to fetch the coffee.

He returned a couple of minutes later with a tray bearing two cups of coffee and, under one arm, a cardboard tube.

'Your picture,' he stated, rather unnecessarily, as he set the tray on the table. 'A Vermeer.'

'Not a Rembrandt then?' Jessica asked.

'No. A Vermeer.'

'Definitely not a Rembrandt?' Jessica persisted, thinking of the time she'd just spent swatting up on the man who'd had two wives.

'Vermeer. Jan Vermeer. Same nationality as Rembrandt. Same time frame come to that, give or take a few years. Both lived and died in the seventeenth century.'

'The Baroque period,' Jessica stated.

'Yup,' Terry agreed, looking appraisingly at Jessica. 'Had its roots in Italian art. Heard of Caravaggio?'

'Rings a bell,' said Jessica, hiding a smile.

'Quite. Well he, Caravaggio, was at the forefront of early Baroque and died in ... sixteen-nineteen, about ten years before Vermeer was born. Of course, although Vermeer lived and worked during the Baroque era, his paintings belonged to the realist influence, and despite being probably *the* Dutch Master of still-life, not too much is known about him except that his output was extremely small. There are only around thirty paintings that have been genuinely attributed to him. He was too busy making babies...'

'Pardon?' Jessica interrupted.

'Babies. He had eleven children.'

'Bloody hell. All with the same woman?'

Terry laughed, 'Don't know.'

Jessica leaned forward, picked up the coffee and took a sip, evaluating the man across the table, impressed by the knowledge on display. She was impressed too by the coffee, better than she'd thought, imparting a deep rich nuttiness.

'So. We've landed a Vermeer,' she said, relaxing back on the sofa. 'Is it worth anything?'

'You're joking?' Terry asked.

'I've no idea,' Jessica informed him.

'Like I said, he only produced about thirty paintings, so...'

'So any new ones, so to speak, that come to light...'

'Are going to be highly sought after...'

'And therefore highly valuable,' Jessica finished.

'Quite,' Terry confirmed.

'Right. Okay.' Jessica leaned forward to collect the tube from the top of the coffee table.

'Might I ask what you're going to do with it?' Terry said.

'You might,' Jessica told him.

'What are you going to do with it?' he asked.

'I don't know,' Jessica replied. 'I don't know. I've got to think about this.'

'Well, while you're thinking, make sure you put it somewhere safe,' Terry warned, accompanying Jessica to the door. As he went to put his hand on the handle, the door opened and in walked Christine.

'Jessica! Haven't seen you since, well, since before Christmas.'

'Christine. How are you?' Jessica asked.

'Fine. Fine. And Alex? Is he here too?'

'No. Just me.' Jessica smiled at her old school friend. No need to give away all my secrets, she thought to herself.

'Well, it's good to see you,' Christine said. She saw the cardboard tube in Jessica's left hand. 'You've collected your painting then?'

'Mmm.'

'Well, be careful. Terry's told me it's worth a fortune.'

'Mmm.'

'Jessica, it's so exciting. Just to think...'

'Yes I know,' Jessica agreed quickly. 'Listen, it's great to see you again, but I've got to rush away. Another time, huh?'

The door was still open and Jessica, not wanting to hang around longer than necessary, passed through the entrance.

'By the way, how's Dan?' Christine called after her.

'Dan?' Jessica asked. Perplexed, she turned around.

'Yes, you know, Dan? Yankee Dan?'

'How do you know Dan?' Jessica asked Christine.

'He called and spoke to Terry. You gave him our number,' Christine explained.

'No I didn't.'

'Well, somebody did,' Christine said.

'He wanted to talk to you,' Terry informed Jessica. 'Told him he had the wrong number and put the phone down...'

'Thank fuck for that,' Jessica interrupted.

'...but not before he'd asked me who I was,' Terry finished.

'You didn't tell him?' Jessica stated.

'Of course. Why not?' Now it was Terry's turn to be perplexed.

'Because Dan would have told Alex and Alex would have put two and two together...'

236

'And?' Terry asked.

'And knowing Alex, he'd've immediately jumped to the wrong conclusion.'

'Which would be?' Terry quizzed Jessica.

'I'll let you work it out for yourself,' she answered.

'Jesus,' Jessica said to herself, her mind in a spin as she walked along Belgrave Road towards Victoria. 'What a fucking mess.' Her guidance system clicked in automatically and allowed her to dodge between the other pedestrians, all of whom seemed to be moving in the opposite direction. She tried to think through her options, mentally ticking them off, one by one. Her first idea, which she quickly rejected, was to call Alex and ask him what he was up to. Then she realized she didn't know where he was. She knew he'd left the house in Barnet. Jack, the pub landlord, had told her when inquisitiveness had got the better of her, and 'Yes,' he'd given her note to Alex, and 'Yes,' he'd met the Americans. 'Nice folk,' he'd said, and Jessica had had to agree with him, immediately feeling a stab of guilty conscience about the way she'd handled the situation in Scotland. No. She decided that she didn't want to talk to Alex, even if she had known his whereabouts.

That left Wolfgang and Michelstraub.

Wolfgang, she thought, was out of the picture; he no longer had the painting. She grinned at the pavement as she recalled the embarrassment on Wolfgang's face when he'd explained that Alex had returned to Germany to collect the Rembrandt. It was almost as if...

'Shit,' she said, as she entered the railway terminus. Forcing herself to remember the conversation she'd had with Michelstraub, she felt hot tendrils of panic crawling up the back of her neck. She recalled exactly what she'd told him. She recalled mentioning her need to visit Germany.

She stopped suddenly, causing people to bump into her, people who had made allowances for her speed and direction, people who found that their calculations had been incorrect. Everybody said, 'Excuse me,' or, 'Sorry,' as they untangled themselves to flow around the obstacle that wasn't supposed to be there. The momentary blip passed, and the dance, the complex weaving of the tide of humanity, continued its unceasing ebb and flow.

'Christ,' she said, unperturbed by her betrayal of clockwork motion, her mind locked on a higher plane. The news must have travelled like greased lightning. She could visualize it flashing from Michelstraub, via Mandie, to Alex, who would've found a way to travel faster than light. Straight to Germany.

'Stupid cow,' she said, annoyed at her own idiocy. 'Stupid, stupid cow.'

'That's nice,' said a female voice at her side.

Jessica looked up. 'Eileen,' she said.

'Yup. Eileen,' her friend agreed. 'It's me.' She smiled at Jessica. 'Who's the stupid cow then?'

'Oh. That's me,' Jessica informed her.

'That's all right then,' Eileen said. 'Do you want to tell me why?'

'Yes, but I need a drink. Right here, right now.'

'Assertive or what?' Eileen laughed. 'Come on then, here's the bar.' She grabbed Jessica by the arm and headed rapidly across the concourse.

They found the one remaining unoccupied table, a circular piece of plastic fixed to the top of a chrome pole, and perched

238

themselves on a couple of stools, smaller pieces of plastic fixed to the top of shorter poles.

'Right. You stay here and guard that with your life,' Jessica said, indicating the tubular container. 'G and T?'

'I think it'd better be a brandy,' Eileen answered.

'Yeah, you're right,' Jessica said as she turned away to get the drinks.

She returned with two cognacs, doubles.

'I've been so stupid,' she said, after they'd both taken generous swigs at their drinks.

'For a change?' Eileen asked, grinning across the narrow space above the table-top.

'Cheeky tart,' Jessica said.

'So tell me,' Eileen said.

'I only went and told Michelstraub just about everything,' Jessica began.

'You mean when you were in the States?' Eileen asked.

'Of course when I was in the States.'

'Well, you're such a jet-setter these days.'

'A trip to America and a trip to Germany doth not me a jet-setter make,' Jessica retorted.

'Okay, so which bit of the "everything" that you told Michelstraub makes you stupid?'

'The bit that informed him that I wanted to go to Germany,' Jessica answered.

'Why?'

'Christ, Eileen. Because Alex will have found out and that's how he managed to get there first.'

'And that's a problem?' Eileen asked.

'Yes. That's a problem. He's got the painting!' Jessica said, exasperation showing uncharacteristically in her voice.

'And you've got your cardboard tube,' Eileen said, glancing towards the tube poking out from under her jacket which was resting on top of a third stool.

'I've got my cardboard tube,' Jessica agreed.

'Tit for tat, then,' Eileen observed. 'All is fair in love.'

'And war,' Jessica added bluntly, completing the aphorism.

'Are you hungry?' Eileen asked.

'Starving,' Jessica replied. 'But I don't want to be out and about too long with this package. It needs to be in a safe place.'

'Absolutely. I'll rustle up something at home. Shall we get a taxi?'

'Good idea. I've still some money from Michelstraub so we'll stop at an offy on the way, buy a couple of bottles of something inspirational.'

3

They had to stand in a queue. The cabs that occasionally slid into the taxi-rank at the front of the station were few and far between, and it took twenty minutes before the two women were safely ensconced on the rear seat of a black cab.

Eileen had given the driver their destination as she'd climbed in through the door, and now she leaned back against the seat and clasped Jessica's left leg.

'What do you think, half an hour?' she asked her friend.

'Half an hour?' Jessica queried.

'To get home,' Eileen explained.

'You'll be lucky,' said the cabbie. 'Look out there. Rain and traffic in all directions.'

'Hey! I thought you were supposed to keep that hatch of yours closed?' Eileen told the driver.

'Nah, never. It'd be back and forth like a shuttlecock. Know what I'm sayin'?'

'No,' Eileen replied. 'Do tell.'

'Well, it's them tourists, innit? They wanna know it all.'

'They do?' Jessica asked.

''Course they do, don't they?'

'Such as?'

'Such as, "Where does the Queen live?" Such as, "Does it always rain like this?"'

'Mind-boggling stuff then?' Jessica said.

'Nah, not really. But the best one is when they ask me if we're on London Bridge. You know, when we're on Tower Bridge?' He chuckled, 'You should see their faces when I tell them that London Bridge is in the middle of a desert somewhere in America.'

'Yeah,' Jessica agreed. 'Arizona.'

' 'Arry owns it, does he?' the cabbie asked, turning to look at his fares.

The girls collapsed in a heap.

Thirty minutes brought them to the middle of Camden, and the taxi was just turning out of Parkway to make its way towards Chalk Farm when Jessica leaned forward.

'No no. Go straight on,' she directed the cabbie.

'What?' he called backwards over his shoulder.

'Keep going straight,' Jessica repeated.

The taxi shot through the lights as they changed to red.

'That's it, nice one. Now,' she said, pointing ahead, 'pull in over there.'

'Over there?' the driver queried.

'Yeah. Bit more,' Jessica directed. 'Go on. Go on. Okay, that'll do.'

They came to a halt next to the pavement, a few yards from Sainsbury's.

'Can you wait, then?' she asked the bewildered cabbie. 'I'll be quick.'

Jessica opened the door, skittered through the rain and disappeared into the maw of the supermarket.

Seven minutes later she reappeared, a plastic bag in each hand. Eileen opened the cab door and Jessica pulled it shut behind her. 'Okay. Off we go,' she announced triumphantly.

The cabbie muttered under his breath as he threaded his cab

through the narrow backstreets of Kentish Town towards Haverstock Hill, before joining the northbound traffic queuing up to crawl past Belsize Park.

'Have you got any cash on you?' Jessica asked Eileen. 'This is going to cost a small fortune and I spent all my money in Sainsbury's.'

Eileen opened her bag and took out her purse. She undid the clasp and rifled through the notes.

'Yup. Should be okay,' she said.

The cab turned in to Wedderburn Road and paused at the crossroads.

'Left or right?' the cabbie asked.

'Just here is fine,' said Eileen, handing him all her folding money. 'And keep the change.' Jessica clanked out of the taxi with her two bags of shopping and Eileen followed with the cardboard tube gripped tightly in her right hand.

'How much, then?' Jessica asked her friend as Eileen fumbled at the front door.

'A king's ransom,' Eileen beamed.

Eileen watched approvingly as Jessica unpacked the bags. First out were the two bottles of wine.

'Open one,' Jessica instructed her friend, 'pour us a couple of glasses, then stick the bottles in front of a radiator to warm up.'

Eileen picked up one of the bottles and peered at the label. 'Looks interesting,' she said, and, falling into a bad French accent, 'a leetle French numbeur, from ze warm fertile vallées in ze Bordeaux région.'

'Don't worry about the pedigree,' Jessica told her. 'Just get it open.'

Eileen opened a drawer, rummaged around and took out her 'waiter's friend' and sliced round the bottle's neck, neatly removing the top of the dark red seal. She folded the blade into the gadget and levered open the corkscrew. Bottle in one hand, corkscrew in the other, she twisted the metal spiral into the cork, caught the metal hook on the lip and, with a soft 'pop', expertly removed the stopper.

Jessica turned to watch as the wine was poured into a couple of glasses, smiling as the rubescent liquid glugged from the bottle. 'What a horrible noise,' she joked as Eileen completed her allotted task. Then, 'Hey? Where are you going?' as Eileen picked up the bottles and walked out of the kitchen.

'To warm the bottles,' Eileen replied, passing through into the living room, 'like how you told me.' She returned a couple of minutes later and sat at the table, picking through the various items of food that Jessica had removed from the carrier bags. 'Mmm, there's some good stuff here, Jessica my friend. Very tasty.'

'Yeah, well, why not?' Jessica said, emptying a bag of mixed baby leaves into a bowl. 'You mentioned something about preparing something to eat at home so, when I remembered there was a Sainsbury's at Camden, I thought why bother cooking?'

'Talking about preparing something, shall I make a dressing?' Eileen asked.

'Yeah, good idea,' Jessica answered, throwing some itsy-bitsy tomatoes into the salad.

Eileen picked a large plastic tub from the table.

'What about these large green olives marinated in a mixture of oil and herbs with large chunks of garlic and wedges of lemon?' she asked, reading from the label.

'Oh. Just take the lid off and we can pick them straight from the tub.'

The preparation didn't take long and soon two large trays were loaded with a tempting array of tasty morsels. The girls had decided to eat their meal in the living room and as there was no coffee table, they placed the trays on the carpet and squatted opposite one another with the food laid out between them.

Jessica noticed the two bottles of wine arrayed in front of a gas fire.

'That wasn't on last night,' she pointed out.

'No. But it adds a bit of cheer, doesn't it?'

'Certainly does,' Jessica agreed. 'And here's to it, a bit of cheer at the end of a dismal day.' She raised her glass towards Eileen, smiled, and took a mouthful of the red Bordeaux, smacking it against the roof of her mouth with her tongue, like a real expert. 'Yeah,' she said, sucking some air through her teeth. 'Not bad. Oaky and a touch of candle wax.'

'Candle wax?' Eileen queried.

'Well, like candles after you've just blown them out,' Jessica explained. 'You know, it's that woody earthy smell. You can taste it as well. Go on, try.'

Eileen raised her glass and hung her nose over the rim. She closed her eyes and took a deep breath. 'Mmm,' she said, before taking a large gulp of the French wine. She sloshed it around her mouth and then swallowed. 'Tastes of sex,' she announced.

'Sex?' Jessica asked, eyes wide.

'Yeah, sex,' Eileen affirmed. 'Earthy and musty, just like ... well, sex.'

'Bloody hell,' said Jessica, gazing at her friend.

'Yeah, bloody hell,' Eileen responded, agreeing. Suddenly she leaned forward over the two trays and kissed Jessica full on her mouth.

Jessica backed away, 'Eileen! What the fuck...?' She was unable to say anymore as Eileen had placed a hand behind her head and pulled her in for another meeting of the mouths. She felt her lips being forced apart and recoiled as she realized that Eileen's tongue had entered her mouth. Thunderstruck, Jessica pulled her head backwards but, due to Eileen's hand, was unable to separate her face from Eileen's. She opened her eyes and found Eileen's staring straight at her, penetrating her brain, boring deep into her soul. Eileen nodded, the movement causing Jessica's head to bob up and down. She felt Eileen's tongue extend itself further into her mouth and, just when she thought enough was enough, their tongues met, briefly. Jessica pulled away again and was able to break free as the restraining hand had been removed. She backed down onto her haunches and wiped a hand across her mouth.

'Eileen!' she shrieked.

'Taste it, Jessica. Taste it.'

'Wha...?'

'Experience the taste on your tongue.'

'Wha...?'

'You know. Attach your brain to your sense of taste.'

Jessica moved her tongue through the air in her mouth, touched the tip against the back of her teeth.

'And?' Eileen asked.

'Mustiness,' Jessica said. She looked up at Eileen. 'Jesus, what the hell's got into you?'

Eileen smiled. 'Okay, listen. Take another mouthful of wine.'

'Why should I?'

'Jessica. Just do it.'

'But why?'

Eileen moved forward and Jessica backed away. Eileen moved further forward and placed a hand on Jessica's chest, just above

246

her left breast. 'It's still beating, you're still alive Jess. You've survived another of life's mysteries. You've lived though it, and you can tell me to fuck off.'

'Yes...'

'But first, drink the wine and tell me what you taste. Do it for me.'

'The olives, we forgot the olives,' Jessica responded, rising to her feet and heading towards the kitchen.

Eileen looked down at the trays, surveying from left to right. Houmous, smoked salmon, peppered salami, French stick, cheese, bowl of salad ... olives. 'No we didn't,' she said to the assorted delicacies. 'Fuck.'

She got to her feet and padded after Jessica. Noticing that the kitchen light hadn't been switched on, she peered into the gloom and saw her friend sitting at the table, head in hands, golden hair cascading down to cover her face.

'Jess,' Eileen said, moving to sit in the other chair. 'Jess, what is it?' She leaned across the table, reached out with both hands and sliding her fingers into the curtain of hair, teased it apart and drew it back on either side of Jessica's head. She tried to smooth it down and fold it behind Jessica's ears, all the while gazing deeply into her friend's face. She watched as a large tear squeezed itself out of Jessica's left eye, tracked down the side of her nose and sort of lodged momentarily on her upper lip. Eileen used a thumb to brush away the tiny pearl of liquid.

'Jessica. I ... I don't...'

'It's me,' Jessica said.

'But...'

'It's me,' Jessica repeated. 'Okay? It's me.'

The two women, separated by the width of the table, sat opposite one another in the darkened room. The silence folded

247

in on itself, formed an invisible barrier and shattered, split asunder by a deafening explosion accompanied by a searing brilliance, illuminating the kitchen as if from within and throwing the two figures into sharp relief.

'Fucking incredible!' Jessica exclaimed, shooting her hands across the table until they came into contact with Eileen's. 'Magnificent. How the fuck did you do it?'

They sat there in the darkness, holding hands, fingers entwined. They sat and listened to the rain clattering onto the brick-weave path that ran along the side of the house. They sat, motionless, in the centre of the all-encompassing noise and witnessed the sound intensify as the rain, galvanised into renewed energy, hurled itself out of the furious heavens. Another flash and then, two seconds later, another crash of thunder. Jessica and Eileen stood up, moved away from the table and embraced, Jessica with her forehead pressed against Eileen's left shoulder, Eileen with her face crushed into Jessica's neck.

'C'mon,' Eileen said. 'The food is calling.'

She led the way back to the living room and the two girls returned to their positions on the carpet, either side of the well-stocked trays.

'Candles,' Jessica said. 'We need candles.' She rose to her feet and wandered off towards the kitchen.

Eileen smiled, shook her head. 'Not again,' she said, and stuffed an olive into her mouth.

Jessica returned with two candles and proceeded to slot them into a couple of holders on the mantelpiece, above the hissing gas fire. She lit the wicks, turned off the light and nodded, pleased with the result. Softly illuminated by the light of flickering flames, the room seemed to diminish in size, closing in, protectively encapsulating the two women in the warm glow.

248

Jessica knelt on the floor in front of the trays, leaned forward and touched her lips lightly against Eileen's forehead. Sinking back onto her heels, she rearranged her legs so that she ended up sitting in the lotus position. She looked across at her friend. 'You're right,' she said. 'Sex.'

'Sex?'

'Oakiness, candle wax and sex,' Jessica expounded. 'The wine has an earthy undertone, a latent muskiness pertaining to the essence of ... sex.'

'Pertaining to the essence of sex, eh?' Eileen chuckled. 'Follow your own guidelines and say what you mean.'

Jessica folded a strip of smoked salmon onto an oval of French bread and held it up to Eileen's mouth.

'I said what I meant,' Jessica told her friend. 'You are correct. The wine has a taste of sex about it.'

'Mmm,' Eileen intoned, biting into the proffered titbit, 'female sex.'

'Eileen!' Jessica exclaimed. 'You're incorrigible.'

'Yes, I am,' Eileen agreed. 'Totally.'

They picked at the food and drained the glasses, their contented munching accompanied by the sounds of the bubbling gas fire and the occasional rumble of thunder, as the storm worked its ponderous way across the low-lying London basin.

Their conversation swung backwards and forwards, taking in the various aspects of the day. Eileen's eyes filled with amusement at Jessica's account of her meeting with Terry. 'You mean you went to all that bother reading about Rembrandt and then the picture turned out to be something else?' She laughed, 'I'd've been well pissed off.'

'Yeah, but all the same it was pretty interesting.'

'Yeah, but you're an intellectual.'

'Never underestimate the power of the pawn,' Jessica stated.

'Porn!' Eileen giggled, then, 'Porn? Are you sure?'

'P – A – W – N,' Jessica spelled it out. 'The piece that supposedly has the lowest value but is still able to cause a lot of hassle if used wisely.'

'See, I was right? An intellectual.'

'No, I'm just a pawn who can't say no.'

'Good. Go and get the chocolate then, pawn.'

Jessica unfolded her legs, stood, and picked up one of the trays. She went out into the kitchen and returned with a couple of Flakes, which she handed to Eileen, before bending down to pick the other tray off the carpet and once again head towards the kitchen. Back in the living room she went to sit beside her friend, who'd moved herself onto the sofa, legs hauled up and tucked away under her bum.

Eileen passed one of the chocolate bars back to Jessica and both women unwrapped and devoured the flakey confectionery in a matter of seconds. They up-ended the bright yellow wrappers, allowing the few remaining chocolate crumbs to slide down the empty tubes and into their mouths.

Eileen held out her hand to take Jessica's wrapper, twisting the two together before tying them into a knot and placing them on the arm of the sofa. 'So. What are you going to do?' she asked.

'About what?'

'Rembrandt and Vermeer,' Eileen replied. 'Let's start with the easy ones.'

'Rembrandt's no longer my problem,' Jessica said, 'and Vermeer, well . . .'

'Let's leave that for a moment,' Eileen butted in. 'What about Alex?'

'Alex?'

'Mmm, Alex. You fucked up big time with him.'

'I did?' Jessica asked, her big blue eyes staring straight at her friend.

'Well, he didn't cause too many problems, did he?' Eileen asked.

'What's your point?'

'And he was generally happy with life, wasn't he?'

'Yes, but...'

'Didn't have any baggage?' Eileen pursued.

'Baggage?'

'The sex was adequate?'

'The sex was fantastic,' Jessica agreed, grinning widely. 'No complaints in that department.'

'So, I don't understand,' Eileen concluded. 'What are you doing here?'

'I don't know, Eileen. I just don't know.' Jessica sighed and looked at the carpet. 'Christ,' she said. 'I sound just like him.'

'Like Alex?'

'Yeah. He said something very similar last time I saw him.'

'When was that?' Eileen enquired.

'Oh, around Christmas.' Jessica looked at her friend. 'I told you.'

Eileen smiled. 'Maybe. Can't remember.'

'Anyway...' Jessica started.

'Anyway, my point is, you've got nothing to lose,' Eileen cut her short.

'Meaning?'

'You need to confront him. Ask him what he intends to do with the painting. Make some sort of deal. Tell him it's better if you work as a team, you know, pool your resources.'

'I can't,' Jessica said.

'Why?'

'I just can't.'

Eileen lay back into the corner of the sofa, put her arms around Jessica and drew her towards her. Jessica realigned her body and lay with her head resting against Eileen's breasts, her legs trailing away towards the far end of the three-seater. She felt Eileen's hand brush against her head, massaging her scalp. Then, two hands. A slow movement across her forehead from a point just above the bridge of her nose, out to the sides and down to her temples. She breathed in, inhaling deeply, filling her lungs and holding them inflated for as long as she could, before slowly releasing the air through her parted lips.

'You're right,' she said. 'Again, you're right.'

'It happens,' Eileen said, softly.

'Mmm. I fucked up.'

'You've got your independence,' Eileen said.

'Not sure I want it,' Jessica responded.

Eileen chuckled, her stomach vibrating beneath Jessica's back. 'Something about beds and lying in them comes to mind,' Eileen whispered into Jessica's right ear.

'Okay, okay,' Jessica acquiesced, 'you win.' She turned her head to look up at Eileen's face. For a breath, a very short breath, time stood still. Jessica felt herself moving upwards, falling against gravity into the depths of Eileen's dark brown eyes. Eileen looked down and searched within Jessica's soul. She inspected the face that seemed to be rising towards her own, saw the dilemma, the question mark burning at the centre of the pupils. She forced her gaze away from Jessica's eyes and examined her mouth. She noticed the slightly parted lips, the dark pink skin contrasting sharply with the white teeth just visible behind the inviting opening. She focused her eyes on Jessica's lips, greedily absorbing the texture, the moistness, and the tenderness. She bent her head forwards and the spell was broken, time recommencing its relentless passage through space.

Eileen's vision expanded when she used the tip of her tongue to explore the surface just inside Jessica's lower lip. She traced her tongue across the width of Jessica's mouth, corner to corner, and did the same with the upper lip. The touch, light as a feather, was precise, and Jessica opened her mouth a fraction wider as the tongue searched and probed, the sensitive tip relaying intimate information gleaned from microscopic nooks and crannies. Jessica parted her teeth giving Eileen full access to her mouth. She lifted her tongue and ran it back along the underside of the intruder, until the tips met and pressed together. After a few seconds Jessica extended her tongue and let it roll around the other, before pushing forwards to begin her own tentative exploration of Eileen's mouth.

She felt Eileen straightening her legs, wriggling underneath, and then she felt her own legs parting and sliding down to rest either side of Eileen's thighs. Still on her back, she felt Eileen's hands slide beneath her blouse, felt the fingers trace random patterns, exquisite sensations across her stomach. She reached up and pulled Eileen's head downwards, towards her own, their mouths melding in hungry kisses. Somehow Eileen had managed to undo the buttons and hooks at the front of her trousers and Jessica rolled over to look into her friend's face. She tensed as she experienced the touch of Eileen's hands worming into the space under the flimsy fabric of her knickers, and again as the warm hands cupped themselves over the tautness of her buttocks and pressed downwards. Jessica stretched herself out, letting her torso blend into the contours of the supine body lying beneath her. Her pelvis came into contact with Eileen's abdomen, her stomach flexed to receive Eileen's rib cage, and her breasts, restrained in their lacy bra, squashed into the space above those of her friend. She let her head fall against Eileen's right shoulder, turned her face into the crook of her neck and nuzzled against the warm flesh. The downward pressure from Eileen's hands increased, forcing the two bodies to come together, to fuse in molten ecstasy.

Jessica woke in the middle of night, startled into alertness by a crack of thunder that shook the house. The concussive report reverberated between the houses lined up on each side of the street, and before the noise had died away, another sharp explosion sliced through the atmosphere. She turned over and glimpsed the outline of Eileen's head resting on the pillow. She was lying on her side, her back towards Jessica, oblivious to the storm raging, fully revived in all its glory, outside the rattling sash window. Jessica slid across the double bed and snuggled her nakedness into the warmth emanating from the unconscious body. She put her arm over Eileen's side and brought it down onto her stomach, drawing herself tightly against her friend's sleeping form. She flattened her breasts into Eileen's back and curled her legs upwards, feeling the curve of Eileen's bottom nestling into her lap. Eileen instinctively reached out from her slumbers and covered Jessica's hand with one of her own.

Jessica went back to sleep.

4

Sunlight flooded into the bedroom and strains of music floated up the stairs. Jessica opened an eye and quickly shut it again, dazzled by the brightness. She placed a hand over her face and opened both eyes, keeping her hand in position until she grew accustomed to the brilliance that filled the room. Mozart and the aroma of fresh coffee filtered through the air, caressing her ears and infiltrating her nostrils. Jessica smiled, delirious as the two senses burst wide open, coruscating intoxicatingly through her cerebral cortex.

She stretched luxuriantly while she looked around Eileen's bedroom. Although roomier than her own, it contained less furniture. In fact, there were only two items; a long, low chest of drawers made of teak, the top drawers very shallow and glass-fronted, and the bed itself, a low-slung wooden-frame structure, plain and featureless. Jessica sat up and swung her legs over the edge of the mattress, placing her feet on the floorboards. She peered down at the highly polished surface and noticed a large volume, Thomas Hardy, *The Complete Works*, poking out from under the bed. She looked at the chest of drawers and noticed that the surface was bare, no pictures, no artifacts, no ornaments, nothing; the room was a shrine to minimalism.

Jessica smiled to herself, it was something she'd thought about in a previous life, a life shared with Alex. It would have been impossible, they had too many bits and pieces scattered in all directions, surfaces laden with the detritus assembled from two lives. She quite liked it, she thought, her eyes roving round the room, the simplicity, the sparseness, the Japanese style, uncluttered and tranquil. You'd certainly be able to focus on yourself in here, she supposed. No distractions, just plain wood, curtains and bed linen.

Jessica left Eileen's room and went to her own bedroom in search of clothes. She pulled on some knickers, slid into a pair of jeans, and scrimmaged about looking for a clean sweatshirt. She sifted through a pile of dirty clothing and found an old sweater, light blue. That'll do, she decided, pulling it over her head as she walked towards the stairs. Drawn by the enticing coffee aroma, she entered the kitchen and witnessed Eileen extracting boiled eggs from a saucepan.

'Morning,' she said, a little sheepishly.

'Hiya. Sleep well?' Eileen greeted her, putting an arm round her waist and planting a kiss on her right cheek.

'Mmm,' Jessica yawned.

'Do you know what day it is today?'

'Um, Sunday?'

'Yes,' Eileen agreed. 'It's Sunday.'

'And?'

'Sunday the fourteenth of February,' Eileen answered.

'Fourteenth, Valentine's Day?'

'Yep. Appropriate, don't you think?'

'Listen, Ei...'

'Yes, I know, it's your first time, etcetera, etcetera.'

'I've never...'

'Felt the way you did last night?' Eileen asked insouciantly.

'I've never done that before,' Jessica said. 'And...'

'And?' Eileen asked.

256

'And I don't think I'll ever do it again.'

'So it was a one-night stand then?'

'It was a one off,' Jessica said, knocking the top off one of the boiled eggs. She stabbed the point of a teaspoon into the heart of the hot yellow yolk and lifted a spoonful of the soft runny gloop into her mouth.

'Cooked to perfection,' she said, smiling at Eileen.

'Well, they do say experience everything once,' Eileen said.

'Yes, they do,' Jessica agreed. 'Don't get me wrong,' she continued, 'I don't think, um, I don't think it was a mistake. It was just...'

'So good, so right,' her friend filled in.

'At the time it seemed right,' Jessica corrected.

'I knew it, you know?' said Eileen.

'How do you mean?'

'I knew it from the moment we jumped into the taxi at Victoria.'

'How?'

'I just did. A feeling. Intuition.'

'And?'

'And there was no way I was going to stop it.'

'Eileen!'

'I wanted it, and... and you needed it,' Eileen said.

'I needed it?' Jessica asked, incredulous. 'What you mean, I needed it?'

'You did,' Eileen insisted. 'You've been fucked about for too long and by too many people.'

Jessica said nothing, and looked at the empty egg shell.

'You needed a little light entertainment,' Eileen went on. 'And I was here to provide it.'

Jessica removed the fragile shell from the egg cup and replaced it with another. She picked up the teaspoon and broke into the top of the egg, keeping her eyes trained on the delicate operation being carried out by her hands.

'It was an experience and I ... I suppose I enjoyed it. But ... it wasn't me.'

'Yes it was,' Eileen informed her, 'and you certainly enjoyed it.'

'It was the wine and the storm,' Jessica countered. 'I go funny when there's a storm brewing, it's all those free-floating negative ions, makes me...'

'Horny,' Eileen told her.

'Anyway, I like cock too much,' Jessica smiled as she scooped the last of the egg white from the shell.

'So do I,' Eileen agreed, 'but I don't like what's attached. They're different, blokes are. They're screwed up most of the time. And it screws me up as well.'

'I don't know,' Jessica said. 'Life, huh? It just seems to go round in circles.'

'Shit. I forgot the bread,' Eileen announced. 'I warmed the remainder of that French stick, it's still in the oven.'

'It's okay,' Jessica replied. 'We can have it with jam. Mmm, bread, jam and fresh coffee. What more could a girl want?'

'Don't start,' Eileen implored, grinning across the table.

'That's it, I've got it,' Eileen announced. 'I think.'

The two were strolling through some long wet grass in a wild, unkempt part of the park near Hampstead Ponds. Jessica, eyebrows raised, peered quizzically at her friend.

'You've got to contact those two in New York.'

'Dan and Mandie?'

'No. Rembrandt and Vermeer. Of course Dan and Mandie.'

'I don't know where they live, don't even have their number. I don't know much about them at all,' Jessica said.

'Your lawyer friend does,' Eileen coaxed.

'They probably wouldn't want anything to do with me.'

'Why?'

'Well, you know. I didn't exactly enhance their visit,' Jessica explained.

'Oh yes, I'd forgotten that,' Eileen agreed. 'Shit.'

They walked on in silence, looping round the far end of the ponds. It was a strange day, the middle of February and surprisingly warm. The storm had cleared the air and the sun had shone from a cloudless sky until about two o'clock, when large ragged chunks of cumulus had begun to drift across the heavens.

'Well, I don't think you've got an option,' Eileen said eventually.

'Even if I did get in touch,' Jessica asked, 'what would I say?'

'I don't know,' Eileen admitted. 'Haven't got that far.'

'Maybe if I went and spoke to Terry?' Jessica suggested.

'Terry?'

'Yes.'

'Why?'

'Well, maybe he'd have some sort of idea.'

'No,' Eileen replied. '*You've* got to be in control of the situation. *You've* got to be the one having ideas and telling people what to do.'

'Yes, you're right,' Jessica agreed.

'Wait a minute. What if you told Terry to ring Alex? Tell him to say that he's finished the work on the Prentiss Pose. That'd get him thinking.'

'Yes. Bugger. No.'

'No?'

'Even supposing he'd agree to do it, he wouldn't have Alex's number.'

'Shit,' said Eileen. Then again, 'Shit, get him to call your lawyer.'

'Straight to the mouth of the horse,' Jessica agreed, smiling.

'Straight to the mouth of the horse,' Eileen repeated.

'Brilliant,' Jessica grinned. 'Quite brilliant. But it doesn't mean I'm going to let you fuck me.'

'Just when I thought it safe to broach the subject,' Eileen grinned in return. The women had navigated a large semicircle and came out of the park onto Heath Street. They started ambling in the direction of the tube station. 'Look, pub,' Eileen said, pointing.

'Yeah, but it's not going to be open at this time of day.'

'Look, coffee shop,' Eileen said, pointing in a different direction. They crossed the road and opened the door to the coffee shop, causing a little ding-a-ling-type bell to go ding, once.

'Cute,' said Eileen, as they sat on high-backed wooden chairs at a table close to a unit displaying a wide selection of hugely tempting, hugely dangerous cakes.

A waitress dressed in black with a frilly white pinafore approached the table and took their order. 'Pot of lemon tea,' she said, jotting it down on a small pad. 'Anything else?'

'Two wedges of that chocolate cake,' said Jessica.

'Which one?' asked the waitress, turning to look at the cabinet.

'That one,' said Jessica, pointing. 'That one up there, top shelf, on the right.'

'Oh, the Black Forest gâteau,' the waitress said. 'Two slices, right?'

'Please.'

They looked round the old-fashioned tea room and caught

260

snippets of conversation from the Sunday afternoon customers. Everyone seemed to be talking about the storm and how it had kept them awake most of the night. Eileen giggled. 'Didn't keep me awake,' she said.

'I noticed,' Jessica told her. 'A loud clap of thunder woke me in the middle of the night and you just lay there, dead to the world, impervious to everything.'

'And what did you do?' Eileen asked, smiling nonchalantly.

'I, er, I turned over and went back to sleep,' Jessica said.

'I know,' Eileen told her, 'with your arm around me, pulling yourself up tight against me.'

'You were awake?'

'Not really. But then I wasn't really asleep either. Just alert enough to feel your body pressing into me. It was nice.'

'Yeah, well, I thought you were asleep,' Jessica said.

'And?'

'Okay. It was nice.'

The tea arrived along with two enormous portions of cake.

'I'll be thinking I'm back in Germany,' Jessica said, digging into the gâteau. 'Look, there are even window-boxes out there.' They looked through the glass and saw the pansies, bright under the winter sun.

5

Jessica and Eileen stood at the top of the steps that led to the fulgent yellow door.

'Two's better than one,' Eileen had said over the coffee and toast. The radio, as usual, had been playing, filling the kitchen with Level 42, and Jessica had been going through her plans for the day when Eileen had suggested that she'd tag along. Initially, Jessica had been a bit anti. 'No, it's okay,' she'd said. 'I can do it. Besides...'

And that's when Eileen had forced the issue with her simple statement. There was no getting away from it, Eileen was right; in the majority of cases two *were* better than one. Jessica found herself thinking back to the numerous occasions when she and Alex had gone through their double act, and they'd been dynamic, the results had been awesome.

'Go on then,' Eileen broke through her thoughts. 'Ring the bell.' Jessica applied finger to button and a frison of déjà-vu passed through her body.

'Yes?' said a voice.

'Terry?'

'Yes?'

'It's Jessica.'

'Jessica? So soon?'

'I need to talk to you,' she said.

'Okay, come on up.' The buzzer buzzed and Jessica leaned on the door. They climbed the stairs and found the door to the apartment open. Jessica knocked in any case as she and Eileen passed through the opening.

'Hello?' she called out.

'In here. Shut the door behind you.' They walked into the living room and found Terry sitting at the desk in front of the French window. He stood up and paced across the room to greet the visitors, his movement displacing the air, imparting a sudden tang of nail varnish.

'Jessica, and...'

'Eileen,' Eileen informed him, proffering her hand. 'Aaah.'

'Sorry,' said Jessica. 'Forgot to warn you.'

Eileen retrieved her hand and nursed it, gently massaging it with her left hand while Terry asked them what it was they'd come to see him about.

'I need your help,' Jessica told him. They'd agreed that it would be the best gambit. Normally, people love it when made to feel useful. It adds to their sense of well-being, boosts their ego, and shuffles great dollops of positive energy around their veins. Yes, they love it, the feeling of power as lesser mortals approach the oracle, seeking advice and words of wisdom.

'Sit down, sit down,' Terry invited, ushering them towards the sofas. 'Now then, how can I be of assistance?'

'I need you to talk to somebody, to tell them that you've finished the work on the canvas,' Jessica explained.

'Is this a good idea?' Terry replied. 'The fewer who know about this, the better.'

'I know, I know,' Jessica agreed. 'But this person is a lawyer.'

'All the more reason...'

'I know,' Jessica said, sensing any advantage that she might have had slipping through her fingers.

'What sort of lawyer is he?' Terry asked.

'American.'

'American?' Terry exclaimed. 'They're even worse!'

'It's a chance I have to take,' Jessica informed him.

'Why?'

'He's the instigator of all this running around and, more to the point, he's got the oth...' Jessica stopped, suddenly realizing that Terry was unaware that the Prentiss Pose he'd cleaned was not unique. Unless, of course, Alex had told him. Bugger, there were too many loose ends.

'The other...?' Terry left the question dangling in thin air.

'The other...' Jessica began, slowly.

'String to the bow,' Eileen slotted in, seeing Jessica's hesitation.

Terry and Jessica stared at Eileen.

'Bow?' Terry queried.

'Well ... purse, actually. He holds the strings.'

Jessica beamed.

'Oh. I see,' Terry said vaguely.

'Yup,' Eileen continued triumphantly. 'Everything has to be approved by him.'

'And he is?' Terry asked her.

'Michelstraub,' Jessica answered, causing Terry's head to swing back in her direction. She met his penetrating gaze with one of her radiant smiles. 'You can do it now,' she told him, glancing at her watch. 'Seven-thirty. It'll be two-thirty over there.'

She opened her bag and searched for the business card that Michelstraub had shoved into her hand only a few days previously.

'Here we are,' she said, handing the card to Terry. 'He should be back in his office by now, fed and watered and ready for his afternoon nap.'

Terry took the card and laid it on the coffee table. 'Are you sure you want to do this?' he asked.

'I'm sure I want to do this,' Jessica assured him.

Picking up the card, Terry got up and walked the few paces to his desk, lifted the phone and dialled the code for the USA, followed by the number on the card.

'Mr Michelstraub?' Terry looked across at Jessica and Eileen, both leaning forward expectantly. 'Ah. My name is Terry Hastings. Yes, Hastings. Yes, I'm calling from England.' He paused for a few seconds, listening. 'That's right, yes, like the battle,' he nodded his agreement at the receiver as his words sped across the Atlantic. 'I've got Jessica here, and ... no, no Alex isn't here. Yes, yes, apparently so. Anyway...' He continued, when allowed, and relayed all the details to Michelstraub.

'What?' The women heard it from across the room as Michelstraub's tinny voice exploded out of the receiver. 'What's that you say?'

'Vermeer,' Terry replied.

'Who?' Michelstraub's voice thundered through the airwaves.

'Vermeer,' Terry repeated a little shakily. He paused and looked across the room.

'Wants to speak with you,' he said, holding the phone towards Jessica. Jessica looked briefly at Eileen before she headed across to take the phone out of Terry's hand.

'Mr Michelstraub...' she began. She was silent for a while, contemplating the carpet, holding the receiver away from her ear as the diatribe came flying out of the little holes perforated into the black plastic handset. 'But...' she started, and then stopped as another string of sentences gushed forth. Jessica hitched herself up to sit on a corner of the outsize desk. She waited, not bothering to jump in. A minute went by, ninety seconds, then, silence. 'Hello?' Jessica asked. 'Hello? Yes, yes.' Another pause. 'No, it was damaged already. We could see... That's right. Yes, there was something underneath.' She gazed across the room. 'Had no idea.' She nodded, 'Yes, it was a risk.' She shook her head, 'No, he's an expert.' She grinned at Terry. 'All right then. Yes. No. No I haven't heard anything.' She looked at her feet swinging in the air as she dangled them off the edge of the desk. 'I don't know where he is,' she paused. 'Okay then, you tell him. 'Bye.' Jessica passed the phone to Terry and he replaced it on its cradle. 'Well,' she said, looking at Eileen, 'the cat's out of the bag now.'

'Well and truly,' Eileen agreed. 'That was masterful. Worthy of a genius.'

'Think so?' Jessica grinned.

'Definitely,' Eileen answered.

'Well, it was your idea,' Jessica responded.

'*Our* idea,' Eileen told her. 'A joint effort.'

'Well, I hope the effort was worthwhile,' Terry said. 'And I hope this Michelstraub keeps the information under wraps. It doesn't want to become common knowledge.'

'It'll be all right,' Jessica assured him, waving a five-pound note under his nose.

'What's that for?'

'The phone call,' Jessica said.

'I was rather hoping for something else,' Terry told her.

Jessica and Eileen exchanged glances.

'What?' Jessica asked.

266

'Recognition,' Terry said. 'Let it be known that it was me who discovered the painting. Well, you know,' he corrected himself, 'that I was responsible for the restoration work.'

'Deal,' Jessica agreed, and stuffed the note back into her jeans pocket.

'Now what?' Jessica asked as they walked towards Victoria.

'We wait for the phone to ring,' Eileen answered.

'Nobody knows the number,' Jessica pointed out.

'Terry does,' Eileen said.

'So?'

'Well, you told me that Dan had spoken to him.'

'Christ, so he did,' Jessica agreed.

'Don't worry about it,' Eileen advised. 'It'll sort itself it out. Pandora's box is open and they'll all come racing out, falling over themselves to find out more.' They giggled as they walked arm in arm along the pavement, imagining the hive of activity, the buzzing phone lines, the questions, the answers, the to-ing and fro-ing, and all because they'd peeled back the covers to reveal the hidden work of art.

''op in then girls,' a voice called out.

'Where's that coming from then?' Jessica asked.

'Over there, look,' Eileen answered, pointing at a taxi. 'Look, it's matey.'

'Who?'

'Matey, from the other evening,' Eileen said, walking towards a cab which had pulled in to the kerb. 'Hiya matey,' she said. 'How's it going?'

'Bloody terrible,' came the reply. 'It's not rainin' so everyone's walkin'. 'Ere, where you goin' then?'

'Finchley.'

'Oh, same place as last week then?' the cabbie said.

'Remember all your fares then, do you?' Jessica asked him.

'Only the pretty ones,' he answered, laughing.

'Right,' said Eileen. 'That'll be us then.'

'Listen, do you wanna taxi or are we just passin' the time of day?'

'Cheeky fucker,' Eileen remarked, grinning at the same time to show she meant no offence.

'Well?'

'Not at your prices,' she responded. 'Not when it's not raining.'

'Tell me abaht it,' lamented the driver. 'Ain't much I can do then.'

'Aw, go on,' Jessica said. 'Come up with something.'

'Can't,' he said.

'How about not turning your meter on?' Eileen suggested.

'Yer 'avin' a laugh, 'intcha?'

'How about half-way then? Turn it on when we get to Regent's Park.'

'Bloody 'ell. Come on then, there ain't nothin' else 'appenin'.'

'All right!' the girls chanted in unison as they clambered into the back of the cab.

''ad a nice day then, 'ave we?' the cabbie asked as the taxi pulled out into a stream of traffic.

'Yeah, not bad,' Eileen answered. 'How about you?'

'Like I say, it's been lousy. Ever since seven there's bin nothin', you know, after the mad rush?'

'Yeah, well, *we're* here now,' Eileen said, trying to cheer him up.

'Yeah, you're here now,' the cabbie agreed, looking in his rear-view mirror. 'Thank Gawd for that.'

268

Twenty minutes later the taxi pulled into their street.

'Here you are then,' said Eileen, handing across the amount of money as dictated by the meter. 'And this is for you,' she added, offering a pound coin.

'Nah, don'tcha worry yerself darlin', thanks all the same.'

'Go on, buy yourself a pint,' she said, forcing the coin into the cabbie's hand, 'and think of us.'

'Gawd bless yer,' he said. 'Everyone should be like you.'

The girls stood in the middle of the crossroads and watched the cab move away into the night.

'Come on,' said Jessica. 'Pub, pie and a pint.'

It was a few minutes before nine when they walked into Eileen's local, and as soon as they opened the door they saw that the place was heaving.

'Two pints of John Smiths and a couple pies please, chicken and mushroom, with peas.'

'You're joking?' the landlord said.

'Don't think so,' Eileen replied.

'You can have your pints, but you don't get the pies.'

'What?'

'No pies,' the landlord stressed. 'It's football night.'

'What's occurring?' Jessica asked, sidling up beside Eileen.

'It's football night. No pies,' Eileen explained.

'Do you still want the pints, then?' the landlord asked.

'Yes we do. And give us a couple of bags of crisps, aircraft-flavoured,' Eileen told him.

'What?'

'Plain,' Eileen said, giggling at herself. 'Whose idea was this then?' she asked Jessica.

'Can't remember,' Jessica replied.

'Yours,' Eileen told her.

They picked up their pints and the two bags of crisps and found a table in a corner, far away from the giant television screen.

'Okay, plan B,' Eileen suggested.

'Which is?'

'Take away. Chinese or Indian?'

'You've got both?' Jessica asked.

'Yeah. This is a great area for takeaways. There's Korean as well.'

'Korean? Don't think I've tried that,' Jessica said.

'No, neither have I,' Eileen admitted.

'Eeny meeny miny mo, grab a...'

'Careful, mustn't say that, you'll offend someone,' Eileen cautioned.

'...Rembrandt by his toe. Chinese then.' Jessica said.

'How do you work that out?'

'I just fancy it.'

'Right. Chinese it is.'

Suddenly, the crowd, huddled around the television at the far end of the saloon, let rip with a giant 'Ohhhhhhh', followed moments later by an equally giant 'Ahhhhhhh', then, 'Yesssssss!'

'Bollocks,' Jessica cried out. The sporting fraternity swung their heads round with one accord, as if they'd all been glued together. They stared at the two women, saw them innocuously sipping their beer and nibbling their crisps and, as one, turned their faces back to the big screen. The girls lifted their pint mugs and spluttered into the smooth creamy ale.

The kitchen table was overladen, cartons of Chinese food lying in every direction. The girls had balanced their plates on their knees and every once in a while they helped themselves to more of the various tasty items. Jessica was attempting to capture a prawn ball and managed to flick it into the beef with chilli sauce. Eileen grabbed it expertly between her chopsticks, lifted it through the air and placed it in her mouth.

'Hey! That was mine,' Jessica complained.

Unperturbed, Eileen wrapped her little wooden sticks around another prawn ball and steered it into Jessica's mouth. 'You know,' Eileen said, 'we were pretty damn dynamic this evening. We had Terry more or less eating out of our hands.'

'Yep,' Jessica smiled across the heaped boxes of food. 'Then there was the cabbie.'

'Mmm, definitely a day for the girls,' Eileen concurred.

'Although now I feel like I'm in limbo,' Jessica announced.

'How do you mean?'

'Well there's nothing I can do. I have to sit and wait.'

'Mmm, I know, but we certainly got the ball rolling,' Eileen said. 'Give it a couple of days and then give Terry a call, see if anyone's taken the bait.'

'Yeah,' Jessica said. 'I just hate waiting.'

'Anyway,' said Eileen. 'What's next for you?'

'Next?'

'Relationship-wise.'

'Oh.'

'Well, I appreciate that you think you're not attracted to women, so ... will you be going back to Alex?'

'Fuck off.'

'Pardon?'

'He declared war, didn't he?' Jessica explained.

'I must have missed something.'

'He pissed off with Rembrandt.'

'It was yours then, was it?' Eileen asked, smiling.

'No. But it wasn't his,' Jessica replied, pouting.

'Anyway, I rather thought it was you who started the war.'

'Me?' Jessica exclaimed. 'How so?'

'You walked out, left him. Left Dan. Left Mandie. Scarpered from Scotland.'

'And? This'll be going somewhere?' Jessica stared at her friend.

'*You* went somewhere Jessica. No rhyme, no reason. You closed the door.'

'Yeah. Jesus, Eileen, why are you so sensible?'

'It's always easy from the outside,' Eileen answered, then laughed. 'Me? Sensible? I don't think so.'

Jessica used the point of one chopstick to chase some lemon chicken round its container. 'Anyway, I've got to get these paintings sussed out.' She looked up, searching for some sort of direction.

Eileen smiled and dug her chopchicks into a mound of congealed special fried rice. 'Well, when it all gets too much, I'll be here, your friendly adviser,' she said.

'Very friendly,' Jessica smiled in agreement.

'Pity. It could be so easy.'

'Too easy, and it ain't gonna be,' Jessica said. She looked at the half-empty boxes. 'You had enough?'

Mixing various dishes together, they piled the remains into containers and put them in the fridge. The empty boxes went into the bin. Jessica picked up the Chardonnay and her glass, 'Come on then, let's relax in front of the fire and listen to some music.' They walked through into the living room and Eileen stretched out on the sofa while Jessica lolled in the armchair, her legs hanging over one of the arms. 'I'll pay you back for this, one day,' Jessica told her friend.

'For what?'

'For this,' Jessica replied, looking around the room. 'For letting me stay here, for putting up with me. For being my best friend.'

'Come on Jess,' Eileen said. 'You'd do it for me.'

'Well...'

''Course you would. Remember? You're just a pawn who can't say no.'

They both collapsed in fits of giggles as Jessica tried to complete the verse.

'This is what it's all about,' said Eileen.

'What is?'

'This. Being able to laugh and joke, sometimes be serious, sometimes be down, but ... but knowing there's someone there for you. Someone who doesn't make any conditions.' She paused. 'Alex didn't make conditions, did he?'

'No, he didn't,' Jessica agreed, looking into space. 'Maybe that was it, maybe it was too easy, too laid back. Nothing was a problem for him, he'd laugh his way round it. Know what I mean?'

'No, not really.' Eileen replied. 'Sounds idyllic.'

'Mmm.' Jessica grinned. 'I'm just a girl who's well fucked up.'

'Look at us,' Eileen said. 'We're free and single. We can do what we want, when we want, and, as for sex...'

'Yes?'

'Well, that's where the single life gets tricky,' Eileen admitted.

'You mean you don't have the answer?' Jessica asked, shocked.

'No. But chocolate is a pretty fine substitute. Do we have any?'

Jessica prowled off into the kitchen and came back clutching a large bar of Fruit and Nut. She went over to Eileen, took her head in both hands and kissed her gently on her forehead. 'That's to say thank you. For everything.'

'Stupid tart,' Eileen giggled. 'Come on, get that chocolate unwrapped.'

Part Four

Coda

1

It was mid afternoon.

After his conversation with Terry and Jessica, Michelstraub had replaced the phone and spent several minutes staring at it. He thought it outrageous that the girl had given the order to have the picture cleaned without consulting him. He felt himself losing control of the situation and, worse, he didn't know what to do about it. Goddamn Brits, he thought, they come over here, take my money, rampage all over Europe and end up ruining my art collection. It suited him to forget that it had been his idea, indeed that it had been his letter, that had brought them out of the woodwork in the first place.

He called his secretary, asked if there were any remaining appointments for the afternoon, and was happy when she informed him that the rest of the day was clear. He opened a desk drawer, took out a huge bunch of keys and went out to his car. 'Mandie,' he muttered to himself as he walked across the parking lot. 'She'll know what to do.'

'Vermeer? That's a wood stain or something, isn't it?' Dan asked.

'Shut up, Dan,' said Mandie.

'It's a painting. It's an artist. No, it's both.' Michelstraub was apoplectic.

'Try to calm down, George,' Mandie told him, a little concerned for his health.

'Calm down, calm down? How do you expect me to calm down?' Michelstraub asked.

'George!' Mandie exclaimed.

He blinked, twice, startled at Mandie's outburst.

'For goodness' sake,' she continued. 'Settle down George, otherwise you're going to burst.'

'Bloody people. Knew I shouldn't have got them involved.'

'Who?' Dan asked.

'The English,' Michelstraub replied. 'Can't trust them.'

'It seems Jessica's putting a lot of trust in you,' Mandie said pointedly.

'Can't understand it, myself,' Michelstraub said. 'She's ruined my picture.'

'What else did she say?' Mandie asked Michelstraub, whilst looking at Dan. It was a strange sort of look, a look implying that doom might be lurking just around the corner.

'Nothing,' Michelstraub answered.

'Nothing?' Mandie repeated. 'Just said she'd discovered this Vermeer?'

'More or less,' Michesltraub said.

'And Alex?' Dan asked. 'No news?'

'Nothing. Jessica doesn't know where he is.'

'What about Terry, did he tell you anything?' Mandie asked.

'Pompous Brit,' Michelstraub said.

'Funny. I got the same impression,' Dan told him.

'Met him, have you?'

'No,' Dan answered. 'Like you, spoke to him on the phone.'

'C'mon guys. This is getting us nowhere.'

Dan and Michelstraub looked at Mandie. Dan shrugged. 'I'm getting a beer. Mandie? George?'

Mandie followed Dan into the kitchen. 'I have to tell him. He has to know. Now.'

'About what?' Dan asked, opening the fridge.

'Rembrandt, the Prentiss, the cover-up, the whole caboodle. Let me handle it.'

'Okay. You're the boss.' Dan removed some beer cans and closed the fridge door. 'Just, you know, be gentle.' He paused, then, pouring a hefty measure of gin into a tumbler, added, 'Find me a lemon.'

They returned to the living area and Mandie handed the G and T to Michelstraub.

'Thought you'd gone to bed,' Michelstraub said. 'What took you so long?'

'Mandie and the lemon,' Dan answered, flipping open a couple of beer cans. 'Come on George, sit down. Stop looking so stressed.'

Mandie had been making a few quick notes on a sheet of paper, and when Dan handed her a beer, she laid the pencil on the paper and took a moment to digest what she'd written. 'So, George. This is where we're at.' She picked up the pencil and used it to tick the items as she mentioned them. 'Seven paintings. Six Prentiss Poses, in Binghamton, and one Vermeer, formerly a Prentiss Pose, in London. What does that tell you?'

Dan and Michelstraub looked at one another, then returned their gaze towards Mandie.

'What does it tell us?' Dan asked.

By way of an answer, Mandie posed another question. 'Remember that night in England, the conversation over dinner?' she asked Dan.

'About the Nazis?' he queried.

'Yup. About the Nazis and the loot they were smuggling out of Germany,' Mandie concurred. She turned to face Michelstraub. 'George,' she said. 'We came up with this theory that your collection of pictures are not what they seem.'

'Actually, it was Jessica and Alex's suggestion,' Dan added.

Michelstraub was confused. 'What do you mean they're not what they seem?'

'They're cover-ups,' Mandie answered.

'And nobody saw fit to tell me?' Michelstraub asked.

'We're telling you now,' Mandie said. 'And there's something else.'

'The day of revelation,' Michesltraub said. 'Finally.'

'When they were in Germany together, Alex and Jessica, they found not just one picture, they found two.'

'Two?' Michelstraub exploded. 'Two?'

'Yes,' Mandie said, looking at Dan. 'And here's the thing.' She transferred her gaze to Michaelstraub. 'George, the second picture is a Rembrandt.'

Michelstraub picked up his gin and tonic, took a long gulp, then set the glass back onto the table. His eyes flashed back and forth like a pair of flippers in a pin-ball machine, flapping about idly awaiting the descent of the ball-bearing. He didn't know whether to focus on Mandie, or Dan. He focused instead on his drink, and again lifted the glass to his mouth. 'Jesus,' was all he could think to say.

'Indeed,' Mandie agreed. 'Sort of ties up all the loose ends.'

'There weren't any loose ends until you went about your ways,' Michelstraub told her churlishly.

Ignoring Michelstraub's barb, Mandie picked up the pencil and wrote 'Rembrandt', adding the name under that of Vermeer. 'It'll be kind of interesting to see what else we've got,' she announced.

'What do you mean?' Michelstraub interjected. 'We know what we've got. Six Prentisses, a Vermeer, a Remb...'

'George,' Mandie said, cutting him short. 'You haven't been listening.'

'But...'

'The Prentisses,' Mandie continued, 'are make-believe. They're a disguise.'

'But...'

'George,' Mandie persisted. 'These paintings, these Masters, are worth infinitely more than your ... what was your expression? Oh yes, your "titillating" Prentisses. Listen, George, this collection is extremely valuable and something has to be done to protect it.'

'Extremely valuable?' Michelstraub asked, a smile gradually replacing his expression of angst. 'How extremely valuable?'

'It's ringing,' Mandie informed them.

They'd exchanged the beer and the gin and tonic for some coffee and biscuits, and had spent a further forty minutes chewing the fat. Michelstraub had been in favour of contacting Terry. 'Might as well talk to the expert,' he'd told them. Mandie and Dan had thought it wiser to speak with Alex; at least they knew him, and having met him and spent time with him, they'd formed a close friendship.

'Alex!' Mandie enthused. 'How are you?' She grinned at Dan while listening to the reply. 'Is it, one o'clock? Shit, I suppose it must be, sorry.' She pulled a face. 'Oh, we're fine, and Dan says hi... Yes. Yes... Now listen, Alex, here's the way it is.' She spoke into the mouthpiece, outlining the plan, idly coiling the phone cord round the index finger of her right hand. 'That's right, Vermeer... Yes.' She laughed, raised her eyebrows at Dan, 'Yes

Alex, she's a stupid bitch... Yes, Dan thinks the same... Oh, okay, hang on.' She looked at Dan. 'You still got that piece of paper with Terry's number?'

Dan nodded. 'It's in the kitchen drawer.' He got up, went to retrieve the piece of paper and handed it to Mandie. She read the number out and paused while Alex repeated it.

'Yup, that's it.' Again, she paused to listen to Alex's voice. 'Okay, hon. Give us a call when it's all set up... Yeah, you too.'

She replaced the receiver on the cradle and put the set back onto the kitchen worktop. 'That's it then,' she said. 'Now we wait.'

'I still don't understand,' Michelstraub said.

'What don't you understand?' Mandie asked him

'Why you didn't tell me earlier?'

'About the Rembrandt?' she queried.

'About the Rembrandt, about the Nazis, about the cover-up, about everything,' he replied.

'It was Alex's idea,' Mandie told him. 'He wanted to keep it under wraps until he was certain, until he had some confirmation or proof about his suspicions.'

'Oh, yes, I understand. Quite so,' Michelstraub said. 'Really quite bright.'

'Who?' Mandie teased.

'The Brits,' Michelstraub grudgingly admitted.

'I think we should go out and celebrate,' Dan said. 'How about the Italian?'

'Yep, good idea,' Mandie agreed. She turned to look at Michelstraub.

'George, you don't mind paying?' she asked him.

'Well, if I must,' he said.

''Course you must,' Mandie told him. 'In recognition of the fact that all your problems are over.'

'Very well,' Michelstraub said, rubbing his hands together. 'Let's go. Oh, and there's another thing.'

'What?' Mandie asked.

'I need a bed for the night.'

'You got yourself a deal,' Mandie said, looping her arms into those of Dan and Michelstraub as they set off down the street to the Italian restaurant.

Nine o'clock on a Tuesday evening and the place was almost deserted. The owner, Luigi, almost skipped across the tiled floor in his eagerness to welcome them, his greeting effusive.

'Bella bella,' he uttered as he took hold of Mandie's hands and guided her towards one of the tables. Dan and Michelstraub followed in their wake. The owner pulled out a chair and slapped at it with a crisp white serviette, before assisting Mandie as she settled onto the leather seat. He unloaded a shedful of Italian as he fussed about rearranging the already perfectly aligned cutlery then, leaning over Mandie's shoulder, he picked her wine glass off the table, inspected it closely, and marched off with it held high, tutting and clicking his tongue. He returned with another glass and set it on the table before producing a bottle of Barolo, which he opened with a grand flourish, explaining that the wine was a gift of the house. He poured it out, filling each glass half-full, then went to attend the only other occupied table.

Left to their own devices, Mandie, Dan and Michelstraub fell into easy conversation which ebbed and flowed across many topics, but had a natural tendency to return to the subject uppermost in their minds.

'I can't believe it,' Michelstraub kept repeating. 'I can't believe that I have six priceless works of art sitting under my nose. It's just too incredible.'

Mandie and Dan nodded agreement.

'They'll have to be authenticated,' Mandie told him.

'I shouldn't think we'll have to worry about that,' Michelstraub said. 'I imagine when they're sold, the auction house would pretty quickly have something to say if they thought the paintings weren't genuine.'

'That's true,' Mandie admitted. 'But people are still going to want to know where they came from.'

'That's where old Charley comes in,' Michelstraub said. 'The paintings belonged to him, and now he's dead.'

'So logically they belong to his wife,' Dan said, and, after a moment's pause, 'and the children and the grandchildren.'

'Eve,' Mandie told them. 'Charley's granddaughter. We have to speak to her.'

'Yes, but technically they belong to the firm,' Michelstraub told them.

'Why?' Mandie asked.

'Because we found the papers in Charley's desk, and Charley's desk was part of the office, part of the firm.'

'But they were Charley's documents, George. Don't you have private papers in your desk?' she asked.

'Yes, of course, but...'

'And do they belong to you, or to the office?'

'Well...' Michelstraub hesitated.

'The question isn't difficult,' Mandie told him.

'I suppose they belong to me,' he admitted.

'There you go,' said Mandie.

'You should be a lawyer,' Michelstraub quipped.

'No no, that's your job,' she replied, 'and I'm sure that

Eve will come to you for advice.'

They'd been so deeply engrossed in their conversation they hadn't noticed that other people had entered the establishment and, as if by magic, two waiters also had appeared.

Luigi materialized at Mandie's side and enquired if they were ready to order. 'Two minutes,' she told him, picking up the menu. 'Two minutes.'

2

'Thirty-one, thirty-two, ah, yellow door.'

Alex's running commentary had guided him round two sides of the square. His sense of location wasn't as advanced as that of Jessica's although, when finally he arrived at the gaily painted entrance, he recognized where he was and recalled the previous occasion when he'd climbed these self-same steps.

He pressed the brass button and announced himself to the voice that came out of the grille.

'Come on up, Alex. First floor.'

He went up the staircase and knocked on the front door. It opened almost immediately and Alex found himself face to face with Christine.

'Hello, Christine,' he said.

'Alex. Good to see you. Been quite a while.'

'Yes,' he replied, 'September, October?'

Christine led him into the living room and Alex saw, right there in front of him, large as life, Jessica. She was sitting on one of the sofas, next to another woman.

'Jessica,' he said.

'Hi Alex,' she replied, a little stiffly. 'How are you?'

'Fine. Thanks.'

'Oh, this is Eileen.'

'Another one of your school friends?' Alex asked.

'Eileen's letting me stay with her while I sort myself out,' Jessica explained.

'Prepared for a long-term resident are you?' Alex addressed Eileen.

Eileen smiled enigmatically.

Terry took a few paces towards the group and coughed, diplomatically.

'Um, are we all ready?' he asked.

Shit, Alex thought, why's everything got to be so fucking awkward? He took a seat on the sofa opposite Jessica and Eileen, thinking of all the places that he'd rather be. He thought back to the last time he'd seen Jessica, her dishevelled appearance, the frantic movement of her eyes. He recalled their silly stilted conversation, the ultra-short sentences that had meant nothing. Fuck, he thought, what the fuck am I doing here? He felt the sofa sag as a body sat down next to him, and looking up from his introspection he noticed Terry inching towards him, making room for Christine, who was lowering herself onto the other end. Alex tried to make himself smaller and pressed himself into the corner of the seat. He looked over at the two girls and for the first time noticed the cardboard cylinder. That'll be the Vermeer then, he thought, shaking his head in amazement as his mind went off at a tangent, trying to work out how many years must have passed since the original painting had last seen the light of day.

'Alex?'

He looked up and saw a sea of faces looking back, quizzically, waiting for him to say something.

'What?' he asked.

'Did you bring it with you, the other painting?' Terry asked him.

'Did I fuck?' Alex responded. 'What is this? She shows us hers and I show you mine?'

'There's no need to get upset,' Terry told him.

'Upset?' Alex retorted. 'What do I need to get upset about?'

'Well, where is it? What have you done with it?' Jessica asked him.

'It's in a safe place,' he assured her, 'waiting to be taken to the States.'

'And who's going to do that?' Eileen asked.

'She speaks,' Alex observed.

'Well?' Eileen pressed him.

'I am,' Alex told her. 'And I'll take that cardboard tube as well, if you don't know what to do with it.'

'I think not,' Jessica said, looking at him.

Alex stared back, waiting for her to continue, waiting for an explanation.

None came.

'I think this is getting...' Terry began.

'Why don't I make some coffee?' Christine suggested.

'Good idea,' Jessica agreed. 'Black and strong.'

Alex twisted himself round to look at Terry. 'Got any gin?' he asked. 'I could murder a G and T.'

'You got it,' Terry replied, relieved that the tension seemed to be subsiding. 'Anyone else?'

'Me too,' Eileen said.

'What, G and T?' Terry asked her.

'Mmm, thanks.'

Alex looked at the woman with the dark hair, saw her reach across to place a hand on Jessica's left leg. Jessica looked round and the two women smiled at each other. What the fuck does that mean? Alex wondered. Bloody typical, they're ganging up on me. The thought crossed his mind that he'd like to be the one sitting next to Jessica, he'd like to be putting his hand on her leg, he'd like to... Then another thought cut in, replacing the first, don't be silly, it'd only end in complications, she's got more hang-ups than a butcher's. He looked up, Jessica was saying something.

'Pardon?'

'Where have you moved?'

'Who says I've moved?'

'Jack.'

'Jack,' said Alex. 'Been snooping have we?'

'No, not really, I just...'

'Listen Jessica. It doesn't matter. There's nothing I can do about it anyway. It was your idea and, yes, I've moved.'

'I know, I know.' Jessica looked down at the table that separated them.

'So what will you do with the painting?' Alex asked her.

'Keep it,' Jessica answered.

'Keep it?' Alex repeated. 'You can't.'

'He's right,' Terry said, putting the gin and tonics on the table. 'You can't.'

'Why not?' Jessica asked.

'It's not yours to keep,' Terry told her.

'So, tell me, whose is it?'

'It's, um, it's...'

'It belongs to Michelstraub,' Alex stated.

'No,' Jessica said. 'It doesn't.'

'I rather think it does,' Terry said, sitting next to Alex. 'You see...'

'It was lost,' Jessica interrupted. 'Then it was found. It was discovered by us, Alex and myself. No one knew of its existence, or if they did, they had no idea where it was. It had disappeared, gone, lost forever. Treasure. Finders keepers.'

'But...'

'There is no "but",' Jessica said. 'If you like, I'll put it back where it was, and after a few years when you've all forgotten about it, I'll dig it up again and flog it.'

Alex was watching the dark-haired woman's eyes, noticed how they gleamed with pride as Jessica expounded. He too was impressed with Jessica's logic, it reminded him of the magic they'd shared, the formidable teamwork, the power of word association.

Bugger, he thought, she was good. She was very good. He looked at Terry, wondering how the expert was going to react.

'I'll have to inform Michelstraub,' Terry told Jessica.

'*You'll* have to inform him?' queried Jessica. 'Why you?'

'Well, okay, *someone* will have to inform him,' Terry replied.

'Have you suddenly become another of his lackeys?' Jessica asked him.

'Lackey no, adviser, yes.'

'What?' Jessica exclaimed.

'He wants me to look at his other paintings,' Terry explained. 'The Prentiss Poses.'

'Did you know about this?' Jessica asked Alex.

'Yes, Mandie told me.'

'Mandie told you,' Jessica repeated his words. 'Why didn't Mandie tell me?'

'Why should she?' Alex replied. 'Besides, she doesn't have your number. Nobody has your number.'

Jessica looked at Eileen, then at Terry.

'Terry does,' she said. 'Why didn't you tell me?' she asked him.

Terry clasped his hands together, looked down at them, and

shook his head. 'Anyway,' he said. 'I think that's about it.' He looked up. 'Alex, are you coming to New York with me?'

'Looks like it,' Alex replied. 'I'll hold your hand on the aircraft and introduce you to Mandie, Dan and Michelstraub.'

'And bring the painting,' Terry reminded him. 'You know, the Rembrandt?'

'That was a pretty sneaky thing to do, zipping over to get that painting from Wolfgang,' Jessica told Alex. They were walking along the pavement in the direction of Victoria, the three of them, with Jessica in the middle.

'No sneakier than you,' Alex retorted.

'Yeah, but you could've told me.'

'Likewise.'

'I didn't know where you were.'

'Likewise,' he repeated.

'Shall we go for a drink then?' Eileen suggested.

Alex and Jessica turned to stare at her.

'You know, drink?' Eileen said.

'Why?' Alex asked.

'Well, you two need to sort this out.'

'Sort what out?'

'Whatever it is that's gnawing at you. At both of you,' Eileen replied.

'And a drink will be the solution, will it?'

'It might help.'

'I don't think so,' said Alex.

'Is that it then?' Jessica asked him.

Alex looked at her, inspected the face of the princess who'd been everything to him. He saw the blue eyes, the long blonde hair falling over her shoulders, the lips he'd loved to kiss. 'Jessica...'

'What?'

'It wasn't my idea. Right or wrong, it was yours. You wanted out, you got out. Live with it.'

'But ... but we all make mistakes.'

'And?'

'And ... sometimes you have to forgive.'

'Jessica, I forgive you,' Alex told her. 'But I don't know if Michelstraub will.'

'Oh that. Like I said, I found it, it's mine.'

'You used Michelstraub's money to help you find it. Anyway, you can't just walk off clutching a work of art under your arm.'

'The Nazis did!'

'That was a war.'

'That made it right then?'

'No, but people had other things on their minds.'

'I really think we should get that drink,' Eileen said as they walked past a pub.

'Doesn't give up, does she?' Alex commented.

As if to confirm his statement, Eileen about-turned and entered the pub. Jessica turned to follow, looked over her shoulder and said, 'Come on Alex, please?'

He muttered under his breath as he followed the girls into the smoky interior.

Eileen was at the bar, picking peanuts out of a shallow dish.

'What's it to be, then?' she asked.

'G and T,' said Jessica.

'Pint of Directors,' said Alex.

'Say please,' Eileen told them.

'Please,' they said, together, shaking their heads.

'Okay, now go find a table.'

They did as commanded, and Alex slumped against the back of the chair and let the general hubbub wash over him. He'd had just about enough. Although he'd anticipated the fact that Jessica more than likely would be at Terry's apartment, to see her sitting there looking so gorgeous, managed nonetheless to knock him sideways. That she should have deemed it necessary to bring someone else only served to knock him further. Still, he'd thought to himself, might as well stand up and wait for another express train to come along and slam into him. He hadn't had long to wait; Jessica's announcement, that she intended to keep the Vermeer, had come out of the blue like a cruise missile. He should have seen it coming, after all they'd been together for three years and Alex reckoned he knew most of her traits. He hadn't. Her statement had taken him completely by surprise, indeed it seemed to have bewildered everybody, apart from Eileen. She'd just sat there looking cool and elegant, seemingly oblivious to the earth-shattering news. But then, Alex supposed, to her it wasn't news; she and Jessica had probably shared deep, meaningful discussions from which Jessica had made her decision. Fuck, Alex thought, if they've held debate on the picture, they sure as hell would have had a heart-to-heart about me. He began to wonder about the friendship between the two girls – how long had they known each other, and why oh why...? He stopped, corrected himself. Who is this Eileen, where did she come from? Two women from Jessica's past and he'd known nothing about them, had heard nothing about them, absolutely nothing. First of all there had been Christine, and now Eileen. Who the fuck is she? He looked to his right as Eileen put three drinks on the table and took the seat next to him. She caught his look and held it, then placed her left arm around his shoulders.

'Come on Alex, do tell.'

'Pardon?'

'Tell us what you've been up to.'

He looked across at Jessica. 'How do you mean, what I've been up to?'

'Okay, where have you been?' Eileen asked, changing the question.

'You know where I've been,' Alex answered, looking at Eileen. Then, transferring his gaze to Jesssica, 'And I know where you've been.'

'Enlighten me,' she said.

'You've been to see Michelstraub and told him that I asked you to go see him. You also told him that I was in Germany. Do you know...?'

'But Alex...'

'Let him finish,' Eileen said, still with her arm resting on Alex's shoulders.

'Do you realize that we were both in Michelstraub's office on the same day, the very same day Jessica? We missed each other by only a couple of hours.'

'So?' Jessica asked.

'So what were you doing? Going into business on your own?'

'No, I was just...'

'Obtaining funds to travel to Germany. I know, Jessica. I know 'cause Michelstraub told me. And let me see... let me guess what you were going to do in Germany. Shouldn't be too difficult.' Alex paused, looked at Eileen and smiled. 'That's it,' he said, 'you planned to visit Wolfgang and collect the other painting. Two's better than one. Two are certainly more valuable than one, aren't they? Then what...? Maybe flog them to Michelstraub, or maybe flog them on the open market? Who knows?'

'Who knows?' Eileen agreed.

Alex lifted his glass and took a long swig at his pint. 'Eileen?' he asked. 'Why have you got your arm around my shoulders?'

'I'm a friendly sort of girl,' she replied. 'And Jessica's told me so much about you, I really wanted to meet you.'

'Bollocks,' said Alex. 'You're both full of bollocks.'

'That'll be your department,' Eileen told him, once again holding his gaze.

'Yeah? Well I'm taking them with me,' he said, getting to his feet. He buttoned his coat and looked at Jessica. 'Jessica, listen. Whatever it is you want, I'm just not able to give it. Obviously I'm not enough for you.'

'Don't worry about it,' she said. 'Why don't you go back to your friends?'

'What friends?'

'Dan and Mandie,' she sneered, putting emphasis on the woman's name.

Alex shook his head and made his way to the door, opened it, and walked out into the night.

Jessica had bowed her head to look at the table top. 'Did he look back?' she asked.

'No,' Eileen told her. 'He didn't.'

Alex got out of the tube at Green Park and got into another. As the train snaked its way under the streets of London he sat back and imagined Brahms. He allowed the violin concerto in D to flood his entire being, the music full of caution yet, at the same time, exploring tangents of optimism. The passages he couldn't remember, he improvised, and when improvisation failed, the clickety-clack of the wheels underscored a few bars of the powerfully haunting music. The train followed the parallel lines of the stave on its journey to the northern suburbs, and Alex was only vaguely aware of the doors as they slid open at each stop, the movement of people in and out, and the tang of burnt electricity. As the music coursed through his veins he tried to understand exactly what it was he was feeling. For the few weeks between Christmas and his visit to Manhattan, his mind had been all over the place, weaving through the distortions, the accusations and counter accusations, the truths and the falsehoods. He began seriously to question his previously held beliefs, the tenets that had been engraved on his heart. He'd become static, trapped, a prisoner to the obfuscations crowding his brain. And then... Then he'd been on his travels and was able to feed on the strength dished out to him by his friends. Alex smiled as he recalled waking up in the New York apartment, the frozen air that skewered into his sleeping brain when he'd opened the window for a millisecond, and the gentle warmth of Mandie's lips when she'd kissed him. He stopped smiling when he realized that the train had pulled to a halt and didn't appear to be going any further. He dragged himself out of his reveries and looked up to see the sign. Cockfosters. Jesus! he thought, normally the journey seemed to take forever. He got out of the carriage and stood on the platform wondering how long he'd have to wait for the next southbound train. He watched as the driver stepped out of the leading carriage and began walking towards him.

'Miss yer stop, mate?' the driver asked.

'Yeah.'

'Get back on, then,' he was told. 'We'll be off in a minute.'

And just when you think everything's against you, he thought. He stepped back onto the train and, sure enough, after few minutes it began to retrace its tracks. Two stops later he disembarked and walked the short distance to his home.

Alex closed the front door behind him, shutting out the world and all its perfidious permutations. Christ, he thought, remembering the evening's symposium and the discourse that had batted to and fro, is this when I start to despair of my fellow man? He climbed the staircase thinking about the tête-à-tête with Jessica and Eileen, and quickly realized his mistake. 'No,' he said to himself, recalling the conversation he'd once had with his toes. 'It's women. They're strange, they come from a different planet, and I don't understand them.'

At the top of the stairs he came face to face with the tower of cardboard boxes, still intact, still untouched. The sight depressed him, so he went back downstairs and consulted with the few CDs he'd found when unpacking the hi-fi. Brahms was amongst the selection, as was Beethoven and of course Mozart, but Alex decided he needed something a little more meaty. He chose Steely Dan, and as the laser beam chewed into 'Black Cow', the sexy combination of bass guitar and a solid steady drum beat, began to dispel his disillusion.

He yanked up the volume and went into the kitchen to make an omelette. He broke the eggs, three of them, into a bowl, mixed in some salt and pepper and then discovered that he had no cheese. 'Bugger,' he said to the eggshells. He looked in the cupboard over the hob and found some jars of herbs and spices; basil, rosemary, thyme, parsley. He threw the lot in to the mixture and placed a frying-pan on top of a high flame. A knob of butter, a drop of oil, and he was away, whistling while he worked. Life ain't so bad, he thought, as he poured the eggs into the frothing butter and watched the mixture slowly solidify. He went into the living room and found a half-full bottle of red wine, its cork pressed into the neck, half in, half out. 'Excellent,' he said to Donald Fagen who'd got into his stride and was singing, 'This is the day of the expanding man.' Alex listened and agreed.

As he sat on the sofa eating his frugal meal he looked around the room, taking in the bare walls, the empty shelves, and yet more packing cases standing in the recess of the bay window. Alex took another bite of the omelette and started to think about the painting that was lying under his bed. What with his visit to New York and Binghamton and the revelations from Michelstraub and then from Jessica, the past two weeks had been quite a scramble, and Alex was astonished to realize that only two days had passed since his return from Munich.

Wolfgang had met him at the airport and Alex had found his friend in pensive mood.

'What is happening, Alex?' Wolfgang had asked as his hand had been pumped up and down in a firm Germanic grasp. 'First there is Jessica, then there is the phone call, and now there is Alex. I am not understanding.'

'Don't worry, Voolfy,' Alex had replied. 'I'll explain everything, but I am only here for twenty-four hours.'

Wolfgang had looked at Alex and shook his head as he led him out of the airport and into the car park. 'You crazy English,' Wolfgang had said.

They'd walked between the rows of cars and had come to a halt in front of a Range Rover.

'Yours?' Alex had asked.

'But of course,' Wolfgang had answered.

Alex had walked around the car, peering into the windows. 'I'm impressed,' he said.

298

Wolfgang had looked surprised. 'It's being necessary, Alex. In the mountains, in the winter, in the snow. We are all having them.'

'And I didn't even know you had a car.' It was Alex's turn to shake his head as he'd climbed into the luxurious interior of the four-by-four.

During the drive down to Lake Tegernsee, Alex did most of the talking. He told Wolfgang about his visit to America and his shock when he'd discovered that Jessica had beaten him to it, had already visited the American lawyer and was on her way to Germany.

'And that's why I had to call you, Voolfy,' Alex explained. 'She already had the Vermeer, and for her to get her hands on the Rembrandt as well would have been ... well, it would have been...'

'Vermeer?' Wolfgang queried. 'What Vermeer?'

So Alex went on to tell him about Terry and the transformation of the Prentiss Pose into the Vermeer. From time to time he glanced to his left, making sure that his Bavarian friend was keeping up with the strange story, which Alex himself was beginning to find a little convoluted, if not a little doubtful. As they neared the northern end of the lake, Alex asked Wolfgang to drive to the kindergarten, the former home of the German general. He grinned widely as he noticed the look of incomprehension streak across Wolfgang's face. 'It's okay, Voolfy,' he said. 'I haven't gone completely mad, not yet.'

The wrought-iron gates had been repaired and re-painted and stood firmly closed, a barrier slung between two enormous brick pillars. Alex opened the car door and slid down to the ground. A set of tyre tracks had been cut into the snow and led under the gates and out the other side to follow the gentle curve of the drive. Alex made his way to the front of the car and then, gingerly placing one foot in front of the other, he followed one of the grooves through the snow. Luckily, the gates had not been locked and Alex was able to slide back the bolt and push them open. He waved Wolfgang onwards and when the car had passed through the entrance, he closed the gates behind it. He climbed back into the warmth of the car and outlined his plan as they drove round to the front of the house. 'I'm hoping that we can still get into the cellars, Voolfy.'

'But why?'

'I'm taking the Rembrandt with me and need something to put it in, and one of those crates would be just the job.'

'Gut gut,' Wolfgang said. 'Zehr gut.'

He brought the car to a halt and they both sat there, staring out at the snowy scene. They noticed that, since their visit in Ocotber, new walls had been built, and they saw pallets full of bricks, metal stanchions, baulks of timber, and all the paraphernalia of construction neatly stacked and covered with protective tarpaulins; modernistic barrows with an icing of snow.

'Jesus, Voolfy, it doesn't look too promising.' They got out of the car and made their way to the front door. As with the gates, the door also hadn't been locked. Alex turned the handle and the huge oak portal swung back easily on well-oiled hinges.

'Bloody hell, look at this,' he said.

Wolfgang peered over Alex's shoulder and together they looked across the expanse of the hallway, amazed at the amount of work that had been carried out. Everything was new, everything was clean. Pine floorboards gleamed under clear varnish, white-painted plaster walls reflected any available light, the place exuded an air of freshness.

300

'Come on Alex, let's be looking,' Wolfgang said, trying to encourage his friend.

'Bloody hell,' Alex repeated as he gazed about him. He followed Wolfgang across the lobby and through an open door. More floorboards, more shining walls. To the right was a staircase leading to the next floor.

'That wasn't there last time,' Alex noted.

'Neizer was the upstairs,' Wolfgang added. 'Remember, it was just a ruin?' They moved to the foot of the stairs and found, hidden behind them, another set of stairs. Stone steps which led downwards. 'See Alex, maybe now we are haffing the luck.' Wolfgang went first, pointing his torch ahead of him, and they made their way slowly down to the basement. Nothing had changed. It was still a brick-lined vault, still awash in dust.

'Maybe Voolfy, maybe,' Alex said. They moved through the cellars, eyes glued to the little pool of light as Wolfgang swung the torch to and fro, and then they saw the work bench. Alex got on his knees and started running his fingers though the layers of ancient dust.

They made their way back out of the cellars and emerged to find that night had fallen. A full moon wheeled itself across the jagged conifers, rising slowly to perch momentarily on top of the tall slender trees. The light reflected from the moon reflected also from the thick layers of snow, the brightness contrasting sharply with the darkness of the surrounding forest. Wolfgang opened the back of the Range Rover and Alex placed the packing case in the rear of the car. They slammed shut the back door and clambered into the front of the car, banging their shoes against the sill to knock off the snow. Wolfgang put the car into a three-point turn and set off towards the gates. They repeated the process of opening, driving through and closing the gates, and resumed the journey to Krohne Stube, Wolfgang's small hotel hidden in the mountains above Bad Wiessee.

He swung the car to a halt next to the large wooden door and the two men jumped out. While Wolfgang opened the front door, Alex collected the case from the back of the four-by-four and they entered the house, closing the heavy door on the cold winter's night.

'Okay. I am preparing something to eat,' Wolfgang declared as he led Alex into the dining room. 'You can use this table to work on,' he said, helping Alex to lay the wooden crate on top of the huge dining table.

Alex had just finished removing the lid when Wolfgang reappeared carrying the Rembrandt, which he set on the floor, leaning it back against one end of the table. Alex took the sheets of oiled paper out of the crate and laid them lengthwise across the open top, then he and Wolfgang placed the painting onto the heavy paper and let it sink slowly into its housing. The crate had been well constructed and Alex was pleased that he'd thought of collecting it from General von Oberstürm's mansion; he'd never have been able to make one as good.

'Ja, Alex, is gut,' Wolfgang said as they stood looking at the painting. 'Come with me and we are finding some things to fix with.'

'Things to fix with,' Alex repeated as he followed Wolfgang into the kitchens. Wolfgang looked in various cupboards and drawers and found a hammer, a screwdriver and a box of screws.

'Well done Voolfy,' Alex said. 'You have everything.'

'Ja, and now I am cooking,' Wolfgang replied, turning to his pots and pans.

* * *

302

They ate their meal in the kitchen, warm, cosy and informal, and over dinner the two friends found much to talk about although, naturally, the main topic hovered around the discovered art fraud. Wolfgang leaned forward, placing his forearms on the knotted surface of the wooden table. 'You know my friend,' he said. 'We Germans are not much liking to talk about the war, about the Nazis und the things they are doing ... did. We are a proud nation und we are knowing these things should neffer haff happened. But, I must tell you, Alex, there are stories you wouldn't be believing, stories that are connecting the past to the present.'

'What do you mean, Voolfy? What are you talking about?' Alex was intrigued.

'They say that there are one or two high-ranking Nazis still living here in Germany. Here, up in the mountains, near the border with Österreich.'

'I thought the Nazi hierarchy was alive and well and kicking its heels in South America?' Alex asked, thinking that it might have been more appropriate to use the word 'clicking'.

'Ja, ja,' Wolfgang agreed. 'Many are. Many. But, with the rising popularity of the National Front, they are saying that one or two elderly Nazis haff elected to come back to the Motherland.'

'Shit.'

'Exactly zo, Alex. Genau.'

'But, Voolfy, I don't understand. Why should this have anything to do with what we've been discussing?'

Wolfgang chuckled and reached across the table to pour more wine into their glasses. He looked up at Alex. 'They are haffing their treasures with them.'

'Christ.'

'Everything. Pictures, chewellery, sculptures, ornaments, gold, silver. Everything.'

'But where did it all come from?' Alex asked, sitting upright.

'Everywhere Alex. From everywhere. All over Europe. From Russia, from Poland, France, Czechoslovakia... Stolen, looted, und of course confiscated from the Jews.'

'So there could be dozens of valuable paintings which never see the light of day.'

'Light of day?' Wolfgang queried. 'What is light of day?'

'Daylight,' Alex explained.

'Oh.'

Alex laughed at the expression on Wolfgang's face. 'What I mean is... What I'm saying is that these pictures are hidden away and will never be seen by the public.'

'Ja. Right. Although, every now und then, there appears a work of art on the market, und the world goes crazy. People are thinking that a new work of Van Gogh, or Michelangelo has been discovered. But, probably, these haff been hanging many years ago in a gallery in Paris, or maybe in a private collection in Amsterdam, Prague or Rome. Alex, you understand? The Nazis removed everything. They erased the records. No traces. They were very clever.'

'Of course,' Alex nodded in agreement. 'I remember seeing it in the papers, the occasional article about a new painting having been discovered. The auction houses in London and New York get very excited.'

Wolfgang pointed over Alex's shoulder, into the darkness in the direction of the lake. 'Over there, the other side of Tegernsee, there is a large house which is looking always deserted. The shutters are closed most of the year and people are rarely seen coming or going. Of course there are bound to be rumours. Some people are thinking it is belonging to a rock star, others maybe a retired Chancellor, but it is strange, no?'

'Weird,' Alex said. 'Nobody lives there?' he asked.

'It doesn't seem zo,' Wolfgang answered. 'Although occasionally, maybe two or three times a year, a large black Mercedes is parked in the drive, but not in front of the house.'

'Goodness. Voolfy, you have to find out more.'

'Ja. But is nothing to find. No people, only rumours.'

'Keep your ears to the ground, Voolfy, and keep them flapping,' Alex advised his friend.

Alex got up, left the sitting room and returned to the kitchen. He put the plug in the drain, ran some hot water into the sink and squeezed a small amount of washing-up liquid into the swirling water. One plate, one knife, one fork, and the frying pan; not too bad, he thought to himself as he scrubbed them clean and put them on the rack to drain. He let the water out of the sink and noticed the mixing bowl, unwashed, standing on the worktop. 'Bollocks,' he said, and turned off the light.

He went back to the living room and sat on the sofa, cradling the glass of wine in his hands. The CD had come to an end and Alex found himself staring at the small blue-green light set into the bottom left-hand corner of the amplifier.

I'm not doing that again, he decided, thinking back to the journey between Munich and London. Normally a light traveller, Alex had found it hell trying to transport the crate, all four foot by two foot six of it, through the terminals and the controls.

'It's a painting,' he'd told the check-in girl when she'd looked incredulously at the packing crate.

'A painting?' she'd repeated.

'Yes, it's a Rembrandt,' Alex had stated.

'Oh ja, okay,' the girl had said, smiling knowingly. She'd slapped a label onto the crate and said, 'Goodbye Rembrandt.'

Alex had watched, fascinated, although he seemed to recall that his heart had been in his mouth.

At Heathrow nobody had bothered to stop him, he'd retrieved the box from the carousel, waited for his bag, then, with both items balanced on a trolley, he had left the concourse and searched for a taxi. No, the controls hadn't been a problem, it was just the hassle of travelling with a cumbersome piece of excess baggage, and it had cost him a small fortune.

Alex took a gulp of the red wine and thought DHL, recalling the television commercials full of broad red arrows flying round the world in all directions. All he had to do, the commercial had indicated, was make a phone call. He looked at his watch.

'Christ, twelve o'clock,' he said, his voice cutting through the silence of the living room. He picked up the bottle from the floor and drained the remnants into his glass. He settled back onto the sofa and thought of Jessica, then his mind transferred to her friend ... what was her name? Eileen, that was it. He wondered what they would be doing, what they would be talking about. He wondered if Jessica was seeing anybody and felt quite pleased that his earlier opinion, about her having a thing with Terry, had been proved wrong. And then he remembered that the idea had not been his own, but had been suggested by Dan, who, having dialled the number that had been supplied by Wolfgang, inadvertently had spoken to Terry. And that's all it takes, Alex realized. How easy to jump to the wrong conclusions.

He started to think about his friends in Manhattan and reasoned that, at twelve-fifteen in London, it would be seven-fifteen in New York, early evening, and therefore a good time to call. Probably.

'Hi, Mandie... Yes, it's me. Yes ... no.' He grinned as he thought of the beautiful face stuck to the other end of the line; the lips, the eyes, the voice.

Mandie was speaking.

'Is he?' Alex asked. Suddenly it all clicked into place. 'Mandie,' he said, 'Listen.'

3

Alex was pacing.

The check-in area was heaving with people flocking out of the country, a vast chunk of the population taking full advantage of an early Easter to leave the cold wet weather behind. All the check-in desks had queues reaching right across the concourse and Alex pounded aggressively up and down the ones attached to American Airlines. 'Where the fuck is he?' he muttered, eyeballing the throng of people.

Jesus, he thought as he paced to and fro, it's a mass evacuation. Whole families appeared to be on the move; babies, toddlers, teenagers, mums, dads and grandparents, and all of them seemed to have brought everything they owned. Christ, Alex thought, knowing that dribble, drool and crying babies didn't feature on his list of survivable situations. He was just thinking that they should all be bundled together and shut into in a Wendy house at the rear of the aircraft – better still, be put in the hold along with the rest of the baggage – when he felt a hand grasp his shoulder. He looked round to see Terry grinning at him.

''kin'ell Terry, you cut it pretty fine.'

'I don't enjoy hanging about,' Terry said. 'Where have all these people come from?'

'Crawled out of the woodwork,' Alex replied. 'C'mon, let's get you checked in.'

They made their way to the end of the shortest queue and

308

took up position behind a couple of Mohican haircuts, one blue, one pink.

'Where's your stuff?' Terry asked.

'Already checked in.'

'And the painting? You have remembered the painting?'

'Already in the States – at least, I hope it is,' Alex informed him.

'But, how...'

'DHL,' Alex cut him short.

'A courier?' Terry asked, looking alarmed.

'Yep,' Alex answered. 'After returning from Munich with a large crate for company, I decided I wasn't going to make a repeat performance.'

'Mmm, well, I suppose you're right.'

'You should try it sometime,' Alex suggested. 'Gordon Bennett, what a hassle.'

The queue lurched forward and Terry and Alex shuffled along behind the Mohicans.

'That was quite an evening, the other night,' Terry said.

'Yes,' Alex agreed. 'It was.'

'Sorry about that,' Terry continued, 'but I couldn't see any other way round it.'

'Nah, it's okay,' Alex told him. 'It was my problem. Well, Jessica's as well.'

'Yeah, but even so...'

'Met up with them afterwards, in a pub.'

'Did you?' Terry asked. 'How'd it go?'

'Lousy,' Alex replied. 'Probably my fault.'

'How so?'

'Well, you know, I just can't seem to forgive her. Although, of course, I told her I did.'

'For what?'

'Exactly,' Alex responded. 'For what? For screwing up a trip to Scotland? For making me look stupid in front of Dan and Mandie? Or for just not being able to communicate?'

'Well, it seems...'

'Sometimes I think it's me, Terry. You know, I can be pretty difficult at times, and I'm very independent. Shit, why am I telling you? I hardly know you.'

'They say it's easier to talk to a stranger,' Terry said. He grinned, 'And they don't come much stranger.'

'You're okay,' Alex told him and punched him on the shoulder.

They reached the front of the queue and walked to the desk. Terry handed his ticket and passport to the check-in man and was told to place his bags on the conveyor belt. The man looped labels through the luggage handles, and Alex and Terry watched as the two bags lurched forwards and disappeared through dangling black leather flaps.

'Why so much luggage?' Alex queried as they trooped off in the direction of passport control.

'Need me bits and pieces, don't I?' Terry answered. 'But most of it's clothes. Gawd knows how long I'm gonna be there, Michelstraub wants me to look at all of the paintings.'

'I'm sure he does,' Alex agreed, chuckling. 'He's all right is Michelstraub. Likes to boss you around mind, but he's okay. You'll like him.'

'Bloody hell, there's two of them,' Alex announced as they wandered, bleary-eyed, through the terminal. 'They're both here.'

Terry glanced at Alex to see where he was looking, to understand what the fuck he was talking about. Then, he saw them, and guessed that the fat one in the suit would be Michelstraub.

'Hey, Alex, how ya doin'?' came a voice from behind.

Alex and Terry turned round to locate the source of the call. It was Sol.

'Make that three,' Alex said. 'They're all here. Well, all except Mandie.' He introduced everyone to Terry and gave Sol a high five. Sol grinned hugely.

'He's coming with me, you're going with him,' Michelstraub said, pointing and nodding at the same time.

'Pardon?' said Terry. He stood there looking doubtful.

'You're coming with me,' Michelstraub told him. 'I want you to start on these Prentiss Poses.'

'George!' Alex and Dan exclaimed in unison. Michelstraub blinked and peered at them through his thick glasses.

'Yes?'

'Easy old buddy,' Dan chuckled. 'The guy's only just arrived. Let's go get some coffee, or a beer or something.'

'Oh, yes,' Michelstraub said. 'Maybe we could get something to eat?'

'Now you're talking,' Dan told him.

Terry looked at Alex as they followed the two Americans into a restaurant.

'Mmm, that's something else you'll get used to,' Alex told him. 'They like to eat whenever they can. You won't starve.'

They settled themselves at a table and watched as Michelstraub, in his element, went through the menu. 'Okay.' He snapped shut the plastic folder. 'Breakfast all round then?' He looked at his three companions, studied their faces.

'Breakfast it is,' he smiled joyously as a waitress approached the table. 'Breakfast for four. Specials, with everything.'

Michelstraub fingered the cutlery laid out on the table in front of him, lining up the individual pieces in the same way that a general might employ toy soldiers when setting out a battle plan. 'Alex,' he said, looking up, looking serious. 'Thanks.'

'My pleasure, George,' Alex replied. 'For what?'

'Oh, I think you know,' Michelstraub smiled across the table. 'By the way, I received the package from DHL two days ago.' He stopped smiling and stared at the formation of cutlery. 'Only one picture?' he asked.

Terry, sitting next to Michelstraub, looked across at Alex.

Alex shifted in his chair. 'Yeah, huh?' he said. 'We need to talk about that.'

'We do,' Michelstraub agreed.

'But you found two pic...' Dan started.

'Jessica decided to keep it,' Alex told him, straight. He returned Michelstraub's stare. 'The other picture, the Vermeer, the painting that Terry discovered hidden beneath the "Pose", Jessica's got it.'

'What?' Michelstraub exclaimed. 'How? Why?' He banged his fist on the table causing the cutlery to dance out of its symmetrical pattern. 'She can't.'

'Well, she has,' Alex said.

'Alex?' Dan said.

'Yeah, I know,' Alex answered. 'It's the way it is. You saw her in action in Scotland.'

'But this is theft,' Michelstraub said.

'Mmm,' Alex agreed. 'Exactly what she said.'

'No, but ... what?'

'Theft,' Alex stated. 'It's what Jessica said. It's how the whole thing started. These paintings were stolen during the war, bundled together and shipped out disguised as erotic fantasies, only, two of them missed the boat.' He grinned as he recalled the same phrase being used by Symond.

'Yes, but...' Michelstraub appeared to be tongue-tied.

312

'She's right,' Dan said. 'But that don't give her the right to keep one of them.'

They stopped talking while the waitress returned with their specials. They picked up their knives and forks and started to attack the mountains of food.

'Treasure,' Alex said eventually, round a mouthful of sausage. 'That's what she called it, treasure. Finders keepers. Said that if you want to go find it, she'll hide it again.'

'Jesus.'

'Shut up Alex, you're spoiling my appetite.' Dan winked at him, shovelling hash browns and egg into his mouth.

Alex shook his head in wonder.

'This is something I'm going to have to sort out,' Michelstraub said, 'but not now.'

'No,' Alex agreed. 'Not now. But, at some stage you're going to tell us who, exactly, is the rightful owner of this collection.'

'I am?' Michelstraub asked.

'You are,' Alex confirmed, nodding his head. He looked across at the lawyer from Binghamton, watched the fluttering jowls as the breakfast disappeared into the large frame. 'So, you don't need me then?' he asked.

'Excuse me?'

'Well, now that you've got Terry here to help you out, seems like I'm redundant.'

'No you're not,' Dan told him. 'We need you. Me and Mandie. We're taking you out tonight. Kind of celebration.'

Alex turned towards his American friend and raised his eyebrows, questioning.

'Mandie's idea,' Dan said.

'Uh-huh?' Alex said.

'C'mon, eat up,' Dan told him. 'We'll get back to the apartment and you can catch up on your beauty sleep. We leave this evening at six-thirty.'

Alex looked round at the others. 'Can't wait,' he said. 'What are we celebrating?'

Dan smirked and Michelstraub stifled a snort.

'Life,' Dan said.

'Rembrandt,' Michelstraub added.

'And Vermeer,' Terry said, not to be left out.

'Shit. Big celebration then.' Alex grinned across the empty plates.

4

'Come on, Alex. We don't want to be late.'

'Yeah, yeah, I'm on my way.'

He shrugged into his overcoat and shuffled towards the door, towards Mandie and Dan.

'Okay bud?'

'Sure.' Alex smiled weakly back at him.

'He'll be fine,' Mandie said, full of assurance.

'Hmm,' was all that Alex could manage in response, wondering what all the fuss was about.

They walked down the street, then another street, and took the subway along Broadway, surfacing at the Lincoln Center. Alex looked about him wondering what they were doing at New York's illustrious cultural centre. Knowing that the Juilliard was housed somewhere in the complex, he felt a little awed to be standing in the shadows of the hallowed halls of musical academe. He noticed a poster featuring a concert by the Chicago Symphony Orchestra at the Avery Fisher Hall and, suddenly, that seemed to be where they were heading. He followed Mandie and Dan into the foyer of the concert hall, managing eventually to catch up with them.

'What are we doing?' he asked.

'We're following Mandie,' Dan told him.

'Oh, that's all right then,' Alex replied. He'd be happy to follow Mandie to the ends of the earth. They wandered here and there, circumnavigating small groups of people engaged in earnest conversation. The general hubbub was at a reasonable level, more like a murmur, punctuated now and again with an outburst of laughter. He lapped it up, immersed in the electric atmosphere of a crowd standing on expectation. He wallowed in the social whirl, the coming together of like minds, and wished he had someone to share it with.

Alex unbuttoned his coat and handed it across the counter to the cloakroom attendant, then waited as Dan and Mandie did likewise. Alex and Dan, both wearing dark suits, watched attentively as Mandie turned away from the counter. She looked fantastic in a black skirt, matched by a black jacket which she wore over a pale blue shirt, crisp, cool and stunningly elegant. The skirt, which stopped just short of the knees, stretched tightly across her body, accentuating her hips and her slim figure.

'Good, isn't it?' Dan asked Alex.

'Yeah,' Alex agreed. 'It's a bit like the Barbican, a glorified meeting place.'

'I meant Mandie's outfit,' Dan said

'Really?' Alex replied, winking.

'Come on, you two,' Mandie called, as she made a beeline across the concourse.

They angled in on the ticket returns office and Alex watched as Mandie walked up to a sylph-like beauty leaning against the highly polished wooden sill. He looked more closely when Mandie put her arms around the woman's shoulders and kissed her on one cheek. Dan grabbed him by the shoulder and steered him towards the two girls. The closer he got, the more he felt his legs turning to porridge, and the last few paces towards the desk were taken as though in a dream, his feet seemingly glued to the floor.

'Dan, you remember Eve, don't you?'

'Yeah, sure I do,' he grinned, bending to kiss her on the cheek.

'And ... this is Alex,' Mandie said radiantly, beckoning him forwards.

'Alex. Hi, I'm Eve.' Her big blue-grey eyes reflected her smile.

'Yes.' Alex said. His mind was in turmoil. 'Umm...' He paused, took a deep breath and held out his hand. He succeeded in meeting her steady gaze with one of his own, his eyes taking in as much detail as possible. His first impression was of height, but possibly this was accentuated by the black catsuit that encased Eve's body from her neck to her ankles. The jersey-like material sheathed her impossibly long legs, stretching forever upwards until, like shrinkwrap, it formed a membrane around her flat behind and tiny waist. The material continued upwards and over her breasts, which looked as though they were straining to be released. The catsuit was cut in a low scoop, showing off perfectly the deep tan of the girl's skin. Over the top, she wore a brilliant-white shirt, unbuttoned and tied in a loose knot at a point somewhere above where Alex imagined her navel would be. Eve placed one of her arms around his waist and guided him gently in the direction of the bar. Mandie and Dan followed closely behind.

A string quartet, lodged in an alcove, serenaded the lobby with renditions of Mozart, Vivaldi and snatches of Beethoven, the music managing to have a calming effect on Alex's state of mind. After a short while he'd recovered sufficiently, and was able to adjust to the situation. Standing between Mandie and Eve, he sipped his Martini, watching and listening as the three friends caught up on the latest gossip. Suddenly he realized who she was.

'Eve!' he gasped. 'Charley! You're Charley's granddaughter.'

'See?' Mandie said. 'We have our very own Sherlock.'

Eve giggled delightfully and kissed Alex on his forehead.

A small bell rang somewhere in the distance, calling the faithful into the auditorium. The two girls sat together and Alex sat between Dan and Eve. The low susurration from the audience ceased altogether as the lights dimmed, and Alex settled back in to his seat, prepared to let the music wash over him, through him and consume him totally. It was superb. Beethoven's Piano Concerto No. 1, by any definition an impressive piece of music but, when sculpted into almost jazzy perfection by the Chicago Symphony Orchestra, the little black dots, one by one, majestically elevated themselves from the score and floated sublimely through the ether.

Alex thought he was in paradise. Inspired by the music, ensconced with his friends, and sitting next to the long, lithe Eve, he reckoned he'd been transported to heaven. Leaving the concert hall after the performance, the four split into pairs, Mandie and Eve following Dan and Alex into the cold New York night. The girls were exchanging idle conversation when Dan turned round and suggested visiting a bistro. Alex turned to look at Eve. She smiled, and took hold of Mandie's arm.

'Come on then,' she said. 'Let's go. Lead on, Dan.'

Alex, who thought the evening couldn't get any better, watched happily as the occasion progressed from being excellent, to being brilliant. The wine bar on Amsterdam Avenue was warm and welcoming. Illuminated solely by candles on the tables and along the bar, the atmosphere reached out and embraced them. Jazz music played in the background, just loud enough to cover the chatter from the surrounding tables.

Alex was entranced. 'This, I could get to like,' he said, as Dan reappeared having ordered the wine.

'Yeah?' Mandie asked.

'Definitely,' Alex said.

'Does that mean you'll be staying?' Eve asked.

'Who wants to know?' he replied.

'We do,' they answered as one.

Alex grinned and pushed the tip of his index finger through a couple of drops of red wine that had splashed onto the table. 'Bloody hell,' he confessed. 'I hadn't even considered it.'

'Oh,' the trio chorused, a little despondent.

'I mean, life in London isn't so bad.' Alex thought about the rain, the empty house, the unpacked boxes of belongings. He thought of the harrowing encounters with Jessica. 'But then again...' he said, and left the remark unfinished.

Later that night, as he lay in bed, Alex recalled the events of the evening. He heard again the fabulous music being played by the world famous orchestra, saw the love and the laughter in the eyes of his friends, remembered the unbeatable mixture of jazz, wine and conversation. He closed his eyes and opened them again, and swimming out of the darkness came the intriguing, beguiling figure of Eve. He saw her almond-shaped blue-grey eyes, her face, her smile, the long, straight black hair, and the incredibly slender waist encased in its catsuit. He remembered her charm, her beauty, her intelligence. Alex let out a long sigh, shook his head gently from side to side and started to think about the past.

Yes, there had been a lot of hassle in the past – and that, he told himself, is where it has to remain, tightly locked up. One has to move on and hopefully become stronger, learning from mistakes, learning from experience. He tried to remember the well-tested maxim – 'seize the day', that was it. Well, it seemed a new day had arrived. He realized that it was no good continually to dwell on the problems associated with previous relationships, life was too short.

'Bugger,' he said softly, the philosopher lost in the darkness of the night. He realized that he had to stand up and decide what sort of future he needed. Decision, he thought, that's what it's all about.

Alex stopped talking to himself and, turning his mind inward, discovered he'd already made his decision, a decision based on his understanding of the past few years. He'd been too easy-going, too ready to accept situations in which he hadn't really believed. Instead of saying, 'No, I cannot accept this,' he'd made the error of being too laid-back and letting things, and life, glide by. No point in tiptoeing around forever, no point in dancing on shards of broken glass. He resolved to quit the uneven playing field which had surrounded him in every direction.

Winter emerges into spring and spring blossoms into summer, he thought, and, continuing along the same thread, realized that when one door closes, another opens.

'Maybe,' he said to himself. 'Maybe.' He closed his eyes and went to sleep. Smiling.